G. E. MORRIS, Jr.

RIFLEMAN DODD
AND
THE GUN

BOOKS BY

C. S. FORESTER

THE GUN

THE PEACEMAKER

THE AFRICAN QUEEN

THE GENERAL

*BEAT TO QUARTERS

*SHIP OF THE LINE

*FLYING COLOURS

CAPTAIN HORATIO HORNBLOWER
(*Originally published in the three volumes starred above*)

TO THE INDIES

THE CAPTAIN FROM CONNECTICUT

PAYMENT DEFERRED

RIFLEMAN DODD AND THE GUN: TWO NOVELS
OF THE PENINSULAR CAMPAIGNS
(RIFLEMAN DODD *was published in England under
the title* DEATH TO THE FRENCH)

RIFLEMAN DODD
AND
THE GUN

*Two Novels of the
Peninsular Campaigns*

BY C. S. FORESTER

BOSTON

LITTLE, BROWN AND COMPANY · 1943

RIFLEMAN DODD

Chapter I

HALF a dozen horsemen were picking their way up a breakneck path. The leader of them was most conspicuous by the excellence of his mount, for his saddle fittings were severely plain and he wore a plain blue cape and coat and an unglazed cocked hat in sharp contrast with the scarlet coats and plumes of several of his followers. But when he pulled up at the brow of the hill and peered keenly forward across the tangled countryside some hint might be gained of the qualities which constituted him the leader. He had an air of authority and of composed self-reliance, and his blue eyes swept across the valley in a glance which noted its features instantly. The big, arrogant nose told the reason why the men in the ranks called him "Conky" and "The long-nosed beggar that beats the French," just as the hauteur of his expression explained why his subordinates alluded to him half ruefully, half deferentially, as "The Peer."

Drawn up below him was a column of scarlet-coated infantry, standing at ease; right ahead keen sight could discern little clusters and groups of men in green, mere dots on the landscape, sheltering behind trees and in dips in the ground. An occasional puff of smoke told that beyond the skirmishing line was the enemy. Lieutenant-General Lord Wellington hitched his sabretache on to his saddlebow, opened a notebook on it, and scribbled a few words on one of its pages, which he tore out. A scarlet-coated dragoon officer walked up his horse alongside as he did so, and took the folded sheet.

"For General Craufurd," was all that was said to him.

The dragoon mechanically repeated "For General Craufurd" and set his horse at the steep slope before them.

"Time for Craufurd to get back, Murray," said Wellington. "Now I want to see the columns across the river."

He wheeled his horse and set spurs to him, and next moment they were clattering down the stony path again, sparks flying and accoutrements clashing as the rest of the staff tried to maintain the breakneck speed and headlong carelessness of danger which characterized the movements across country of the Commander-in-Chief. The dragoon officer would have a busy time trying to find his way back to his post of duty after delivering the order which sets this tale in motion.

A bugle was sounding out to the left.

"Fire and retire," said a Lieutenant to himself, listening to the high long-drawn notes. "And not too soon, either. Where's that picket?"

He strode away along the top of the little hill to look for it, with his crooked sword trailing at his side. To the conservative military eye his uniform was a ludicrous mixture. It was dark green instead of the scarlet which had won honour for itself on fifty battlefields; the black braid on it, the busby, the pelisse hung across the shoulders, all indicated, absurdly in an infantryman, an aping of Hussar equipment accentuated by the crooked sword. Yet it was only natural, because the Ninety-Fifth Foot were supposed to inherit some of the traditions set up by the Hussars when they were the most irregular of irregular horse. On the other hand the colour of the tunic, and the bugle horn badge, were no legacy from the Hussars — they recalled to the memory the fact that the first rifle regiments employed by the British Government had been recruited from the huntsmen of German princelings. Nevertheless no one now dreamed of sneering at this fantastic attire; the Ninety-Fifth Foot — the Rifle Brigade — had in the short ten years of its existence won itself a reputation worthy of the envy of any older unit.

"Fire and retire," repeated the Lieutenant to himself, as the bugle called again more insistently. There was a scattering rifle fire out to the left now, to endorse the urgency of the call. The dozen riflemen standing awaiting the Lieutenant's decision on the top of the hill showed no signs of agitation. They knew their officer and trusted him, despite the fact that he was not yet nineteen years old. They had twice followed him across Spain, to Corunna and Talavera — to say nothing of the dreary marshes of Walcheren — and they knew they could rely on him. The

Lieutenant shaded his eyes with his hand, but as he did so there was a clatter of equipment down in the valley and the missing picket came running up the hill.

"You're late, Sergeant," snapped the Lieutenant.

"Yessir. We was nearly cut off and had to get round them," explained the Sergeant, and then, apologetically, "Dodd's missing, sir."

"Dodd's missing?"

"Yessir. I sent him forward and — "

"Do you know what happened to him?"

"No, sir. Didn't hear any shots fired out his way."

The bugle rang out again amid a spatter of musketry.

"We can't wait for him," said the Lieutenant, with a decision acquired in a hundred rear-guard actions. "Sorry for him, but I expect he'll find his way back to us. Fall in, there. Left in file. Quick march."

And the half company moved off, their rifles at the trail. The Ninety-Fifth were part of Craufurd's famous Light Division, whose boast was that they were always first into action and last out. Now they were covering the last stages of Wellington's retreat to the lines of Torres Vedras — the retreat during which they captured more prisoners than they left behind. But to-day they would have to report at least one "missing" — Rifleman Matthew Dodd, cut off from his unit by the fortune of war.

Chapter II

Rifleman Matthew Dodd was already aware that he was cut off, although at the moment he was too occupied in saving his life to consider the consequences. He had been making his way back through the olive groves to his picket when he had heard strange voices ahead and had glimpsed strange uniforms. Bent double, and sweating under his pack, he had scurried through the undergrowth in the valley trying to make his way round the enemies who had interposed across his line of retreat. Half an hour of violent exertion had, he thought, brought him clear, when at that very moment a shout told him that he was observed by some other detachment. A musket rang out not far away from him and a bullet smacked into a tree-trunk a dozen yards away. He turned and ran again, uphill this time, in a direction which he knew took him away from his friends but which alone, as far as his skirmisher's instinct told him, was still not barred by the French advance-guard. There were more shouts behind him and a crashing among the undergrowth which told him that he was closely pursued by a dozen men.

He dashed along up the steep slope, his pack leaping on his back, and his ammunition pouches pounding on his ribs. Soon he emerged from the olive grove on to an open, heather-covered hillside. There was nothing for it but to continue his flight without the protection of the friendly trees — either that, at least, or to turn back and surrender, and Dodd was not of the type which surrenders too easily. He ran heavily up the hill. Twenty seconds later the first of his pursuers reached the edge of the grove, and had him in clear view. They raised their muskets and fired at him, one after the other as they came up, but Dodd was a hundred yards away by now, and no one could hope to hit a man a hundred yards away with a musket, especially when panting from heavy exertion. Dodd heard the shots, but hardly one of the bullets came near enough for him to hear it. He climbed on up the steep slope until, when the last shot had been fired, he deemed it safe to spare a moment to glance back. Half a dozen Frenchmen were reloading their muskets; half a dozen more were starting up the hill after him. Dodd plunged forward again through the clinging heather.

The hill, like all the hills in Portugal, was steep and rocky and seemingly interminable, rising bleakly up from between two wooded valleys. He laboured up it, his steps growing slower and slower as the slope increased. Half-way up he stopped and looked back again.

The Frenchmen had ceased their pursuit and had drawn together to go back down to the road. Dodd's jaws clenched hard together. He threw himself down among the heather and pushed his rifle forward; an outcrop of rock provided a convenient rest. He cocked the rifle, saw to it that the priming was still in place, and then looked along the barrel. Although a musket might miss a house at a hundred yards, the rifle could be relied on to hit a group of men at twice that distance. He pressed the trigger, and the flint fell. The priming took fire — in dry weather not more than one shot in ten missed fire — and the rifle went off. Through the smoke he saw one of the Frenchmen down the slope lurch forward and fall, rolling down the incline a little way before he lay still.

A yell of rage went up from the Frenchmen, and they turned to pursue him again, but Dodd leaped to his feet and ran once more up the slope. One or two ineffectual shots were fired after him, but they went wide. And after a hundred yards or so more the Frenchmen abandoned the pursuit again, and went back to where some of them were still stooping over the wounded man.

Dodd had taken his revenge for being chased off his best line of retreat. It was annoyance at this fact which had caused him to fire that parting shot, for in the Peninsular War casual shootings were not encouraged by high authority: the General commanding in chief had confidence in the persistence of the "offensive spirit" among his men without any additional stimulus.

Chapter III

A DOZEN French soldiers were marching down a Portuguese by-road. They were a shabby enough group in appearance, for their blue uniforms had been badly dyed originally and now, after months of exposure to the weather, had changed colour in patches, greenish and whitish and reddish, here and there, and every coat was torn and darned in sundry places. Their shakos were dented and shapeless, and the cheap brass finery which adorned tunics and shakos was dull and dirty. Up to the knees their legs were white with dust, and their faces were grimed and bearded. Every man marched bent beneath a mountainous pack, round which was looped his greatcoat, and from which depended all sorts of curious bundles, varying with each individual save as regards one bundle, the most curious of them all. Each man carried one of these — eight hard flat cakes, irregularly square, strung on a cord, through holes in the middle, for all the world like monstrous Chinese coins. The likeness had been noted in the French Army, and these cakes were always alluded to as "cash." Each weighed one pound, and represented one day's rations.

A French general considered he had done his duty by his men if he issued one pound of this flinty bread per head per day — anything else they needed he expected them to gain from the countryside. When the advance was resumed after the defeat at Busaco, every man was given fourteen of these one-pound biscuits, and told to expect no further issue of rations until Lisbon was reached; from which it can be deduced that these men had been six days on the march from Busaco. Six days ahead of them lay the Lines of Torres Vedras, barring them eternally from Lisbon, but they did not know that. No one in the French Army as yet knew of the existence of the Lines.

Sergeant Godinot was in command of the party, and the six men behind him were his particular friends: Boyel, Dubois, little Godron, and the others. Two hundred yards ahead marched the "advance-guard" of two men; two hundred yards behind came the "rear-guard," for although the detachment was marching in the midst of the French Army, precautions had to be taken against ambush, for in Portugal every man's hand was against them. Even when Godinot called a halt, and the exhausted men lay down to rest at the side of the road in the shade, one man was detailed to patrol round them.

"How much farther before we find this uncle of yours, Sergeant?" asked Boyel.

Godinot had an uncle who was a general in Soult's army in the South; for eight hundred miles of marching the Sergeant had been encouraging his section with descriptions of the golden times he and his friends would enjoy when they came under his command. Godinot shrugged his shoulders.

"Patience," he said. "We'll find him sooner or later, never fear. Have I not brought you safely so far?"

"You can call it safe, I suppose," said little Godron. He was lying on his back with his legs in the air to relieve his aching feet. "Marching for six months. One good meal a week when we've been lucky. A battle once a month and a siege every Sunday."

"There's gratitude," said Godinot, grinning so that his white teeth flashed brilliantly in contrast with his sunburned face and black moustache. "Who was it found that jeweller's shop when we took Astorga? Why, there are three gold watches ticking in your pack this very minute, you — you ungrateful viper. How you've kept them I don't know. That little Spanish girl at Rodrigo took all my loot from me. But we'll get some more before long. Just wait till we find my uncle. He's the chap for me."

"Don't believe old Godinot's got an uncle," said some one. "He got us to join his regiment under false pretences."

"And where would you be if I hadn't seen you at the depot and taken you under my wing?" demanded Godinot. "Shivering in Poland or somewhere I expect, with no Daddy Godinot to wipe your nose for you. You blues don't know when you are well off."

A "blue" in the French Army was a recruit — because until he grew used to it, the recruit went blue in the face under the constriction of the uniform stock.

"Why," went on Godinot, "perhaps — "

But Godinot's speech was interrupted by a loud challenge from the patrolling sentry, followed immediately by a shot. All of the detachment scrambled to their feet and grasped their muskets, following Godinot in his rush to where the sentry, his musket smoking in his hand, stood peering through the olives.

"A green Englishman," said the sentry, pointing. "That way."

"After him!" said Godinot. Since the day of Busaco every one in the Eighth Corps knew what a green Englishman was.

The detachment began to struggle through the olive groves, crashing among the branches on the trail of the hurrying rifleman. Five minutes of hot pursuit brought them to the edge of the grove, where a high, bare hill mounted up in front of them. The dark-clad Englishman was toiling up the slope a hundred yards ahead. Godinot dropped on one knee, trying to calm his laboured breathing, and fired hastily, without result. The others as they came up pitched their muskets to their shoulders and pulled the trigger.

"Enough of that!" snapped Godinot. "Reload. Come on, you others."

He pressed on up the slope with half a dozen men beside him. But the Englishman had the longer legs or the stouter heart. At every stride he increased his distance from them.

"Oh, let him go!" said Godinot at length. "The dragoons on the left will catch him."

The men pulled up, panting.

"Come on back," said Godinot. "We'll never reach the battalion to-night at this rate."

They began to plod down the hill again, leaving the Englishman to continue his climb up it. The incident meant little enough to them; every day for a month they had been accustomed to exchanging shots with English outposts. Yet even as they began to dismiss the incident from their memory it was sharply recalled to them. A shot rang out behind them, and Boyel pitched forward on his face, and rolled a little way down the hill, blood pouring from his throat. Every one shouted with rage. Little Godron dropped on his knees beside Boyel; the others, with one accord, turned to climb the hill once more in pursuit. A puff of smoke hung in the still air to show from whence the Englishman had taken aim. Yet as they set themselves to the climb the Englishman leaped once more to his feet and ran labouring up the hill, and five minutes more of pursuit told them how useless it was. They turned back again, to where Godron, with tears running down his cheeks, was kneeling with Boyel in his arms. An ounce of lead had torn a great hole in his neck and his tunic was already soaked with blood.

"Give my regards to your uncle, Godinot, when you see him," said Boyel weakly. "I shall not have the pleasure."

And blood ran from Boyel's mouth and he died.

Godron was sobbing bitterly as Godinot knelt and made certain Boyel was dead.

"He has died for the Emperor," said Godinot, rising.

"The first of us," said Dubois bitterly. "Six of us joined you, Sergeant. Now we are five. To-morrow — "

"To-morrow it may be four," agreed Godinot harshly. He was as moved as were the others, but he was in a position of authority, and had not so much time for sentiment. "But we must join the battalion to-night, all the same."

He was running his fingers deftly through the dead man's pockets and equipment.

"Money," he said. "Observe, eleven francs. You are witnesses. That is for the regimental funds. Cartridges. Here, divide these among you. Socks. Anybody want them? Well, they'll fit me. Nothing else of importance."

He took the dead man's musket and walked across to a rock, where he smashed the stock and the lock with half a dozen blows.

"Take his bread, some of you," he said. But the others hung back. "Take his bread, I say. Dubois, Godron, you others. One biscuit each. Never waste bread on a campaign. Now come along back to the road."

"But aren't we going to bury him, Sergeant?" protested Dubois.

Godinot looked up at the sun to judge the time of day.

"There is no time to spare," he said. "We must join the battalion to-night. Come along, all of you."

They obeyed reluctantly, trooping down the hill and through the olive groves to the road. They formed up and resumed their march, but of the six friends who had joined under Godinot's charge at the depot nine months before there were now only five, five men with heavy hearts and hanging heads. The sixth lay out on the bare hillside, where he would continue to lie all through the approaching winter, a noisome, festering mass until the carrion crows picked his bones clean to bleach in the sun and the rain.

Chapter IV

RIFLEMAN MATTHEW DODD went on up the hill. As soon as he was safe from immediate pursuit he sat down in the cover of a whin-bush to reload his rifle — reloading took so long that it was always advisable to do it in the first available moment of leisure, lest one should encounter danger calling for instant use of the rifle. He took a cartridge from his pouch and bit the bullet — a half-inch sphere of lead — out of the paper container. He poured the powder into the barrel, all save a pinch which went into the priming pan, whose cover he carefully replaced. He folded the empty cartridge into a wad, which he pushed down the barrel on top of the charge with the ramrod which he took from its socket along the barrel. Then he spat the bullet into the muzzle; it only fell down an inch or so, for it happened to be one of the more tightly-fitting bullets — extreme precision of manufacture was not demanded or considered necessary by those in authority. Since he could not coax the bullet down the rifling, he reached behind him to where a little mallet hung from his belt by a string through a hole in the handle. The fact that Dodd carried one of these tools proved that he was one of the careful ones of his regiment — it was not a service issue. Standing the rifle up on its butt he rested the ramrod on the bullet and tapped sharply with the mallet; musket and ramrod were so long that only a tall man could do this easily. The blows of the mallet drove the bullet down the rifling until at last it rested safely on top of the wadding; then Dodd hung the mallet on his belt again and replaced the ramrod in its groove. After that he had only to make sure that the flint was in good condition, and then his rifle was ready to fire again. Dodd went through all these operations mechanically. Months and months of drill had been devoted to making him mechanically perfect in loading, so that he would not in a moment of excitement put the bullet in before the powder, or omit to prime, or fire the ramrod out along with the bullet, or make any other of the fifty mistakes to which recruits were prone.

It was only then that he had time to consider his position and think what he had to do. He settled himself down in the shelter of the whin-bush, easing his pack on his shoulders; three years' campaigning had taught him the importance of making the most of every moment of rest. Somewhere to the south of him was his regiment, which meant to him his home, his family, his honour and his future. To rejoin his regiment was the summit of his desires. But the regiment — so his extensive experience of rear-guard actions told him — had been marching hard in retreat for the last two hours, while he had, perforce, been going in the opposite direction. The regiment was ten miles away by now, and between him and it was not merely the enemy's advance-guard but probably a whole mass of other troops; the detachment which chased him would not have been moving isolated in the way he had found it if it had not been well behind the front line. Merely to follow his regiment would simply carry him into the arms of the enemy.

Military instinct called upon him to find a way round — that was the earliest tactical lesson the regiment had taught him, five years ago on the high Downs at Shorncliffe, with Sir John Moore on his white horse riding up and down to see that every recruit learned his part. South-east from him ran the Tagus, and along the Tagus bank he knew he would find a road which would take him to Lisbon and the Lines — he had tramped that road a dozen times already. To reach it he would have to get across the pursuing French Army and pass forward round its flank. Dodd had never seen a map of Portugal in his life, and could not have read it if he had: he had learned his geography by experience. With his face upturned to the sky he visualized from memory what he knew of a thousand square miles of country. He knew the two main roads by which the French were advancing. There was a chance — a faint chance — that he could reach the third road and find it unguarded. It would be one, two, three, four days' march with luck to the Tagus, and two — three, perhaps — to the Lines at Alhandra from the point where he would meet the river.

In his haversack there were two pounds of what the Army termed "bread" — unleavened biscuits only a shade better in quality than the French — and a beefbone with some stringy meat still adherent. Dodd was a careful soldier; he had saved that meat from his last night's ration, knowing well that when on rear-guard duty it was no unusual thing for camp to be pitched long after midnight, much too late for the wretched ration bullocks to be slaughtered and cut up and cooked. In the twin pouches on his belt there were fifty-five cartridges and a packet of flints — he felt to make sure. His rifle was loaded and his sword bayonet hung on his hip. He was as well equipped as a private soldier could hope to be. He wasted no time repining over the shortcomings of his outfit; he heaved himself to his feet, looked cautiously round him for signs of the enemy and, finding none, began to plod stubbornly south-eastwards through the heather. The hillside was bare and open, and there was no possible chance of concealing his movements for a mile or so.

But the rifle-green colour of his uniform was some slight protection, all the same; a scarlet infantryman — and nine tenths of Wellington's army was scarlet infantry — would have been absurdly conspicuous. And his buttons and badges were black, with nothing to catch the sun and reveal his presence. The brave old Duke of York at the Horse Guards might not be very receptive of new ideas, but once he could be induced to accept an innovation he could be relied upon to see that it was carried out to its logical end. In the same way the long bayonet which tapped on Dodd's hip was really a short sword, because skirmishers and sharpshooters might find their marksmanship impaired if they had to aim with a fixed bayonet, although at any moment they might be called upon to fight hand to hand. So to this day the Rifle Brigade flaunts its black buttons and badges, and "fixes swords" when its fellow regiments "fix bayonets," and carries its rifles at the "trail" instead of at the "slope."

The dark green dot moved slowly along the hillside. At its end the hill sank in an abrupt shoulder, dropping down into a tortuous valley winding its way through a tangle of other hills, in which Dodd guessed he might find a rushing stream, and probably some sort of track, or possibly a real road — but that was not very likely, for roads were few in Portugal. He approached the sky-line cautiously, and when he reached it he sank down upon his face in the heather, hitching himself forward with his elbows to see what lay before him.

There was the little stream he had expected, much contracted now at the end of summer and making its way tortuously among masses of boulders. But beside the stream there was a little house, walls and roof of grey stone, standing in the midst of a tiny field which generations of patient work had cleared of rocks and made fit for cultivation.

Houses spelt danger to an isolated straggler. Dodd lay long and patiently staring down at it. He could see no sign of life. There was no smoke, no movement. That was not specially surprising, because he knew that the country had been swept clean of inhabitants at Wellington's order. Food was to be all destroyed, women and old men and children were to be swept back into the Lines — Dodd had seen much of the pitiful processions during the retreat — while every one who could handle pike or musket was to go up into the hills and feed as best he might while hoping for the chance of catching an isolated Frenchman.

So that the house should be empty of its owners was only to be expected; what was to be feared was that there might be Frenchmen there. Down in the courtyard, close by the grey stone wall which divided it from the field, was some whitish bundle — even Dodd's keen countryman's sight could not make out what it was. Probably an abandoned household bundle. At last Dodd decided that although he could see no sign of a Frenchman he had better not approach the house. He scanned the valley of the stream, noting the twisting path which followed it. By keeping to the hillside, above the sky-line, he could work his way safely to the next valley. There he could see a coppice, and he could go through that down to the little stream and reach the path unobtrusively. He hitched himself back above the ridge, peered round, and walked over the hill down towards the coppice.

Among the trees he moved with caution. He had the slope of the ground to indicate his direction to him, but that was a treacherous guide, as he well knew. And there might be enemies within ten yards of him. He peered round each beech trunk in turn as he came to it, looking for Frenchmen and planning his next advance. It was ironical that with all this elaborate caution he should have been taken by surprise. Something hit him on the shoulder. It was only a beechnut, but it made him leap as though it had been a bullet. Some one was peering at him through the yellowing leaves high up in a tree — he had forgotten to look upwards.

"P'st! P'st!" said whoever was there. "*Inglez?*"

"Yes," said Dodd, "*sim.*"

He could not raise his voice above a whisper, standing there in the silence of the trees. There came a scrambling among the branches. Two legs appeared dangling down, clothed in fantastic garments, fantastically ragged, half breeches, half trousers, with two filthy feet emerging at the end. Their owner dropped lightly to the ground, and came towards him with a wreathing, dancing step, his swarthy face grimacing with triumph, presumably at having identified Dodd as an Englishman, despite his green uniform, by the caution of his movements. He was only a youth, and he was crazy.

He mouthed out a few halting words, but Dodd could make no reply. His knowledge of Portuguese was practically limited to the few words necessary to buy wine. The idiot took his hand and led him to the edge of the wood, pointing to the little grey house, only two hundred yards away. Again he spoke, and again Dodd could neither understand nor reply. The idiot seized Dodd's hand once more, and started to draw him along towards the house. He noticed Dodd's reluctance and guessed the reason for it. He spoke once more, and, seeing the uselessness of speech, he fell into pantomime. Shading his eyes with his hand, he peered round the countryside, and then made an emphatic negative gesture. Clearly he meant that the neighbourhood was clear of enemies. Dodd did not resist when the idiot drew him towards the house again.

Everything was very still. The sound of the little stream boiling over its boulders was all that could be heard as they approached the desolate little building. Inside the courtyard, beside the house door, Dodd halted abruptly. A dead man lay there in a pool of blood. He was a very old man, white-haired, and his face was calm.

"*Sim, sim,*" said the idiot, pulling still at Dodd's hand. He led him behind the house.

The whitish mass which Dodd had observed there from the top of the hill was revealed now as a dead woman. Her grey hair was soaked with blood, and her open hands were lacerated as though they had been cut when she seized the weapon which destroyed her. Her ragged clothes were bundled up round her breast, and she lay there in pitiful nakedness.

The little group made a striking picture there beside the house at the foot of the hills — the tall, burly soldier in his green uniform, the idiot mopping and mowing beside him, and at his feet the naked corpse. Dodd stood there in silence, until the idiot broke into his sombre reverie.

"*Morran os Franceses!*" said the idiot suddenly.

Death to the French! That was the cry which was echoing through Portugal at that moment. He must have heard it often enough.

Dodd started out of his black mood. He made to go out of the courtyard, but, struck with a sudden thought, he stooped, and with a rough tenderness he pulled down the bloody clothes about the dead woman, and he folded the lacerated hands upon the breast. Then he turned to go, with the idiot beside him. The courtyard beside the house was littered with the little belongings of the dead couple. Dodd had seen looted cottages often enough before, but this particular sight moved him inexpressibly.

"*Caballeros,*" said the idiot. He pointed to signs on the track indicating that horses had stood there beside the courtyard gate.

Dodd nodded; this was not the first time he had seen the handiwork of the French dragoons. The idiot pointed to the gate, and went through the pantomime of mounting a horse and then of riding. Then he pointed along the track and down towards the hills away from the little wood of their first encounter. Dodd was glad of the information. He knew cavalry must be somewhere about. At the point where he had been cut off from his regiment the country had been so tangled that rear-guard and advance-guard had been composed of infantry, but out on the flanks the cavalry were fulfilling their usual rôle of screen. The fact that he had come into their zone indicated that he had made some progress towards his goal.

"Well!" said Dodd, with finality. He could do nothing here; it was his duty to push on. He pointed south-eastwards. "Tagus?" he said interrogatively, and then, remembering the native name of the river, "*Tejo?*"

The aspirated "*j*" was a stumbling-block, but he thought he had pronounced the name recognizably. Yet no sign of recognition came into the idiot's face.

"*Tejo?*" said Dodd again.

The idiot muttered something, which Dodd strongly suspected not to be even Portuguese, but gibberish. Dodd could do no more. He turned away and began to tramp along the rough track beside the stream. A second later the idiot came pattering after him. They left the desolate house behind, with its deserted corpses, and walked on down the valley — the English soldier and the capering idiot.

When they emerged from the woods of beech and cork oak the sun was low in the horizon. Dodd began to think about making preparations for the night. He was not the man to risk losing his way by walking in darkness. In the essence of things he must sleep where no man was likely to come near, which meant, of course, sleeping on an open hillside. He could have no fire, for that would attract attention. Lastly, he must drink — the iron discipline of the Light Division had accustomed him to dispense almost entirely with water during the heat of the day, but at the same time had given him the habit of drinking immense quantities at night-fall.

His simple demands were readily fulfilled. The stream was beside him, and he knelt to drink. He emptied his water-bottle — "canteen" was its Army name in these days — of its lukewarm contents, filled it, and drank, filled it again, and drank again, filled it again, and looped the strap over his head once more. The idiot beside him drank without so much formality. With his toes on the bank he rested his hands on two boulders protruding above the surface in mid-stream, and, lowering his mouth to the water, he drank great gulps as it flowed past his nose. Dodd was reminded of a chapter in the Bible he had heard read in church during his plough-boy days, about some old general who had picked his men for some special enterprise by the curiously arbitrary method of selecting those who lapped at a stream instead of drinking from their hands.

Darkness was now falling rapidly. There was a towering bare hill to their left and, leaving the path, Dodd set his face to it. Nearly at the summit was a little cluster of whin-bushes, and of these Dodd selected the easterly side. They would give him a little shelter during the night if the west wind brought rain. He slipped his arms out of his equipment, and unrolled his greatcoat, which he put on. Then he harnessed himself again with his pack, so as to be ready for instant action if an alarm should come during the darkness. The idiot had watched all these actions attentively, and when Dodd pulled out his bread and his beefbone from his haversack he crept nearer in the twilight and held out his hands in supplicatory fashion.

Dodd was torn between two emotions. He wanted to feed the starving creature, and yet he had only two days' food to carry him through the ten days of marching which lay between him and his regiment. Duty told him to conserve his rations, pity told him to give. He hardened his heart and munched stolidly, ignoring the pitiful appeal. The biscuit was terribly hard, the beef was terribly tough. As a matter of fact the ox which supplied it had been driven one or two hundred miles on woefully poor food before it had been slaughtered; it had been cut up and subjected to the ill-directed attentions of the regimental cooks as soon as the breath was out of its body, being boiled in a cauldron for an hour or so, the longest that the fierce appetites of the men last evening could wait. But Dodd had known little better food during his five years in the Army, and before that he had been the eleventh child of a farm-labourer earning ten shillings a week and had fed even worse, so that he bit into the tough fibres with contentment.

Yet when he began carefully to pack the remainder away in his haversack the idiot uttered a low wail of despair. He thrust forward his hands, he made pleading noises, and withal so gently and so movingly that Dodd could not resist his appeal. Cursing himself for a helpless fool, he broke a lump from a biscuit and thrust it and the remains of the beef into the idiot's hands. The pleading noises changed to sounds of delight. It was quite dark now, but Dodd heard the biscuit being crunched between the idiot's teeth. From the quality of the sounds he even suspected that the rib of beef was receiving the same treatment.

He sat huddled in his greatcoat for a few minutes, brooding over the day's events before going to sleep, when the sight of a glow in the sky far off brought him to his feet again. He seized his rifle and strode over to the edge of the hill, and the light was explained. Across the valley, stretching to right and left as far as the eye could see, were rows and rows of twinkling points of fire — the bivouac fires of an army. It was a sight he had seen often enough before; looking down at the irregular pattern, he could make a rough guess at the strength of the force encamped there; he could even, by noticing the size of the patches of darkness which broke the continuity, guess at the extent of the horse-lines and consequently estimate the proportion of cavalry and artillery. He did not trouble to do this. He had no report to make to an officer, nor would have for days; it was of no consequence to him if twenty thousand or forty thousand men were there. It was sufficient for him to know that these must be the main column of the French left wing, across whose line of march or behind whose rear he must pass next day. They were five miles away, and it was scarcely possible that their outposts would trouble him here on his bare hillside.

He went back to his bushes, with the idiot rustling through the heather beside him. Loosening his equipment belt a couple of holes, he hitched his pack up under his back until it made a pillow under the back of his neck. He saw to it that his greatcoat was over his legs, and prepared to go to sleep, his face upturned to the stars which glowed brilliantly overhead — far more brightly than ever they did in misty England. A little wind was blowing, very gently, but he was in the lee of the bushes and it did not chill him much. Somewhere near him the idiot seemed to be flattening out a nest for himself in the heather, like a cat, and muttering to himself in monosyllables.

As Dodd was dropping off to sleep there passed through his mind another fragment of what he had once heard in church — something about birds having nests and beasts holes, while the Son of Man had nowhere to rest his head. Dodd did not realize it, but that quotation passed through his mind every time he composed himself to sleep in a bivouac. It was indicative of the fact that he would be asleep in two minutes' time — and, sure enough, he was.

Even now it was only eight o'clock in the evening. Dodd was merely giving a demonstration of that ability to sleep at any hour which has characterized the English private soldier, and has been remarked upon by diarists from generation to generation, from the time of Marlborough's wars to the present day.

Chapter V

AT intervals during the night Dodd stirred and shifted his attitude. He was still fast asleep, but if at those times there had been the slightest suspicious noise near him he would have been broad awake on the instant. But nothing came to disturb him. The shrieking of owls and the barking of a fox were natural noises which the mechanism of his brain filtered out and did not permit to interfere with his sleep. He was a veteran soldier.

He woke easily when the first suspicion of daylight came to lessen the pitch darkness of the night. There was a light rain falling; the coarse frieze of his greatcoat was spangled and silvered with it. He sat up a little stiffly, and looked round him. The idiot sprang into wakefulness when he moved, but beyond that there was no sign of life. He walked to the brow of the hill, but the fine rain drifting across the valley limited the range of vision so that nothing could be seen.

He made his preparations for the day. First he changed the powder in the pan of his rifle, sheltering it under his bowed body as he did so. Then, standing the weapon carefully against a bush, he unbuckled the straps of his pantaloons and drew off his shoes and stockings. There was another pair of stockings, worsted ones, in his pack, and he put these on after he had bathed his feet in the wet heather, being careful to put on his left foot the stocking which he had worn two days before on his right. He put on his shoes and buckled his straps again, ate a mouthful of biscuit and swallowed a mouthful of water, and he was ready for another twelve hours of marching. Grudgingly he tossed a fragment of biscuit to the idiot, who gulped it like a wolf. The poor wretch was shivering and stiff with cold.

Dodd started across the hill. From the ridge, as far as the rain would permit, he made a mental note of the lie of the country and its inconsequent tangle of hills, comparing it with what he had seen of the bivouac fires of the night before. It would be a dangerous march to-day, across the rear of the advancing column. He might encounter foraging parties or marauders or stragglers as well as units on the march. Beyond the road there would be the cavalry of the wings to reckon with. Within the next two hours he might be dead or a prisoner, and captivity or death would be imminent all through the day. But at present he was alive and at liberty, and, soldier fashion, he did not allow the other possibility to depress his spirits.

The rain grew heavier as he plodded on. The legs of his trousers were soaked with wet before very long and, although his greatcoat kept it out admirably, little trickles of moisture began to run down his neck inside his clothes and cause him a good deal of discomfort. The wretched idiot at his side was soon whimpering with distress; Dodd, as he walked along, tried not to think what the rocks and boulders which they sometimes had to cross as they continued along the hill-tops were doing to the poor devil's naked feet. After all, as he told himself, he had not asked him to attach himself to him.

After two hours of difficult going Dodd grew more and more cautious. He must soon be nearing the high road. He strained his eyes through the driving rain to catch a glimpse of it, but the rain was too heavy to allow him to do so. The one element of comfort in the situation was that the wind was coming from the northwest, as nearly as he could judge, so that by keeping his back to it he not merely was preserving his direction but was also walking as comfortably as the comfortless conditions allowed. They came to a stream. Already, in that rocky country, the rain had swelled its volume and it was boiling among the boulders. As Dodd splashed across it, holding up the skirts of his greatcoat and wet to the middle of his thighs, he realized that a continuance of the rain would seriously limit his power of moving across country because of the deepening of the streams. And this one ran southwestward — he still had not yet crossed the main watershed between the sea and the Tagus.

Above the stream rose yet another precipitous slope, up which Dodd set himself doggedly to plod. The wind was working up to gale force, and the rain was whirling across the country with the torrential violence which can only be realized by those who have witnessed an autumnal storm in the Peninsula. The top of this hill was rounded instead of scarped; Dodd had to toil across it for some distance before the next valley opened up before him. What he saw there, dimly through the rain, caused him to drop hastily to the ground.

The high road crossed the valley diagonally before him, from his left rear to his right front, mounting the steep incline with a contempt for gradients which made one wonder at the boldness of the engineers, and it was crammed with men and animals and vehicles. Apparently it was by this leftmost road that the main train of the French Army was being directed. Dodd's arrival synchronized with the disappearance of the last of the marching troops and the beginning of the interminable mass of impedimenta which an army of a hundred thousand men must drag behind it. Dodd lay in the heather while the rain poured down upon him, watching the march of the column, while the idiot whimpered at his side. Even an idiot could appreciate the necessity of lying still when French troops were at hand.

As far back as Dodd could see, and doubtless for miles beyond that, the road was jammed with wheel traffic. There were fifty guns and fifty caissons, there were the heavy waggons of the train, there were hundreds of country carts — the most primitive vehicle invented; each consisted of a long stout pole upon which was bolted a clumsy box-like framework of solid wood, much broader at the top than at the bottom. The wheels were solid, and immovable upon their axles, which rotated stiffly in sockets on the pole to the accompaniment of a most dolorous squeaking. Each cart was drawn by eight oxen, yoked two by two, goaded along by sulky Spanish or Portuguese renegades, and in each cart lay three or four sick or wounded Frenchmen, jolted about on the stony path, exposed to the rain, dying in dozens daily. Yet their lot, even so, was better than if they had been left behind to the mercy of Portuguese peasants.

Guns and waggons and carts were all of them short of draught animals — Dodd could see that nearly every gun had only five horses instead of six. And the hill they had to climb while Dodd watched was far too much for their failing strength. Only a few yards up the slope each vehicle came to a stop despite the shouts of the drivers. Then a team had to be unhitched and brought to reinforce the overworked animals. Then with whips cracking and drivers yelling the horses would plunge up the hill a little farther until some stone of more inconvenient size and shape than usual baulked their progress and the men would have to throw themselves upon the drag ropes and tug and strain until the obstacle was negotiated and a few more yards of the hill were climbed. And so on, and so on, until at last the top of the hill was reached and the vehicle could be left there while the doubled team descended to drag up the next; hours of agonizing effort, stupefied by hunger and rain and wind — a dozen such hills a day, and a hopeless future ahead of dozens more of such days.

Dodd could only lie where he was and wait for the slow procession to crawl past him. He wanted to reach the other side of the road; if he went back up the road to pass the rear of the column more quickly he would only have to retrace his steps once he was across. So he lay there with the rain beating upon him and the wind shrieking overhead; soon he was soaked to the skin, but still he lay, with the inexhaustible, terrible patience acquired in years of campaigning.

It was late afternoon before the last of the vehicles passed out of sight over the hill; it was followed by a mass of sick and wounded men on foot, staggering along blindly over the stony road, and after them came a battalion of infantry in rear-guard formation. Yet even when the rear-guard had disappeared Dodd still waited for fear lest stragglers and marauders should be coming behind. There were none, however. The French did not straggle to the rear nowadays, when they knew that the Portuguese who followed them up had a habit of roasting their prisoners alive, or boiling them, or sawing them in half.

Just before twilight came Dodd was able to descend to the road, and cross it, and mount the hill the other side. The rain had ceased now, but the wind was backing round to the north and blowing colder every minute. He was glad of the chance of exercising his shivering limbs — the idiot who still came with him was so cramped with cold that he fell down every few yards and shambled on all fours until he could rise to his feet again.

Bitter cold it was, but the wind and the exercise did at least have the effect of drying their clothes. Dodd plunged on through the gathering darkness, bent upon putting as much distance between him and the road as was possible before nightfall. He thought of the men of his regiment, gathering round roaring fires, with, if they were lucky, roast pork or boiled beef for supper, and perhaps a nip of brandy. There would be no fire for him to-night, as near to the French as he was, and there would be little enough supper.

It was on an open hillside again that Dodd stopped for the night. He would not camp in a valley or in a wood — that was the sort of place patrols would explore. Philosophically he chose once more the lee of an isolated patch of bushes, but there was comfort to be found in the sight of the glow of the French bivouac fires behind him this evening. With any luck there would be a clear road before him to-morrow back to the Lines — back to his regiment. Strangely, the idiot wanted no supper that night. Dodd could hear his teeth chattering where he lay some distance off.

And in the morning, before it was yet light, it was the idiot who woke Dodd. He was calling out in a loud voice, so that even as Dodd awoke and got to his feet his hand went out to his rifle and he stared through the twilight for an approaching enemy. He could see nothing; he could hear nothing save the idiot's voice, and as he went towards him the voice rose an octave and broke into laughter. Dodd knelt beside him; there was just enough light for him to see that the idiot was lying on his back with his arms thrashing about while he laughed and laughed. Then the laughter changed to words — terror-laden words obviously — while he struggled up to a sitting position and then fell back again. The poor wretch was delirious and in the grip of pneumonia — "fever," Dodd called it to himself. Dodd had to decide what to do; he made his decision in the course of his preparation for the day's march.

If he stayed by the idiot they would starve together. If he burdened himself with his weight he would never catch up on the

marching French, never rejoin his regiment. All he could do was
to leave him there, to starve if the fever did not kill him first. He
made a pitifully feeble attempt to make the idiot comfortable
among the heather, and then, sick at heart but fierce with resolution, he turned away and left him chuckling anew at some comic
thought which had penetrated his fevered idiot's mind. The last
Dodd heard of him was a new shout of *"Morran os Franceses!"*
— a fitting cry enough. Dodd left him there, shouting and laughing, to sink into exhaustion and coma and die, alone on the wind-
swept hill. After all, a soldier had much more important work to
do than to ease an idiot's last hours, as any one would agree who
did not have to make the decision.

Chapter VI

Dodd had promised himself that he would not continue across country after noon that day. By that time he ought to be fairly safe from patrols, and would take the first cross-road that bore in approximately the direction he wished. Before the morning was half over he came across a tempting path which he resolutely kept away from. Twice he saw grey villages in the distance and went cautiously round them out of sight; there was smoke rising from one of them, but smoke might at that point indicate the presence of French as much as Portuguese. He found a stream — a raging torrent after yesterday's rain — which gave him fresh heart because it was running in the right direction, towards the Tagus and not towards the sea. He marched on, never slackening his pace. A man who had marched with Craufurd to Talavera could do without rest. In the nearly roadless desert of the Lisbon Peninsula it was easy enough to keep straight across country, avoiding all the habitations of man. He kept to the hills, away from the sky-line, as much as possible, only descending into the valleys when his route compelled him to do so, and hastening across them with extreme care. All through that morning's march he saw no one, no man working in the fields, not a cow or a sheep, nothing save a herd of wild swine in a beech wood.

That was only to be expected, for it was by Wellington's orders that the country had been swept clear of every living thing before the advance of the French. The crops were to be destroyed, the fields laid waste, the villages left deserted. An enemy who relied for his food on what could be gleaned from the countryside was to be taught a lesson in war. And the ruin and desolation caused thereby might even constitute a shining example to a later generation, which, with the additional advantages of poison gases and high explosives, might worthily attempt to emulate it.

Dodd indulged in no highfalutin meditations upon the waste and destruction. He had been a soldier from the age of seventeen.

His business was solely concerned with killing Frenchmen (or Russians or Germans as the ebb and flow of high politics might decide) while remaining alive as long as possible himself. If by ingenious strategy the French could be lured into starving themselves to death instead of presenting themselves as targets for his rifle so much the better. It increased his respect for "Conky Atty" — "Long-nosed Arthur," Viscount Wellington, in other words — but roused no other emotion. And as a last word in the argument it was only Portuguese whose farms were being burnt and whose fields were being laid waste, and Dodd had enough insular pride to consider Portuguese as not quite human, even now, although Portuguese battalions were now considered worthy of inclusion even in the ranks of the Light Division, and had fought worthily alongside the Ninety-Fifth at Busaco and the Coa and the other battles to which he looked back with pride.

Somewhere right ahead of him came a spatter of musketry fire, and Dodd's nerves tautened. Fighting indicated the presence of both enemies and friends. He pushed on cautiously, with his rifle ready for instant action. His instincts took him to the highest ground in sight, whence he might have an opportunity of discovering the military situation. He was throbbing with hope that perhaps there were English soldiers there. It seemed almost impossible, but there was a chance that he had wandered somehow into a rear-guard action.

The hill below him fell away into a steep, rocky precipice — the gorge of the rushing stream which coursed along its foot with a rough track running along its banks. The firing had nearly ceased now — Dodd could hear only very occasional shots and they were a long way away. Then, out of sight to his right, where the track turned round a shoulder of the hill, he heard the rapid staccato of the hoof-beats of a horse, galloping as hard as he could be driven along the stony path. Round the corner there appeared, far below him, the little figure of a man on foot, running faster than ever Dodd had seen a man run before, and twenty yards behind him came a French dragoon, his sabre flashing as he swung it in the air, leaning forward over his saddle as he spurred his horse in mad pursuit.

For a moment Dodd wondered why the man on foot did not have the sense to take to the hillside where the horseman could not follow him; he decided that he must have lost his head with fright, and pushed forward his rifle to stop the pursuit. It was a Frenchman he was aiming at; he was sure of that — he had aimed at French dragoons often before. He recognized the bell-shaped shako, and the horse's tail was undocked, in the French fashion. He cocked his rifle, aimed and pulled the trigger. But it was incredibly difficult to hit a man at full gallop two hundred yards away with that rifle. Dodd must have missed, for the dragoon continued without a check. Then, while Dodd was frantically reloading, the Frenchman caught up with the man on foot. The sabre flashed again as he swung it round, slashing like a boy with a stick at a nettle. The man on foot staggered, with his arms round his head, but he fell beneath a second slash. The dragoon slashed again at his writhing body, leaning sideways off his horse to do so; he stabbed at it, and then, wheeling his horse round, he spurred it and reined it back until he forced the reluctant animal to trample on his victim, over and over again. Then he trotted back, his whole bearing full of conscious triumph.

Still Dodd had not contrived to coax a fresh bullet down his rifle barrel. He was cursing vilely at the weapon, for he saw clearly there would be no chance of a second shot. Then, when the dragoon was about to turn the corner, a ragged volley sounded from the other side of the gorge. The horse plunged and fell, pitching the dragoon over his head, and instantly a little group of men came leaping down the opposite hillside, splashed across the stream, and seized him just as he was sitting up, dazed. There appeared to be a brief consultation round the prisoner, and then the group, dragging him with them, mounted the side of the gorge almost to where Dodd lay watching.

They were Portuguese peasants, he could see — friends, that was to say. He walked along the crest to where they were gathered round the helpless dragoon. At sight of him they seized their weapons and rushed towards him. Some of them had pikes, two or three of them had muskets, one of them with a bayonet fixed, and apparently with every intention of using it.

"*Inglez*," said Dodd hastily, as they came running up — that green uniform of his made this explanation necessary. The Portuguese always expected to find an Englishman in a red coat.

They looked their unbelief until their leader pushed past them and inspected him.

"*Sim, Inglez,*" he decided, and turned to pour out a torrent of rapid explanation to his followers.

Then he turned back to Dodd and said something which Dodd could not understand. He repeated the phrase, and then, seeing that it meant nothing to Dodd, he reached forward and shook Dodd's rifle.

"*Espingarda raiada,*" he repeated impatiently.

"Rifle," said Dodd.

"Rye-full," said the other. "*Sim, sim, espingarda raiada.*"

To his friends he repeated the word along with more explanation and a vivid bit of pantomime illustrating the rotation of a rifle bullet in flight. Clearly he was a Portuguese of more than average intelligence.

The party drifted back to where the wretched dragoon lay among the rocks, his hands behind his back and a cord round his ankles. His face lit up with hope when he caught sight of Dodd's uniform. The Portuguese leader kicked him in the face as he came up, and then, as he fell back among the stones, kicked him in the belly so that he moaned and doubled up in agony. That was enormously amusing; all the Portuguese hooted with joy as he writhed, and when he turned over on his stomach one of them stuck the point of his pike into the seat of his breeches so that he cried out again with pain and writhed over again on to his back, enabling them to kick him again where it hurt most, amid shrieks of laughter.

It was more than Dodd could stand. He pushed forward like the chivalrous hero of some boys' book of adventure, and cleared the brutes away from the prostrate man.

"Prisoner," he said, and then, in the instinctive belief that they would understand him better if he shouted and if he spoke ungrammatically, he continued in a louder tone, pointing to the captive. "Prisoner. He prisoner. He not to be hurt."

Looking round at the lowering expressions of the Portuguese, he realized that they still did not understand, and he tried to make use of what he knew of Spanish and Portuguese grammatical constructions.

"*Prisonerado,*" he said. "*Captivado. Não damagado.*"

The leader nodded. Clearly he had heard somewhere or other of some silly convention that prisoners were not to be tortured. He broke into rapid speech. Two of his men under his instructions hoisted the dragoon to his feet so that he stood swaying between them. And then, under his further instructions, before Dodd could interfere, three more of his men lowered their pikes and thrust them into his body. The Frenchman, mercifully, was not long dying then, while Dodd looked on horrified and the others grinned at each other. When he was dead they tore his bloodstained clothes from his corpse; one man put on the blue tunic with the red shoulder-knots, while another pulled on the white breeches. Stained and torn as they were, they were better garments than those discarded in their favour. Then they made ready to move on. The leader tapped Dodd on the shoulder and by his gestures clearly indicated that they expected him to accompany them.

"*Inglezes?*" demanded Dodd, pointing.

The leader shook his head and pointed in nearly the opposite direction, and once more insisted in pantomime on his accompanying them. His verbal explanation included the word "*Franceses*"; obviously he was trying to tell Dodd what he knew already, that the whole French Army lay between him and the English. Dodd pointed to himself and then south-eastwards.

"*Tejo,*" he said. "*Alhandra. Lisboa.*"

The leader nodded and shrugged. He had heard vaguely of the Tagus and of Lisbon, but the river was fully fifty miles away and the city a hundred; he had no real belief in their existence. He sloped his musket and signed to Dodd to come with them. The southerly route they seemed determined upon was not far out of his way, so that he joined them in their march without misgiving.

Two months of guerrilla warfare had already taught the Portuguese some elements of military methods. At orders from the leader one man went out far to the right, another to the left, a third ahead. With flank-guards and advance-guard in this fashion there was small chance of their meeting the enemy unexpectedly. They trooped down the steep slope, and turned their faces up the path. The dead horse lay there, already stripped of everything worth carrying away. Farther back lay the dead Portuguese. Some one waved his hand towards the body and made some remark about João. Everybody laughed a little — laughed at the memory of the dead João who did not have the sense to take to the rocks when pursued by a horseman. That was all the epitaph João received.

Dodd never discovered, to his dying day, what had been going on just before his arrival on the scene of the skirmish — who had been fighting, and in what numbers. He could only guess that some reconnoitring or foraging party of dragoons had collided with some detachment of the irregulars. How the men he was now accompanying came to be in their strategical position overlooking the gorge when clearly there had been hand-to-hand fighting higher up he could not conceive, nor what had happened to the rest of the combatants, nor why his friends displayed no anxiety to rejoin their main body. Portuguese irregulars were not distinguished for the discipline which prevailed, for example, in the Ninety-Fifth Foot.

They knew their way about the country. They quitted the good track upon which the march had begun in favour of one much less obvious and practicable, and tramped along without hesitation, up hills and down them, over fords and through forests, the while the sun sank lower and lower. Then they turned into a path which led straight up into the highest hills. It wound round the edge of some precipices and went straight up the face of others, becoming indistinguishable from a dry watercourse in the process. Even the marching powers of a man of the Ninety-Fifth were strained to the utmost. Dodd had fed badly for two days now, and he had marched much. His head began to swim and his heart to beat distressfully against his ribs as he toiled along behind the big Portuguese leader. He began to slip and fall at the difficult parts, borne down by the weight of his weapons and pack. When he fell the man behind trod on his feet while the man in front

made no attempt to wait for him. Darkness fell, and still they
struggled along the stony way, while Dodd felt as though he
must soon sink under his fatigue.

What roused him at the end of that nightmare climb was a
harsh challenge from the slopes above, which was instantly answered by his party. The pace slackened; they stumbled over a
few yards more of rocky path, and round a corner where Dodd
had the impression of a vertical drop hundreds of feet high on his
right hand. Here there was a clear space — a wide shelf on the
mountain side, apparently, where a score of bivouac fires were
burning, with little groups seated round them.

The leader tapped Dodd's shoulder and led him forward through
the lines of fires to the farthest end of the shelf. Here a corner of
the rock made some sort of shallow cave, at the mouth of which a
big fire was burning, and where two lanterns on poles shed additional light. Seated by the fire were two priests in their black
clothes, and between them a burly man in a shabby blue uniform
with faded silver lace at collar and wrists. Dodd's guide approached and made some sort of salute and, as far as Dodd could
understand, accounted for Dodd's presence.

"*Capitão Mor,*" he continued explanatorily to Dodd, and then
left him.

A "Capitão Mor" — Great Captain — as Dodd vaguely understood, was a great man in Portugal, something midway between a
squire and a Lord-Lieutenant, ex-officio commander of the feudal
levies of the district. This one looked Dodd up and down and said
something to him in Portuguese.

"*Não comprehend,*" said Dodd.

The Capitão Mor tried again, speaking with difficulty in what
Dodd guessed must be another language — French, presumably.

"*Não comprehend,*" said Dodd.

The Capitão Mor turned to one of the priests at his side, who in
turn addressed him in some other language, concluding with the
sign of the cross and the gesture of counting his rosary. Dodd
guessed what that meant, and hotly denied the imputation.

"*Não, não, não,*" he said. There were Roman Catholics in his
regiment, good enough fellows too, but Dodd's early upbringing

had laid so much stress on the wickedness of Popery that even now
he felt insulted at being asked if he was a Roman Catholic. He
would not put up with being questioned by Papists and Portuguese any longer. He pointed to himself and then out into the
night.

"*Tejo,*" he said. "*Lisboa.* Me. To-morrow."

The others made no sign of comprehension.

"*Tejo,*" he repeated angrily, pounding on his chest. "Lisbon.
Tejo, Tejo, Tejo."

The three conferred together.

"*Tejo?*" said the Capitão Mor to Dodd interrogatively.

"*Sim. Tejo, Tejo, Tejo.*"

"Bernardino," said the Capitão Mor, turning to one of the
groups at the fires.

Some one came over to them. He was in the usual rags, but on
his head was an English infantry shako — the regimental figures
"43" shone in the firelight. He was only a boy, and he grinned at
Dodd in friendly fashion while the Capitão Mor gave his orders.
Dodd heard the words "*Tejo*" and "*Lisboa*" — blessed words.
Bernardino nodded and grinned again. Then the Capitão Mor
turned to Dodd again with words and gesture of polite dismissal,
and Bernardino led him away to another fireside.

Over this fire hung an iron pot from which came a smell of
onions which to Dodd's famished interior was utterly heavenly.
Bernardino politely made him sit down, found a wooden dish
from somewhere, and ladled into it a generous portion of stew
from the pot. He brought him a hunk of bread, and, still grinning, invited him to eat — an invitation Dodd did not need to
have repeated. He pulled his knife and spoon from his pack and
ate like a wolf. Yet even at that moment, dizzy with fatigue, the
ruling passion asserted itself.

"*Lisboa? Tejo?*" he asked of Bernardino.

"*Sim. Sim.*" Bernardino nodded and said a good deal more,
until, realizing that he was quite unintelligible, he fell back on
pantomime. It takes much complicated gesture to convey the ab-
stract of "to-morrow," but he succeeded at last, and Dodd was
satisfied. When he had finished his meal his head began to nod on

to his breast. He coiled himself up in his greatcoat and fell asleep, revelling in the delicious warmth of the fire. But he mistrusted the military efficiency of the Portuguese. He took off neither his equipment nor his boots, and he slept with his rifle within reach.

Chapter VII

DURING the three days' march that followed Bernardino was almost convinced that this big Englishman whom he had been deputed to guide was slightly mad. He had only one thought — it might be said he had only one word. What he wanted was to reach the Tagus. Nothing else would satisfy him. He would not rest a moment more than necessary; he was always up at the first streak of dawn; he insisted on striding along even when Bernardino was whimpering with fatigue. Bernardino had not heard of the Indian pilgrims whose one wish it was to bathe in the Ganges, but once or twice he had encountered Spaniards or Portuguese who were set on visiting some particular shrine — Santiago di Compostella or some other — and who also were slightly mad, and he came to class Dodd with them in his mind. He explained to every one they met that he had a mad Englishman in his charge whose one wish in life was to set eyes on the Tagus; in Bernardino's opinion this was just as remarkable as that the long rifle which the Englishman carried would (so he had been assured) kill a man with deadly accuracy at half a mile. Bernardino's ambition was, after having gratified the Englishman's strange passion for the Tagus, to lure him into sight of a Frenchman and then see the feat performed.

There were plenty of people for Bernardino to tell all this to, because the country through which they were passing was not laid waste. The proclamations commanding this to be done had been issued — every priest and every alcalde had one — but the country was not in the direct line of march of the contending armies and Wellington had not been able to come there in person and see his orders carried out. It would take more than a mere proclamation to make a wretched peasant burn his crops and his farm and send his womenfolk to Lisbon while he himself went up into the hills to starve. Here and there were patches of ruined country where some Capitão Mor of unusual energy had swept the district with his militia, but elsewhere there were flocks of sheep and herds of cattle, and fields under the plough making ready for the winter sowing.

Dodd shook his head at sight of all this; if the French Army should come this way they would be able to demonstrate their practice that every village should be able to feed a battalion for a week or a division for a day. He was surly towards the village people on whom Bernardino billeted him each night. He could not even accept the pleasant advances of the women in his billets; the women ran delighted eyes over his burly inches, and would have liked to tell him how much they missed their husbands whom the conscription had swept away, but Dodd turned away from them angrily. Their refusal to destroy all their possessions was imperilling his regiment.

There came a day when the road along which they were marching climbed up a small slope, and then descended into a green valley. At the crest Bernardino stopped and pointed forwards dramatically.

"*Eis!*" he said. "*Tejo.*"

He gazed at Dodd expectantly to see what effect this long-wished-for spectacle would have upon him, and he was woefully disappointed. For Dodd merely gazed for a moment across the flat land to where the vast green river ran turbulently in its rocky bed, and then strode on carelessly. And when the country track they were following joined the main high road above the river's bank he turned along it to the right without stopping for Bernardino's guidance and without another glance at the river he had been asking for, for at least the last three days — the river he had walked sixty-five miles to see. Bernardino pulled him by the sleeve to call his attention to it again, but Dodd merely shook him off.

"*Lisboa,*" said Dodd, pointing forwards.

Bernardino could only resign himself to another sixty-five-mile march to Lisbon.

Only for brief stretches does the Tagus run through fertile, cultivated land. Before very long their march took them once again into a stony, sandy desert, a high plateau towering far above the water's edge, and cut up here and there by ravines, at the bottom of which torrential watercourses boiled over their rocky beds on their way to join the main river. The great high road passed across this plateau as straight as a bullet, leaping each ravine in turn by a high stone bridge; at rare intervals a little village lay beside the road, whose inhabitants gained a scanty living by keeping flocks of stunted sheep on the scanty herbage of the hills.

Dodd had twice marched along this road with his regiment; he remembered its main features, and as each remembered characteristic came into view he grew more fevered in his expectancy, and pressed forward until Bernardino was really running to keep pace with him. The morning came when Alhandra, the town where the Lines came down to the river, was only thirty miles away — one long march. Inside the Lines was the British Army, the regiment, everything that Dodd held dear.

Then they met a group of Portuguese irregulars beside the road, at a point where the river left it to make a great loop round the end of a mountain spur. They were not quite as irregular as some Portuguese Dodd had seen; some had genuine fragments of uniform, most of them had muskets, and some of them had bayonets and military cross-belts. They stopped Dodd and Bernardino, and the leader addressed them with harsh questions. Bernardino answered with the loquacity and self-importance natural to him — a long explanation of the Englishman whose one wish was to see Lisbon again, whose rifle would kill a man at a mile, the orders given them by the Capitão Mor, and much more besides.

The man addressed laughed harshly at all this, shaking his head. He told Bernardino that the French barred the way to Alhandra and Lisbon, and Bernardino looked blankly at Dodd. But Dodd understood nothing of what was said, and strongly disapproved of all this waste of time over idle gossip. He made to push through the group.

"*Lisboa,*" said Dodd. "*Alhandra.*"

They held him back, explaining to him in voluble Portuguese. He caught their drift at last; he heard the word "*Franceses.*"

"*Franceses?*" he asked.

"*Sim, sim, Franceses,*" they answered, pointing down the road. And at that moment, as if to accentuate their words, the sentry a quarter of a mile down the road uttered a loud shout, and came running towards them, gesticulating. Every one looked to see to what he was calling their attention; they climbed on the stone wall bordering the road, and gazed along it. A long column of horsemen was trotting towards them; it only took one glance to recognize French dragoons.

At once every one was seized with the confusion of the undisciplined. Some made to run away, some towards the dragoons. Some even pointed their muskets towards the French, who were ten times as far away as a bullet could reach. Dodd alone produced a practicable plan — he had fought in so many skirmishes by now that his reactions were instinctive. He glanced back at the last bridge — but he decided that he could not rely on these feeble soldiers to hold a bridge against a charge of dragoons. To the right the ground sloped away smoothly, and save for a few stone walls offered no protection against horsemen. Only to the left was there safety — the ground rose steeply only one field away, and was rocky and broken.

"This way!" shouted Dodd. "Come this way, you fools!"

The universal language of gesture and example explained what he wanted. Everybody bundled over the stone wall and across the field and up into the rocks. Somebody's musket which had been carried at full cock went off without hurting any one. Once they had started running they would have gone on until they dropped, doubtless, but Dodd yelled himself hoarse, dropped behind a convenient rock, and the others at length imitated his example. Bernardino, squeaking with excitement, was kneeling beside Dodd and peering over the rock.

"*Tirar!*" he was saying, or some such word.

What he meant was obvious from the way he pointed to Dodd's rifle and then at the French. But Dodd shook his head; the range was far too long. Bernardino wailed his disappointment.

The Colonel commanding the dragoons down in the road had no thought of attacking the light-footed men among the rocks. He had had too many lessons in guerrilla warfare by now — he had led his men the length and breadth of Portugal and Spain in incessant contact with pests like these. All he wanted to do was to take his regiment along the road in peace and find out whether there were formed troops along it; the presence of irregulars could be taken for granted. What had to be done was to keep the enemy from the roadside so that they could not take long shots into the vulnerable column. At his orders a troop of dragoons trotted into the field, dismounted on the far side, and while some stayed holding the horses the remainder took their short carbines and scattered among the rocks, while the rest of the long column of horsemen filed along the road. Dodd gazed down at the scattered dragoons. In their long boots and hampered by their helmets and their trailing sabres they were the most unwieldy skirmishers imaginable. He had no fear of them, and it would be tempting to evade them and harass the long column behind them. He looked round at his motley companions; they were looking to him for a lead. With a yell he sprang to his feet, waving his arms to his men, and ran, not towards the road, but parallel to it, along the steep side of the hill. The others hesitated, but Bernardino seemed to have grasped Dodd's plan, and when he called to them explanatorily they followed. The covering dragoons fired at them ineffectually with their carbines; not a shot told, and Dodd, with the others yelling behind him, ran panting over the rocks diagonally down to the road again where the dragoons were riding three by three. He fired into the thick of them, and a man fell from his saddle. Instantly the others fired too; it seemed as if one or two of the bullets miraculously hit their marks. There was confusion in the road. Some young officer who still had not learnt his lesson drew his sword and set his horse at the rocks calling to the others to follow him.

Horses fell with a crash among the stones, and Dodd, reloading with the speed of years of drill, shot the officer whose horse alone kept his feet. Other dragoons fired wildly from the saddle; a few dismounted and began a more careful fire from the side of the road. It was only then that the covering flank-guard began to come into action again. The clumsily equipped men had had to labour along the field and over the walls along to where the irregulars had preceded them. Dodd saw them coming and yelled again to his men. Bernardino, mad with excitement, abetted him shrilly. Next moment they were all running diagonally up the hill again, leaving their clumsy pursuers far behind. They made their breathless way again along the spur to head off the column once more, and then again they rushed down the slope to fire at the helpless horsemen.

There was no pity in Dodd's mind; it was his business to kill Frenchmen, and if the Frenchmen were not in a position to try to kill him in return so much the better. He fired pitilessly into the long column, reloaded and fired again, and his companions did the same when they came up. The flanking party came up belatedly to drive them off, but for yet a third time they were able to get along the spur and repeat their manœuvre. The maddened dragoons down in the road could do nothing. It had been their fate to be sniped at thus over a thousand miles of road — small wonder that they burnt in their exasperation the villages through which they passed, and hanged any one unfortunate enough to fall into their hands.

To-day relief came to them where the mountain spur ended and the road came down close to the river bank. Dodd eyed the narrowing triangle between road and river and called his men off. He would not risk being hemmed in there, and he was wearied with much running among the rocks. He shouted, and he gesticulated, and then he walked back up the spur. Below him the cavalry trotted on down the road. The last man in the long column turned in his saddle and shook his fist and shouted his exasperation, at which every one with Dodd laughed hysterically.

It was an exhilarating introduction to war for the Tagus-side militia. There were half a dozen dead men and half a dozen dead horses along the road, to be stripped of their clothes and accoutrements, and not one of their own party had been hurt. They looked at Dodd respectfully now, and, as for Bernardino, his eyes shone with admiration for the big, burly rifleman in his black-braided green coat. He walked along beside him looking up at him almost with a dog's devotion, and when Dodd sat down on a boulder overlooking the road, with his chin on his hands, Bernardino sat down too, quietly, so as not to disturb the great man's meditations.

There was much for Dodd to think about. This, the last road towards Lisbon, was blocked with French troops, apparently. He was cut off from his countrymen and his regiment. He had failed in his endeavour to march round the French Army. The latter seemed to have swerved to its left and then recoiled, which made it appear most likely that they had reached the Lines. The one hope left was that they might be in retreat — the cavalry were certainly on the road towards France, but the movement of a single regiment of cavalry was by no means indicative of the movement of a whole army. Far more probably they were only looking for means of crossing the Tagus. All that Dodd could decide was that he must find a secure shelter until he could discover enough about the French movements to make fresh plans now that his first plan was upset.

Dodd was not exasperated or cast down at the new development. The soldier with years of campaigning behind him has, perforce, acquired a philosophic outlook towards turns of fortune. If one plan goes wrong there is need to make another, that is all. And, as for despair — there was no room for despair in Dodd's make-up. The regiment had taught him that he must do his duty or die in the attempt; a simple enough religion fit for his simple mind. As long as there was breath in his body or a thought in his mind he must struggle on; as long as he went on trying there was no need to meditate on success or failure. The only reward for the doing of his duty would be the knowledge that his duty was being done. That was how honour called; and glory — the man in the ranks did not bother with glory, nor did the men a century later who died in the poison gas at Ypres.

The Portuguese round Dodd were chattering like a nest of magpies, telling each other over and over again of their individual exploits in the recent skirmish, and every time with embellishments and additions. They displayed their trophies to each other, they romped and they gambolled. They were not like the hardbitten militia of the Beira whom Dodd had encountered earlier, who had fought in three invasions of Portugal, who had seen their homes destroyed and their women ravished; this was the first time the tide of war had reached these out of the way banks of the Tagus.

Dodd wondered grimly what these men would do in action against a French light-infantry regiment, and realized that he would probably see it happen soon enough. He must make preparations against the arrival of the French Army. First, he must discover their village, their headquarters. He searched in his mind for words of Portuguese. He poked the leader in the ribs and tried the word for "town."

"*Vilha?*" he asked.

The other seemed dazed at the question. Truth to tell, there was no town within thirty miles. Dodd thought again, and inspiration came to him.

"*Posada?*" he asked. Where the wine shop was, there would be the village.

A great light dawned upon the faces of the listening Portuguese. Of course there was immediate need to visit the *posada*. They could not understand how they had come to forget the possibility of celebrating the recent glorious victory. Every one shouted at once. Every one caught up his bundle of booty and began to bustle about in preparation for a triumphant return home. With beckonings of welcome they led Dodd down to the road, a mile or so along it, and up a narrow, rocky lane over the spur of the hill. There, nestling in a little valley surrounded by towering rocks, lay their little village, twenty stone houses in all. The houses were grouped with no method about a central open space; there were huge stinking heaps of manure here and there; a little rivulet rushing through the village down to the Tagus served at once as a source of drinking water and as a sewer. The women and old men and children turned out to witness their triumphant entry. Lean chickens scrambled about the stones; four long strips of hand-picked land stretching down towards the green river showed where the villagers wrung their wretched living from the ungrateful soil. There were pigs to be seen, and up the sides of the valley were tethered cows just managing to keep alive among the few blades of grass among the rocks.

The ragged women and the nearly naked children — no child wore more than one garment — stood wondering as they marched in, waving their weapons and their trophies.

The men gathered outside the wine shop, escorting Dodd with ceremony to a seat on the stone benches.

Wine made its appearance at once, in wooden cups. Every one was drinking, talking, shouting. Every one eyed Dodd as he was pointed out as the marvellous Englishman who had beaten the French with the necessary assistance of the valiant villagers. As an afterthought Dodd's cup, half empty, was taken from him, and a new one brought him, full of the best wine the *posada* boasted — *vinho valeroso,* as he was assured on every side.

When Dodd made the gesture of eating they brought him food, and every one else, like a child, decided he must eat too. The men squatted here and there round the *posada* while the women brought food, but eating did not interfere in the least with conversation or — most decidedly not — with drinking. The situation had every appearance of developing into a wild village spree, one of those few marvellous days when the frugal Portuguese peasant could forget the cost of anything, forget the need to work, forget the precariousness of existence. Bernardino, who naturally had the morals of a muleteer, seeing that was his profession, was caressing a girl in a secluded corner. Already some one had produced a guitar, and some were singing and some were dancing, when Dodd heaved himself to his feet. All eyes turned upon him while he picked out three of the young men and beckoned them to follow him. He led them out of the village up the stony lane again. Two of them he stationed within sight of the high road. He handled their muskets; he pointed up and down the road, peering out under his hand; he seemed to catch sight of something on the road, pointed the musket, called out "bang," held one of the two still, and pushed the other with the gesture of running back to the village. They grasped his meaning, grinning broadly and nodding. Pointing to the sun, and then to the west, he indicated the length of their watch. The third man he sent up the hillside where the view was more extensive.

Then he went back to the village. There was no position that he could see where twenty peasants could defy the attack of a hundred thousand men, although there was comfort to be found in the sight of the precipitous, rocky heights on each side of the ravine. He walked down to the river bank. The turbulent green water was pouring down over its rocky shelves, the whole surface marked with ripples and eddies. So wide was it that details on the farther bank were hardly to be made out.

Then, far down the river, something appeared round the bend which made him catch his breath with excitement. It was a white boat; as he looked he saw the flash of oars. He picked his way along the stony water's edge towards it. It was fighting its way upstream, taking advantage of the eddies inside the curve. There was something unusual about the deliberation of the strokes of the oars; Dodd recognized the rhythm at once — he had been landed from so many transports that he could not help but know the Navy stroke. The boat drew nearer and nearer. Dodd could see the gun mounted in the bow and the flutter of the white ensign at the stern. He could see the officer at the tiller and the men bending over the oars. He rushed along the bank, waving and shouting; but the boat pulled steadily on. In the long pull up from Alhandra so many Portuguese had waved to them from the bank that the crew did not give him a second thought. If only he had been wearing a red coat!

The boat rounded the curve and the officer stood up in the stern sheets to look up the next reach. Satisfied that no French were trying to cross the river he sat down again and pulled the tiller over. The boat swung round and edged into mid-stream to catch the full force of the current; its patrol was over. The current whirled it back round the curve at four times the speed at which it had ascended. Dodd still ran and waved and shouted, to no avail. The officer found time to wave a friendly arm to him, and a few minutes later the boat had vanished round the curve, beneath the beetling cliffs. There was nothing that Dodd could do save to plod back to the village and resume his plans for the discomfiture of the French in this quarter.

Chapter VIII

"PRECIPICES! My God, nothing but precipices!" said Sergeant Godinot, staring up at the Lines of Torres Vedras. "And there is a fortress as strong as Rodrigo on the top of that hill — look at the guns in the embrasures. We shall have some fighting to do before we reach Lisbon after all, you men. Three miles of precipices so far."

"You didn't tell us about this at the depot, Sergeant," said Fournier, where he stood beside him.

"The English had not seen fit to inform me of it," said Godinot, and added, under his breath, "Nor any one else either."

"What in the name of God is that in that ravine?" asked Dubois, pointing.

Every one looked, but no one offered an explanation. All they could see was that a whole valley penetrating the Lines had been stuffed up with something or other. At that distance it was impossible to see, and from their experience it was impossible to realize, that a hundred thousand olive trees, roots, branches and all, had been flung into the ravine to make an entanglement that not even a mouse, let alone a man, could penetrate.

"More precipices," said Godinot, as the march of the company opened up a view of a new sector. Another long strip of a bare hillside had been dug or blasted away, leaving a ten-foot scarp that a man could mount only with a ladder; and redoubts at each end of the scarp, with guns mounted to enfilade it, indicated what would be the fate of any one who attempted to do so.

"Red-coats up there," said Godron, pointing. The British Army was in position behind the Lines to support the hordes of militia who manned the redoubts.

Still the company marched on. The French advance-guard was feeling to its left in an endeavour to find if there was any end to this line of fortifications against which it had stumbled. Sergeant Godinot and his friends were in the extreme flank company, marching continually southwards parallel to the Lines. On their right a bare valley, three quarters of a mile wide, extended to the foot of the entrenchments, and this valley had been swept clean as if with a broom. Not a tree, not a bush, not a fragment of rock had been allowed to remain. Troops forming up for an assault would do so under heavy fire and without a vestige of cover.

"Somebody's worked damned hard," growled Fournier.

"Not as hard as you'll have to work soon, old boy, when we break through," laughed Godinot, expressing an opinion he did not feel in the least.

"Break through? Do you think we're going to break through *that*? Never in your life," said Fournier. He had only been a soldier for a year, but he knew the militarily impossible when he saw it.

"Well, we'll find a way round," said Godinot optimistically.

A puff of smoke shot from a redoubt, and a cannon-ball screamed over their heads and plumped into the hillside above them.

"We are trespassing on Their Excellencies' territory," said Godinot.

The Captain at the head of the company took the hint, and led the little column diagonally up the hill a trifle before marching on.

There were frequent stumbles and oaths in the ranks, for there was only the rough countryside to march upon. There was no road, no track even, here outside the Lines. Before long every man in the ranks was cursing and complaining as he staggered along over the uneven ground, bowed under his pack, until at last there was no breath left even for curses, and the only sounds to be heard were the clash of nailed boots on rock and the creaking of ac-coutrements. Once or twice there was a welcome halt, but each time the Colonel rode up and the company had to move on again. As much information as was possible must be gained in the short-est possible time regarding this amazing phenomenon, and these stony hills were no place for cavalry. Up hills they went, so steep that progress had to be made on hands and knees, and down valleys. The intervals between companies was growing longer and longer, as Sergeant Godinot saw when he looked back; the advance-guard was growing desperately thin. Still they marched, until at the last crest they saw ahead of them what must be a river valley — the Tagus at last.

"Did you say we were going to find a way round, Sergeant?" asked Fournier with a sneer, pointing to their right front.

In that direction there was a gleam of water, a hint of marsh and of flooded fields, stretching clear down to where two more huge redoubts towered above the Tagus bank. A tributary of the Tagus had been dammed at its mouth to make a morass four miles long to fill the gap between the fortifications in the hills and the Tagus. Even Godinot, conscientiously anxious to keep his section cheerful, had no reply to make to that. He could only look wordlessly, and he continued to look when the order to halt was given and the exhausted men sank to the ground. Three staff officers who had accompanied them on foot, their bridles over their arms, gazed down at the river with their telescopes. Then they turned back, wordlessly.

Godinot guessed what sort of message they would have to take back to headquarters — they displayed their disappointment and dismay in every gesture — still he did his best to be cheerful.

"They'll have found something better than this out on the right," he said.

But his tentative optimism was received with a chilling silence. Even men stupid with fatigue and hunger had more sense than to imagine that an enemy who had so carefully fortified this end would leave the other end unguarded.

That, of course, was an eminently correct deduction. This outer line (there were inner ones too) extended for twenty-two miles across the base of the triangle enclosed between the sea and the Tagus, so that in the top of the triangle, in Lisbon and the surrounding country, the British Army and the Portuguese population could find secure shelter while the enemy starved outside. British ingenuity and Portuguese hard work could make a position impregnable even in the days before barbed wire and machine guns.

The Captain summoned his four sergeants and issued his orders.

"Sergeant Bossin's section will do picket duty to-night. I will attend to the posting of the sentries myself. The other sections may bivouac and cook."

The Captain tried to meet the eyes of his sergeants when he said this, but his gaze wavered. It was hard to say those words and face the reproach in the faces of the others. There was a chill wind blowing, and a thin rain was beginning to fall.

"Do we bivouac where we are, sir?" asked Godron.

"Yes. Those are the orders."

The Captain knew that it was a bad disciplinary move to blame the hardship the men had to suffer upon higher authority, but he had to excuse himself.

Back went the sergeants to where the exhausted men lay upon the bleak hillside. So weary were they that the news that there was to be no issue of rations was received without a complaint. The men had ceased, in fact, to expect a ration issue, and, marching as they had been in contact with the enemy, they had had no chance to plunder food.

Wearily they made their preparations for the night. Half a dozen volunteers — the ones whose feet were least damaged — began to crawl about the hill cutting bushes for fuel. Fournier and Lebrun, who boasted the possession of a blanket which they carried turn and turn about, began to erect it like a tiny tent. Soon half a dozen wretched little fires were alight, giving much smoke and very little heat. Only round one fire was there any bustle of expectation. Here a pot was actually being hung over the flames, and one man was preparing the meat for the evening meal for himself and his intimate friends. It was a little white dog he had seen at the beginning of that day's march, and had instantly shot. For the rest of the day he had carried it slung by the paws from his belt and now, in quite a matter-of-fact way, he proceeded to skin it and disembowel it and joint it, throwing the meat piece by piece into the pot. Other men looked on hungrily, but it was only a little dog, and they could not expect a share.

Some one carried a platter of the stew to the Captain in his solitary bivouac, but although he looked at it with longing, and sniffed at its heavenly savour, he refused it sadly, and turned again to gnawing at his flinty bread. He could not eat meat unless all his men had at least a taste of it.

Darkness fell, and the fires began to die away. The wretched men huddled their cloaks closer about their ragged bodies, and tried to burrow into the earth in an effort to shelter themselves from the penetrating cold. They were only boys, these men of the Eighth Corps, new recruits bundled together into hastily formed battalions and sent out on the long and dreary road to Portugal, untrained, unseasoned, ill-equipped. The man who sent them was at that time progressing about his provinces displaying to a dazzled people the marvellous new wife he had won by right of conquest — a real Hapsburg princess, daughter of fifty emperors.

The wind blew colder with the falling of the night. The men muttered and groaned as they turned backwards and forwards seeking some sort of warmth or comfort. Yet their rest was not broken when the sentries challenged, for that was a cry to which they were accustomed. For the Captain went the rounds three times that night, to see that the sentries were alert and at their posts. Vigilance was necessary, for Portuguese had been known to creep into the ranks of sleeping men and cut half a dozen throats before crawling away again undetected.

Chapter IX

EVEN the young soldiers of the Eighth Corps could look at a river and guess by the direction of its flow whether they were in advance or retreat.

"What's this, Sergeant?" asked young Bernhard. "Are we going home?"

For the regiment was at the head of a long column marching up the high road along the Tagus bank away from the Lines.

"Perhaps God knows, but I don't," said Godinot.

"Perhaps we're going to find Godinot's uncle," said Fournier.

"Let us hope so," said Godinot. He himself could not hope so; he could not imagine that they were about to pass the bridgeless Tagus and join with the distant Army of the South.

"No," said Fournier, "Bernhard is right. We're going home. Back to decent billets. And all of us are to be given a new pair of shoes and let us hope Godron will get another pair of breeches before the Spanish ladies lay eyes on him and swoon in ecstasy."

There was a laugh at that. The boys could actually laugh, now that a definite move had been made and they were marching in a new direction.

They passed a dead horse at the side of the road.

"The dragoons are in front of us, then," said Godinot, looking at the thing, which was just beginning to swell with corruption.

"Why should it be one of ours?" asked Godron. There was no fraction of its equipment left on it.

"By the brand on its flank, son," replied Godinot. "When are you going to learn your trade?"

"But if it's one of ours," said Bernhard thoughtfully, "and the dragoons are in front, it looks like a retreat, doesn't it?"

"Maybe," said Godinot, and then he hardened his heart, for he did not want these boys' hopes raised too high. "But they'd be sent back out of the way whatever we were going to do —

attack the lines or stand still. I expect we're only sent this way
to act as flank-guard to look after the river."

That cast them down: the prospect of lingering further in
Portugal was abhorrent to them. There was no further conversation until another incident occurred to stimulate it afresh.

A staff officer came clattering up the paved road along the column to where the Colonel rode at the head.

"Orders," said Bernhard sagely. "And orders always mean
trouble."

He was right. Somewhere farther back the road had diverged
from the river in order to cross at a more convenient point a
double-headed spur of hills which ran at right angles down to
the river. Up into the mass of tangled country lying between road
and river diverged a narrow, stony lane. Here the battalion halted
for a moment, and the rumour — as always, no one knew who
was responsible for it — ran down the ranks that billets lay at the
end of the lane. But the Colonel clearly did not expect a hospitable
reception at the billets, seeing that he pushed the battalion up the
lane in advance-guard formation.

"This looks like the end of our retreat," said Godron.

"But billets to-night, boys," said Fournier. "And soup for
supper."

At that very moment a shot rang out at the head of the column,
followed by half a dozen more. The column halted, went on,
halted again, while the firing increased and died away and revived. Godinot's friends at the rear of the column did not bother
to crane their necks to see what was happening in front. This sort
of skirmish occurred two or three times a day to a column marching in Portugal. Then the Captain came back down the column,
his drummer behind him. He scaled the steep side of the lane and
stood looking up the hills for a space before he turned and beckoned to his waiting company. They climbed the bank with stoical
nonchalance.

"Chase those fellows over into the river," said the Captain.

Every one knew what he had to do. The company spread out
in a long thin line and pushed slowly up the steep hill. Right at
the summit occasional shots and puffs of smoke indicated where

the advance-guard was in action. For some distance they met with no opposition, but half-way up the hill a puff of smoke jetted out from behind a rock and a bullet crackled overhead. The man who fired it sprang up and dashed ahead of them up the hill. The line of skirmishers bulged for a minute as some of the hotheads made as though to run after him, and then settled down again to a steady advance. Higher up there were more men in ambush, more shots fired. Some one in the skirmishing line fell with a crash and a clatter. Here and there men fired back.

"Wait until you are sure," shouted Godinot to his section.

Some of them looked round at him and grinned. In the friendly relations which existed between non-commissioned officers and men in the French Army they had often had arguments with him regarding marksmanship.

They were nearing the top of the hill. Whoever was opposing them there would find his retreat cut off if he was not careful.

"There's an Englishman there!" suddenly shouted Fournier. "A green Englishman!"

They all caught sight of him; he was calling and gesticulating to the men gathered at the summit. Every one recognized his uniform, and, further, every one realized the purport of his gesticulations. The Captain, waving his sword, rushed to the front and called to his men to follow him in a final dash, but the green-coated soldier had timed his stand to a nicety. He and his band turned and ran helter-skelter along the summit, neatly avoiding being driven down into the river.

Without orders, the French inclined to their right and ran to head them off, while the advance-guard with whom the Portuguese had originally been engaged followed in hot pursuit. One of the Portuguese missed his footing and fell rolling down the slope, and before he could regain his feet Godinot's bayonet was through him. Fournier at Godinot's side, wild with excitement, stabbed him too, and the man died writhing with rage and pain.

The skirmish lost all trace of order up here on the wild mountain top. When a skirmishing line begins to run in broken country and with frequent changes of direction it soon ceases to be a line. The two French companies broke into little groups ranging hither and thither over the hillside, while the sky grew dark and torrents of rain poured down to add to the confusion. In that nightmare country of tall rocks and scrubby trees and low bushes the battle was fought out to an indecisive end. The timorous and the weary among the French found ample opportunity of withdrawing from the struggle, and crouching for shelter and concealment in clefts in the rock, while the brave and the headstrong lost their way. Yet there were still musket shots spitting out here and there in the gathering gloom. Men were still meeting their deaths in the disordered battle.

Godinot, pushing up a little ravine with two or three followers, met Lebrun and Fournier coming down it, and between them they were half leading, half carrying some one else — Godron.

"The Englishman shot him," explained Fournier.

"The Englishman?"

"Yes, by God!"

"Where's he wounded?"

"In the stomach."

There was a pause at that. Every one knew what a stomach wound involved, and every one knew — it had been enjoined upon them so often — that only the cowards withdrew from a fight to help the wounded home. Yet every one knew, too, that they could not leave a wounded man — not even a dying man — where Portuguese irregulars might reach him.

Godinot was saved from the dilemma by the long roll of a drum far behind him. Then the drum beat to a new rhythm, a long roll and three beats followed by a short roll and three beats, repeated. It was the retreat. A greatcoat with two muskets thrust through the sleeves and pocket slits made some sort of stretcher for Godron, and between them they carried him back to where the two companies were reassembling on the crest above the lane. The sun had set now, but the clouds had parted in the west, and permitted a little watery, dying light. The Captain was a sad man as the sergeants made their reports. So-and-so was missing, and some one else. And some one else was dead — they had seen him fall, and brought back his things from his pack. The Captain looked darkly up the hill, and over to the fading west. This was a defeat, and he could not avenge it as yet. He could not think of plunging his weary men into that tangle of rocks in darkness. He could not even think of trying to find the missing men. He hoped that they were dead rather than in Portuguese hands. He kept the company waiting while darkness fell, to be rewarded by the return of one or two of the missing, and then, reluctantly, he led the company down the hill and down the lane to where a cluster of stone cottages marked the billets of the battalion.

That evening, while little Godron was dying under the surgeon's hands, there was rejoicing in the battalion. Not merely did every one have a roof over his head — were it only the roof of a filthy cowshed — but every one had enough to eat. There was a field of potatoes between the village and the river, and although, apparently, efforts had been made to dig them up and throw them into the Tagus, there were still great quantities to be found for the digging. And as they had marched in a nanny-goat with two kids had also entered the village, bleating pathetically. That meant soup for every one, and more than a taste of meat; and not only that, but some one had grabbed a stray, lone chicken running round the dunghills which would be a welcome addition to the officers' mess. There was fuel too — fences and palings in such quantity that there was no need to cut down the fruit trees. Every one could sit near a great, roaring fire and get warm for the first evening in weeks.

It was sad about the wine. Some one had smashed in all the casks of wine in the cellar of the inn; wine was running everywhere, but for all that there was still enough in the casks for the officers and enough could be scooped off the floor for the men to make them all thoroughly happy. It was a perfectly splendid, riotous evening.

No one gave a second thought to the fact that the goats and the chicken were the only living creatures to be found in the village: they were used to that. Of course it would have added to their enjoyment if a woman or two had been kind enough to remain to help in their entertainment. But that was not important at present; the men had marched too fast and too far lately to have many thoughts to devote to that subject. They were all very happy eating and drinking and revelling in the warmth.

Fournier came and sat down heavily beside Sergeant Godinot.

"Godron's going to die, I suppose," he began.

"I'm afraid so, poor devil," said Godinot.

Fournier hesitated awhile before he continued: —

"Do you remember that day when we were rejoining the battalion after that fatigue we were left behind to do?"

"You mean the day Boyel was killed? Yes."

"Boyel was Godron's friend."

"He was my friend too."

"The same man killed them both," said Fournier.

"Not likely. How do you know?" asked Godinot.

"It is. I swear it. I saw him as plain as my hand when he killed Boyel. And to-day — I saw him twice along my musket barrel. How did I come to miss him? How did we all come to miss him the other time? Tell me that."

"Gently, gently," said Godinot, noticing the expression on Fournier's face. "More bullets miss than hit, you know."

"It will take a lot of bullets to hit that one," said Fournier.

"Go to sleep and forget about it," said Godinot. "You will feel better in the morning."

Yet it took more than that kindly offhandedness to soothe the superstitious Fournier; it was late when Godinot succeeded.

The fires died down. The battalion slept while the sentries paced their beats round the village. The sentries were on the alert, as well men may be whose lives depend upon it. But no sentry's beat extended down to the river beach, and no one saw a score of dark shadows creep along the water's edge across the mouth of the ravine, leaving the hill of that day's battle for the other one beyond the ravine.

Chapter X

NEXT morning the battalion were delighted to hear that they were not to march. Settled here in comfort, with enough to eat and shelter from the weather, they had forgotten their yesterday's yearnings to retreat. But they were not to remain idle, not all of them. Two companies were to stay in their billets to guard the fort and mend their clothes and do whatever else might seem necessary. The other four paraded in light marching order — carrying nothing but their arms and their ammunition — and proceeded to sweep the hill where they had fought yesterday, in search of the brigands who had had the better of them.

It was a careful and highly scientific operation. Three companies were extended until they covered the whole width from road to river, a dozen yards between each man. The four sections of the fourth company were distributed at intervals along the line to supply a solid mass to deal with the brigands when found — the twenty men of a single section could be relied on to do that. Then, with infinite trouble in preserving distance and dressing, they swept across the hill. There were seven miles of it to where the high road came down to the river again, and it took them all day — seven hours of cursing and slipping and stumbling, of dreary waiting in the rain while the line straightened, of beating through dripping wet bushes for hidden enemies, and they found nothing. A few men fired their muskets, but they were only the sort of fools who fire muskets when there is nothing to fire at. There was nobody on the hill at all; the only sign that there had been any one was the presence of a few naked corpses lying in the rain, one or two of them unknown and therefore Portuguese, the rest the missing Frenchmen of yesterday. They were all infuriated, wet, and exhausted when towards evening they stumbled on the pickets of the next battalion down the river and knew that there was no use in searching farther. They marched back through the drenching rain of the bitter night along the high road with its ankle-twisting *pavé*.

It was some consolation when they at last staggered back into the village to find that the headquarters guard had fires ready for them, and hot soup — even though the soup this night had not even a taste of meat and was hardly to be distinguished from plain potatoes and water.

In exasperating three hundred men like this, and wearing out three hundred men's shoe leather, Rifleman Matthew Dodd had done his duty. It had been simple enough, even though it had been tiresome explaining his wishes to the village, not in the least aided by Bernardino's hopeless misinterpretations of his signs.

The hardest part had been persuading the villagers to destroy what food they could not carry off. They would leave their homes for the hills, they would take their cattle with them, but to destroy food was almost a sacrilege to their frugal minds. Dodd had had to set to work single-handed digging up the potatoes and wheeling them down to the river's brink before they would come to assist him. And he had had to stave in the wine-casks singlehanded. Nevertheless, much had been done in the course of the thirty-six hours granted him between the passing of the dragoons and the arrival of the infantry. And when that arrival was at last signalled it had only been elementary strategy to attack them from one hill while the women and the animals had taken refuge in the other; nor was it much more to transfer his men under cover of night to the other hill to evade the more searching attack which Dodd foresaw (he had been a soldier for five years and knew much about the military mind) to be inevitable on the morrow. Simple strategy, but most remarkably effective.

Dodd, that night, sitting by the concealed fire close to the bank of the Tagus, saw no reason at all why he should not continue this harassment for the further two or three days that the French would be in the vicinity before want of food drove them into retreat so that he could emerge and rejoin his beloved regiment.

Two or three days, thought Dodd: the French would have

eaten up the supplies by then. Dodd did not estimate correctly what French troops could endure, nor the iron will of the Marshal in command, nor — well as he knew his subject — to quite what lengths of nightmarish, logical absurdity war could be carried. He could not foresee that for three whole months the French were to stay here on the Tagus, starving, while disease and hunger brought down victim after victim, until one man in three had died without setting eyes on an enemy while the English rested and waxed fat in the shelter of the Lines. The ships streaming into Lisbon Harbour would bring them English beef and English pork and English bread so that they might rest in comfort until their grim, unseen allies had done their work, until the French Army might be sufficiently reduced in numbers to make it possible for them to sally out and engage them on an equality.

It was a strategy as simple as Dodd's, but in both cases it called for iron resolution and contempt for public opinion to carry it out to its fullest, most destructive extent. To compare a simple Rifleman with his Commander-in-Chief may seem sacrilegious, but at least they had been trained in the same school.

The village had worked hard enough in all conscience at saving food from the invaders. The children had been packed off into the hills with the animals while men and women toiled at emptying the big village barn. Sacks of corn and of maize had been dragged up the steep slopes, women showing themselves as strong as the men at the work. First of all two little side ravines, where arbutus grew thick, had been filled with sacks of corn. When it came to taking the flour, the people had at first appeared to raise objection to Dodd's plans. They talked to each other in loud voices, and turned and explained to Dodd over and over again, but he could not understand. At last big Maria, the mother of the pretty Agostina whom Bernardino favoured, seized Dodd by the arm and dragged him after her, bowed though she was beneath the sack of flour. Over the summit of the hill they went, by a tricky, winding goat track, and down the other side, where the river coursed green and immense at the foot of the slope. A thin track ran down here to the water's edge and ended there abruptly. On each side of the little beach where the path ended the bank of the river rose again in big, beetling cliffs, forty feet high, and the water, running in its winter volume, washed the very foot of them.

Without hesitation Maria hitched up her bulging dress and plunged barelegged into the water, still calling Dodd to follow her. Just below the surface, and responsible for the foaming, frightening eddy here, lay a long ridge of rock. Dodd followed Maria along it, with the water boiling round his knees. Round a corner of the cliff they went, and then before them Dodd could see the ideal sanctuary. It was a little beach in an angle of the cliff, which here had been undercut so that observation even from above would be difficult and most unlikely. There was a small cave, which could be easily enlarged by a few hours' work with a pick. There was no other approach to the beach at all; there was only this underwater ridge — exposed at times of drought, doubt-less, which was how the village knew of it — whose existence no one could guess at.

Dodd displayed his enthusiasm for this hiding-place by all the antics of which he was capable, and the village gathered round and revelled in his approval. Hither the old folk were brought, and what few household valuables existed, and as much food as could be carried in the limited time available — the climb was far too long and too steep to permit of everything being done which could be considered necessary. Much of the corn, as has been already mentioned, had to be hidden on the hillside — some even was only poured into a silo near the barn and the mouth of the pit covered with rubbish. The forty-eight hours which opened with the battle with the dragoons and concluded with the battle with the infantry had been busy enough.

Since the last skirmish there had been peace. Dodd, with Ber-nardino chuckling delightedly at his side, had lain out on the hill and seen the elaborate attack launched on the other hill — the one they had evacuated. He had counted the force left in the village, and had decided that it was ten times at least too large for him to risk an attack upon it in the absence of the main body. He had seen two graves dug and two men buried in them — one had been little Godron, whom he himself had wounded the night before, although he did not know that. He could easily have lobbed a shot or two at long range among the groups moving among the cottages, but he refrained. There were valuable sheep and cows on the hill behind him, and he did not want to offer any temptation to the French to come up this way and find them.

As they made their way back to the river something on the distant bank caught Dodd's attention — it looked like a long row of glittering beads on an invisible thread. He looked again — the distance was well over half a mile and details were obscure. But his first guess had been correct. The glittering beads were the helmets of a long line of horsemen trotting along the road on the farther bank. It was a long distance to ascertain their nationality. Dodd gazed and gazed, and was still not sure.

"*Portugezes*," said Bernardino briefly, looking at them under his hand.

Bernardino's eyesight was perfectly marvellous — even better than Dodd's — and Dodd was content to take his word for it. He thought he could see high crests to the helmets, and was inclined to agree with him.

So the farther bank was occupied and would be defended against the French should the latter by some miracle find means of crossing the roaring half-mile flood. Dodd nodded his head in solid approval of my Lord of Wellington's arrangements. Could he himself cross over he would find himself among friends who would pass him back to Lisbon and the regiment. But there was no way in which he could cross. There seemed to be no boats at all — that was one matter in which Wellington's order had been obeyed — and Dodd could not swim a stroke. He could only look longingly at the Portuguese dragoons trotting along the opposite bank and turn once more to his present duty of keeping himself out of the hands of the French.

Chapter XI

THE fourth battalion of the Forty-Sixth *Infanterie de Ligne* had time now to look about itself — for the first time, be it said, since it was formed. Until recently a French infantry regiment had consisted of three battalions, but when the war with Austria was over and the war in Spain was rising to a climax the masses of eighteen-year-old recruits — harvest of two successive anticipated conscriptions — which cluttered the depots had been swept together into battalions which had arbitrarily been labelled as belonging to regiments already serving in Spain and packed off as reinforcements for the great offensive to be launched against Wellington. Unmilitary bodies they were: some hundreds of untrained boys, a dozen officers scraped up from here and from there, a few sergeants from the depot. What little they knew about soldiering had been acquired in the long, long march from France to Portugal, during skirmishes with Spanish guerrillas and Portuguese irregulars and British outposts. At the one pitched battle, Busaco, this unhappy Eighth Corps had been kept discreetly in the background while Ney had led the veterans of the other Corps to red ruin against the British line.

They had never known as yet the kindly sensation of being included in a regiment, a properly constituted regiment with staff and transport and efficient officers. The half-dozen pack-mules they had been allotted had broken down months ago on the heart-breaking mountain roads of Spain. Even the battalion papers and accounts — those masses of notes so dear to the French official mind — had vanished. Even the *cantinière* which every self-respecting French unit could boast had deserted them. She had gone off to some other unit which was more experienced and could be relied upon to steal a mule for her when necessary and protect it — and her dubious virtue — from the assaults of hostile irregulars. The fourth battalion of the Forty-Sixth owned nothing, literally nothing, which had not been carried into Portugal on the backs of its aged officers or its eighteen-year-old privates. Since leaving France it had depended for its food on what it could glean from a harried countryside, and it had cooked it by the light of nature supplemented by the instruction of its half-dozen overworked sergeants. Small wonder, therefore, that of eight hundred men who had entered Spain only six hundred had entered Portugal and only five hundred had lived to assemble in the little village.

The Colonel roused himself from his contemplative languor long enough to issue orders for the village and the fields to be swept clear of food which was to constitute a regimental reserve — even his lack-lustre eyes had brightened at the words "regimental reserve," because the battalion had never owned a reserve of food apart from the bundles of "cash" which dangled from the men's belts. And yet when it was all brought in and the men had lived on it for a couple of days little enough remained. Five hundred starving men can eat all that is to be found in a little village when the villagers have had time to make their escape. There was a little heap of potatoes, and a sack or two of corn scraped from the corners of the barn, and that was all. In a couple of days' time the battalion would be back again in its normal state of semi-starvation, unless, miraculously, the headquarters which seemed to care so little should do something about it.

The Colonel roused himself again. Twice he sent out a company across the high road, and each time by good luck they came back with food. Once they caught a little girl herding sheep, and took all her flock and left her weeping. An older regiment would have given her, young as she was, something more to weep over. Once they found a solitary farm, deserted, and found much corn and maize there, so that the whole foraging party was not merely able to load itself but also filled a cart with the food which they dragged back by hand to the village. But all this only managed to stave off starvation for a day or two. Five hundred men eat an enormous bulk of food every day. Even twenty sheep do not go very far among five hundred men. And they loathed the corn rations. The mill beyond the road had been burnt, and the men could only pound their corn between two rocks and then boil the product into a sort of porridge which revolted the stomach after the fifth meal.

And when it came round to the turn of Sergeant Godinot's company to go out foraging beyond the high road there was an unpleasant surprise awaiting them. They encountered a column of troops before they had marched five miles — French troops, hard-bitten veterans of Reynier's Second Corps. The officer in command of the new-comers halted his men and rode up to the company. The men heard every word of the dialogue between him and their Captain.

"What are you doing here? Foraging?"

"Yes," said the Captain.

"You have no right here. The General's order gave us this area for foraging."

"But we must — the battalion has nothing."

"You must not. I will not have it. We need all we can find here for ourselves. Take your miserable recruits away out of my district."

The Captain refused to be browbeaten.

"I have orders from my Colonel to forage here. I insist upon going on."

"You insist, do you?"

The Colonel turned and bawled an order to his waiting battalion. There was a long ripple of steel down the line as they fixed bayonets.

"Now, sir," said the Colonel, "please do not waste any more of my time or my men's. I mean every word I say. Take your blues away out of my district."

The men of the Second Corps — veterans of Austerlitz, who had fought in four campaigns in Spain — would use their bayonets on their own fathers if it came to a question of food, and both sides knew it. All that the Captain could say was that his Colonel would protest to headquarters about this outrage.

"He can protest as much as he likes," shrugged the Colonel. "Meanwhile my Captain Gauthier will escort you back to the high road just in case you are thinking of looking for another way into my territory after leaving us. Good day to you, Captain."

All that the company could do was to march back with their

tails between their legs, while oaths rippled along the ranks — oaths which were re-echoed when the rest of the battalion in the village turned out to welcome them on their return and heard the news that they had come back empty-handed. They saw the Captain, after making his report, ride off on the Colonel's horse — the only animal the battalion possessed — and they saw him come back late in the day dejected and unhappy. Headquarters had confirmed the order regarding the foraging area allotted to the fourth battalion of the Forty-Sixth.

Still, there remained the mountain by the river for them to seek food upon —not a very hopeful prospect, apparently, at sight of the rocks and gullies which was all it seemed to consist of. Next morning four companies were paraded to search the mountain. There were little, straggling paths winding here and there up the mountain side, goat tracks where men could walk in single file.

"We ought to find goats up here," grumbled Lebrun, slipping and stumbling as he made his way up the path behind Godinot. "They are the only creatures who could live here."

"Goats will be good enough for me," said Bernhard, the optimist. "A nice collop of goat, with onions."

"The people we chased away when we first came here must be somewhere near," said Dubois, joining in the conversation. "And their sheep and their cattle. I would rather have a beefsteak than any collop of goat."

"Beafsteak! Listen to the man!" said Lebrun. "Served on silver, I suppose, by attentive naked damsels."

"That would be better," agreed Dubois.

Somewhere ahead they heard a musket shot, beyond the head of the long, straggling column.

"That's one of Dubois's damsels," said Lebrun. "Out with her blunderbuss. She wants a collop of Frenchman for dinner to-day."

The column still pushed on up the path. Occasionally a shot or two sounded at the head of the column. After a while they passed a dead man lying at the side of the path — a dead Frenchman, with a blue hole in his forehead and his brains running out on to the heather. Lebrun made no joke about him.

Then word was passed down the line for Sergeant Godinot's

section to take the path to the right, and the order had no sooner reached them than they reached the path named — another goat track diverging from the one up which the company was advancing. Godinot led his twenty men up the path. Away to their left they could hear the rest of the company still stumbling and climbing up the slope, but they had not gone twenty yards before they could no longer see them, so broken was the hillside and so thick the undergrowth.

"I was right about my goats," muttered Lebrun, pointing to the ground.

"Goats be damned!" said Fournier. "That's sheep, man. Sheep! Stewed mutton for dinner!"

There were sheep's footprints and sheep's dung all along the path, and the men pressed forward eagerly.

There was more firing away to the left. Godinot strove to see what was happening there, but he could see nothing at all. Then a shot or two were heard to the right; clearly the battalion was extended over the hill, but still they could see nothing, neither friends nor enemies. Now the path through the bushes began to descend. It was no fortuitous dip, either: the descent was too prolonged and too steep for that. At one corner they had a glimpse of the wide, green Tagus below them, before a turn in the path hid it again from view. Then they went on down the descent until the river came in view again, closer this time. And in the end the path ceased abruptly at the water's edge, and Godinot and his men looked at each other.

"The sheep seem to have found another way round, Sergeant," said Fournier.

"We'll find them all the same," said Godinot. "Up this path, boys."

They turned their backs on the river and plunged up the hill again. Right ahead of them they heard more firing. Godinot halted his men and listened carefully. It seemed as if they must have penetrated the enemy's skirmishing line by some unguarded gap. They must be in the rear of the Portuguese. Then they heard a shot from close ahead. Godinot beckoned to Fournier and Bernhard and the three of them crept cautiously forward, leaving the others behind. They tried to move silently up the stony path and through the thorny undergrowth. They heard something moving ahead of them, and crouched silently by the path. Then some one came running down towards them. Godinot gathered his limbs under him and sprang, and he and the man upon whom he had leaped fell with a crash on the path. Fournier and Bernhard came up to them and helped secure the prisoner — an old Portuguese peasant, very old, very wrinkled. His face was like an old potato, brown and lumpy. And it was as expressionless as a potato too. He crouched while the Frenchmen stood round him, gazing before him without moving a feature. They dragged him back to where the rest of the section awaited them.

"Get out and scout," said Godinot. "You, and you, and you."

Three of the men seized their muskets and plunged up and down the path to guard against surprise while Godinot turned to the prisoner, raking through his mind for the few words of Portuguese which he had picked up. He wanted to ask for food, for sheep, for cattle, for corn.

"*Alimento*," said Godinot, bending over the prisoner. "*Ovelha. Gado. Grão.*"

The prisoner said nothing; he merely sat on his haunches gazing out into infinity. Godinot repeated himself; still the prisoner said nothing. Godinot set his teeth and cocked his musket, and thrust the muzzle against the peasant's ear.

"*Alimento*," said Godinot.

The prisoner drew a long shuddering breath, but otherwise he made no sound.

"*Alimento*," said Godinot again, jogging the man's head with his musket barrel, but it was still unavailing.

"Here," said somebody. "I'll do it, Sergeant. Where are those sheep, curse you?"

The man's bayonet was fixed; he stuck an inch of the point into the peasant's arm and twisted it. This time a groan escaped the prisoner's lips, but he said nothing articulate.

"That's enough," snapped Godinot, his gorge rising. "We'll take him back with us. Bring him along."

Some one fastened the man's wrists behind him, and, dragging him with them, they climbed the path. So broken and overgrown was the hillside that they could see nothing of the rest of the battalion, and it was only with difficulty that they found their way over the hill back to the village, where the old man gazed broken-hearted at the ruin the invaders had caused.

The Sergeant-Major, Adjutant Doguereau, was overjoyed at their appearance.

"A prisoner, Sergeant? Excellent! He will tell us where his food is hidden."

"He would tell me nothing," said Godinot.

Doguereau glared down at the old man, who had collapsed at Godinot's feet. Blood was still dripping from his sleeve where the bayonet had pricked him.

"Indeed?" said Doguereau. "I expect he will tell *me*. Me and Sergeant Minguet."

Adjutant Doguereau had served in Egypt; he knew something about making prisoners talk. His swarthy face was twisted into a bitter smile.

"Bring him along to the prison and then tell Sergeant Minguet to report to me there."

Sergeant Godinot never knew what Adjutant Doguereau and Sergeant Minguet did to the old man in the cottage room which had been set aside as a prison; nor did any one else, because Doguereau turned out from it the two soldiers undergoing punishment there before he set to work. But the battalion heard the old man scream pitifully, like a child.

And later in the day Doguereau called for Sergeant Godinot and a working party, and came out of the prison dragging the old man with him. The prisoner found difficulty in walking, but he led them out of the village to the fields, and there he indicated a pile of rubbish at one corner.

"Dig here," said Doguereau.

The working party fell to and swept away the rubbish. Underneath was a board flooring, and when that was pulled up a treasure indeed was revealed. The funnel-shaped silo pit beneath was full of maize, heaps and heaps of it, and when they began to rake that away there were jars of olive oil underneath.

"Take all this to the regimental store," said Doguereau, rubbing his hands.

"And what about the prisoner, *mon adjudant?*" asked Godinot. The poor old man was lying by the pit, his face wet with tears. "Shall we let him go?"

"No, not a bit of it. Take him back to the prison. I expect he will find more yet to tell us later on when I attend to him again."

But the old man never did reveal any other hidden stores, for he hanged himself in his cell that night.

There was rejoicing in the battalion. Besides the ton of maize which had been found, and the gallons of oil, another section ranging the hillside had found four head of cattle hidden in a gully, although they had not found the person minding them. Altogether there were provisions for the whole five hundred men for nearly a week, and for that it was well worth having a man killed and two wounded in the ambushes on the hill.

Chapter XII

DURING the days that followed Adjutant Doguereau had working parties all over the village and the fields looking for further hidden supplies. They pulled every pile of rubbish and rock to pieces, they probed the floors of the cottages and the edges of the fields, they hunted everywhere, but unavailingly. When provisions were beginning to run short again Doguereau issued orders that another prisoner must be taken. Various small expeditions had been pushed across the mountain top, without success. The peasants who had taken shelter there had grown too cunning, apparently; and no one had ever yet succeeded in finding where their central place of concealment might be.

"All that is no use," said Adjutant Doguereau. "If we want to catch a man we must employ other methods. I want parties of five or six men to go up to the hill at night, and hide there. When morning comes some one will fall into your hands, mark my words. Act intelligently."

So that midnight found Sergeant Godinot and a small party creeping up the hill, feeling their way up the path as silently as they might, and hiding in the undergrowth when they had penetrated far into the tangled summit. It rained heavily that night — it always seemed to be raining now — and a cold wind blew. They huddled together in the darkness for warmth, not daring to speak lest some one should overhear them. They were all friends together, these men, Sergeant Godinot and his particular intimates, Fournier and Dubois and Lebrun and Bernhard, and two more from his section, Catrin and Guimblot.

When morning came it was, perhaps, inevitable that Godinot should be dissatisfied with the position he had taken up in the darkness. It was not a good ambush: it did not overlook the goat track properly and it did not offer sufficient concealment. What Godinot wanted was some position at an intersection of paths, giving a double chance of making a capture. He got his men together and moved up the path again, every man stooping to keep concealed, and creeping up the stony hill as quietly as he might. They ranged over the hill for some time, seeing nothing, hearing nothing. It was hard to find the perfect ambush. They began to feel that they had been sent out on a fool's errand, although they realized that twenty parties like theirs were out on the hill, and it would be a fortunate chance if in a day one single prisoner were caught. They were only young French soldiers; they had not the patience to lie in the cold rain waiting for their opportunity; they had to move about and seek it.

And the result was perhaps inevitable. There were others on the hill who knew the paths and the contours far better than they, and who could move more silently, and more swiftly. The Frenchmen had come to lay an ambush; instead they walked into one. Sergeant Godinot for the rest of his life felt a feeling of shame when he remembered it — the stupidity with which he had led his party to their death, the panic which overwhelmed him in the moment of danger. A high shelf of rock overlooked the path here, and it was from the shelf that death leaped out at them. There was a crashing, stunning volley and a billow of smoke, and through the smoke the enemy came leaping down at them. Men fell at Godinot's left hand, and at his right. Some one screamed. Two impressions remained printed on Godinot's memory — one of Guimblot coughing up floods of blood at his feet, another of the wild charge of the enemy with the green Englishman at their head, bayonets flashing and smoke eddying. Some one turned and ran, and Godinot ran too, down the path, and as he began to run panic gripped him and he ran faster and ever faster, stumbling over the stones, tearing his clothes on the thorns, running so madly that pursuit dropped behind and in the end he was able to slow down and try to recover his breath and his wits.

Dubois was with him. He was wounded, as he said stupidly over and over again — a bullet had gone through his arm. Fournier came up a moment later brandishing his musket.

"I fired at him again," said Fournier, "but I missed him clean. He is hard to hit, that one."

"Where are the others?" asked Godinot. He knew the answer

to the question, but he asked it merely for something to say.

"Dead," said Fournier. "They shot Bernhard through the heart. Guimblot — "

"I saw Guimblot," said Godinot.

They looked at each other. Godinot was ashamed of his panic.

"They're coming! They're coming again!" said Dubois, seizing Godinot's arm. A twig snapped somewhere in the undergrowth, and the noise started the panic in their minds again — perhaps it was Dubois's fault, for he was shaken by his wound and panic is infectious. They fled over the hill again, running madly along the paths, until Dubois fainted with loss of blood. They tied up his wound and dragged him down to the village. There was an unpleasant interview with his Captain awaiting Sergeant Godinot when he had to explain the loss of more than half his party. There is no excuse for defeat in the military code, just as success excuses everything. But other parties had sustained loss and defeat, too, it appeared, when they came back in driblets from the mountain; there were several wounded to bear Dubois company in the hospital; there were several dead left among the rocks. And several men had seen the Englishman in green uniform, and several shots had been fired at him, all unavailingly.

In the evening Fournier came to Sergeant Godinot.

"I want some money, Sergeant," he said. "Give me some."

Sergeant Godinot could see no use for money here in these uninhabited billets, and he said so.

"Never mind that," said Fournier. "I want some money."

Godinot bowed to his whim and pulled out two or three copper coins — enough to buy a drink had there been drinks to be bought. Fournier thrust them aside.

"I want *money*," he said.

What he was really asking for, as Godinot came to realize, was silver — in French the same word. Godinot found him a Spanish pillar dollar, one of four which Godinot kept sewn in his shirt in case of need. Fournier weighed it in his hand.

"Give me another one, Sergeant. Please give me another one," he pleaded.

Godinot did so with some reluctance, looking at him oddly. It was only later in the evening, when he saw Fournier sitting by the fire with an iron spoon and a bullet-mould, that he realized part of what was in Fournier's mind. He was casting silver bullets to make sure of hitting the green Englishman at the next opportunity. The others round the fire were not given the chance by Fournier of seeing exactly what he was doing. They made jokes about shortage of ammunition and Fournier's diligence in replacing it, but they did not know it was silver he was using, and in consequence paid no special attention to his actions. After all, bullet-moulding was a pleasantly distracting hobby, and men who were really fussy about their marksmanship were often known to mould their own bullets in an endeavour to obtain more perfect spheres than the official issue.

Yet Sergeant Godinot felt much more ill at ease when at next morning's parade Private Fournier was found to be missing. Every one realized that it could not be a case of desertion — no one could desert to the Portuguese, and to have deserted to the English would have called for a journey through the cantonments of half the French Army. Sergeant Godinot could only tell his Captain what he knew of Fournier's motives, and express the opinion that he was out on the hill somewhere trying to shoot the green Englishman. And the Captain could only shrug his shoulders and hope that Fournier would return alive.

He never did. Godinot awaited him anxiously for several days, but he never came back. Godinot never found out what happened to him. He was the fifth of that little group of friends to die — Boyel had been the first, and little Godron the second, and Lebrun and Bernhard had been killed in the ambush a day or two before, and now Fournier was gone and only Dubois was left, with a hole in his arm.

So one day after an announcement by the Colonel, Sergeant Godinot came to visit Dubois in the battalion hospital.

"We are going to Santarem to-morrow," said Godinot.

"Who is?"

"We are. You and I. We are going carpentering or ropemaking or boatbuilding — they want men for all those."

"Who does?"

"Headquarters. The Colonel announced this morning that all men with a knowledge of carpentry or boatbuilding or ropemaking or smith's work were to report to the adjutant. So I reported for you and me. I didn't have to tell him more than the truth. When I said that my father owned one third of the Chantier Naval, and that you and I had spent half our lives in small boats in Nantes Harbour, he put our names down at once. We are to report at Santarem to-morrow."

"Santarem?" asked Dubois vaguely.

"Santarem is twenty kilometres down the river," said Godinot. "Heaven bless us, man, don't you remember marching up through it?"

But since the conscription had taken him from his home a year ago, at the age of seventeen and a half, Dubois had marched through too many places to remember half of them.

"So that arm of yours must be better by to-morrow," said Godinot. "Half a bullet ought not to keep you sick longer than that."

The missile which had been extracted from Dubois's arm had been half a musket ball — apparently the Portuguese sawed their bullets in two in order to double their chances of hitting something.

"It is better," said Dubois. "I was to report for light duty the day after to-morrow. Do you think they'll issue rations to us at Santarem?"

"They'll have to if we're doing other work," said Godinot, and the two of them looked at each other. Food was already short again in the battalion — that day's ration had only consisted of a litre of maize porridge. "It's Headquarters at Santarem," he continued. "Those brutes in the Second Corps will have to send in some of the beef they get beyond the road."

Every one in the battalion was firmly convinced that the Second Corps in its foraging area beyond the road was revelling in beef every day — an extraordinarily inaccurate estimate. Dubois smacked his lips.

"Beef!" he said. "With thick gravy!"

He said the words with the same respectful awe he had once employed in speaking about the Emperor Napoleon.

Adjutant Doguereau had weeded out a great many of the applicants for work at Santarem. Quite half the battalion had hurried to report to him after the regimental announcement, full of stories about their knowledge of carpentry or ropemaking. Every one was anxious to escape from the battalion, from the dreariness of life in cramped billets, the shortage of food, the endless, ineffectual skirmishing with the outcasts on the hill. They had told the most fantastic lies about their experience with boats and their ability to do smith's work. But Adjutant Doguereau had seen through all the lies of these lads fresh from the plough and the cart's tail. There were only thirty men paraded under Sergeant Godinot and sent off to march down the road to Santarem.

Santarem was a long, narrow town of tall, white houses squeezed in between the road and the river. When they marched into it there was no sign of civilian life — every inhabitant had fled weeks ago — but the long, high street was all a-bustle with groups of men working here and there. The red woollen shoulder-knots of the engineers were much in evidence. They saw white-haired old General Éblé, whom every one knew and liked, striding stiffly along the road followed by his staff. A sergeant of sappers took them in charge and led them to their billet — a big warehouse on the water's edge.

"Here, you blues," said the Sergeant of Sappers, "is where you will live for the next month or two. And where you will work. My God, how you will work!"

"But what is the work, Sergeant?" asked Godinot.

"We are going to build a bridge to cross the river. A pontoon bridge. And after that we are going to build another bridge. That makes two."

Godinot looked out of the open warehouse door, across the quay, to where the river rolled in its green immensity. Two pontoon bridges to cross that width of rushing water — bridges capable of bearing artillery — would be an immense task.

"Yes, you can look," said the Sergeant of Sappers. "The calculation is that we shall need two hundred pontoons. And some pontoons will need four anchors, some only two. And we shall need about ten kilometres of cable for the anchors and the roadway.

And the roadway, as you see, will be about a kilometre and a half long for the two bridges. That will have to be made of timber."

"Have you got the timber and anchors and things?" asked Godinot, a little bewildered.

"No," said the Sergeant. "But we have a good many houses in the town. We are to pull the houses down and use the joists. And we shall have to save the nails when we pull the houses down because we have no nails. And before we start pulling the houses down we shall have to make the tools to do it with, because we have no tools except a few hammers we have got from the farriers. But there is plenty of iron in the balconies. We have got to make hammers and saws and axes and adzes out of that. And of course we have no hemp for the cables. We have got to make cables. There are three warehouses full of bales of wool. We have got to try if woollen ropes will suit, and if not — well, we have got to try ropes made of linen, or hay, or straw, or we shall have to tie together every odd bit of rope the Army can find in its billets. And there is no tar, of course, for the bottoms of the pontoons. I don't think General Éblé has thought of a way round the difficulty of the tar. There is olive oil, however. Is there any one here who knows how to make a durable paint out of olive oil? I thought not. But they have begun experiments already down the road. If you sniff attentively you may be able to smell them."

This long speech by the Sergeant of Sappers was received with a chilly silence by his audience. The French recruit takes none of the delight in extemporization which his counterpart across the Channel displays. This talk of building bridges to cross a half-mile river out of floor-joists appeared to their minds to take far too much for granted. The Sergeant of Sappers knew it, but he could do nothing in the matter except change the subject.

"Five o'clock," he said. "Too late to start work to-day. Report with your party at five o'clock to-morrow morning, Sergeant."

Godinot instantly broached the subject which lay nearest to their hearts.

"What about rations, Sergeant?" he asked.

"Rations? *Rations?* Do you blues mean to say you want rations? I don't know why you have come to Santarem, then. You must hurry to the quartermaster's stores and see what there is. They served out the day's rations an hour ago."

"What was it, Sergeant?" asked Dubois.

"Maize," said the Sergeant of Sappers. "Unground maize. One pound per man. That is what they were issuing an hour ago. There may be some left, but I doubt it."

As it happened, the doubts of the Sergeant of Sappers were ill-founded. Every man in Sergeant Godinot's party received his pound of maize. It only remained for them to pound it as well as they could, and then boil it into porridge over a fire made of what wood they could steal. It constituted a poor day's food for men engaged in hard physical work.

Chapter XIII

LIFE among the outcasts in the rocky mountain by the river settled down extraordinarily quickly into routine. The Portuguese peasants had been accustomed all their lives to unremitting hard work, and gladly took up what labour there was to be done — it irked them to be idle. So that it was quite willingly that they did sentry-go along the brow of the hill, and slaved to enlarge the cave by the river so that there might be shelter in it for all. It was the women's task to look after the cattle on the hill and move them from point to point so that they might find herbage here and there — scanty herbage, but enough to keep them just alive. The constant fear of attack by the French kept every one from quarrelling.

It was all very matter-of-fact and obvious. When shots from the brow of the hill told that an attack was developing there, every one knew what he had to do. The little flock of sheep was driven down to the river's brink and carried one by one on the backs of men and women over the secret ford to the little beach outside the cave. The women drove the large cattle into hidden gullies and left them there, perforce, while they came down for shelter to the cave as well. The men took their muskets and went out on the hillside to skirmish with the enemy. There was ample time for everything to be done, because on the precipitous goat tracks through the rocks and the undergrowth the French soldiers moved so slowly that an interval hours long occurred between the firing of the first warning shots and the arrival of the French anywhere where they might be dangerous.

The very first attack, made only a few days after the arrival of the French, was perhaps the most successful. It was only a short while after daybreak that a musket shot told of the danger, and Dodd had seized his rifle, and, with Bernardino at his side, had hurried to the broad flat rock on the summit which the peasants called "the table" to see what was developing.

It was the usual sort of attack — four columns of men pushing up the hill by perilous goat tracks through the bush. Dodd could catch glimpses of each in turn making the slow ascent whenever the conformation of the ground brought them into view. Each column consisted of a company; even at that distance he could see in the clear air that one column wore the bearskins of the grenadiers of the battalion and another the plumes of the *voltigeurs* — "light bobs" Dodd called them mentally — the remaining two companies of the battalion had been left behind, of course, to act as headquarters guard. The progress of the attackers was inordinately slow. They had continually to halt to enable the rear to catch up with the head. The three sentries who had given the alarm were able to slip round by other paths and take long shots into the caterpillars of men crawling up the slope. Dodd and the other half-dozen men who gathered round him had ample time to choose their course of action and glide along the crest away to the flank and by heavy firing there bring one of the columns to a complete stop.

Yet it was a damaging day. The other columns had broken into smaller parties, which had ranged very thoroughly over the top of the mountain — as thoroughly, that is to say, as twelve small parties could range over an immense hill-top seamed and broken with gullies. One such party must have found the cattle, the four draught bullocks who had drawn the village plough in the days before the French came. And perhaps another such party had found Miguel. However it was, Miguel was missing. He might be dead, and his body might be lying somewhere out on the hillside. No one knew what had become of old Miguel, and the women in the cave that night wept for him — more bitterly, perhaps, than the men bewailed the loss of the draught oxen. They sought him next day over the hill without finding him, but later in the day one of the watchers on the brow of the hill came in with news of him.

He had seen Miguel brought out of the village and buried by the fields; he was sure it was Miguel, even at that distance. The French must have dragged him into the village and murdered him. There was more wailing among the women. Miguel had led a solitary life lately; his wife was dead and his sons had been conscripted into the Army, but every one in that village was related to every one else; they had intermarried for generations, even (as was not unusual in those lost villages) within the prohibited degrees. Miguel was mourned by cousins and nieces and daughters-in-law.

The other information which the watchers on the hill brought, to the effect that the French had discovered the hidden stores of food in Miguel's silo, went almost unnoticed in the general dismay.

Nevertheless, Miguel's death was not long unavenged. There came a morning when Bernardino, flushed with excitement, came hurriedly to Dodd and the others and led them to "the table," where they gathered with infinite caution. Bernardino pointed down the hill, and every one followed his gesture. Far down the slope they could see half a dozen men crawling along a path. They were bent double, and moving with such ludicrous care that Bernardino could not help giggling as he pointed to them: it was so amusing to see them picking their way with so much caution and ignorant that they had been observed.

It was Dodd who laid the ambush. He guessed the future route of the little party, and brought his men hurriedly across the slope to where they could await their arrival unseen. He had lain on his stomach with his rifle pushed out in front of him ready for action, and the others had imitated him. And, when at one point of their course the Frenchmen had shown up clearly and just within range, he had turned his head and had glowered at his men with such intensity that they had restrained their natural instincts and had not fired, but had waited instead for the better opportunity which Dodd had foreseen.

The volley at ten yards and the instant charge which Dodd had headed had been effective enough. There were three men dead and another one wounded, whose throat Pedro had cut the instant Dodd's back was turned, and the survivors had fled down the path as though the devil were behind them. Dodd would have been glad if they had all been killed, but to kill seven men with a volley from seven muskets even at ten yards was much more than could be expected — a pity, all the same, for Dodd could guess at the moral effect it would have had on the battalion if a whole detachment had been cut off without trace.

He had forbidden pursuit, calling back Bernardino who had begun to run down the path after the fugitives. There was no sense in running madly about the hill where other enemies were to be found; there might indeed be danger.

Instead, Dodd made the best move possible in taking his men back to "the table" and scanning the hill for further parties of the enemy, and when he saw none he pushed out scouts here and there to seek for them. Two other little groups were located during the day, and Dodd brought up his men to attack them, creeping cautiously through the undergrowth. But neither attack was as successful as the first — the first burst of firing had set them on the alert and it had not been possible to approach them closely. They could only follow them back to the village in a long, straggling fight in which much powder was expended and very few people hurt — several of the Portuguese received flesh wounds.

All the same, it had been a glorious day. The new French plan of pushing small parties up the hill under cover of darkness had been heavily defeated. And every man on the hill now had a good French musket and bayonet and ammunition, taken from the corpses of the slain.

Next day there was a stranger incident, which Dodd never fully understood. It was quite late in the afternoon when Dodd, crossing the hill with Bernardino at his heels, felt a bullet whiz by his face, and heard the crack of a musket from the bushes to his right. He dropped instantly to the ground, and peered in the direction whence the shot had come. A wisp of smoke still drifting through the bushes indicated clearly enough the position of the man who had missed so narrowly. Whether there was one man there or twenty Dodd did not know. He crawled to cover behind a rock and sighted his rifle carefully on the neighbourhood of the hiding-place of the enemy. Bernardino began to crawl like a snake up the path again — perhaps to turn the enemy's flank, perhaps to direct the attack of the other defenders of the hill who would be attracted to the spot by the firing.

Dodd gazed along the barrel of his rifle. Soon he saw the bushes in movement, and he knew what was moving them — he had played this game so often before. Some one there was trying to reload his musket; it was a terribly difficult thing to do when lying down trying to keep concealed. Dodd did his best to judge by the amount of movement the position of the head and feet of the man who was loading. Then he sighted for the mid-point between them and fired, instantly rolling behind his rock again. No shot came in reply. Dodd wriggled on his belly away from his rock, down the path, until a journey of twenty yards brought him to a dip in the ground which promised complete concealment. Here, lying on his back, he contrived to reload. Fortunately on this occasion the bullet did not jam in the rifling, but slid sweetly down to rest on the wadding. He laid the weapon down beside his head, rolled over on his stomach, and took hold of it again. Then he wriggled away to another rock from which he could bring under observation the area of scrub into which he had fired.

He pushed his rifle forward and took aim, but he could see no sign of movement. His straining ears could just detect the sound of some one creeping through the bush higher up, but that was doubtless Bernardino — it came from his direction. Dodd lay very still, with all his senses on the alert, scanning the thick bushes all round for any sign of an enemy — they might not all be in the same spot; they might be creeping upon him from any point of the compass. With dreadful patience he lay still. His ears actually twitched, so tensely was he tuned up, when some particularly clumsy movement on Bernardino's part made more noise than usual.

Then, at the end of a very long time, he saw far out to his right the top of an English infantry shako appear above the bushes. That was Bernardino, employing the age-old trick of raising his hat on a stick to draw the enemy's fire. It was specially useful in this case, because it told Dodd where Bernardino was. With the knowledge that that flank was secure, he was able to assume the offensive. He set his rifle at half-cock — Dodd was far too careful a man to crawl through undergrowth with a cocked rifle — and began another very cautious advance. He writhed along through the bushes, raising no part of himself off the ground, using his toes and his elbows, moving inches at a time at the cost of prodigious exertion.

At last the time came when he could see his enemy — a part of him, at least. He could see the top of a black gaiter and a bit of the leg of a pair of extremely dirty white breeches. Change his position as he might within moderate limits, he could bring no other part of the enemy into view as a result of the lie of the land. He took careful aim at the knee of the breeches, and fired. He was sure he had hit the mark; he thought he saw the leg leap before the smoke obscured his view, but when he looked again the leg was still lying there. Once again, after carefully moving away from where he had fired, Dodd performed the difficult contortionist's feat of loading while lying down. Then he writhed forward again in a narrowing arc. He put his hat on his ramrod, and holding it at arm's length, raised it above the bushes. It drew no fire, and, after a time, the signal was answered by Bernardino from a position right in his front. They had turned both flanks of the enemy on a wide curve, apparently. There could be no one else near save whoever it was — be it few or many — at the point whence the first shot had been fired. Dodd began to suspect the truth of the matter, but he was far too cautious and patient to risk his life by a rash testing of his suspicions. He resumed his tedious, difficult advance, creeping through the scrub, changing his direction every yard or so to avoid having to crawl over some lump of rock which might lift him an inch or two above the skyline.

At last he reached the position of the enemy, and found that his suspicions were correct. There had only been one man there all the time, and Dodd had killed him with his first shot. The bullet had hit him in the groin, and, bursting the great artery of the thigh, had drained the life out of him in twenty seconds. He lay tranquil on his left side in the midst of a great pool of congealed blood. Only a few drops of blood had trickled from his other wound in his right knee, which must have been inflicted after death.

Bernardino, when he arrived a few seconds later, was intensely amused that they had expended so much time and energy on stalking a dead man. But he displayed admiration at the fact that Dodd had hit his man twice with two shots, both of them at a range of over fifty yards. The dead man lay on his left side. His ramrod was in his right hand, clearly indicating that he had been killed while reloading. His left hand was clenched, but when Bernardino turned him over to go through his pockets something fell from it — the bullet which he had been about to ram into his musket.

It did not have the usual dull grey colour. It had a bright, frosted appearance. Dodd picked it up idly. It was not as heavy as usual; it did not seem to be a leaden bullet. Dodd fancied, but he could not believe, that it must be a silver one. He could not believe it to be silver; he came to the conclusion that the French must be running short of ammunition and casting bullets out of scrap metal. He tossed it away idly into the bushes.

That was not the only puzzling item in the business. The dead man must have lain hidden there for a long time — since before dawn of that day, most probably. He must almost for certain have had opportunities of shooting at several other people before Dodd came in range. There was no obvious reason at all why he had come alone into the enemy's territory, nor yet why, having come there, he should have waited to fire at Dodd in particular. Dodd simply could not understand it. He had never heard of the superstition that to kill a very important person, or one with diabolical powers, a silver bullet is desirable. Modestly, he could not imagine — it never came within the farthest possibility of occurring to him — that he might have come to bulk so large in poor Fournier's tortured imagination. Dodd gave up puzzling about the business once he had decided that it had no important bearing upon his own welfare and that of his followers. No one else of the party seemed to give the matter a second thought, as far as Dodd could ascertain. It was merely one more Frenchman dead, another little step in the right direction. They turned from the death of this Frenchman to planning the death of the next.

So day succeeded day. Still the battalion huddled in its overcrowded cottages and outhouses down in the village, and still the Portuguese starved and shivered on the hill. There were days and days of torrential, drenching rain and bitter winds, which largely explained the inactivity of the French. There was spasmodic starvation in the village, and more ordered starvation on the hill. Dodd had begun to guess that the French were going to stay where

they were until privation drove them out. It would be a starving
match, and he wanted to see that his side could starve longest. The
precious flour and corn were hoarded religiously, even though the
damp had begun to make them mouldy. The five cows were killed
and eaten first — it was hard to feed them and there was always
the danger that the enemy might capture them in some new attack on the hill. Then the sheep were eaten, beginning first with
the ones which died of starvation and exposure. The Portuguese
grew restless under this diet of unrelieved meat — they were never
great eaters of that commodity at any time. They clamoured for
bread, but Dodd set his face resolutely against their demands and
old Maria, who had taken charge of the stores at the end of the
cave, backed him up. She seemed wiser than the others, and met
all their demands for bread and for cakes fried in oil with a resolute "Não, não," whose nasal tones seemed to voice all her contempt for the masculine half of humanity in every branch of
human activity, from housekeeping to planning a campaign —
although in this kind of warfare those two particular objectives
were not specially distinct.

The wretched peasants, of course, saw utter ruin ahead of them.
Their fields were being left untilled, their buildings were being
ruined, and now they were being compelled to eat their livestock
without leaving any nucleus at all which might multiply in the
years to come. The score or so of diseased and starving sheep which
were carried twice daily across the secret ford represented now
their sole wealth; when that was gone they would have nothing,
literally nothing. They would starve whether the French re-
treated or whether the French stayed. Yet it was not a matter in
which any principle could be debated except for the small details,
because there was always one great outstanding fact — it would
mean far more certain death to yield to the French now than to
stay up here in the mountain and starve. Every one remembered
the fate of Miguel.

Dodd by now could understand a little of all this which was
being said round him. He had to learn the language as a child
learns his native tongue. When Dodd used a noun and a verb and
made a sentence out of them he had not the least consciousness of

these three operations; he did not know what was a noun or a verb or a sentence. Being unable to read or write naturally made learning difficult for him. He progressed eventually into the condition of an eighteen-months-old child — he understood most of what was said to him, but all he could employ in reply was a small collection of nouns and verbs which made not the slightest attempt to agree with each other. Yet his prestige never suffered on account of the ludicrous things he said; he was far too adept at killing Frenchmen ever to appear in the least ridiculous in the eyes of the peasants.

Chapter XIV

THERE was little enough that went on in the village where the fourth battalion of the Forty-Sixth rotted in stagnation which was unobserved by the keen-eyed watchers on the hill. The sentinels saw everything. They could report the continual and mostly unsuccessful search which went on in the arable land for food. They could see little parties of men — ever armed and vigilant — seeking nettles and edible weeds to add to their meagre diet. They reported whenever a small grudging convoy of food reached the battalion from headquarters — which was not very often. They knew when sickness smote the wretched troops, because they could see sick men staggering up to the hospital-cottage, and they could see the corpses being carried out for burial, and they chuckled over it. Dysentery, it was, the inevitable result of weeks of exposure and bad food. They explained the nature of the disease to Dodd with a vivid explanatory pantomime, and Dodd nodded grimly. There was not a soldier alive who did not know a great deal about dysentery. Bernardino grinned broadly when from the brow of the hill he pointed out how greatly extended were the battalion latrines and how continually crowded they were.

Naturally, Dodd realized, there were no medicines for the French down there; there were no medicines for the whole French Army huddled in its billets around Santarem, and there was no means of obtaining any. The hundred and fifty miles of mountain road which lay between the French and the frontier even of Spain were quite blocked by the hordes of starving irregulars whom Wellington had mobilized. Not so much as a letter — far less a convoy — had reached the French since the time, three months back, when they crossed the frontier. In all that time, while conducting sieges, fighting battles and worried by skirmishes innumerable, they had lived on what they could find in a country naturally poor and which had in great part been laid waste before them.

On the only occasion when they had been able to send news of themselves back to France the messenger had been escorted by six hundred men who had had to fight every yard of the road and had left half their numbers by the wayside. Even Dodd, who knew much about the French military capacity, marvelled at the way in which they hung on to their uncomfortable position; Dodd, of course, knew nothing of the fierce determination of the Marshal in command; he had never even heard of the siege of Genoa ten years back, when this same Marshal had defended the town with troops fed on a daily ration of half a pound of hair-powder the while the prisoners he took ate each other because they were given nothing to eat at all. No one could bring himself to believe that the Marshal would try to repeat his exploit, and would hold on until thirty thousand men were dead of disease so that it was dangerous to linger further before an English army making ready to sally out upon them.

Besides, Dodd could not imagine any object at all in this hanging on. He did not know anything about high politics, and so could not appreciate the fact that England was going through a Cabinet crisis which might quite possibly result in the assumption of power by the Opposition and a prompt withdrawal of Wellington from his impregnable position. Nor could he envisage at first the major strategical situation, and grasp the main military reason for this fierce retention of the position along the Tagus. What initiated the train of events which in the end gave him an insight into the matter was the sound of guns down the river.

Faint it was, and yet distinct enough. Dodd, walking in the dawn on the hillside, heard the distant rumble and stopped, listening intently, with his heart beating faster because of the possibilities which the sound implied. It was distinctly the firing of big guns. It was not a big battle — there was not enough gun-fire for that. Nor was it a siege, for the firing was in no way continuous. Yet guns were firing, and to Dodd that was terribly important. For it must imply that the French were in contact with the regular enemy not far away. And any enemy of the French must be Dodd's friends; they must be British or Portuguese, and formed troops at that, because of the artillery. If he could only join them he would be back in his regiment almost at once — the regiment, his home. Every good soldier must rally to his regiment.

He listened again to the firing; it was not in salvos, but he could detect individual shots, and from their loudness he could estimate by experience how far away they were. Certainly not at the Lines — the firing was a good deal nearer than that. What was there down the river a dozen miles away? The only point of any strategical value that he could think of was Santarem, but he was not sure how far off Santarem was. He turned to Bernardino.

"Santarem?" he said. "Where?"

It took a little while for Bernardino to realize what he was being asked, but he gave the right answer at last.

"Five," he said, and held up five fingers.

Five Portuguese leagues meant ten miles or a little more; the firing was certainly at Santarem.

"We go," said Dodd, with decision. He turned back to the cave to make his preparations for the move.

Down in the cave the news that their English leader was about to go to Santarem roused mixed emotions. Some wanted to accompany him; some wanted him to stay. Dodd swept away their arguments with the few words at his disposal. They must stay; there was still food to guard, there was still the battalion to worry. Moreover, he foresaw a dangerous march through the French cantonments. One or two men might slip through where a party of a dozen would be detected. Bernardino must accompany him of course — Dodd could hardly now imagine any risky march through Portugal without Bernardino, and he would be extremely useful to explain matters in the very likely event of encountering any further parties of Portuguese irregulars. Dodd filled his haversack with unleavened bread from the pile Maria was slowly accumulating in the cave — the result of continuous small bakings in a makeshift oven over a screened fire. He strapped on his greatcoat, saw that he had his ammunition and flints, filled his canteen from the river, and was ready. Bernardino had made similar preparations, imitating each of his actions like a monkey. Then they set out, up the steep path, across the stony mountain, and down to where the little lane ran from the village over to the high road.

Caution was necessary here: there might be patrols or sentries or stray parties moving along the lane. They edged cautiously down to the top of the bank, and peered through the rain this way and that. When they were satisfied that it was safe they plunged down the bank, across the lane, and up the other side. They climbed hurriedly until the rocks and bushes gave them cover again.

Now they were on the long, low hill which had been the scene of their first skirmish with the battalion. They picked their way up it cautiously, ready to fall flat at the sight of Frenchmen. But the driving rain was a good screen. They saw no one. Dodd directed his course diagonally over the hill, threading his way through rocks and bushes until once more they were over the Tagus bank. Dodd did not wish to be too far from the river, not so much because of its use as a guide — the high road beyond the hill would have been as useful in that respect — but because he knew instinctively that the river was the most important strategical factor in the situation; that anything which might affect his destiny must, in the present conditions, happen on the river. He gazed down, as he strolled along with Bernardino beside him, at the broad, green mass of water pouring sullenly down between its rocky banks, and at the floating stuff which swirled in its eddies.

He had seen a British gunboat pushing its way up here once, but he had no hope of seeing another; he guessed that the French must have established shore batteries down by Alhandra to stop such voyages. Yet at the same time he had a strong suspicion that the gun-fire at Santarem must be due to activity on the river by the British forces, though what form that activity was taking he could not imagine. The more he thought about it, the more he hurried his pace without relaxing his strained alertness lest the enemy should appear. The merest possibility that he might find a chance of rejoining his friends was enough to rouse passionate excitement in his breast.

Dodd never stopped to think that perhaps he was doing better work for England out here organizing the irregulars than if he were inside the Lines lost in the ranks of the Ninety-Fifth; that would have been a form of presumption quite foreign to his nature. He knew his place and his duty. England had spent a great deal of money and the deepest thought of her keenest minds on making a good soldier of him; she could have made a useful citizen of him for one-half the expense and trouble if there had been no war — except that in that case she would have judged it better policy to save her money.

The gun-fire had largely died away as the day went on; there were only a very few distant reports to mark the fact that the activity at Santarem, whatever the reason for it, still continued to a small extent. It was late afternoon before they came to the end of the hill, where the river came back to the road, and had to stop to consider their next movements. Santarem was not more than four or five miles farther on, but here the plain came down nearly to the river's bank, and only a short distance ahead of them was another little village lying along the main road. A village meant French troops and the need for infinite caution.

Dodd scanned the landscape from the river side of the hill without seeing any safe route for further progress. With the puzzled Bernardino trailing behind him he crossed the hill-top and examined the lie of the land from the side by the main road. Nor from here could he see any means of pushing on: it was level plain land for a great distance, dotted here and there with villages and farm buildings. At more than one point he could see parties of French troops moving along the paths out there. Clearly it would be a dangerous enterprise to try to make his way through that country. Bernardino voiced his disgust at the prospect; he was for turning back again, and a man less obstinate than Dodd might have yielded, or one with a lower ideal of military duty. But the British Army had not won the distinction it now possessed by turning back at the first sign of difficulty; nor would Dodd turn back now.

Certainly he did retrace his steps a little way, but that was in search of another way round. Bernardino grumbled bitterly when he realized that Dodd was not turning homeward, but Dodd paid no attention to his complaints — he only understood one word in twenty of them, anyway. A mile back along the hill the other side of the main road was bordered by a thick wood, stretching

inland for some considerable distance. At the farther end of it
a view could be obtained which might throw fresh light on the
situation. Dodd picked his way cautiously down to the road,
scuttled across it when he was sure no Frenchman was in sight,
and then plunged into the forest.

It was in the heart of the wood that they found the man who
was to help them. The encounter was a surprise to all three of
them. They were all making their way cautiously from tree to
tree, listening hard for the enemy, when simultaneously they
caught a glimpse of each other across a glade. All three of them
dived for cover and reached for their weapons instinctively, but
Bernardino had had a clear view of the stranger for a tenth of a
second, and saw that he wore no uniform. He called to him in
Portuguese and received an answer in that language, and, finally,
prodded by Dodd, he stood up and moved into the open. That
was taking a slight chance, because a hunted Portuguese might
possibly fire first and answer questions after, but in this case the
move was successful. The other man came forward into the glade,
and Bernardino was able to explain the situation to him. The
stranger was a stunted little man, with a knife at his belt and a
musket in his hand; he glanced keenly up and down Dodd's burly
form as Bernardino explained the presence of an Englishman.
The stranger led them away through the forest, and then on his
hands and knees plunged into an insignificant tunnel into a tangle
of undergrowth. A few yards farther in, the bushes ceased for a
space around the trunk of a great tree, and against the tree was
built a little three-sided shelter of twigs and branches. On the
ground inside the hut, with a few rags spread over him, lay an
old man, with a mop of tangled white hair and beard, moaning
and muttering to himself.

"My father," said the stranger, by way of introduction, and
then he knelt beside the pitiful form, trying to give him a little
comfort, whispering little words to him as though to a child.

He was dying from one of the diseases of famine or exposure,
typhus or plague, or pneumonia — pneumonia, most likely, to
judge from his rapid laboured breathing and the fluttering of his
nostrils. There were tears in the stunted man's eyes when he

backed out of the shelter again and turned to face Dodd and Bernardino; tears which ran down his cheeks and lost themselves among the sparse hairs of his beard.

Bernardino was too young, and had seen too much of war lately, to be much moved by the sight of the illness of an old man who was bound to die rather sooner than later anyway. He explained that Dodd was anxious to see Santarem, to inspect the cause of the gun-fire there. The stunted man shook his head, and indicated his father. He said he could not leave him. An argument developed there in the little clearing, while the light faded and the rain dripped dismally among the branches. Dodd played his part in the argument.

"I go Santarem," he said, and then, his small vocabulary failing because he did not know the Portuguese for "cannon" or for "see," he looked out under his hand and then said "Boom, boom."

The stunted man nodded; Bernardino had already given quite an adequate account of what this Englishman wanted to do. But the stunted man pointed to his father and shook his head. He would not leave his father to act as a guide to them. Bernardino demanded if they could make their way to within sight of Santarem without his guiding them, but the stunted man shook his head again. There were very many Frenchmen in the way. It would be quite impossible. He could take them by night, but no one who did not know the country could hope to get through.

There was nothing for it but to wait for the old man to die; fortunately that did not take long — only thirty-six hours. Dodd and Bernardino helped the son to bury him — Bernardino very sulky and dodging as much of the work as possible. He looked on it as very unnecessary labour and none of his business; but the stunted man wept bitterly, and constantly bewailed the fact that his father had died unshriven, and without a priest to bury him, and with uncounted years of purgatory before him in consequence. Dodd was not much moved anyway. His trade was in death, and he had seen much of it of late years. He was engaged in war, and war without death was a quite unthinkable thing. And seeing that England had been engaged in one continuous war since he was a child in petticoats, a world without war was equally unthinkable. And Dodd had far too much practical common sense ever to begin to think about such a fantastic notion as a world without the possibility of war. He was far too deeply occupied, moreover, with his present business of killing Frenchmen, or aiding them to starve to death, or tormenting them with disease.

Chapter XV

WHEN night fell again after they had scooped the shallow grave in the leaf-mould and had covered up the wasted body and the white hair, they set out again for Santarem. The stunted man had been speaking the truth when he had said that they could not find the way by night without his aid. They crept across several fields, following a zigzag route through the rainy darkness, apparently to make sure of their direction by going from one landmark to another — a tree or a disused plough. At one place the stunted man enjoined special precaution. They could just see him in the darkness lower himself down into a drainage ditch alongside a field, and crept after him along it — there was a trough in the bottom of the ditch and they could walk with one foot on each side of the water. Only thirty yards away they heard the challenge of a sentry and the reply of the visiting rounds — apparently they were creeping past a village. After a long wait they crept along the ditch. Some distance along they emerged, crept across the *pavé* of the road, and plunged into another ditch. Then there was more creeping and crawling. They crossed a field thick with weeds, apparently, and at last they heard the rushing gurgling sound of the Tagus close at hand. Soon they were on its very bank, and could just discern the dark surface of the water. They crept along above the river for a few more yards, and then their guide checked them, and lowered himself with infinite precaution over the edge. They followed him, and, guided by his whispers and sharp pokes from his fingers, they lay down under the edge of the bank. Here the river rose within ten feet of the level of the surrounding country; it had reached its maximum winter level now. The strip of vertical bank still exposed was covered with vegetation dragging out a miserable existence among the rocks — myrtle bushes, Dodd thought. They afforded very fair cover, and here they waited for the dawn, wet and weary. Bernardino's teeth chattered.

Morning came with a mist from the river, which only later
dissolved into the perpetual rain which had been falling for weeks
now. It was only occasionally that the weather cleared sufficiently
to afford a good view. During those bright intervals it was evident
that their guide had done his work well. Looking across the arc of
a wide bend in the river they could see the white houses of Santarem ranged along the quays of the town, and on the quays they
could see a good deal of bustle and activity. Then on the farther
bank they saw something which set Dodd's heart beating strangely
— a line of red-coats; the watery sun was reflected from the
sloped musket barrels. There was British infantry across the river,
then — Dodd had seen Portuguese cavalry there a long time ago.
The red streak moved steadily along the river bank down stream;
as he watched, a dip in the contour of land gradually swallowed it
up. So that enough troops had been spared from the garrison of
the Lines to establish a solid force beyond the river. The French
were properly ringed in now, between the Lines and the irregulars
and the river and troops across the river. But that still did not
explain the cannonade at Santarem; they had to wait a little
longer for the explanation of that.

Soon guns boomed from the farther bank, and were instantly
answered by guns from Santarem. Dodd, gazing anxiously across
the bend, tried to make out at what the British guns were aimed,
but it was hard to detect the fall of shot at that distance. Then he
saw something else. A long streak of smoke shot from the bank,
and described a wide curve across the river, ending among the
houses of Santarem. Another followed it, and another, while the
fire of the French guns was redoubled.

Dodd scratched his head in some bewilderment before he hit
on an explanation of the phenomenon. Rockets! There had long
been one or two rocket batteries in the English Army, the source
of a good deal of amusement to everybody. Rockets were such
unreliable and irregular weapons. They might serve to terrify
savages, perhaps, or to — Dodd guessed their purpose now. There
was something in Santarem which the English were anxious to
set on fire. Presumably that something must be within sight of
the farther bank, and therefore must be close to the water's edge.

Dodd was enough of a soldier to guess what it must be — a bridge or bridging material, boats or pontoons and roadway stuff. Dodd pulled at the bristling beard which had sprouted on his chin during the last few weeks and fell into deep thought.

Rocket after rocket curved across the river, while the guns from Santarem strove to put the rocket battery out of action and the guns on the other bank strove to silence them. In the middle of the action they heard a noise overhead which startled them. They looked at each other in fear and cowered back amid the myrtles. There came a cracking of whips and a clattering of harness and loud orders in French from the field under whose edge they lay. Horses neighed and men shouted. Dodd knew what was happening, but he dared not make a sound to enlighten his companions, even if his command of the language had enabled him to do so. He knew the sound of a battery going into action well enough.

Bernardino and the stunted man did not have to wait long in ignorance. With an appalling crash the six guns fifty yards behind them opened simultaneously. They had been moved up here to take the English in flank. The powder smoke from the guns, keeping low along the ground, came drifting down upon them. It would have set them coughing had they dared to allow themselves to cough. They heard the orders of the officers correcting the direction and elevation, and then the guns roared out again, and again, and again. Dodd was too low down to see what they were firing at, and he certainly was not going to try and find out. They were in deadly peril here in their hiding-place. They crouched down among the myrtle bushes, striving after complete concealment. Bernardino's lips were moving in prayer, but he was stupid, because he allowed the noise to add to his terror; despite his common sense, he could not make himself believe that the appalling explosions added nothing to their danger.

A moment of far greater danger came, all the same, a few minutes later, when some one came to the edge of the river some distance away and looked over at the water. The three of them lay frozen among the bushes — a searching glance from the new arrival might have disclosed them nevertheless. But he was not looking for men; he would have been extremely surprised to find an English soldier and a couple of Portuguese hidden under the very muzzles of his guns. He was looking for a place to water the horses, and the immediate neighbourhood, with a ten-foot drop to the surface of the river, was clearly not suitable. It was at a place three hundred yards away that the horses were eventually led to the water's edge — dangerous enough, but not too much so.

Dodd and Bernardino and the stunted man cowered among the bushes all day long, while the guns roared above them at intervals whenever their target was not obscured, while the horses were being watered quite close at hand, and the rockets still strung their arcs of smoke across the river. As far as Dodd could see, they produced not the least effect. For a rocket to start a fire while a numerous and vigilant fire-fighting party was on the watch would call for a far more propitious combination of circumstances than could ever be expected; and, anyway, no rocket could be expected to come to earth less than a hundred yards from the point aimed at. In fact, in Dodd's opinion, every one concerned was simply wasting gunpowder.

Perhaps the British officer in command of the rocket battery and artillery beyond the river came to the same opinion as the day wore on, for the firing died away. The battery in the field above the trio ceased fire, presumably because the enemy had withdrawn from sight, and silence descended again, broken only by occasional bursts of laughter and conversation from the unseen artillery men, and by the unceasing gurgle of the eddies of the river below them.

Later in the afternoon their good fortune displayed itself once more. They heard the clink and clatter of harness as the horses were put to the guns again, and they heard the whip cracking and shouts of the drivers as the beasts were stimulated to the wild effort necessary to heave the guns out of the earth into which they had sunk under the impulse of their firing. Then the guns jingled and clattered across the field, and they heard the noise of their progress rise to a roar when they reached the paved high road, and the roar gradually died away with the increasing distance.

The battery had departed, and Bernardino, with the impatience of his years and inexperience, began to stretch his cramped limbs as a matter of course; he intended to climb up and look over the edge of the cliff to see if any of the enemy remained above them, but Dodd seized his shoulder and forced him into passivity again. Whether the enemy had gone or not they would not be able to move from their present position until nightfall. To look over the edge was running a risk for no reward save the satisfaction of curiosity, and although Dodd's curiosity in the matter was just as acute as Bernardino's he had no intention of imperilling himself on that account. No comfort of mind or body could compare in Dodd's opinion with the negative comfort of remaining alive as long as duty permitted — this opinion of Dodd's goes far to explain why he had been able to survive five campaigns.

They stayed for the rest of the day immobile among the bushes, wetted through at intervals by the rain. They would probably pay no immediate penalty for that; colds in the head are very infrequent among people living all their time out of doors. Yet they could boast no such immunity from pneumonia or rheumatic fever, and in after years, were they to live so long, they would be bent and crippled and agonized with rheumatism — say in thirty years' time. But men in the early twenties — least of all soldiers — do not often stop to think about possible illness in thirty years' time.

All Dodd's cogitation during the afternoon led him no nearer any definite decision. There was bridging material at Santarem which the English wanted burnt; that made it his duty to burn it if he could. That was clear enough; it was none of Dodd's business to bear in mind the fact that the motive for desiring the destruction of the bridge might be very slight indeed — no stronger than the result of the very ordinary decision that it ought to be a good move to destroy anything that the enemy considers it desirable to construct. If horse, foot and guns had been brought up to burn the bridge, then Dodd ought to try as well; the unanswerable question at the moment was how to do it.

He could see Santarem clearly enough, and the towering warehouses on the quays. There were several thousand men there; at night (such must be the crowding in the town) there would be men asleep or on guard all round the stuff, and upon it and underneath it. Reluctantly he decided that it would be an impossible task — as far as he could judge at the moment — to penetrate into Santarem and set fire to the bridge. It might be done by a man not in uniform, but to discard his uniform would make him a spy, liable to the death of a spy, and Dodd, with the usual fantastic notions of military honour, refused to consider it, although he knew well enough that if the French were to catch him this far within their cantonments they would probably shoot him or hang him anyway.

Yet, although the business seemed so impossible, Dodd did not entirely put away all thought of it. Some other way round the difficulty might present itself. Prolonged reconnaissance from the inland corner of the wood where they had found their present guide might suggest something — Dodd could not imagine what, but he hoped. So as dusk crept down upon them he made ready with the others for a return to the stunted man's hiding-place.

In the twilight they allowed Bernardino to satisfy his earlier wish to climb up and look over the top of the little cliff; sure enough, the field beyond was deserted and the way to the main road was clear. When it was fully dark they started stiffly out upon the return journey, over the fields and along the ditches, past the village where, at this early hour in the evening, the fires blazed with their full volume, until not very much past midnight they reached the edge of the wood, and could warm themselves by a sharp walk to the hut where the old man had died.

They were all desperately tired and hungry and short-tempered. Dodd was disappointed at the unsatisfactory result of his investigations, but he was not half so annoyed as his companions. They had gone short of sleep for two nights, they had spent a day in unutterable discomfort and a great deal of terror, they were wet and muddy and cramped, solely because of his unreasonable wish to see Santarem — that was how they expressed it to themselves. Even Bernardino's faith in Dodd was shaken for the moment. He had failed to produce any new ingenious scheme for the discomfiture of the French, and Bernardino was one of those who demand new things. He grumbled and complained as they crowded into the little hut seeking its not-completely-effective shelter from the rain. He objected violently when Dodd's knees and elbows dug into him in their cramped sleeping space. But he was too tired to keep it up. Soon they were all three of them fast asleep, packed together like pigs in a sty, and nearly as dirty. The rain dripped monotonously through the trees.

Chapter XVI

In the wet morning the usual three military problems of offence and defence and supply presented themselves. They shared the last of their bread with the stunted man — there was no knowing how he had been maintaining himself before they met him; badly enough, presumably — and tried to discuss the next move. Bernardino, in fact, was so disgruntled by recent events that he presumed to press plans upon Dodd. He wanted to go back to the village, taking the stunted man with them as a fresh recruit, and resume the harassing of the battalion there. To Bernardino it was obviously the thing to do. On the hill there was food and there were friends and an enemy to attack. Here in the wood there seemed nothing. When Dodd said "See Santarem" and persisted in saying it he grew exasperated. He knew nothing of strategy; he could not grasp the possibly supreme importance of the bridging material at Santarem.

The stunted man contributed little to the discussion. If he had ever had any initiative — and there was no means of telling — it had all evaporated with the death of his father. He wanted to kill Frenchmen, but he seemed willing enough to do it under the direction of others. He said nothing when Dodd said "See Santarem" in a tone of finality and rose and hitched his rifle on his shoulder and set off towards the far corner of the wood, although Bernardino stamped his feet with annoyance.

Bernardino followed Dodd, sulkily, in the end, and the stunted man came too, without a word. There was small satisfaction to be gained from the distant view of the land front of Santarem. The little town was walled on this side, with gates, which would make it supremely difficult to achieve an unobserved entrance. Bernardino fidgeted with irritation while Dodd looked this way, and that way, and tried to ask the stunted man questions.

In the end coincidence brought about a dramatic change in Dodd's plans, and delighted Bernardino's heart. Across the half or three quarters of a mile of flat land which lay between them and the town they suddenly saw signs of some important move outside the gate on the up-stream end of the town. They saw a little column of troops march out. After them came a waggon — at that distance they could make out no details, but Dodd was sure it was a waggon and not a gun. There came another waggon, and another, and another, and another. Waggon followed waggon until Dodd was sure that he was not observing a minor military move — the transfer of a convoy, or something of that order. It became pressingly important to his mind to discover what this was.

"Go to road. See," said Dodd.

He turned and hurried back into the wood, with Bernardino delightedly following him, for that must be the direction they must follow to return to the village.

They hurried through the wood at the best speed possible to them when they had to be on guard at every step lest some French patrol should be prowling near at hand. Even in the heart of the forest they could hear the sound of the waggon train on the *pavé* — a low rumble rising a note or two in the scale whenever a waggon crossed over a culvert or a bridge.

At last they reached a point in the wood whence they could look down on the high road, and Dodd threw himself on his face and edged forward to peer round the trunk of a tree. The others crouched near, and ever the rain poured down on them. The head of the column, with the vanguard of troops, had already passed, but what followed was far more interesting. Dodd had been right when he had suspected the French of bridge construction. The first vehicles were odd-shaped things, each composed of two artillery caissons linked together. On these were piled pontoons, huge, clumsy boats nested into each other, four or five together. Their number was great — section after section lumbered by. Dodd took note of the animals drawing them along — wretched, under-fed horses with their ribs starting through their coats; it was a wonder that they could drag themselves along, to say nothing of the loads behind them. The French soldiers driving them displayed little care as to their condition, flogging the poor brutes along as they slipped and stumbled over the cobbles. Dodd readily decided that a few weeks more of this underfed life would leave the French Army with no transport animals at all. To the pontoon-laden caissons succeeded, at length, service waggons and country carts heaped with all the miscellaneous accessories of military bridges; there were four carts laden with rope and quite thirty laden with timber.

But before the last caisson had gone by Dodd had resolved to do what he could to interfere with the march of the bridging train. No one knew better than he, who had served in so many convoy guards, how helpless is a long train of waggons strung out along the road. And he knew, too, that to kill one of the enemy's horses was quite as helpful as killing one of the enemy's men. He looked round at his two followers.

"*Caballos*," he said, "*caballos*," and pushed his rifle forward.

They took aim beside him, and the three shots rang out almost together. One horse in a team of six fell in its traces; another, plunging and kicking on three legs, made evident the fact that the fourth was broken. Instantly Dodd leaped to his feet and dashed back among the trees, with the others at his heels, to where he could reload undisturbed.

"Horses," said Dodd again, as he rammed the bullet home.

The others nodded. They could understand this method of warfare. Dodd pelted through the wood parallel with the road for a short space before changing direction to the edge again. There was confusion in the convoy. The waggon at whose team they had fired was stationary and helpless, and everything behind it was pulling up. Drivers were seeking their weapons, men were shouting, horses were plunging — there was all the confusion of a sudden surprise attack. The escort parties at the head and rear of the column were each of them half a mile away or more; the three were safe for some time from any counterattack, for the drivers had, as was only to be expected, an exaggerated idea of the force attacking them, and were hampered by the necessity of looking after their teams. A young officer came galloping up the road to the place of the jam. For the moment Dodd pointed his rifle at him, but he refrained from pulling the trigger when he guessed what order the officer was going to give. He glowered round at his companions to enforce on them the same self-restraint. At the officer's order the waggon behind the one which was stationary pulled out of the line and began to go up past the point of stoppage; the rest of the long line made preparations to follow. Just when the overtaking waggon was diagonally across the road Dodd fired again, and next second the jam was complete; two helpless waggons completely blocked the narrow paved road. Drivers raved and horses kicked while Dodd reloaded with all the speed five years of practice could give. A third volley brought down more horses still and perfected the work. After that for several hectic minutes each of the three loaded and fired at will, bringing down a horse here and a horse there, until Dodd made his companions cease fire. He had to shake them by the shoulders to compel their attention, so excited had they grown. Some of the drivers had found their muskets and were blazing back at random into the wood; bullets were rapping sharply on trees here and there, but that was not the reason for Dodd's cessation of fire. There was a body of troops hurrying back from the head of the column; another hurrying up from the tail. They were still some distance off when Dodd ran away, intent on living to fight another day. As they ran breathlessly through the wood, Dodd found himself regretting that he had not thirty men with him instead of two; there would be a fine game open to them then in the attack on this long vulnerable column. Three were too small a force altogether.

When the escort reached the point in the road whence the firing had come they halted for a moment at a loss, for there was no firing now. In the end they plunged into the wood, but only for a short distance. They could find no trace of the enemy, and as they plunged about in the undergrowth the officers were uneasily conscious that meanwhile they were leaving the line of waggons unguarded — an uneasiness which was greatly accentuated immediately afterwards by the sound of firing from high up towards the head of the column. It was a lively day for the convoy escort as well as for the drivers. The escort spent their time running up and down a couple of miles of road in hopeless dashes after an enemy which fled at their earliest approach and yet was always ready to reappear elsewhere and resume its harassing attacks. If the three hundred men of the escort had been strung along the road trying to guard every point they would have been just as useless — one man to every ten yards. Meanwhile the drivers were engaged in cutting out injured horses, in replacing them with animals from the few teams which could spare them, and getting the waggons along somehow.

In the end, the situation was relieved by the arrival of reinforcements. A battalion — the fourth of the Forty-Sixth — was called out of its billets in a village some distance up the road, and another came up from Santarem, which the convoy had just left. Then they were able to post guards in sufficient strength along the dangerous length of road, and even to spare men to man-handle teamless waggons out of the way. Yet all this took time; by the end of the day the waggon train had progressed exactly three miles.

Dodd, crouching with his two companions at the far end of the wood, whither they had been driven by the new arrivals, could feel pleased with his day's work, despite the fact that they were all three of them so exhausted that they could hardly stand. He had regained his old ascendancy too. Bernardino was enormously amused by what they had done; despite his fatigue he still broke into little chuckles at the recollection of the exasperated waggon drivers and the jams and confusion of the train and the harassed running about of the escort. It had taken a thousand men in the end to guard those waggons against three enemies.

It is to be feared that Dodd enjoyed undue credit on this account — both Bernardino and the stunted man believed (and the difficulties of language prevented a clearing up of the situation) that this attack on the convoy had been planned from the first, and that the dangerous visit to inspect Santarem, which they had condemned so bitterly earlier, was a necessary part of the scheme. It sent up Dodd's stock with a bound. Several times Bernardino told Dodd, who did not understand what he said, and the stunted man, who did not appear specially interested, all about what they had done that day.

Even Bernardino's excitement died away in time, and allowed him to meditate upon the matter which was now occupying all Dodd's attention — the matter of their hunger and the absence of means to satisfy it. Bernardino's ebullition of spirits had changed to peevishness, when suddenly the stunted man rose and walked away through the darkness under the trees. Bernardino was actually too tired and hungry to ask where he was going. Dodd pulled in his belt and tried to reconcile himself to an evening without supper and the prospect of a morrow without breakfast. He had actually sunk into a fitful doze when they heard the stunted man, seeking them, call to them in a guarded tone. They replied, and he appeared, a shadowy shape, through the trees. He pressed something wet and faintly warm into Dodd's hands, and presumably made a similar present to Bernardino.

"What is this?" asked Bernardino.

"Horse," said the stunted man, who was a man of few words.

For once one of Dodd's subordinates had been cleverer than he — Dodd had forgotten all about the dozen dead horses along the edge of the main road, but the stunted man had remembered them, and had found his way to one. Not merely that, but he had used his wits well when he had reached his objective. Even in the dark and in the imminent danger of being surprised by a stray enemy he had remembered that it would be far too dangerous to light a fire for cooking with so many of the enemy near, and he had realized that a lump of muscle hacked from a starving horse might well defy their teeth were it uncooked. So he had ripped open the horse's belly and had plunged into its still warm entrails in search of its liver, from which he had cut the generous portions which they were now considering.

Dodd had eaten horse before — no soldier could serve five campaigns in the Peninsula, where small armies are beaten and large armies starve, without doing so — but always before it had at least made a pretence at being cooked. But he had never been as hungry before as he was now, and it was too dark to see what he was eating and, anyway, he had led the life of a savage for two months. He took a tentative nibble at his lump, and followed it with another, and yet another. Before very long he had made a good meal in the darkness and so had the others. And the fact that they had all been living lives of hard physical exertion in the fresh air for so long blessed them with digestions which could master even uncooked cart-horse.

After that they all slept well and deeply until Dodd woke and roused his companions — he had the knack of being able to wake at any hour he decided upon before going to sleep. It was two hours before dawn and they were stupid and weary, but they followed Dodd when he began to make his way back through the wood to the high road. They crossed the road safely, for it was still dark, and went up into the hill opposite, and then it dawned upon Bernardino what was in Dodd's mind, and he clapped his fist into his hand with delight. For by the end of yesterday the convoy had progressed beyond the point where the forest bordered the road; any further attack upon it would have to be made from the hill this other side, the hill whence weeks ago they had harassed the dragoons, and fought their first skirmish with the Forty-Sixth.

But there is nothing so fragile as a military plan. When dawn revealed the convoy breaking up its ordered ranks from its camp in the fields at the roadside beyond the wood, and drawing out its cumbrous length on the road, they could see that the reinforcements for the convoy escort which had arrived yesterday evening had stayed with it and were prepared to march with it to-day. Instead of having merely a hundred and fifty men both at the head and at the tail of the column, a mile and a half apart, there were now detachments of very considerable strength all the way along. Dodd looked down at the column from the crest of the hill, and decided not to interfere with it. Long service under a general who never lost a gun in action had taught even the men in the ranks of his army the distinction between bold enterprises and foolhardy ones. Neither of Dodd's followers questioned his decision: their faith in him was profound.

They dragged their weary limbs after him as he walked along the hill-top towards the village. Perhaps Bernardino experienced a feeling of pleasurable anticipation at the prospect of returning to Agostina's embraces; perhaps he was too tired.

The nearer they came to the village the more cautious were their movements, until at last they reached the point where they could look down the slope to where the village nestled between the two hills. Everything seemed much as usual. There were only a few French to be seen moving among the houses — Dodd guessed that it was from here that most of the reinforcements for the convoy escort had been drawn. There were a few engaged on their eternal hunt for something edible, for nettles at least if not for hidden stores of food, and a few sick and wounded limping about here and there. Across the deep valley, on the slopes of the other, steeper hill, they could see nothing at all of importance, but that was only to be expected. It was not the custom of the outlaws to expose themselves.

Dodd changed their direction away from the river over towards the stony lane, which they crossed with all due precaution, just as Dodd and Bernardino had crossed it in the opposite direction five days before. Now they were very near to their friends. Dodd felt quite pleased at the prospect of seeing them again. He increased his pace as he scrambled up the steep paths, as much as the steepness would allow, and the necessity for taking care not to run into either a French patrol or a Portuguese sentry too ready to fire.

They found no sentry at the summit of the path, even though Dodd had purposely chosen a path which led towards a point where a sentry ought to have been found. Dodd clicked his tongue with annoyance as he halted there for breath; the sentry's absence seemed to indicate slackness on the part of the garrison unless some important duty had called him elsewhere. Even if they were certain that the greater part of the enemy was away on the high road they should still keep their watch unbroken. Dodd looked round, but the hillside was far too irregular and overgrown for him to see far. He pushed on over the brow of the hill, down the dip, and up the next slope.

And then both he and Bernardino caught sight of something which made them halt abruptly where they stood, and look, and look again, not understanding what they saw. There was a little level stretch of ground here, where the rocks were more naked than usual, and the bushes lower, but at the farther side of it a

thorn tree maintained a precarious existence. The branches of
the thorn tree grew downwards a little, so as partly to screen
whatever was underneath them. Through this screen they could
faintly see two men leaning against the trunk in attitudes of
strange abandon. One was bent oddly forward with his arms
hanging queerly limp, the other was lolling back in a manner
which made it appear strange that he did not slip down to the
ground.

It was all very mysterious and eerie. Dodd cocked his rifle as he
picked his way over the rocks towards the tree. It was not until
he was close to it that he could see the details. The two men had
been nailed to the tree with bayonets — their own, presumably,
as their scabbards were empty — although it was apparent that
whoever was responsible had been merciful enough to shoot them
afterwards. Dodd looked at the dead faces. He knew them, despite the distortion of the features. They were two Portuguese,
two of the men who had helped him defend the hill. One of them
was Pedro who had cut the wounded Frenchman's throat after
the ambushing.

Bernardino at Dodd's elbow was pouring forth prayers and
oaths intermingled. The stunted man, as ever, said nothing. To
him this was only two more corpses in a land where Death took his
hundreds daily. Dodd, in the end, forced himself to take the same
view of it, although the sight had strangely unnerved him and left
him pale under his tan. He turned away and resumed his journey
over the hill. Bit by bit the whole tragedy revealed itself. The
hill had been stormed during their absence. Another dead man,
one of the garrison, lay in the path down to the river. Old Maria
lay dead at the mouth of the cave beyond the secret ford. It was
possible to guess a little of what had happened to her before she
died.

But it was not possible for Dodd to guess all the details. He
could not guess, and he never would know, that the Colonel of
the battalion in the village had at last brought himself to confess
his own weakness and had borrowed the services of two battalions
of Ney's Sixth Corps to help him clear the mountain of the brigands who plagued him there. Dodd never knew of the onslaught
of these terrible men who had marched by night to launch a sur-

prise at dawn. He never knew, fortunately perhaps, of the torture which was applied to one of the captives to make him reveal the secret of the ford, nor of what the brutes did to Agostina and the little girls.

But it became clear enough in the course of the day that the mountain was deserted and empty. The men and the boys were dead. The women — save old Maria — and the girls were missing. Thirteen hundred men, attacking concentrically from all round, had swept the place bare, and left no living thing upon it. Nor could Ney's men be really blamed for what they had done to their prisoners. They had carried on a nightmare war in Spain and Portugal for three endless years now. Often had they seen what the enemy did to their friends. The men they had captured had been taken with arms in their hands and without uniforms, and so deserved to die. The women were as bad as the men, and anyway soldiers needed relaxation during three years' campaigning. And if the poor fools had only sense enough to submit to the all powerful Emperor the women would not be interfered with quite so violently.

All food, of course, had been taken away. Dodd found consolation in the thought that what would make thirty days' food for twenty people would only make one day's food for five hundred, and actually, although he did not know it, thirteen hundred men had shared it — barely more than a mouthful apiece.

To Dodd and Bernardino the hill seemed accursed. They remembered the jolly people with whom they had lived there so long, people who had faced death at their sides over and over again. Dodd was too serious-minded a man to be able to smile — as many soldiers would — over the fact that the mere coincidence that he should have decided at that moment to go and see why the guns were firing at Santarem should have preserved his life when the others died.

Dodd would allow nothing to be done, all the same, to alter the things on the hill. The two dead men remained nailed to their tree to rot, Maria still lay in her dreadful attitude at the mouth of the cave. There was too much chance that anything he might do in the matter would disclose to any fresh exploring party from the village that there were still some survivors on the hill.

Chapter XVII

SERGEANT GODINOT came to find that, despite the desperately hard work demanded of him and his men, life in Santarem was far more to his liking than life with the battalion in the village. The very work was a blessing; they were at least doing something instead of rotting in their billets while the eternal rain drummed on the roofs, and the hard-bitten veterans of the Second and Sixth Corps were far better working partners than the helpless disease-ridden recruits of his own battalion — except for Dubois, of course, who was his boyhood's friend. They got the town mill working soon, and the town ovens, so that the men could have bread to eat instead of the pestilent corn porridge. With the light-heartedness of the best type of French soldiers they soon organized among themselves a town band which gave concerts whenever work permitted. The officers walked about the streets with women on their arms, which made the place very homely, even though some of the women wore men's uniforms and none of them as they flaunted through the town could possibly be mistaken for other than what they were.

There were other women in the town, too, women who avoided men's eyes and slunk along by the walls, women who wept and women who sometimes killed themselves, women whom Ney's godless veterans of the Sixth Corps had caught in their foraging expeditions inland.

The bridge made rapid progress towards completion, thanks to old General Éblé. He was everywhere at once, urging and commanding and inspecting. There was always a flurry and a speeding up whenever he appeared, whether it was in the forges where men laboured to make steel saws and adzes out of wrought-iron balcony rails, or in the nail recovery workshop where men laboriously straightened and repointed nails, or in the row of houses which men were feverishly pulling down for the sake of their timber, or in the paint works, or in the boat-building shed where

Godinot spent most of his time, or in the rope works where men were trying to perform miracles.

Perhaps the most popular employment was the housebreaking — literally housebreaking — because the old houses which were being pulled down were infested with rats which could often be caught in the course of the work. A roasted rat made a splendid addition to one's daily ration during the frequent weeks when no meat was issued. Men who had been lucky in the matter of loot earlier in the campaign were known to pay as much as a silver dollar for a fat rat, although it was hard to find sellers here where there was nothing for money to buy and no apparent prospect of ever reaching home.

That was the worst part of the life, even worse than the food. No one knew what was happening outside the ranks of the army in which they were serving. The Emperor in whose name they were fighting might be dead, the Russians might be in Paris, or the other armies in Spain might have been pushed back to the Pyrenees leaving them isolated here in Portugal. They knew nothing whatever save that they were holding a patch of country twenty miles square from which they would have to wring their food until something — no one knew what — should happen. The building of the bridge was an anodyne for despair, but not a satisfactory one. Old soldiers could not picture the army crossing the river by perilous pontoon bridges while an active and vigilant enemy was ready to fall upon them in the act of passing. And if they should pass, there lay on the other side of the river only the barren plains of southern Portugal. And, if they stayed, they starved. And the only retreat open to them was over the awful mountain roads by which they had come, which was a prospect just as appalling as the other two. The dreadful feeling of helpless isolation demoralized every one.

There were bitter jests made in the workshops about Godinot's uncle — Dubois had told the others of the relationship. The only route by which a new factor could enter into the situation was from the south, where, two hundred miles away beyond the Tagus, Soult with General Godinot's aid was holding down Andalusia. If he should abandon his principality and march to the

Tagus something fresh might happen; most of the men believed that it was in consequence of this possibility that the bridge was being constructed. Every day some jester would ask Godinot if there were any news from his uncle, and when they would have the pleasure of meeting him. In fact, the bridge was alluded to by most of the men as Godinot's uncle's bridge. But Godinot's uncle never came, however often they asked about him.

The construction of the pontoons progressed, nevertheless, in the face of difficulties and discouragement. It was heart-breaking work. Everything had to be botched and makeshift. The knees and ribs of the boats which ought to have grown naturally to shape had to be hacked out of floor-joists with badly-tempered saws and axes, which bent like lead when they were incautiously used. Bending the rotten timber into shape for the strakes was a tedious business, which had to be repeated over and over again before a result remotely satisfactory was attained. Nails were truly and literally more precious than gold; they had to be employed with niggling economy and every one had to be accounted for. The gaping seams left open by unavoidable bad workmanship had to be caulked with any odd materials that came to hand. Yet the caulking must be perfect, for when an army of a hundred thousand men with guns and waggons is pouring over a bridge there must be no delay to bail out pontoons. The paint which the experimenters produced was almost useless — when daubed on wood and immersed in water as a test most of it floated up to the surface in an hour or two. The experimental cordage stretched and snapped and disintegrated. The one problem which was solved to the satisfaction of every one was that of the anchors — in Portugal there could not be any difficulty in finding a sufficiency of big rocks for that purpose.

As soon as each pontoon — great, lumbering, over-heavy things that they were — was completed it was brought down to the quay and launched into the river by the slipway Godinot helped to build. Here it swung to moorings while being tested for staunchness and stability; quite two out of three of them demanded further attention before they could be passed as fit to bear a roadway to carry an army. Then they were hauled out and stacked on the quays, alongside the growing mass of roadway material and cables.

The river ran torrentially; it boiled along the quay, and in the prevailing westerly winds its surface was whipped, by the action of the wind against the current, into big, lumpy waves crested with foam. Godinot used to look out across the mass of mad water with gloomy forebodings. A bridge laid across it would bank up the current against itself. If one cable were to break, one anchor to drag, he could picture the whole bridge breaking into fragments and being swept down stream, leaving the army if it were crossing at the time divided into two helpless halves.

Godinot saw more than that when he looked across the river. Already the presence of Portuguese cavalry had been noted on the low, featureless, opposite bank. One morning Godinot caught Dubois's arm and pointed. There was a red stripe showing against the neutral grey-green, a stripe which moved steadily across the landscape, up and down the slight undulations, and along its upper edge the stripe was bordered with a rim of flashing steel. There was a brigade of red-coats marching there.

"Englishmen!" said Dubois, staring, while Godinot turned hastily away to report his discovery to the nearest officer.

When he came back he found Dubois still standing on the quay, staring with parted lips at the next development. There were half a dozen little things like caterpillars on the opposite bank now, and as Godinot reached Dubois's side they all swung round and broke into halves, and there was infinite bustle among the little dots above the water's edge. Then a white puff like a ball of cotton-wool appeared for a second, a sudden fountain of water from the surface of the river just in front of them, and a cannon-ball, ricochetting, sang over their heads like a hive of bees and then crashed into the upper story of the warehouse behind them. Another immediately afterwards hit the edge of the quay some distance away and caused such a spray of flying chips of stone that it was a miracle no one was hurt.

"It appears to me," said Dubois, aping the imperturbability of a veteran, "as if the English have begun to take notice of our activities here."

Then the next cannon-ball splintered a door close at hand and Dubois dropped his nonchalance and ran to cover behind the warehouse as fast as Godinot did.

For the moment all work ceased in Santarem. Mounted messengers clattered through the streets and dashed out of the gates to bring batteries into action to drive away these insolent interrupters, while cannon-balls came crashing into the town at regular intervals. Then a shell exploded with a sharp crack overhead, and sprayed shrapnel bullets over the exact centre of the main street, causing several casualties among the crowd gathered there. That caused annoyance to supersede interest. The British artillery was the only one to employ this new missile, and it was universally disliked and dreaded by the French.

However, the shells that came over were few, because the enemy had come to destroy bridging material and workshops, not men. Godinot, peering round the corner of the warehouse, saw a moored pontoon fly suddenly into fragments when a round-shot hit it fair and true in the middle. There were gaping holes now here and there in the solid walls of the warehouses. A sudden enormous clatter of hoofs announced the arrival of some one specially important; so it was — no less a person than Marshal Masséna himself, the general commanding in chief, with General Éblé and Marshal Ney and a couple of score of aides-de-camp and his renegade Portuguese advisers and three dozen mounted orderlies.

Masséna climbed down from his horse and hobbled stiffly down a side alley to the river. He grabbed Dubois by the arm and made him stand out beyond the corner of the warehouse so that he could rest his ponderous telescope on his shoulder. Godinot, watching the expression on Dubois's face, could not help but be amused. There was doubtless honour in supporting the telescope of a Prince of the Empire, but it was an honour Dubois could have done well without when it involved standing clear of all cover while a bombardment was going on.

Masséna gave back his telescope to his aide-de-camp and turned away without a word, and Dubois scuttled gratefully back to Godinot behind the warehouse. It was not long before guns came clashing and clattering into the town and took up position in the alley ways leading to the river and opened fire on the enemy. Down stream they heard other guns take up the chorus. Whoever the British general was across the water, his hopes must far have outrun his judgment if he expected to destroy the French bridges with a single six-pounder horse battery. Soon thirty guns were firing in reply, with all the advantages of concealment and cover. The British battery stood up to a good deal of heavy punishment, but it was more than flesh and blood could stand in the end, and they limbered up and went away.

Then the French officers were able to collect their workmen at last and begin the day's work. Not much damage had been done. A single pontoon had been sunk and the workshops had been a little knocked about; that was all. Later in the day the British horse artillery tried new tactics, galloping up suddenly to an unexpected position and putting in a few hasty shots which came crashing into the houses, but each time they were driven off speedily by the counter-batteries awaiting them. Not even the British artillery, with its brilliant officers and magnificent material, had yet devised a method of firing the guns from a concealed position while a forward observation officer controlled the aim.

Yet the British were not easily deterred from an objective on which they had set their hearts. Next morning revealed to the French a series of low mounds on the opposite bank; the British had started to throw up earthworks for gun emplacements there, and not all the fire of the French guns during the day could knock them to pieces.

And the morning after that the earthworks were completed. The guns were mounted there, and only their muzzles, peeping through the embrasures, could be seen from the French bank, while the men were afforded almost complete protection. There were other instruments of destruction besides guns too. With a hiss and a scream a long trail of smoke shot up from the earthworks and came curving over to the quays, falling with a splutter of blue fire beside a warehouse. Fortunately, perhaps, there were very few occasions when the rockets made as good a shot as that. The workmen, Dubois and Godinot among them, were paraded under cover with buckets and barrels of water ready to fight fires, but their services were hardly called upon. Some of the rockets dived straight into the river; others curved away in the wind and fell absurd distances away. One or two even soared into the air and fell back on the English side.

Yet despite all this bad practice, and despite the fact that French artillery was sent far out to right and to left in an endeavour to enfilade the English earthworks, Godinot knew that this English demonstration would be effective enough in one respect. There were enough roundshot coming into the town to make work in the workshops risky, but a more important consideration was that the operation of casting bridges over the river at Santarem (if ever it were contemplated) would now be so difficult as almost to be impossible, now that there was artillery in solid works to oppose the passage. When, late in the afternoon, carts and waggons and artillery caissons — as much transport as the whole army could boast, Godinot guessed — began to stream into the town his suspicions were confirmed.

"We shall move to-morrow," he said to Dubois, nodding at the waggons parking in the main street.

"How do you know?" asked Dubois, the ever sceptical. "There are lots of reasons why — "

"Mark my words," said Godinot, "we shall move to-morrow, if we don't move to-night."

He was quite right. In the evening all the bridge builders were hard at work loading their nearly completed bridges on the waggons. It was an immense task, for the amount of material they had put together was colossal. The only means that could be devised of transporting the pontoons themselves was by tying the artillery caissons together in pairs and balancing the big, clumsy boats on top. For the actual hoisting of them up, the blocks and tackle once used for lifting wool bales, hanging outside the upper windows of the wool warehouses, came in exceedingly handy, and it was in devising ways and means of bringing these God-sent appliances into use that Godinot earned a word of praise from General Éblé. The cordage and, above all, the roadway timber, occupied an immense number of waggons. Every one was tired out and wet through — for of course the rain which had fallen at intervals during the day settled into a steady downpour at nightfall — by the time the loading was finished. Yet the order was given for the bridging party to be on parade at five o'clock in the morning — only three hours hence.

Even getting the immense convoy under way when morning came was a huge business. The emaciated horses slipped and fell on the cobbles, traces broke, lashings broke. But it was done at last. Carefully closed up, in obedience to the strict orders given, the convoy, a solid mile and a half of vehicles, began its slow course out of the town, in an up-stream direction, towards, as Dubois was actually able to work out for himself, the village where the fourth battalion of the Forty-Sixth was billeted. He and Godinot were marching with half the bridging party at the head of the column. Every one was tired and sick and hungry and exceedingly bad-tempered, and no one, save, presumably, the officers, knew whither they were going.

The pace was funereal. Every few minutes they had to halt in the rain to allow the dragging column to catch up with them, and every minute they grew wetter and at every halt they grew colder. Godinot, struggling and slipping on the *pavé*, was glad that he still possessed a good pair of boots. Boots were growing scarce in the French Army; half the men round him, especially those detached from the Sixth Corps, had none at all. Their feet were, instead, tied up in bags of raw hide obtained from the carcasses of the ration animals or from dead horses. They were comfortable from one point of view, in that worn with the hair inside they kept the feet warm, but in every other respect they were horribly unsuitable, and they were liable to wear out suddenly and leave their wretched possessor to tramp barefoot on the stony roads. Most of the men, too, were in rags barely sufficient for decency; a few had civilian clothes, coats or breeches, some of them significantly marked with bloodstains. Altogether they looked more like a mob of beggars than the bridging section of a regular army — dispirited beggars, moreover. The obvious check to the Army's plans at Santarem had taken the heart out of them.

So that when, almost as soon as the convoy had started, there came the sound of distant musketry far down the column, every one cursed and grumbled. A message from the rear halted the head of the column, and turned the escort about on a hurried dash back to the focus of the trouble. Executed at the double, it was a long run for men underfed and overworked. When they arrived there was not a glimpse of the enemy, which was just what they expected. There were traces of their handiwork, all the same — waggons with half their horses dead, jammed across the road, wounded horses plunging and kicking, drivers trying to control their teams, officers swearing. The road here was bordered by a thick forest, in which, as the cursing escort realized, there was no chance at all of catching their elusive enemies. Moreover, hardly had they halted, panting, at the edge of the wood, than other shots were fired back towards whence they came, and half of them, the unfortunate Godinot and Dubois among them, had to run back again, only to find just another crippled team there to add to the difficulty of getting the convoy along.

As the blaspheming soldiers said, a guard of three hundred men ought to have been sufficient for a waggon column moving in the middle of the cantonments of an army of a hundred thousand, but in the Peninsula ordinary military axioms did not apply. In that broken and difficult country three hundred men could not guard a convoy a mile and a half long against an active enemy, and it was only too obvious that the enemy was still active here in the heart of the French territory.

Exactly how many of the enemy there were attacking the column no one really stopped to consider. Every one took it for granted that not less than fifty at least would have the boldness to pester a large force in this way, which complicated enormously the question of breaking the escort up into detachments, or pursuing the enemy into the forest. And when the road set itself to the task of climbing over the spur of mountain which here ran down to the Tagus from the backbone of the Lisbon peninsula matters grew more difficult still, because now "tracing" had to be resorted to — taking the team from one waggon to reinforce that of another to climb part way up the hill before descending to pick up the one left horseless. This naturally made for a long break in the column, and at either end of the break a muddle of stationary vehicles, with horses being taken out or put in, and everybody busy and distracted — an ideal mark for any one who cared to take a long shot into the thick of it from the shelter of the forest.

A subtle difference in the quality of the sound of some of the shots fired caught Godinot's ear. There was a peculiar ring about them; they were the sounds of a rifle and not of a musket. He had heard that noise before, often enough. And listening carefully, he was sure only one rifle was firing. Then he guessed who was responsible — it was only natural, for it was just in this locality that his battalion had first fought the irregulars whom the green English rifleman had led. It confirmed Godinot in his notion that there must be a large party attacking them, for the green Englishman had been at the head of a considerable band at their last encounter. If Godinot and his companions had only known that the pests who were worrying them numbered only three in all they would have been considerably astonished, but they would not discover it if Dodd could help it. Dodd had learned his trade under a soldier with an acute ability to estimate relative values — the last man in the world to abandon a strategical position in order to score a tactical point.

So Sergeant Godinot did not know what to make of things when, at the end of a terribly exhausting day, he was chatting with Adjutant Doguereau of his battalion, which had been brought down from its billets to help bring the column through. Adjutant Doguereau gave Godinot the latest battalion gossip, and told Godinot of how they had just cleared — with the help of a couple of battalions from the Sixth Corps — the hill above the village of the gang who had plagued them.

"We wiped them out," said Adjutant Doguereau. "Every blessed one of them. The ones we caught we shot — you fellows of the bridging gang haven't left us with enough rope even to hang a brigand when we catch one. And the others we chased all over the hill and got them all. One tried to swim the river. Poor devil! And the women! Oh, sonny, the women!"

Adjutant Doguereau smacked his lips, as he recalled that part of the affair, before he went on to tell Godinot the interesting story about the cave and the secret ford which led to it. Somehow Sergeant Godinot could not take much interest in that part of the story which told of how Ney's men had caught a child — a little boy — who had refused to disclose the secret even when threatened with death, but who had given it up readily enough when suitable methods were employed upon him.

"But what about the green Englishman?" asked Godinot.

"To hell with you and your green Englishman!" said Adjutant Doguereau. "Half the battalion is still talking about a green Englishman. There never was one. *I* never saw him. Nor did any one else that day."

"You didn't catch one on the hill then?"

"No. There wasn't one, I say. There never was one."

"Oh," said Godinot, "he's back in that forest there now."

"How do you know? Have you seen him?"

"No," said Godinot, "but I heard him. I know a rifle shot when I hear one."

"Bah!" replied Doguereau. "And I know imagination when I hear it too."

That sort of argument went no way towards convincing hardheaded Sergeant Godinot.

The matter was so much on his nerves that it was a very decided relief next day that the column was not harassed in its march by a human enemy. Although the road had left the forest behind, the opposite side of it was flanked by the twin hills, the long, lower one and the short, steep one, between which lay the headquarters of the Forty-Sixth, and which constituted an ideal base for an attack by a force of any size on the lumbering convoy, even though the latter was now guarded by over a thousand men. Yet not a shot was fired all day; Godinot formed the opinion that the Englishman's force must indeed have been greatly diminished by the successful assault on the mountain which Doguereau had described. The fact that the Englishman himself had escaped tended to strengthen the suspicion which even the matter-of-fact Godinot had begun uneasily to cherish, to the effect that the Englishman must have some kind of supernatural power.

Godinot, however, did not have much time to think about it on that day. He was kept far too busy in the work of the convoy, for the steep descent on the other side of the spur proved to be more troublesome even than the ascent of the previous day. The rain still beat down relentlessly, and the road was full of pot-holes in which the overworked horses slipped and stumbled and broke their legs. Waggons fell over into ditches, and waggons out of control crashed into the ones ahead. A culvert, weakened by the rain, gave way under the weight passing over it and held up the whole line until the labouring bridging party had botched up some kind of new road-bed, across which doubled teams and a manhandling party a hundred strong could haul the stubborn waggons. Nightfall still found them short of their destination, and compelled to bivouac wretchedly by the roadside in the rain, on half-rations — and half-rations in this army meant quarter-rations. Nor was anybody's temper improved by the rumour which ran rapidly round the ranks next morning to the effect that a sentry had been found with his throat cut.

That afternoon, however, found them at the point to which they had been directed. It was a wild corner of Portugal. There was a little stone village here — Punhete it was called, Godinot understood, but clearly it was not on account of the village that the bridging train had been sent here. It was because of the river, the Zezere was its fantastic name, which came boiling down here from the mountains to lose itself in the broad waters of the Tagus. The bridging train established itself here, half a mile from the confluence, where the English artillery on the other side of the Tagus could not annoy it, and where it was out of observation. The portion of the bridges which had been completed was to be stacked here, and sheds were to be built to protect it from the weather, and launching slips for the boats were to be set up on the bank while the bridges were being completed. The theory was that here the pontoons could be launched, and even large sections of the bridge coupled together, before being floated down to the main river, to take the English by surprise as soon as the passage of the Tagus was decided upon.

Sergeant Godinot looked at the racing mountain stream, and the rocks, and the eddies, and shook his head when he considered this plan. He knew something about the handling of boats on swift rivers, having spent many happy boyhood hours among the shoals of the Loire, and he could picture the muddle the unhandy lands-men of the bridging train would make of the affair. In his opinion it was just as well that sufficient material for two bridges was being constructed; when the attempt was to be made there might be just enough preserved from shipwreck and from being swept away down stream to make one bridge.

Godinot began to suspect that the building of the bridges was merely a gesture, something exactly comparable with the blind lunges of a strangling man — indeed the comparison between a strangling man and the French Army in Portugal is a very apt one. The French felt themselves dying slowly, and were expending their energies in ill-directed efforts. Yet if no use were to be made of the bridges it would imply that soon they would have to re-treat, and beyond the Zezere Godinot could see the mountains of central Portugal, rising up in peak after peak to mark the dif-ficulties of the road over which they would have to go.

Yet the work had to be taken in hand all the same. The men were set to the colossal task of levelling an area beside the Zezere, and building sheds, and completing the bridges with materials taken from the village of Punhete. The men themselves had no billets this time; they had to construct little brushwood huts for themselves — as the veterans of the Second and Sixth Corps had long ago learnt how to do — in which they dragged out a miser-able existence in the continual rain while they lived upon insuf-ficient and irregular convoys of food sent up by a reluctant head-quarters. As Dubois dolefully pointed out to Godinot, they had chosen the wrong job. When food is short the men who have the obtaining of it will see that they have enough before passing on any surplus to those who have none.

Chapter XVIII

THE three vagabonds out on the hill were faced with the usual pressing military problem of supply. They were as ever horribly hungry, and they did not know where food was to come from. It is true that they had breakfasted in the morning off what was left of the horse's liver which the stunted man had gained for them the night before, but there had not been much, and what there was had been eaten twelve hours ago. Now it was growing dark, and cold, and the world seemed a gloomy place.

Dodd could pull in his belt and philosophically endure the pangs of hunger, but Bernardino had not the temperament for that. Besides, Dodd was worried about the future. He could see no likely chance of gaining more food. What they could do was more than he could guess. Slow starvation up here on the hill was probably as pleasant a death as the French would provide for them if they were to go down and surrender. And even if he were assured of good treatment the prospect of surrendering was very nearly as hateful to him as death. He wanted to live. He wanted to rejoin his regiment. He wanted to find out what was the destination of the bridging train, and to do something towards destroying it.

This last desire marked a slight but significant change in Dodd's mental outlook which had been accomplished by the experiences of these last few weeks of independent action. Before that, even though he was a light infantryman and accustomed to some extent to acting by himself, he had been thoroughly imbued with the army tradition of looking for orders and doing nothing more than those orders dictated. That was all a private soldier was expected to do; indeed, to go beyond that usually meant trouble. Even in those days the usual retort of a non-commissioned officer was "You thought? You're not paid to think. You're paid to obey orders" — a speech which has endured word for word even down to our day.

The rifle regiment tradition had never been as rigid as that of the line regiments, for in action the rifleman had more to do than merely to keep in step and in line with a thousand of his fellows whatever happened, but it was firm enough for any variation from it to mark out Rifleman Dodd as a man of some originality; five campaigns had already shown him to be a man of brute courage and resolution. It was a far cry from the skirmishing line at Busaco, farther still from the barrack square and the parade ground, and even farther from the bird-scaring and sheaf-binding and hay-making at the foot of the rolling Sussex Downs where he had spent his boyhood, to trying to play a part in the plans of Marshal the Prince of Essling and Lieutenant-General Viscount Wellington, K.B.

Yet highfalutin plans would not fill Dodd's belly, and were no use at all to the hungry Bernardino. It was a very depressed and discontented Portuguese who resigned himself at last to a supperless bed amid the rocks at the side of Dodd. All the same, there was a ray of hope, because the stunted man, who never seemed to want to sleep, had gone out when they settled down, clearly — although he did not waste words on explaining his motives — to see what he could find to eat. Yesterday he had brought back a fine lump of horse's liver. Bernardino pinned his faith on the efforts of the stunted man, and such was his hope that he actually went to sleep, hungry though he was.

Some hours after midnight, when just the faintest suspicion of greyness was come to relieve the blackness of night, Dodd awoke with a start. His ear had caught some strange noise, some noise which was not a natural one, and his sub-conscious mind had sifted it out from the other noises, and considered it, and finally had passed it on to his active mind and had wakened it instantly. Dodd sat up with his rifle in his hand; beside him Bernardino stirred and came to a slower awakening. There was a noise down the rocky slopes. Dodd listened with pricking ears. There was a mist over the hill to reinforce the lessening darkness, and Dodd could see nothing. Then they both heard something, a clash and a clatter, unmistakably like the sound of a horse slipping on the rocks. Dodd was on his feet in one motion, gliding silently off to the flank to investigate the new threat of danger from a safer angle, like a poacher's dog.

He heard the clatter again, and then a voice speaking in Portuguese — the stunted man's voice. Dodd walked towards it, and soon he saw him looming up through the mist, and by his side, elephantine in its appearance in the weird light, a big, raw-boned mule, one-eyed, harness-galled, with flapping lips revealing yellow teeth. The stunted man clapped the mule on the shoulder.

"Food," he said. He was always a man of few words.

The delighted Dodd saw the commissariat problem solved for days and days. Bernardino came up and grinned broadly. Between them they led the one-eyed mule over the hill down well below the crest, close above the river. Here Dodd judged that the smoke of a fire would be best concealed; in the prevailing mist and rain it would be safe enough here. The stunted man took the knife from his belt and held it to the big artery in the mule's throat; he was about to make the fatal stab when Dodd noticed that the knife was all smeared with dried blood, and so were the stunted man's hand and forearm. Dodd guessed what the blood was — one can rarely steal a mule from a convoy's horse lines without killing at least one sentry. Dodd may have been leading the life of a savage for some time past, but he was not as much a savage as to care to see his meat killed with a weapon stained in that fashion. The other two tried but failed to conceal their amusement at this attitude of his, and Bernardino took the knife, scrambled down to the riverside, and washed it with painful elaboration. Then he brought it back and handed it to the stunted man.

The knife went home among the great blood-vessels of the throat, but the mule's convulsive jerk at the prick of the knife caused him to break the halter which tied him to a stump, and his subsequent plunges bade fair to pitch him into the river. The stunted man saw the danger, and, regardless of the lashing hoofs, threw his arms round the mule's neck. When Dodd's plans for the destruction of the bridge are allowed for, it seems permissible to assume that the future course of European history might turn upon the plunging of a harness-galled mule with its throat cut.

The stunted man achieved his object. The mule fell with a clash of shod hoofs, but he lay on his side among the rocks and had not fallen into the water. He made one or two unavailing efforts to rise, but the blood spouting in great jets from his severed carotid drained his strength away, and soon he lay still and dead.

Then there was a great business to be done. Dodd gave orders as well as he could.

"Fire," he said, handing over his precious tinder-box to Bernardino, and then, pointing to the mule, "Much, much, much."

Bernardino ran about gathering fuel, and then with flint, tinder and slow-match set himself to kindle a fire. The stunted man began to flay and remove a quarter of mule. Dodd himself, his military instincts quite ineradicable, went rifle in hand up the hill again to take up a position on "the table" — ignoring the two dead men who still hung nailed to the thorn tree close beside it — to keep guard lest the smoke of the fire, or pure chance for that matter, should bring up stray parties of the enemy. There was no real need to worry, although he did not know it. Nearly all the battalion billeted in the village were still on the road escorting the bridging train. Only enough sound men remained to guard the sick.

It was a Gargantuan feast which that mule provided. Bernardino and the stunted man ate until they could eat no more, and then the stunted man came up the hill to where Dodd was on guard, pointed back to where the fire was, and obviously set himself to keep guard in Dodd's place. He was a far more thoughtful man than Bernardino.

Dodd went back to where Bernardino, all slimed with the mule's blood, was holding great chunks of meat on a ramrod before the fire. Dodd ate gluttonously, and by the time he was satisfied Bernardino found that he had regained a supplementary appetite and was able to start again. Dodd let him eat as much as he could hold; he had a good many days of half rations to make up for and — so Dodd's plans dictated — a good many days of half rations yet to come, against which he might as well make as much preparation as he could. Yet when he simply could hold no more, and the grateful warmth of the fire was tempting him to stretch himself beside it and make up for nights and nights of broken rest, Dodd kept him stirred into activity.

He had to keep on bringing in further supplies of fuel, and assist Dodd in the task of grilling more and more meat. Bernardino's face, no less than Dodd's, was toasted a bright scarlet. The heat of the fire was such that they had to shield their hands from it as they turned the stickfuls of meat before the blaze. It was the most primitive cookery imaginable. Dodd insisted on the meat being very thoroughly roasted, until it was quite dry, in fact, and naturally it became charred at the edges, but that could not be helped. The meat was coarse and tough and fibrous and had a peculiar sweetish flavour, but to men who have been hungry enough to eat raw horse roast mule is a positive luxury.

Anyway, Dodd had never known what good food was, not once in all his life, nor had Bernardino. It was mere irony that the money and effort wasted in the war in which they were fighting were sufficient to keep every single man engaged in it in Lucullan luxury for all their days.

The pile of roast meat, steaks and succulent chunks from the ribs grew larger and larger, despite the fact that every now and then both Dodd and Bernardino discovered that they could manage another bite or two of some particularly attractive fragment. Bernardino looked at the colossal pile of meat with wondering eyes; he could not see the reason for it at all. But it was impossible to ask questions. He just went on toasting meat and gathering fuel, all that livelong day. It was not until something over a hundredweight of meat had been cooked that Dodd appeared satisfied, and Bernardino could go to sleep, lying like a cat before the glowing embers of the fire. The warmth and his unwontedly full belly made him sleep for thirteen solid hours, right round until the next morning, in fact.

He woke to find Dodd and the stunted man making evident preparations for a further journey. They were loading themselves with the cooked meat, stuffing every available pouch and pocket with it, and so did Bernardino have to do when he got to his feet. It was a grievous burden which each carried when they started, some forty pounds of meat each. But Dodd was happy. That would mean rations for three weeks provided the meat kept good — or even if it did not, for the matter of that. Maggoty mule meat is better than none at all. Dodd, although he had never heard the expression "a balanced diet," and although the word "calory" had not yet been invented, would gladly have exchanged half the meat for an equal weight of bread, but since such an exchange was quite impossible he wasted no regrets over it. That careful cooking of the meat to an extreme point of dryness had for its object the preserving of the meat for the maximum possible time, and it was still cold, although spring was so close at hand.

It was a perilous journey upon which they were setting out, although perforce only Dodd could know its objective. They came down the hill to the main road, and started to pursue the convoy. But here the river and road ran close together in an up-stream direction, and the country beside the road was for some way more open and level, and there were troops in the little hamlets which dotted it. Their progress was terribly slow — it was a matter of crawling along ditches, and sneaking furtively from coppice to coppice, and lying concealed for long periods when any of the enemy were in sight.

Yet this was the only way of moving through this country. Stratagems and disguises would have been of no help at all, for such was the state of the war in Portugal that there was no chance of posing as peaceful civilians making a journey for private reasons. There were no peaceful civilians, and private reasons had ceased to exist. The French would hang or shoot — if they did not torture — any one they caught who was not a Frenchman; they had been doing so for so many weeks in this area that few natives were left, and these were living like wild beasts — like Dodd and his two companions, in fact — in secret lairs.

Nor was the notion of moving along the high road by night any more practicable. There were military posts and villages along it in such numbers as to necessitate incessant detours, and Dodd had far too much sense to contemplate prolonged movement by night across unknown country. They were out of the stunted man's area by now, and Bernardino's muleteer's knowledge of the country could hardly be expected to extend to cover every ditch

and thicket. All they could do was to struggle along in the fashion
they were following, taking what precautions they could to ensure that on their detours away from the road they did not over-
shoot the mark and go past the bridging convoy, which with
twenty-four hours' start was somewhere ahead of them, destined
for a locality which Dodd was very anxious to ascertain.

The chances were against their getting through alive. Dodd
had known it when he started, but he had come so far along the
road to thinking for himself that he judged it to be his duty
to risk his life without orders on an objective chosen by himself rather than preserve it like the one talent to be given back
unprofitably to the regiment when the great day should come
when he could rejoin. He guessed that his life was of small importance compared with the bridge the French were building, and
so he imperilled it, not cheerfully, but not despondently either;
equably is perhaps the best expression, for there was nothing of
resignation about Dodd.

The fiendish difficulty of the journey displayed itself at once
when they began it, creeping along ditches and furrows. It was
dreadfully fatiguing, and the continual tension was trying. Afterwards Dodd could not remember the order of events at all; he
could not even remember how many days and nights they had
spent on the journey before they were discovered and chased. Yet
little things remained printed indelibly on his memory — details
like the pattern of the leaves in the patch of undergrowth where
they lay hidden half a morning awaiting an opportunity of crossing an exposed stretch of land, and the brown mineral stain of
the water of one of the little streams where they were cowering
when a picket caught sight of them.

The long, heart-breaking pursuit which followed could not be
remembered with the same clarity. It was like a nightmare, recalled as something horrible but blurred in its outline. Dodd remembered the view halloo which greeted them, and the line of
shouting Frenchmen which chased them. He remembered how
his heart laboured, and how his legs grew weaker and weaker
under him while the load on his back grew intolerably heavy. He
remembered how a fresh patrol appeared in front of them head-

ing them off, attracted by the yells of the pursuers, and he remembered always what an effort of will was necessary to change the direction of his flight and to urge his weary legs once more to another spurt while he seemed unable to draw another breath or take another step. He remembered Bernardino falling to the ground exhausted, and then the stunted man, and how he had to fight against the temptation to stop with them and end all this toilsome business in one last glorious fight.

He could hardly bring himself to believe it when he found at last that he was no longer pursued, that he had no longer to force one leg in front of the other, that he could fling himself on to the ground and gaspingly regain his breath and wait for the sledge-hammer beating of his heart to subside. When the time came that he could move once more, he crept along to peer through the thorn bushes over the crest of the hill to where his late pursuers were gathered round the foot of a tall, isolated tree. They were hoisting the banners of their triumph, in celebration of having caught two more bandits. Strange flags they were, which mounted up to the horizontal branch, black flags, which flapped in a curious, contorted way. They were Bernardino and the stunted man, his last two friends, no less dear to him despite the fact that of one of them he never knew the name. Apparently the unit which caught them had kept back from the bridge builders a supply of rope for the hanging of bandits.

There was sorrow in Dodd's heart as he looked down on the pitiful scene, but it did not prevent him from turning away and setting himself to survey and plan the next adventurous quarter of a mile of his route. There are many who give up, and many who procrastinate, but there are some who go on.

After this the nightmare-like quality of Dodd's Odyssey persisted. There was loneliness to be contended with now; it bore heavily on Dodd in the end. Often he found himself, as he crawled and crept on his way, muttering directions to himself — usually in the baby Portuguese which was all he had spoken during the last months. Loneliness and fatigue and strain and bad food made a strange dark labyrinth of his mind, but they did not prevent him from creeping steadily along on his self-set task. He ate very little of his roast mule meat, for he never seemed hungry, but he still went on.

It must have been the very day when Bernardino was hanged that the cannonade began, to maintain a continual monotonous accompaniment to Dodd's thoughts. It was very distant — a mere dull growling, very far off. But it went on and on and on without a break and without variation. There was only one kind of cannonade which could make that kind of sound — a siege. Somewhere an army was pounding away to bore a hole in a stone wall with cannon-balls while some one else was firing away trying to stop them. Dodd heard the sound, and sometimes stopped to listen to it. But it was away to the south, fifty miles away or more, and whatever it portended it could only make the destruction of the bridge of greater importance than ever. Dodd went on all day, and all the next day, and all the next, with that dull muttering in his ears. So persistent was it that at nightfall when it ceased his hearing remained at attention, conscious that something was missing.

It was in the afternoon that Dodd reached the Zezere, and it was evening when he set eyes again on the bridging equipment. In a straight line it is twenty-five miles from where Dodd started to Punhete; Dodd's route with all its zigzags and detours must have stretched to fifty — the greater part of which he had done on his hands and knees or on his belly.

Chapter XIX

DODD reached the river unexpectedly and halted in some dismay above its ravine. He had passed several streams already, and had been able to splash through them, but this was a raging river, running white amid its rocks, and apparently impassable. If down stream there were any means of passing, between this point and the confluence with the Tagus, he guessed it must be well guarded by the enemy. If he had to cross he must go up stream, in search either of an unguarded bridge left intact — a most unlikely possibility — or else of a spot where the river grew sufficiently small to cross; as far as the mountains which gave it birth, perhaps. Before he plunged thus into the interior he had better make one of his periodical reconnaissances of the main road, to make sure that he was not leaving the bridging train behind him.

He slid down the nearly vertical fifty-foot bank of the ravine and began to pick his way along the water's edge with the river roaring beside him. It was difficult walking, for the river filled its bed, and the side of the ravine ran nearly vertically down to the water. And at frequent intervals Dodd had to climb this bank to peer over the edge, both to look for the enemy and to see if the high road were yet in sight. As he made his way down stream the sides of the ravine became not merely lower but less sloped. Dodd began to fear that soon he would be deprived of the cover of this deep, natural trench. Indeed, he actually formed the resolution to leave it because the ravine had grown so shallow that it was no shelter at all, but, on the contrary, an added danger. Accessible running water always increased the chance of meeting Frenchmen, who might be there watering horses or washing clothes.

But just as he reached this decision he saw the bridging train. There was no mistaking it, assembled down there on the river bank with just a glint of the Tagus showing in the distance. There were the pontoons, stacked in orderly piles just above the water, and the great masses of timber roadway, and heaps of cables, and

Dodd could see men busily at work putting up a low roof over the mass of material, and others above the water hammering away at what Dodd guessed to be runways for lowering the pontoons down to the river.

It was nearly dark by now, and Dodd had but a short time to observe these things. As twilight fell he picked his way up stream again and chose a lair for himself — a stony hollow in the side of the ravine, where he could rest. That night, just as on most of the other nights and most of the days, it rained heavily and a cold wind blew. Dodd still, before going to sleep, found passing through his mind that old Biblical passage about foxes having holes and birds having nests.

Yet if he had been asked — it is quite impossible, but assume it to have happened — if he were happy, he would not have known what to reply. He would have admitted readily enough that he was uncomfortable, that he was cold, and badly fed, and verminous; that his clothes were in rags, and his feet and knees and elbows raw and bleeding through much walking and crawling; that he was in ever-present peril of his life, and that he really did not expect to survive the adventure he was about to thrust himself into voluntarily, but all this had nothing to do with happiness: that was something he never stopped to think about. Perhaps the fact that he did not think about it proves he was happy. He was a soldier carrying out his duty as well as he knew how. He would have been the first to admit that under the wise direction of an officer what he had done and what he proposed to do might be more successful, but as it was he felt (or rather he would have felt if he had thought about it) he had nothing with which to reproach himself. And that condition is not at all far from true happiness. At the same time he would have been utterly astonished if he had ever been told that some day a real printed book would devote paragraphs to the consideration of his frame of mind.

The usual shuddering misty morning succeeded the watery dawn, and Dodd stretched to loosen his stiffened joints and peered about for an enemy before making his way down the rushing river again to the point from which he could see the bridge-building preparations. He was terribly aware that he must enter into this adventure as well prepared as possible. He was all alone; if he should fail there was no one now who might repeat the attempt after him. From what he could see time was not of pressing importance. He proposed to devote the whole of to-day — longer, if necessary — to observing what was before him.

He selected a little embrasure of rocks where he could hope to be quite concealed unless any one passed very close, and from here he stared down the stream at the bustle going on there. Nearest of all was the actual boat-building section. There were two skeletons of pontoons on which men were busy nailing the strakes. A little farther from the river there were cauldrons boiling over fires, set in the angle between two rough hoardings to screen the work somewhat from the wind. Here men were trying to bend their nearly useless timber into shape. Dodd could not guess what they were about, but he saw that there was fire there, and he gulped with hope when he realized how much that might help him. Beyond that clearly some one was painting the bottom of a pontoon — daubing something over it, anyway, something which was contained in another cauldron which stood there. Farther down were two sheds full of rope, and beyond that again was a rope-walk. Dodd recognized that; he had seen one at work at Dover on one occasion, when he had walked into that town from Shorncliffe Camp. Beyond that there was an immense long pile of timber, neatly squared and stacked, which Dodd guessed must be the roadway, ready for laying across the cables when — if — the pontoons should ever be moored in position.

All day long Dodd watched and stared. It was a difficult task he was setting himself. He was trying to familiarize himself with everything he could see to such an extent that he would be able to find his way about there in the dark. He marked the route thither, making mental notes of a bush here and a gully there, so that he would be able to pick his way to the workplace from point to point however dark it might be. He watched without fretting and without restlessness; it was a task for which all his education and training — or lack of them — had made him eminently fitted. His uneventful boyhood as an agricultural

worker, and his severe schooling in patience during his years as
a soldier, were a help now. His mind did not constantly demand
new little activities. He could lie and chew the cud of his obser-
vations as placidly as a cow.

Yet he redoubled his attention when the long day reached its
close. It was important to ascertain if sentries were placed over
the work, and if so, how many, and where. When evening fell
he saw the workmen cease their labours and troop off up the
bank to where a double row of wigwams — rough huts of twigs
and branches — awaited them. Then, in the last glimmer of daylight, he saw the guard mounted and the sentries posted. There
were only two of them on the works, each of them allotted a beat
along half the long line of works. Dodd guessed that they were
not there to guard against attack — nothing could be farther
from the minds of the French. Knowing the ways of soldiers, he
realized that they were posted there to prevent men from stealing
the material of the bridge to make fires; the life of a private soldier often resolves itself into one perennial search for fuel, and
no soldier is very particular about the source of his supplies. Already Dodd could see the glimmer of fires from among the wigwams.

Dodd might have made his attempt upon the bridge that night,
but he exercised his judgment and his patience, and resolved to
wait another day. To-night, exceptionally, there was a moon. It
was wan and watery, but it gave sufficient light to add danger to
anything he might attempt. He would not be sorry to have the
opportunity of a night's watching; he wished to find out all he
could about the routine of visiting rounds and sentry-changing
at this point. With the ordinary French system of outposts he was
familiar enough — he had so often done picket duty in the rear-
guard or advance-guard within earshot of the French screen —
but he wanted to note all he could to-night. He could see that he
might need as much as an hour undisturbed to carry out the plans
which his slow but logical brain was constructing.

He stayed on in his hiding-place through the night, dozing
for long intervals, but waking up abruptly at every unusual noise.

In the clear, still night he could hear everything that went on down there, three hundred yards away. By the time morning came he had all the information he wanted.

Next morning the weather changed again, to a blustering day of much wind and occasional sharp showers, but it was distinctly warmer — a day which was clearly the herald of the coming spring. Dodd still stayed in his hiding-place, lashed at intervals by the rain, but sometimes amazingly warmed and comforted by little spells of sunshine which beat gratefully on his upturned back. When the sun came out he took the opportunity of spreading out his remaining thirteen cartridges to rid them of possible damp. He had taken tremendous care of his ammunition all this winter, but despite all his care he had found two of his cartridges unfit to use. He had no idea how many more might prove to be the same, and, once rammed home, a charge which refused to explode was a crippling nuisance.

Yet Dodd did not allow this simple little duty to interfere with his business of observation. He watched all day long the work down the river. He saw another pontoon completed — the second since he began his watch — and he saw more cable added to the pile in the sheds. In the afternoon he saw two soldiers stagger up from the distant village, each with a cauldron which they put down at the boat-painting place. That would be paint or tar or grease, obviously — if it had been merely water the cauldrons would have been filled from the river. That was helpful for his plans, and he saw no new development which might interfere with them.

When night came he ate temperately of his dried mule meat. He had to force himself to eat at all. Partly it was because even the stolid, philosophic Dodd could feel excitement sometimes, as when about to embark upon an adventure of this sort; partly it was because he had eaten nothing except cold roast mule for a week now; partly it was because the meat, never very attractive in the first place, was by now beginning to grow even more unpleasant. All the same, Dodd made himself eat, because he did not know when he would eat again should he survive the night's adventure. He emptied his pack and his pockets of their encumbering stores, and laid them on the ground in his hiding-place. He might be able to return for them, or he might not. It was a harder struggle to decide to leave his rifle. No good soldier ever parts from his weapon; without it, in fact, he ceases to be a soldier. That is a tradition which has come down from prehistoric wars. It irked Dodd sadly to leave his rifle behind. The act of leaving it, besides, indicated too surely that he was going to do his work with his bayonet used like a knife, which savoured strongly of assassination and unsoldierly warfare. Yet the fact remained that the rifle would be an encumbrance, while if he had to use it it would only be because his attempt had failed. It would be far wiser to leave it behind. And because it was wiser, Dodd did so, in the end.

He slid the frog of his bayonet-scabbard along his belt until the weapon hung in the middle of his back; in that position it was least likely to catch or clatter while crawling over rocks. He saw that the bayonet lay free in the scabbard, he made certain that his precious tinder-box was in his pocket, and then he started on his adventure.

He kept to the brink of the river, as offering the route most likely to be clear of the enemy. He crawled on his poor sore elbows and knees over the sharp rocks. The appearance of the moon from behind a cloud kept him motionless in a gully for nearly an hour until it went in again. The flying clouds which obscured the moon brought more than darkness; they brought a sharp spatter of rain which gave him splendid cover for the remainder of his crawl. Finally he settled down, not moving a finger, stretched on his face, behind some low rocks only twenty yards from the end of the sentry's beat.

There he waited; it was not yet midnight, and he could afford to spend several hours in awaiting the best possible combination of circumstances. It was nervous work. At fairly regular intervals he could hear the measured step of the sentry approaching him, and then receding again. Sometimes there would be a pause before the sentry turned back along his beat. That was agonizing, for Dodd, lying on his face, could not tell whether the sentry had halted to rest, and to gaze at the turbulent stream rushing by, or whether he was staring at the dark mass behind the rocks making up his mind that it was human and hostile. But he was not discovered, and sometimes there was a blessed interval of relief from tension when the sentry was at the other end of his beat chatting with his fellow.

The hours stole by; the sentries were twice relieved. Dodd was almost beginning to wonder whether it might not be better if he were to act at once, when the first thing he was waiting for occurred. One of the sentries challenged sharply, the "*Qui vive?*" ringing through the night. The challenge was peaceably replied to. It was the officer of the day on his rounds. Dodd settled himself to wait a little longer; events were working out satisfactorily. A quarter of an hour later came another challenge. This time it was the Sergeant with the relief. Dodd heard the sentries changed and the guard march off again. He waited, very keyed-up now. It was his business to judge of sufficient passage of time for all to be quiet again; it is hard to estimate the passage of twenty minutes when one has nothing whatever to do during that time.

Finally, he waited until the sentry's step was receding, and then he went forward silently to where another rock, twenty yards farther on, lay close by where the sentry would pass on his return. He drew his sword bayonet and crouched there. He heard the sentries exchange a few words, and then he heard the sentry on his side coming back towards him, and he tautened up his muscles in readiness. Then, as the sentry came near, he sprang, silent and swift, like a leopard.

The rifle regiment sword bayonet was an ideal weapon for silent assassination, long and sharp and slender, curving a little at the tip. Dodd thrust upward with it, with all the strength of his arm. It went up under the sentry's ribs, through his liver and diaphragm, upwards until the long, slender point burst the great blood-vessels beside the heart. Private Dubois, of the fourth battalion of the Forty-Sixth, died without even a groan. He died on his feet. Dodd's left hand grasped the stock of Dubois's sloped musket; his right hand quitted the bayonet's hilt and his arm shot round the man's waist in time to catch him as he fell and to ease him to the ground without a sound.

That disposed of one sentry. Dodd stooped and with fierce effort tore the bayonet from the corpse, and thrust it back, dripping as it was, into the scabbard. Then he picked up the Frenchman's heavy musket with its fixed bayonet, and started back with sloped arms down the sentry's beat. He stopped in the darkness behind the shed; the other sentry, as he approached, could see only a dark, erect figure and the glimmer of a bayonet as Dodd stood at ease. Nothing could have been farther from his thoughts than that it was an Englishman who stood there and not his acquaintance Dubois, whom he had last seen only two minutes ago. He said something as he came up. Presumably his last thought must have been that Dubois had suddenly gone mad, as the dark figure stepped forward and brought the musket butt crashing down on his head.

There was less need for silence to kill only a single sentry, and the butt is more certain than the bayonet to ensure instant inability to give warning. Such was the strength with which Dodd struck that the musket stock broke at the small of the butt; the heavy base, attached now by only a few fibres, waggled heavily as Dodd brought the weapon back ready if another blow were needed.

None was. The man had fallen instantly. Dodd's expression hardened in the darkness as he stooped over him. Soldiers do not kill wounded men, but in this case, with the fate of a campaign dependent on a man's silence, Dodd would not have hesitated at the cutting of a throat. But it was not necessary; the man's brains were running out of his shattered skull like porridge.

Dodd was free now to go on with his plan. The visiting rounds had been made; sentries would not be changed for nearly two hours. An hour ought to be sufficient for the completion of his work. He listened intently for an instant to see if the dull sounds had caught the attention of the soldiers up the bank. He heard nothing, and he burst into rapid action. He hurried round to the river front of the works. In the cable sheds he found masses of loosely twisted, hairy rope, and with his sword bayonet he cut an armful of two-feet lengths of this. Then he groped his way to where he had seen put down the cauldrons of liquid for daubing the bottoms of the pontoons. There was still plenty in them. By touch Dodd ascertained that their contents were a semi-liquid grease that ought to burn furiously. He soaked his lengths of rope in the stuff, and put them among the stacked pontoons.

Cutting himself a fresh supply he soaked these too. There was still place for some more among the pontoons. The others he took along to the piled road-bed timber. He pushed his oily wicks among the planks. For a second he debated the risks of delay against the advantages of more inflammables, and decided that delay was justifiable, so he cut yet more lengths of rope, soaked them, and thrust them among the timber. Then he poured what was left in one cauldron over a pile of pontoons, and what was left in the other over some of the mass of rope in the shed. Then he went up the bank to where he had seen the fires. Digging with his foot among the ashes disclosed a mass of red embers. They would save him a good deal of trouble with all the paraphernalia of flint and steel and tinder and slow-match.

He tore off his battered old shako, shovelled embers into it with his foot, and ran, clumsily yet fast, down to the sheds. He poured the embers out on to the oil-soaked cables. That ought to make a fine blaze. The cables were the easiest stuff to burn, and if they were destroyed Dodd guessed that they would be difficult to re-place, so that their destruction might be equivalent to the destruc-tion of the whole bridge. The oil spluttered and sizzled; there rose to his nostrils a smell like the frying he had often noticed in Portuguese kitchens. Then a wisp of cable took fire; the little flame sprang up, sank, sprang up again, and spread to the whole thickness of the cable, which burnt like a torch. Dodd watched it for a moment, watched the flame spread to the other ropes and then, catching up a burning length, he raced along the works with it. He stopped wherever he remembered having inserted a piece of oily rope, which he lit. They burnt nobly. Soon all along the heaped masses of timber, and among the stacked pontoons, there were little roaring flames. From the time of the first bringing of the fire until now not more than five minutes had elapsed.

It was at this moment that there came a shout and a bustle from the bank where the French were, and Dodd knew that he had no more time for destruction. He flung his torch in among the pontoons, and ran away in the darkness up stream. If he had had his rifle with him he might have stayed longer, firing a shot or two to keep the French back so that the flames might gain a better hold, but his rifle was up in his hiding-place. And a glance at the piled cables just before he fled showed him that it was not necessary: the sheds were a roaring furnace already. The sight of that mass of flames cheered Dodd immensely as he ran for his life up the river bank. The men who were now rushing down at top speed to the works would find that blaze hard to extinguish. From the French huts came the long roll of a drum.

Chapter XX

It was after the bridge builders had been established for two days on the banks of the Zezere that the faint sound of a distant bombardment came to their ears. It was a very distant droning noise, coming from far away to the south, and every one could guess from the quality of the sound that it implied a siege. Exactly which town was being besieged, and who was besieging and who besieged, no one in the ranks could really guess. Not even the men of the Second and Sixth Corps in their marchings to and fro across Spain had ever been led south of the Tagus, and a knowledge of Spanish geography beyond the river was not very usual among them. It was Colonel Gille, in command of the bridging party under the general command of General Éblé, who supplied an explanation.

"That sounds like your uncle, Sergeant," he said to Sergeant Godinot, in an interval of inspecting the work on the pontoons.

"Oh, yes, Colonel?" said Godinot.

"That must be the Army of Andalusia besieging Badajoz," said Colonel Gille. "They are on the move at last. But — "

Colonel Gille bit his sentence off sharply, and swallowed the end. Not even the loose discipline of the French Army, which permitted of quite free conversation between a Colonel and a Sergeant, quite allowed the Sergeant to ask questions of the Colonel. Godinot could not press Colonel Gille to continue his sentence, but that "but" had told him a great deal. He could only wait for the Colonel to resume his conversation.

"Your uncle is a fine officer," went on Colonel Gille. "I knew him well when I was on the Prince of Eckmühl's staff in Poland. I would give something to see his brigade come marching up to the other side of the river. If only the Duke of Dalmatia — "

Colonel Gille left another sentence unfinished.

"Oh, well, we shall see, we shall see," he concluded lamely before going off to another part of the works. "This is good work you have been doing here, Sergeant."

Sergeant Godinot, even if he could not divine the details of Colonel Gille's thoughts, could at least guess that the sound of the bombardment of Badajoz was not as comforting to the staff as might be supposed. It proved that the Army of Soult (the Duke of Dalmatia, as Colonel Gille punctiliously called him) was on the move, but it proved also that the move would be an ineffective one. Instead of marching with all his army to their aid, Soult had merely thrust a detachment of his army into the nest of fortresses guarding Southern Portugal. He was besieging Badajoz now. If he was successful in his attack there, he would next have to take Elvas, which was a larger and a better designed and a better garrisoned fortress. And after that there were half a dozen smaller fortresses — Albuquerque, Olivenza, and so on. It would be months before he could appear on the Tagus by this route. Months? And the French Army there was dying of sheer starvation, at the rate of hundreds a day. No wonder that the sound of the distant bombardment was the knell of the hopes of the French staff.

Sergeant Godinot could not guess these details, of course, but he could guess that there was despair at headquarters, and so could his fellow-soldiers; if confirmation was needed it was supplied by the fact that the miserable daily rations were being reduced even below their previous unhealthy standard. On their first arrival on the Zezere the men used to take their muskets and go out into the neighbouring country and shoot little birds, using bags of tiny stones in place of small shot, but the practice was discontinued almost at once by general order. The Army, with no reserves of ammunition, could not waste powder on sparrows, nor even on thrushes. Ragged, barefooted, hungry and diseased, the French Army in Portugal was in imminent danger of going to pieces.

Still, despite the rumours of retreat which sped through the ranks, the bridge building still went on. The carpenters still laboured over their unpromising materials, and the rope makers still twisted cables, and the boat builders still built boats. The work was very nearly complete now, and every one knew that even when it was finished they would still have to stand by to lay the bridge when the time came. The men dragged on their uncomfortable existence in the huts above the river, the officers their hardly less uncomfortable existence in houses in the village, save for the officer of the day, for whose use the men built a wooden shed at the end of their row of huts, next door to that devoted to the guard.

Naturally, guard duty was not heavy. In daytime two sentries out on the hill, and at night two additional ones to guard the bridging material from the pilferings to be expected of men chronically short of fuel, were all that were necessary. Fifteen men and a sergeant and a drummer supplied these guards — it was only once in three weeks that a man's turn came round.

The day when Sergeant Godinot was Sergeant of the Guard had begun no differently from any other. True, a messenger had come from Santarem to summon General Éblé to headquarters — the orderly had told them his message, and they had seen the General ride off — but that might not mean anything of importance. The duties of the Sergeant of the Guard at this point were not in the least onerous. There were no drunkards to be dealt with, for not one of the men had drunk anything except water for six weeks. Equipment inspections brought no defaulters, for every man's equipment had been reduced by wear and tear to a nullity. Desertion was impossible on this wing of the army: no man would willingly leave the frying pan of life in the ranks for the fire of capture by the irregulars — the English were far away. All that Sergeant Godinot had to do was to post his sentries and relieve them at the proper time. The rest of the time he could sit and doze in the doorway of the guard hut while his men snored away their four hours' off duty inside.

Night came with a gusty wind and showers of rain and an intermittent moon. Everything was very quiet in the camp. From where Godinot was sitting he could just hear the gurgle and splash of the turbulent Zezere. He had ample time to sit and meditate on his hunger, and to try to work out what would be the future course of the campaign, and to look back on the golden days when he had been a schoolboy in Nantes, sailing boats on Sundays, and with always enough to eat and with never a tear in his clothes lasting for more than a day. His shako was on his knees, and he smoothed his scalp thoughtfully — before he had been promoted and transferred to the new fourth battalion he had served in the grenadier company, and the bearskin of the grenadiers tended to make a man's hair thin on top. The last change of sentries had left young Dubois on guard down by the river. Godinot hoped that Dubois would come safely through the campaign. All the others — Boyel and little Godron and Fournier and the rest — were dead. And he knew all their mothers in Nantes — women who would weep and would say he was to blame. The poor women did not know yet that their sons were dead, although it was as much as three months since Boyel was killed. They never would know as long as the Army remained isolated here in Portugal. But that could not last much longer. Soon they must move — and Godinot found his thoughts beginning the circle again. He shook them off and rose to his feet, glancing at the guard-house watch — the one watch which remained in working order in the whole detachment — hanging on the wall. There was still an hour before sentries had to be changed again. He stepped out into the night, stopped, rubbed his eyes, and looked again.

Down on the river's brink there was a dull red glow like a fire. On each side of it were a row of twinkling points of light, like candles. As he watched, one of these points of light expanded and brightened and reddened. There was another point of light moving about down there. Some one was setting fire to the bridge — the bridge was on fire already!

"Guard, turn out!" roared Godinot. "Turn out, you bastards. Quick!"

He kicked the men awake as they turned over sleepily. He grabbed the drummer by the collar and stood him, still half-asleep, on his feet.

"Beat to arms! Do you hear me? Beat to arms! Come on, you others."

He dashed down the slope with the sleepy guard trailing behind. As he ran, he saw tall flames shoot up from the cable sheds.

As a gust of wind blew, the sound of the burning rose to a roar.
Then he tripped and fell with a crash over a dead body. He paid
it no attention, but plunged on to try to save the precious bridge.

The cables were the most precious, and were burning the most
strongly. He plunged into the mass of flames, and tried to drag the
stuff out, but the heat drove him back. He turned to the men who
came up behind him.

"Buckets! Water!" he said. "Use your hats — anything."

Up the bank the roll of the drum roused the sleeping soldiers.
Soon they were all pouring down to the river. Men ran with
buckets, with cooking cauldrons. A bucket chain — a double
bucket chain — was formed from the river's brink to the rope
sheds. But it was not with mere bucketfuls of water that that
blaze could be extinguished. Men dragged out masses of burning
rope and tried to beat out the flames with bits of wood. But there
was so much to do. There were flames roaring up the sides of
stacks of pontoons. The timber for the road-bed — dry brittle
stuff — was burning in its huge piles, each the size of a cottage.
Gusts of wind were carrying sparks everywhere. Men with crow-
bars tried to tear the great heaps to pieces and roll the burning
stuff down the bank, but that was stopped after two great masses
of timber had been swept away to be lost in the wide waters of
the Tagus. Timber adrift in the Tagus would be as much lost to
the French as if it had been burned.

The officers had come running up from their billets in Punhete
in all stages of undress and helped to direct the efforts of the men,
with Colonel Gille in chief command. The heat and smoke were
terrible — at one time and another there were as many as a score
of men stretched out on the bank recovering from their effects.
No one in the mad struggle noticed the coming of the dawn. No
one paid any attention to the despatch rider, who turned up in
the middle of the confusion calling for Colonel Gille. The Colonel
merely snatched the note and crammed it into his pocket before
plunging into the battle with the flames again.

They got the fire under at last, but it was a hopeless sight on
which their eyes rested in the bleak light of the early morning.
Quite three quarters of the cable were burned, and half the pon-

toons; the other half were burned in patches where flames had licked up the sides of the stacks of pontoons. Pontoons with one side burned off lay about here and there above the water's edge. A little tangle of rope represented all that remained of the heaps of neat coils which had lain in the sheds. A good deal of the road-bed timber remained, but that was the most easily replaced of all. Taking it all in all, the bridge was utterly ruined. To rebuild it would call for much time — and all available material had already been used.

The men and the officers, utterly worn-out, lay about exhausted on the bank, looking gloomily at the charred remains. No one said anything, no one did anything. Gloom and depression had settled upon them all. No one even stirred when white-haired old General Éblé came trotting up the slope on his emaciated horse. They looked dully at him as he cast his eyes hither and thither over the scene of destruction. Sergeant Godinot was too tired and sick at heart even to feel the apprehension which as Sergeant of the Guard he ought to have felt. With Dubois dead he had no heart for anything. Colonel Gille and the other officers rose to their feet as General Éblé rode up, and stood shakily at attention. Every one heard what the General said.

"There is still a lot of timber, boats, rope, all over the place. Why have you left them like this?"

Colonel Gille's teeth showed white in his smoke-blackened face as his lips writhed at this bitter irony.

"Yes, my General," was all he was able to say.

"Do you call this complete destruction, Colonel Gille? It is as well I came here to see that my orders were obeyed."

Colonel Gille could only stand to attention and try to take this chastisement unmoved.

"Come on, speak up, man. The men ought to have been on the move an hour ago. Why did you not finish your work?"

By this time doubt had begun to display itself in the expressions of the sapper officers. In this nightmare campaign anything might happen. The General might be mad, or they themselves might be mad.

"Oh, for God's sake, Colonel," snapped General Éblé, showing anger at last. "Pull yourself together, man, and your men too. Why have you not obeyed my orders?"

"Orders?" repeated Colonel Gille stupidly.

"I sent you orders three hours back that the bridge was to be burnt down to the last stick and the bridging detachment returned to their units. The army retreats to-morrow."

A lightning change came over the officers' faces. Even Colonel Gille smiled. With a flash of recollection he put his hand in his pocket and pulled out the despatch which had been handed him in the middle of the rush to extinguish the flames.

"Get these pontoons stacked together again," he ordered briefly. "Bring that rope and pile the whole lot together and burn it. And set fire to the roadway timber again. You see, it was like this, my General . . ."

But there is no need to follow Colonel Gille into the ramifications of his explanation to General Éblé on how the bridge came to be set on fire prematurely and extinguished again. When an army is about to set out on a dangerous retreat in face of an active enemy there is little time for explanation.

Once more the crackle and roar of the flames made themselves heard above the gurgle of the river, and the wind blew a long streamer of smoke across the countryside. Soon all that was left of the bridge on which hundreds of men had laboured for three months was a long row of piles of white ashes, still smoking a little.

Down on the high road there was already a long string of artillery marching down towards the concentration point at Santarem. They were the guns which had been brought up to be set in batteries at the confluence of the rivers to cover that hypothetical crossing.

After the guns went the two battalions of infantry who had been waiting here for the same purpose. It was easy to see that they were intended to be battalions, for each was divided into six companies, and of each six one company wore the bearskins of grenadiers and one company the green plumes of the *voltigeurs*. Had it not been for that it might have been guessed that the column represented a single battalion, so short was it. That was the effect of a winter without food.

General Éblé pointed down to the moving column and spoke to Colonel Gille.

"Hurry up and give these men their orders, Colonel," he said. "They ought to have left before those. Now half of them will never reach their regiments."

It took some time to issue *feuilles de route* to every non-commissioned officer in charge of a detachment. Nearly every regiment in the French Army was represented in the bridge-building column. However, there were no rations to be issued as well; the army staff could not be expected to have sent up from their almost non-existent store rations for men who were to march in towards them that very day. It was long past noon now, and none of the men had eaten since the day before, and now they were faced with marches of twenty miles or more. No wonder there was gloom upon the faces of the men as they marched off.

Sergeant Godinot's party was the worst of all. Its twenty men (there had been thirty at one time; the other ten lay in the graves where sickness had overtaken them) were at once weak in body and mutinous in soul. The unfortunate sum of their military experiences — they were only one-year conscripts, after all — had left them without any more desire to serve their country at all. Already Godinot had caught bits of conversation among them which proved that their one ambition was to desert to the English — they would have deserted to the Portuguese if there were the least chance of doing so and surviving. And the very last thing they wanted to do was to march back with the French Army through the awful mountains they already knew too well, with the English pressing on their rear and the hated irregulars all round them. Yet as they were all of them still only boys who had not yet attained their full growth, the months of underfeeding and exposure had left them very weak, and such was their present hunger that they could hardly stagger along. Some of them, however, retained just enough spirit to burst into hoots and catcalls when General Éblé and the other officers rode past them, overtaking them on the road towards Santarem. Sergeant Godinot could not check them.

Sergeant Godinot reflected ruefully that he had to march these men twenty-five miles before dawn next morning, with the prospect of another march, and perhaps even a battle, immediately on arrival. With Dubois dead, there was no one in the detachment he could trust. It was going to be a difficult time for him. He would be glad when he got into Nossa Senhora do Rocamonde — that, he learned for the first time from his *feuille de route,* was the surprising name of the village where the Forty-Sixth had lain so long billeted.

The march was far worse than he anticipated. The whisperings that went on in the ranks behind him boded no good, he knew. He guessed that the men were realizing that twenty men, banded together, might be safe from the irregulars and be able to find their way to the English outposts. He might at any moment be faced with mutiny. Certainly he was faced all the time with disobedience of orders and with mutinous arguments. The men kept calling out that they were tired, they kept asking for rests, and when a rest was granted they were sulky about starting again. Godinot had to plead and urge and beg. He did not dare use violent methods. Even although military law justified him in threatening to shoot those who disobeyed, the situation did not. At the first sign of a physical threat he would have found a bayonet through him or a bullet in his brain. If there had been even one man among them whom he could trust, one man to guard his back, he might have cowed and overawed those mutinous dogs. As it was he could only plead and joke, and pretend to ignore the *sotto voce* insolences which reached his ears.

After dark the trouble became much worse, naturally. Sergeant Godinot marched at the tail of the little column, slipping and stumbling over the stones. He urged them along, keeping an eye open lest any should take advantage of the darkness to leave the ranks. He tried to cheer them up by drawing vivid pictures of the rations which would be issued to them when they reached the battalion — but that was not successful. The men remembered what sort of rations had been issued before they were detailed to the bridging train, and they could form a shrewd guess as to what they would be like now, after two months' further starvation.

The moment came when the whole section flung themselves down on the roadside and swore they could not move another step — not for all the sergeants in Christendom. Godinot did his best. He reached into the darkness and seized what he thought to be the ringleader by the collar and hauled him to his feet, and then the man next to him, and then the next. If he had been an unpopular man they might have killed him then, but, as it was, they spared his life in the scuffle which flared up there at the side of the road. Somebody kicked Godinot; somebody pushed him back. Somebody else, more vicious, took his musket by the muzzle and swung the butt end round in the darkness close to the ground, like a scythe. It was a blow delivered with all the lout's strength; it hit Godinot on the leg and he fell with a cry. Then they all ran off in a body, like a pack of schoolboys (they were hardly more than that) detected in a piece of mischief, leaving Godinot on his knees on the road, trying to get to his feet.

Godinot found that even when he managed to get on his feet he could not long retain the position. The small bone of his right leg was broken; it was agony to walk or even to stand. He could only make the slowest possible progress along the road, and the others never came back to help him. What happened to them, whether they eventually rejoined their battalion, or achieved their ambition of deserting to the English, or died of starvation, or fell into the hands of the Portuguese, will never be known.

After two days the Portuguese irregulars found Godinot. Terrible creatures these Portuguese were — half naked, reduced to skeletons by starvation, as mad with rage at their sufferings and those of their country as was Godinot with pain and hunger and thirst when they found him. They had come creeping across the Zezere, closing in remorselessly on the French Army when it gathered itself together to make its retreat. Godinot was the first of the stragglers they picked up, and he was not to be the last by any manner of means. Although he was crazy when they found him, they did not spare his life.

Chapter XXI

RIFLEMAN DODD was not disturbed in the hiding-place to which he fled after setting fire to the bridge. Even if any one had seen him as he ran away when the alarm was given they were all too busy fighting the fire to trouble about a single fugitive. Dodd reached the shelter of the rocks, and assured himself that his rifle and the rest of his gear were there. In his hand he found, rather to his astonishment, that he still held the battered remnants of his shako. It had been so soaked with rain that the glowing embers had only burned one or two small holes in it. He pulled it on again over his mop of hair and passed the chin strap over the tangle of his beard. Down the stream he could see the flames of the burning bridge, with the figures of the fire-fighting party rushing about round them like old-fashioned pictures of devils in hell.

He watched their exertions with as much excitement as his exhausted condition would allow, and the longer the fire burned the more assured he could become that his efforts had been successful. He felt some elation, but not nearly as much as he would have done had he been fresh and strong and fit. Indeed, now that his efforts had been crowned with success, he was mainly conscious only of weariness, and of something which oppressed him like despair. It was home-sickness — not the desire for the green Sussex Downs, but the desire to be once more with his regiment, marching along with the green-clad files, exchanging jagged jests with his fellows, squatting round the camp fires, leading a life fatalistically free from anxiety and responsibility.

He had almost to force himself to take an interest in the scene of ruin which daylight disclosed — the heaps of ashes, the half-burned boats, the exhausted bridging train lying about the ruins of their handiwork in attitudes clearly indicative of despair. His interest revived when later in the day he saw guns and infantry on the move down stream along the distant high road, and when the bridging party pulled themselves together and wearily set about the task of piling together the debris of the bridge and completing the destruction. All this looked uncommonly like the beginnings of a retreat. Then the bridging party began to march away in small detachments, some by the high road, others by the two paths running diagonally inland from the village. The last to leave were a group of mounted officers and orderlies, and when they had gone the banks of the stream were left desolate, with only the great heaps of smoking ashes to mark where had been the farthest limits of the French Army.

Certainly these moves indicated a concentration, and a concentration could only mean one of two things — an attack on the Lines or a retreat. Dodd knew far too much about the condition of the French Army to consider an attack on the Lines in the least possible. There only remained a retreat — and he can hardly be blamed for believing, with a modest pride, that it was he who had caused the French Army to retreat. And a retreat meant that he would soon have his path cleared for rejoining his regiment, and that prospect caused him far more excitement than did the consideration of his achievements. He had to compel himself to remain where he was until next day, and then, with all due precaution, he started back across country — over much the same route as he had previously followed largely on his hands and knees — back towards Santarem.

What he saw confirmed him in his theory of an immediate retreat. The French had burned the villages and hamlets in which they had found shelter through the winter, just as the Germans were to do in France one hundred and six years later. They burnt everything, destroyed everything; the smoke of their burnings rose to the sky wherever one looked. In truth, the area which the French had occupied was horrible with its burnt villages and its desolate fields, ruined and overgrown, where not a living creature was to be seen. There were dead ones enough to compensate — dead men and dead animals, some already skeletons, some bloated corpses, with a fair sprinkling of dead men — and women — swinging from trees and gallows here and there. Yet it was all just a natural result, even if a highly coloured one, of war, and war was a natural state, and so the horrible landscape through which Dodd trudged did not depress him unduly — how could it when he was on the way back to his regiment?

As for the wake of death which Dodd had left behind him — the Frenchmen whose deaths he had caused or planned, the Portuguese who had died in his sight or to his knowledge, from the idiot boy of his first encounter to Bernardino and the stunted man a week ago, all that made no impression at all upon Dodd. Five campaigns had left him indifferent regarding the lives of Portuguese or Frenchmen.

Santarem when Dodd reached it was a mere wreck of a town — only as much remained of it as there remains of a fallen leaf when spring comes round. And just beyond Santarem Dodd met the first English patrol; the English were out of the Lines. Great minds sometimes think alike: the conclusions reached by Marshal the Prince of Essling and General Lord Wellington had been identical. The former had judged that his army was too weak to remain where it was on the very day that the latter had issued orders for his army to sally forth and fall upon the weakened French. Advance and retreat exactly coincided. The Light Dragoons came pushing up the road on the heels of the French from one direction just when Dodd came down it in the other.

The Lieutenant in command of the patrol looked at Dodd curiously.

"Who in God's name do you think you are?" he asked.

Dodd thrilled at the sound of the English language, yet when he tried to speak he found difficulty; he had spent months now struggling with a foreign language.

"Dodd," he said at length. "Rifleman, Ninety-Fifth, sir."

The Lieutenant stared down at him; he had seen some strange sights during this war, but none stranger than this. An incredibly battered and shapeless shako rested precariously on the top of a wild mane of hair; beneath it a homely English face burned to a red-black by continual exposure, and two honest blue English eyes looked out through a bristling tangle of beard all tawny-gold. With the British Army Dodd shared the use of a razor with Eccles, his front rank man; with the Portuguese Dodd had never once set eyes on a razor. The green tunic and trousers were torn and frayed so that in many places the skin beneath could be seen, and only fragments of black braid remained, hanging by threads, and there were toes protruding through the shoes. Yet the Lieutenant's keen eye could detect nothing important as missing. The rifle in the man's hand looked well cared for, the long sword bayonet was still in its sheath. His equipment seemed intact, with the cartridge pouches on the belt and what must have been the wreck of a greatcoat in its slings on his back. The Lieutenant's first inward comment on seeing Dodd had been "Deserter" — desertion being the plague of a professional army — but deserters do not come smiling up to the nearest patrol, nor do they bring back all their equipment. Besides, men did *not* desert from the Ninety-Fifth.

"Are you trying to rejoin your battalion?" asked the Lieutenant.

"Yessir," said Dodd.

"M'm," said the Lieutenant, and then, slowly making up his mind: "They're only two miles away, on the upper road. Sergeant Casey!"

"Yes, sir."

"Take this man up to the Ninety-Fifth. Report to Colonel Beckwith."

The Sergeant walked his horse forward, and Dodd stood at his side. The Lieutenant snapped an order to the rest of the patrol, and he and his men went jingling forward along the main road, leaving Dodd and his escort to take the by-lane up to the other wing of the advance-guard.

The Sergeant sat back in his saddle well contented, and allowed his horse to amble quietly up the lane, while Dodd strode along beside him. They exchanged no conversation, for the Sergeant was more convinced than his officer had been that Dodd was a deserter, while Dodd's heart was far too full for words. The sun was breaking through the clouds, and it bore a genial warmth, the certain promise of the coming spring. Away to their left a long column of troops was forming up again after a rest; it was the First Division, for the leading brigade were the Guards in their bearskins and scarlet. Dodd saw the drum-major's silver staff raised, he saw the drummers poise their sticks up by their mouths, and he heard the crash of the drums as the sticks fell. "Br-rr-rrm. Br-rr-rm," went the drums. Then faintly over the ravaged fields came the squealing of the fifes —

> Some talk of Alexander,
> And some of Hercules,
> Of Hector and Lysander . . .

— as the river of scarlet and black and gold came flooding down the lane. Farther off more troops were in movement; a kilted regiment headed a column marching over a low rise of ground. The sun gleamed on the musket barrels, and the plumes fluttered as the long line of kilts swayed in unison. Dodd breathed in the sunshine with open mouth as he looked about him; he was well content.

They found the Ninety-Fifth on the upper road, just as the Lieutenant had said. They were drawn up on the roadside waiting for the word to move, because for once in a way the foremost skirmishing line had been entrusted to the Fifty-Second and the Portuguese. Sergeant Casey brought his man up to where Colonel Beckwith with his adjutant and other officers stood at the side of the column, with their horses held by orderlies.

"What's this? What's this?" demanded the Colonel. Beckwith, the beloved Colonel of the Ninety-Fifth, was popularly known as "Old What's-this?" because that was how he prefaced every conversation.

The Sergeant told him as much as he knew.

"Very good, Sergeant, that'll do," said Beckwith, and the Sergeant saluted and wheeled his horse and trotted back, while Beckwith watched him go. If there was any dirty linen to wash, the Ninety-Fifth would not do it in front of strangers.

"Well, who the devil are you?" demanded Beckwith, at last.

"Dodd, sir. Rifleman. Mr. Fotheringham's company."

"*Captain* Fotheringham's company," corrected Beckwith absent-mindedly. Apparently there had been some promotion this winter.

The Colonel ran his eye up and down Dodd's remarkable uniform. Just as the Lieutenant had done, he was taking note of the fact that the man seemed to have done his best to keep his equipment together.

"Dodd," said Colonel Beckwith to himself. He was one of those officers who know the name and record of every man in the ranks. "Let me see. Why, yes, Matthew Dodd. I remember you. You enlisted at Shorncliffe. But you look more like Robinson Crusoe now."

There was a little splutter of mirth at that from the adjutant and the other officers in the background, for the comparison was extraordinarily apt, save in Dodd's eyes, for he had never heard of Robinson Crusoe.

"What happened to you?" asked the Colonel. He tried to speak sternly, because the man might be a deserter, as the Sergeant had tried to hint, although men did *not* desert from the Ninety-Fifth.

"I was cut off, sir, when we were retreating to the Lines," said Dodd, still finding it hard to speak. "Been out here trying to rejoin ever since."

"Out here?" repeated the Colonel, looking round at the desolation all about them. That desolation was in itself a sufficient excuse for the state of the man's uniform. And the man looked at him honestly, and despite himself the Colonel could never help softening to the pleasant Sussex burr whenever he heard it.

"Is there any one who can answer for you?" asked the Colonel.

"Dunno, sir. Perhaps Mr. — Captain Fotheringham — sir — "

"I can remember when you were reported missing, now you remind me," said the Colonel musingly. "Matthew Dodd. Nothing on your sheet. Five years enlisted. Vimiero. Corunna. Flushing. Talavera. Busaco."

The glorious names fell one by one from the Colonel's lips, but the Colonel was being matter-of-fact: he did not realize what a marvellous opportunity this was to sentimentalize.

"Yes, sir," said Rifleman Dodd.

"We can't have you back in that state," said the Colonel. "You'll have to go back to the advanced depot."

The great wave of relief in Dodd's soul was instantly flattened by the realization that he could not rejoin at once.

"Oh, sir," said Dodd. It took more courage to protest to the Colonel than it did to burn the Frenchmen's bridge. "Can't I — can't — ?"

"You mean you want to fall in now?" asked the Colonel.

"Yes, sir. Please, sir."

"Oh, well, I suppose you can. Report to the quartermaster this evening and tell him I said you were to have another pair of shoes and a coat and trousers to hide your nakedness. And for God's sake have that hair and beard off by to-morrow morning."

"Yes, sir. Thank you, sir."

Dodd was about to salute when the Colonel checked him.

"What happened to you all this time?" he asked curiously. "How did you live? What did you get up to?"

"Dunno, sir. I managed somehow, sir."

"I suppose you did," said Beckwith thoughtfully. He realized he would never know any details. There might even be an epic somewhere at the back of all this, but he would never be able to induce these dumb Sussex men to tell it. "Very well, you can fall in. Join your old company for the present."

The epic would have to wait long before it would be written. It would only be pieced together with much difficulty, from hints in diaries here and there — diaries of French officers and English riflemen. Dodd would never tell it in its entirety. Sometimes little bits of it would come out over the camp fire, on a long evening when the brandy ration had been larger than usual or some one had looted a quart or two of the wine of the country, and would be noted by some of the many diarists to be found in the ranks of the Rifle Brigade. Many years later, when Dodd was a rheumaticky old pensioner, mumbling in approaching senility in the chimney corner, he would tell bits of the tale to the doctor and the Squire's young son, but he never learned to tell a story straight, and the tale of how he altered history — as he thought — was always so broken up among reminiscences of Waterloo and the storming of Badajoz that it was hard to disentangle. Not that it mattered. Not even trifles depended on it, for in those days there were no medals or crosses for the men in the ranks. There was only honour and duty, and it was hard for a later generation to realize that these abstractions had meant anything to the querulous, bald-headed old boozer who had once been Rifleman Dodd.

Chapter XXII

DODD's mates greeted him with laughter when they recognized him; he joined his section bashfully enough, at Captain Fotheringham's orders. Rifleman Barret, the company wit, promptly labelled him "the King of the Cannibal Islands," a nickname which was much approved. They could afford to jest; they had just spent a winter in comfortable cantonments, and every man was well fed and properly clad, in startling contrast with the barefooted, naked multitude of living skeletons which Dodd had been harassing. And they were in high spirits too. The Army knew, even if England yet did not, that the tide of the war had turned. All the unembarrassed might of the French Empire had fallen before them, and not merely the French Army but the French system — the new terrible style of making war which had overrun Europe for nineteen years — had failed.

When the bugles blew and the men fell in to resume the advance they did so light-heartedly. They were marching forward, and the French were falling back before them in ruin. They could guess at the triumphs yet to come, even though the great names of Salamanca and Vittoria were still hidden in the future. There was exhilaration in the ranks, and jests flew backwards and forwards as they marched. As for Dodd, he might as well have been in heaven. He was back in the regiment, in the old atmosphere of comradeship and good-fellowship. Up at the head of the line the bugle band was blowing away lustily with half the buglers, as ever, blowing horribly flat. The very dust of the road and the smell of the sweating ranks were like the scent of paradise. The tread of marching feet and the click of accoutrements were like the harps and cymbals. He tramped along with them in a dreamy ecstasy.

At the allotted camping ground the Portuguese guard turned out and presented arms; they were saluting the Ninety-Fifth; there was no thought of saluting the man who had just returned from an adventure calling for as much courage and resolution and initiative as any that the regimental history could boast. Dodd would have scoffed at any such idea. He was looking forward to his bread ration; he was hungry for bread. And there would be salt too; it was weeks since he had tasted salt — there had been none with which to savour the stinking mule meat of his recent meals. And there would be a go of brandy, too, with any luck.

As he sat and munched, warming himself deliciously at the fire, his eye caught sight of a twinkling point of light far away on a hill-top, beyond the lines of the English fires. He did not think twice about it; it might be the fire of a French outpost or of a party of irregulars.

Actually, it had been lighted by irregulars; in it they were burning Sergeant Godinot to death. Dodd did not know. He did not know there had ever been such a man as Sergeant Godinot. What he did know was that he had borrowed an extra lot of salt from Eccles. He dipped his bread in it luxuriously, and munched and munched and munched.

THE GUN

Chapter I

A DEFEATED army was falling back through the mountains from Espinosa. Such was its condition that an ignorant observer would find it easier to guess that it had been defeated than that it had been an army. The twenty thousand men of whom it was composed were strung out along twenty miles of road; its sick and its dead littered the edges of the road for a hundred miles to the rear. At the head came such of the cavalry as were fortunate enough still to have horses to ride; they felt safer there than in their proper place, covering the retreat. Next came the infantry, in groups, in herds, or in ones and twos. Their white Bourbon uniforms were now in strips and tatters, and their skin, blue with disease and cold, showed through the rents. Perhaps half of them still retained their muskets, and of these perhaps a quarter had bayonets as well. Here and there little groups still displayed some soldierly bearing, and marched steadily beneath the cased regimental colours, but these groups were few, for most of the colours had been lost at Espinosa.

The long column of misery tended continually to grow longer, as the more robust struggled forward to get as far as possible from the pursuing French, and as the weaker fell farther and farther behind. There were enough weaklings, in all conscience; even in summer the men had been badly clothed, and even in victory insufficiently fed, and now it was winter, and Espinosa had been fought and lost, and the route of the retreat lay away from the fertile plains and up into the inhospitable mountains. The rain had fallen upon them in deluges for days, and now, as they climbed higher, it was turning into sleet, and a bitter cold wind blew. Ahead of them they could see the snow lying thick on the mountain passes through which they would have to climb, without food or fuel or rest, and with the terror of the French to urge them on. Disease had come, inevitably, to complete the work so well begun by hunger, exposure, and the sword. The typhus — the Black Death — was in among them, along with dysentery and rheumatism and pneumonia. Men dropped dying in the very middle of the road, to be trodden and spurned by comrades too sick and weary to step out of the way, and whose shoeless feet left blood at every step.

If such were the state of affairs at the head of the column, the condition of the rear can hardly be imagined. Here were the men whose legs had given way beneath them, and who still tried to struggle along on hands and knees. Here were the women and the children, left ever farther and farther behind, gazing back apprehensively down the road to see when the dreaded helmets of the French dragoons would appear over the rise. Here were the last few relics of the impedimenta of the army, all that had survived the disaster of Espinosa and the hundred miles of the retreat. The horses were all dead, and the few guns and wagons were being dragged along by dying mules, goaded by the drivers who limped along at their sides. It was bad luck on the sick who fell in the highway incapable of moving, for the gun teams were quite incapable of hauling the guns out of the deep central ruts; they could only go straight on, regardless.

If any part of the wretched Spanish Bourbon Army could boast *esprit de corps* and devotion to duty, it was the artillery. The gunners of the few guns which had escaped from Espinosa had no real motive in imperilling their lives in dragging their guns on in this fashion. They knew that if they were to cut the traces and leave their pieces behind no one would ever have the energy to make inquiries into the matter. But either their own natural obstinacy or that ingrained by discipline had caused them to drag the things thus far.

The very last unit in the Spanish column — if we except the dying — was a bigger, heavier, and more imposing gun than the iron six-pounders which led the artillery column. Thirteen feet long, it was, and two feet in diameter at the breech, and a foot in diameter at the muzzle. It was an eighteen-pounder bronze gun, of that handsome dark alloy which is still known as "gun-metal." Around the vent and forward along the barrel it was ornamented with blazonry and heraldic traceries, beautifully designed, and cast as part of the gun itself; it was evidently a gun which had had a mould made expressly for itself at the time of casting, and had clearly been intended as an ornament for some wealthy noble's castle. Round the muzzle, in boldly raised lettering, was a Latin inscription, a fragment of the liturgy of Nocturne — "And our mouths shall show forth Thy praise." The gun must have been one of a pair; its brother must have borne the inscription "Oh, Lord, open Thou our lips," and the two must have stood one each side of the entrance ramp of a castle in the South. When the Spaniards rose against the French invaders, and the nation flew to arms after a French army had been engulfed at Baylen, these two guns must have been taken from their ornamental duties to help eke out the woefully inadequate equipment of the Spanish artillery. The other gun had fallen into French hands at some one or other of the disasters which had befallen Spain when Napoleon in his wrath led the Grand Army across the Pyrenees — at Gamonal, perhaps, or Rio Seco, or Tudela, and was probably relegated again by now to ornamental duties at the Tuileries or at Compiègne, to grace Imperial splendour.

It seemed likely enough that the same fate would overtake its fellow, trailing along at the rear of Blake's defeated army. The dozen mules which were dragging its three tons of weight along the rocky road were in the last stages of exhaustion. To force them to take every single step the drivers had to stick their goads into their raw and bleeding sides; the big lumbering gun surged forward only a yard at a time, and every yard with pain and difficulty, crashing and bumping over the rocks which surfaced the road. They reached a point where all the gradients which they had already climbed up into the mountains were inconsiderable, compared with the one which now faced them. It seemed to rise before them like the sides of a house; ahead they could see it at intervals winding on interminably, looping back and forth up the mountain side, as far as the eye could see through the driving sleet. At every hairpin bend the pull of the long string of mules was necessarily at an angle to the length of the gun, with much consequent wastage of power. The drivers shouted, and stuck their goads into the mules' sides until the blood ran in streams; the gunners toiled at the spokes of the wheels with what feeble strength was left them. The wind shrieked round them, dazing them with its force and with the sleet which it hurled along with it. Then the inevitable occurred. One last spasmodic effort carried one wheel up to the top of the rock which had been impeding it; the mules lunged forward under the goads, and the whole thing tottered and fell over on its side in the midst of the road, dragging the limber over with it, and the wheelers in their traces, and they the pair in front, and so on, until half the team was down, while the gun lay, huge and ungainly, on its side with one wheel still slowly rotating.

In this fashion the question was settled for the gunners. It would take hours to put that three tons of bronze on to its wheels again. And the mules were past further effort. Those which had fallen lay quietly on the rocky road, their only movement being the distressed heaving of their flanks. With most of them no amount of goading or kicking or cursing could get them on their feet again. When a dying mule finds himself lying down, he nearly always decides to lie and die quietly, and no stimulus whatever will get him on his feet again to expend his last few breaths in the service of mankind. The wretched animals who were still on their feet huddled together and tried, as well as their traces would allow, to turn their tails to the sleet-laden wind. At any moment the dragoons might appear in pursuit; the gunners had seen them in among the rear-guard once or twice already during the retreat, slashing about with their swords like a schoolboy among thistles. The wind and the cold and fatigue and hunger had left the gunners too dazed for intelligent effort with levers and ramps. They had just sense enough to open the limber and allow its small content of ammunition to cascade into the road, and then, detaching the limber from the gun, they were able to right the former and hitch the last few mules to it. With this light load, they were able to struggle forward again up the interminable mountain road, into the fast falling winter night, while the gun still lay grotesquely with one wheel in the air and the dying mules around it, like some fantastic god surrounded by sacrificed animals — a simile which is not so far from the truth.

The Spanish Army went on its way, leaving the gun behind it. Thirty thousand men had fought at Espinosa, and twenty thousand had escaped from that disaster. The march through the mountains, and a winter among their desolate slopes, left some eight thousand fever-ridden phantoms alive next spring to appear again in another corner of Spain and to be sacrificed in some further foolish battle. For the French left their retreat unharried from the morning of the day when the gun was abandoned. Not even a French army could penetrate farther into that desolate tangle of mountains, with no more motive than the destruction of a beaten enemy; they wheeled aside and marched down into the plains to Madrid.

Chapter II

THE men of the mountain valleys, the charcoal burners and the miners, found the gun still lying in the road when next they descended it. They eyed it with curiosity; for familiar though they were with small arms, a cannon was a rare sight among those precipices. So far, in this lost corner of the Peninsula, the war had barely touched them. Indeed, they had suffered more up to now from the depredation of the starving Spaniards than from the French. The sight of the long desolate road, littered with dead men and dead animals and all the pitiful paraphernalia abandoned in a retreat, was their first introduction to the horrors which were to overwhelm Spain during the next four years. They were men of the mountains, not of the towns. The news that the French Emperor had kidnapped their king and had determined on setting his own brother in his place had been slow in reaching them, and these Galician peasantry did not feel the same intense national pride as did the Castilians and the townsfolk. It was the sight of the dead men along the road, and the tales told by the few living stragglers, and the shameful news of Espinosa, which roused them at last to take their part in the national uprising.

In every mountain village the parish priest mounted his mule and rode off to the nearest town for news, and came back with stories of the formation of provincial governments, of decrees of universal military service, of the organization of new armies to take the place of the old. So that when Father Ciro Prieto came riding up the road in reply to a hurried message, and saw the group of peasants round the gun, he reined in and dismounted with a thrill of pleasure. Artillery was rare among the mountains.

"Good morning, children," said Father Ciro Prieto, shaking his cassock out of the disorder consequent upon riding astride.

"Good morning, Father," said they respectfully, and waited

for him to take charge of operations. He was a little man with sharp grey eyes, and a great snuff taker, and much respected all round about as a fount of wisdom. Those sharp eyes of his took in the whole story; the wheel marks in the road, the position of the gun, turned over at a bend, and the dead mules, made it all obvious to him.

"The French are no farther off than Camino Real," he said. "The sooner we get this gun into a place of safety, the better."

"Yes, Father, certainly," said Vigil the woodcutter. "But how?"

The priest spread his hands.

"I leave that to you, my sons," he said. "Use any means you think will serve."

Father Prieto's worldly wisdom stopped short at the problem of righting three-ton guns, but he was not going to admit it. He sat at the edge of the road holding the reins of his mule and taking snuff, while his parishioners bustled about the task.

At first their efforts were feeble and ill advised. It was hard for them to realize the enormous weight with which they were dealing. Their early pullings and pryings availed them not at all. It was the copper miners among them who initiated the correct method; they were more used to such difficulties. Two woodcutters were despatched to get a couple of big tree branches as levers. When these were brought back, there was at last a real promise of progress. A little hole was dug beneath the barrel of the gun, just in front of the swell of the breech, and the end of a lever thrust into it. Then, when ten men flung all their weight upon the other end, behold, the gun moved! It stirred a little in the rut in which it had buried itself. Every one else promptly flung himself upon the lever. It sank under the combined weight, the gun lifted itself a full foot, and then, the lever slipping from under it, it fell again with a shattering crash upon the road.

"Gently, children, gently," said Father Prieto from the roadside. His life's experience among these wild mountain people had taught him that they needed far more to be restrained from headlong excess of zeal than to be urged on.

"Gently, you fools," said Comas the miner. "That is not the way. Listen — oh, Mother of God!"

Already the wild enthusiasts had pushed the lever under the gun again and were swinging on to it.

"Listen to Andres," said Father Prieto sharply, and his flock ceased their heavings while Comas gave a hurried lecture on the use of alternating levers. This time, when the gun was heaved up out of its bed, Comas was ready. He pushed the second lever under the gun, and a rock beneath it as a fulcrum, and in response to his shouts, half the party now flung themselves upon the second lever. The gun rose farther still — Andres' wild exhortations, backed up by Father Prieto, just sufficed to stop them overdoing it again. While the gun hung precariously on the tip of the lever, Comas built yet a higher fulcrum, rested the first lever upon it, thrust the lever under the gun, and called to the others to heave again. In this fashion the gun rose steadily, turning over with its carriage to an upright position. There was a tense moment when the rim of the lower wheel took the ground and the gun began to rise upon it. Comas imperilled his life by rushing beneath the swaying mass to pile rocks against the wheel rim when it threatened to slip. As the fulcrums grew higher and higher, the effort of turning the gun grew greater and greater; to the very end success hovered in the balance. Just before the gun was ready to fall into the upright position, it seemed as if they would never be able to lift it the last necessary six inches. Every one piled upon the lever, their feet seeking out some grip which might increase their weight; they tugged and they strained, their joints cracking and the sweat running in streams in the cold mountain air. At last Father Prieto left his mule by the roadside and ran to the lever. He found a foot of it unoccupied, grasped it, and lifted his feet from the ground, his legs kicking absurdly within his cassock. His little additional weight turned the scale. The gun swung over, falling with a crash upon its other wheel, tottered, and kept its position, on its two wheels again, pointing with defiance down the road towards the French, while the lever, slipping from beneath it, deposited the whole mass of mountaineers in an ungraceful heap on the road.

Everybody rose, panting and full of pride. They swarmed about the gun, examining it with curiosity. They plied Father Prieto with questions about it, most of which the poor man was quite unable to answer. The minute education of a Spanish parish priest did not extend to a knowledge of siege artillery. He could tell them nothing about the employment of the elevating screw and wedge beneath the breech, but he could at least read out the legend round the muzzle — they heard the Latin words with a respectful intake of breath — and translate it for them — "And our mouths shall show forth Thy praise" — and he found the touchhole for them (the gun did not boast the elaborate firing arrangements with lock and lanyard which modern artillery possesses) and was able to explain how to load and fire. His flock could understand that; it was just the same simple method that they used with their own muskets, and Father Prieto's economic use of the little knowledge he possessed quite concealed from them his complete ignorance of anything like laying and elevating an eighteen-pounder. They were quite enthralled by his little lecture. Diego Cabrera picked up one of the half-dozen rusty cannonballs which the gunners had spilt from the limber, and weighed it in his hands. Every one looked longingly at every one else. The thought was in the minds of all, big children that they were, that it would be fine to load the gun and fire it off, just once. But they looked at the width of the bore and at the cavernous depths of the barrel. A single charge for the monster would consume as much powder as the whole community possessed. Diego let the cannonball fall reluctantly from his hands.

"Now, into a place of safety with it, children," said Father Prieto.

That started a new discussion. Any one could guess that an enormous team would be necessary to drag the gun up the mountain side. Although these peasantry were ready enough to risk their lives, they were all of them peculiarly unwilling to risk their cattle. Horses and mules and draught oxen had been hur-

ried away, along with the flocks and herds, into safe recesses of
the upper valleys even before there was fear of the French coming — the unpaid Spanish armies were just as careless about the
rights of property. But no one could disclaim the possession of
draught animals to neighbours who knew every detail of his
affairs, whatever tales he was willing to tell to commissaries and
tax gatherers. Each in turn was gradually provoked into offering the use of a mule or a yoke of oxen, and at last there was a
general dispersion to assemble a team, while the few unpropertied
men remained behind with the gun, fingering the relief work
along its barrel, peeping into the muzzle to see the tiny bit of
light which crept in through the touchhole, passing wise comment on the solidity of the carriage work, while all the time the
gun, huge and impassive, stood glaring defiantly down the
mountain side. It was well that the French made no move.

Then, when the team was got together, in the late afternoon,
and harness had been devised, a new difficulty arose. They began
by attaching the traces to the iron loop at the tip of the trail
of the gun, and found that thus it was impossible to pull the
thing along. The trail was devised for limiting recoil and simply
dug itself into the ground when they applied any pull. Clearly
the trail must be lifted, and the muzzle depressed, and the gun
drawn along in that position. But no cattle on earth were strong
enough to maintain sufficient tension on the traces to hold the
ponderous weight of the trail in the air. Even Clemente Cagorno's renowned yoke of draught oxen, weighing a ton and a
half between them, were dragged backwards as though they had
been no more than a pair of nanny-goats, while the trail sank
back to the ground.

A stray memory came into Father Prieto's mind at last, illuminating it like day. It was a memory ten years old, of an occasion when he had ridden into Burgos, an enormous journey, to
consult with the Bishop's secretary. In Burgos he had seen an
army on the march, on its way to the Pyrenees to fight the
French, who were then Red revolutionaries instead of Imperial
king makers. There had been guns with that army, clattering
through Burgos, and by an excruciating effort Father Prieto

remembered how they had been pulled along. The trails of the guns had been swung from limbers — stout two-wheeled carts, to which the horses were harnessed.

With dignity Father Prieto intervened in his parishioners' despairing discussion and explained how the thing should be done, and every one instantly saw the soundness of the advice. And at the same time every one — save one — instantly decided who should supply the cart which would take the place of the limber. Isidoro Botto had been the least helpful of any of the group. He had not done much in the matter of righting the gun, and his contribution to the team had been only one unhappy ass, which every one knew to be sixteen years old if a day. Yet he was the wealthiest of them all, and they knew he owned just the right cart for the business. Each solid pair of wheels was of one piece with the six-inch axles, and they were attached to the wooden cheek pieces with iron staples of best Galician smiths' work, and every bit of wood was of solid Spanish oak. A clamour arose for Botto to offer his cart. He demurred; it was unsuitable for the job in hand; it was out of repair; he had lent it last week to a man from the Asturias; he could not afford to be without it. But he swallowed his objections when Diego Cabrera drew his knife and was imitated by half a dozen others. He went sullenly off with them to his farm to fetch the cart.

It was nearly nightfall when they returned, and humorists declared they could still hear Granny Botto's imprecations, which she had hurled at them when she saw that beloved cart being commandeered, and was presumably still continuing to hurl, some four miles away.

And now the trail of the gun was swung up and fastened to the back axle of the cart, and the motley team was harnessed up. Those who had whips cracked them joyfully; those who had goads plied them with a will, and those with neither ran up and down, shouting encouragement. Cart and gun lurched, heaved, and then unmistakably got under way. The difficult corner was rounded, and they set themselves to the climb. Lanterns made their appearance from here and from there, and by their light each successive hairpin bend was negotiated, and the rising of the moon found them over the shoulder of the mountain. Then every one decided he had done enough for that day.

The further progress of the gun into the heart of the mountains can hardly be followed in so much detail. Certainly it was the very next day that the would-be gunners discovered a truth which the artillery teamster learns speedily enough — that going downhill is more difficult even than going uphill. Three tons of solid metal on a steep slope constitute a Juggernaut which exacts a cruel toll of lives and broken limbs. The first runaway was only terminated by a crash into the ditch at a bend, with half the team disabled, and incredible labour necessitated in the way of building of ramps and working with levers to get the thing on the road again. If the wheels were locked for a descent, they ploughed so deep into the road that it was necessary to dig them out again. And if the strain on the ropes which locked the wheels rose above breaking point, so that one wheel was suddenly released, that meant another capsizing and more heartbreaking toil to right the gun. Diego Cabrera and Clemente Cagorno and the others came to hate the huge thing which had taken possession of their lives. Isidoro Botto watched with dismay the gradual disintegration of his beloved cart under the shocks and strains to which it was subjected.

But there was some compensation in the fact that the passage of the gun through the mountain villages excited enormous attention. Men who were still hesitating to take up arms were carried away by the spectacle and attached themselves to the party, which increased in snowball fashion. To those unsophisticated mountaineers a force of a thousand peasants with an eighteen-pounder appeared an irresistible army. Father Prieto, rather to his dismay, found himself at the head of one of the most considerable forces of the province, and in consequence a man of weight in the councils of the Junta, when the point of concentration was at last reached.

It was one of Fate's bitter ironies that not one of these men who had toiled so Homerically to bear the gun on its way was to see it in action. For more news reached the Junta. The tide of war had oscillated violently back and forth across the Peninsula. Madrid had fallen to the French, despite all the boastings of the Government. Moore and the English had struck their blow, and had marched the length and breadth of Spain, pursued by treble numbers, even along a part of the very road where the gun had been abandoned. Now Moore's army had taken ship at Corunna, leaving their beloved leader buried in the ramparts, and the rumour sped round the countryside that their baulked pursuers were to plunge on through Galicia to complete the conquest of the country. Every available man must be marched by the quickest route to head them off. Father Prieto's Galician band must come, of course. With any luck, Soult might be completely surrounded and compelled to surrender, which would bring more glory to Galicia than Baylen did to Andalusia. The gun could not accompany them, however. The route would be by mountain paths, and their experience even on roads had shown how slow was the movement of an eighteen-pounder. Every moment was precious when resounding victory was so near their grasp. The gun must be left, and the men must march at once.

To Father Prieto's credit, he improved on the hot-headed Junta's instructions. Perhaps he may have foreseen disaster. The gun was not left standing, as the Junta's orders would have had it, in the street of the little village where they found themselves at the moment. It made one more journey, to where a quarry, unworked now in these turbulent times, had been hacked out of the side of a hill at the edge of the road. The gun was hauled into the basin of the quarry, and lumps of stone were heaped on and around it, until a cairn was formed over it. No one would ever suspect that a siege gun was concealed within that mass of stones; the passer-by would naturally assume that the latter was a pile formed during the working of the quarry.

And having completed this good piece of work for Spain, Father Prieto and his men marched on to the promised surrounding and destruction of Soult. Of course that promise was not fulfilled. Soult and his veterans of the Grand Army tore their way through the flimsy lines of armed peasants. They rubbed in their easy victories by shooting or hanging or dropping over precipices the prisoners they caught — as indeed they were authorized to do by the laws of war, because their opponents wore no uniform. Father Prieto, poor little man, they hanged in the market square of Vigo, because it was well to make a special example of priests; and most of his followers who did not die by violence died by disease. Only a few crept back to their farms and forests among the mountains to try and eke out a living from what was left to them after the exactions of Spanish irregulars and French armies had been met. The gun stayed where it was, hidden in its cairn of stones, month after month, until two years of the interminable war had gone by. French armies came and went; more than once they passed actually beside the gun without discovering it, on their occasional expeditions into the mountain country in pursuit of what they called brigands and the Spaniards called *guerrilleros.*

Chapter III

AT the end of that period of two years a man stood on the southernmost ridge of the Cantabrian Mountains, gazing down into the fertile plain of León. The contrast between the scenery close about him and that on the horizon was astonishing. The Cantabrian sierras are formed of row on row of mountain chains, each roughly parallel to the southern coast of the Bay of Biscay, each rocky, steep, and scarped, clothed with forests for most of their height, and their summits nothing more than jagged peaks of naked rock. They are pierced by few paths and by fewer roads, although here and there they enclose rich upland valleys.

But at the very foot of the escarpment above which the man stood gazing down began the plain land, the *"tierra de campos,"* the "land of fields," the richest portion of all Spain. Here, as far as the eye could see, stretched rolling cornfields, unbroken by hedges, with hardly a tree to diversify the scene. There were numerous roads which formed a network of yellow streaks over the surface, and which connected the villages which dotted the plain — clusters of one-storeyed cottages, for the most part constructed of sun-dried bricks, whitewashed. There were no rivers to be seen, but the man gazing down from the sierra knew that there were many, that the plain was one of the few Spanish plateaux rich in water. For the rivers had cut themselves beds far below the level of the plain, and flowed at the bottom of deep-sunk ravines, so that only a very keen eye could discern from the mountain top the dark marking of the cañons as they wound about through the folds of the plain. The best way of ascertaining their course, in fact, was to note the little white bridges at the points where the rivers were crossed by the country roads.

The man who stood on the sierra looking over the plain was a *guerrillero* chief, whom his followers knew as *"El Bilbanito,"* "the young man from Bilbao." The Spanish habit of conferring nicknames on any one of note, from kings to bullfighters, was specially in evidence in the case of the *guerrillero* leaders. There were the "*Empecinado*," the "swarthy one"; the "*Cura*," the "priest"; and the "*Marquesito*," the "little marquis" — and a hundred others. Between them they were teaching a new lesson in war to the Napoleonic armies who had themselves taught so many to the rest of the world. Unstable and fickle and wayward as they were, the Spanish irregulars were never discouraged, never wholly put down, and were always ready for some new raid on a vulnerable point in the widespread French Army of Occupation.

El Bilbanito, looking out over the plains as he had looked scores of times before, had an additional motive to-day for longing to strike a new blow. His forces had just received a most irritating and annoying defeat of a kind to which they were unaccustomed. Two companies of French infantry, marching by night from the plain, had attacked them at dawn, after scaling a path which El Bilbanito had been quite certain was unknown to any one in the French Army. There had been a few casualties, although most of the men made their escape easily enough over the face of a precipice and through forest paths where the French had not dared to follow, but what was more exasperating was the loss of everything the band possessed save what was on their persons. Half a dozen pack mules had fallen into the hands of the French, all they had save one, and after two years of war a pack mule was worth its weight in gold. With them had been taken five hundredweight of powder, quantities of cartridges, some salt meat and biscuits, and much of the treasure which had been accumulated by much harrying of Frenchmen who had already harried Spaniards. The band was sorely annoyed and El Bilbanito's position was badly undermined; indeed had not Pablo, the ambitious second in command, been killed in the fray by a stray bullet (which might possibly have been fired from El Bilbanito's musket) he might have been already deposed. The need to achieve some striking feat of arms was therefore all the more pressing.

Yet by itself the sight of those rich plains was enough to rouse El Bilbanito's zeal. For two years now French garrisons had held those plains, plundering them only moderately, growing fat on their ample products, and with their dominion hardly challenged. No Spanish force could face the French on those plains, for the French possessed discipline, artillery, and cavalry, in all of which the Spaniards were conspicuously lacking. Not even a raid could be attempted on account of those cursed rivers. At every strategic point — which in the plains meant at every river crossing — the French had set down a small sedentary garrison, established sometimes in some strong isolated building or in field-works built for the purpose; some of them were visible to El Bilbanito's keen eye. That did not in itself stop raids, for a small party could cross the rivers anywhere, by night if necessary. But sooner or later that small party would encounter a superior force and would have to retreat. And what then? There could be no crossing of those difficult ravines when closely pursued, probably by the dreaded dragoons. They would be hemmed in, taken, and hanged for certain. Before they could run that risk, they must make sure of a line of retreat, and to do that they must hold the bridges, and to do that they must capture the covering works. And to do that they must have artillery, which no *guerrillero* band possessed, or could possess, considering the hunted life they led among the mountains.

El Bilbanito followed up this train of thought for the hundredth time, and for the hundredth time came to the same exasperated conclusion. The thing could not be done, although its desirability was so apparent. He stamped with vexation as he turned away from his viewpoint, and walked back along the ridge, over the perfect green turf which the abundant Cantabrian rains caused to grow here, halfway up the mountain side. He was a picturesque enough figure in his loose black trousers, and his red sash with the pistols and the knives in it, and his blouse with the big gilt buttons, and his flowing black cloak, buttoned at the neck and billowing out behind him with the speed of his step.

A quarter of a mile along the ride there was a narrow neck which joined this outpost of the mountains to the main mass of the sierras. At each side here a steep path ran down into the plains, and, uniting, continued along the neck and steeply up-

wards to the forest-clad slopes. Here, as was to be expected, a
sentry was posted, keeping watch along the protruding ridge
and down both paths. He stood aside for El Bilbanito, but with
small enough respect, so that El Bilbanito watched him out of
the corner of his eye as he went by, and felt a creeping of the
skin over his spine as he went on up the path, lest a shot in the
back should end his career then and there. Something would
have to be done to keep these mutinous dogs busy.

The path plunged into the pine forest, rising sharply all the
time, and only when he had turned a corner among the trees
out of sight did El Bilbanito breathe more freely again. His
sense of his own dignity had withheld him from looking back.
Deep in the forest at a dividing of the ways was another sentry,
who displayed a little more deference.

"Jorge has returned, Captain," he said, as El Bilbanito went by.

El Bilbanito's only reply was a growl which might have meant
anything, but he quickened his step until he reached the clearing which was his temporary headquarters. Of the hundred men
of his band, the one or two energetic ones were busied making
themselves little huts of pine branches. Half a dozen more were
occupied at the fires; apparently Jorge had brought back food
from his raid into the mountain village. Perhaps fifty, wrapped
in their cloaks, were stretched out here and there in the clearing,
indulging in their siesta; the rest were sitting idly about, awaiting his arrival.

As he made his appearance, one of these men arose and came
to meet him; it was Jorge, the big smiling boy from the Rioja,
who was tacitly assumed to have taken the lately deceased Pablo's
place as second in command and was naturally suspected of having designs on that of El Bilbanito himself.

"We have laid our hands on the criminal, Captain," said
Jorge, with his usual grin.

"Which one?" snapped El Bilbanito.

"The one who caused us to be attacked last week. He is here,
Captain."

El Bilbanito brushed Jorge aside and walked over to the seated
group.

"He has confessed already, Captain," said Jorge, hurrying after him.

"Why did you not hang him at once, then?" demanded El Bilbanito.

"Because — " but Jorge's explanation was cut short when El Bilbanito reached the group round the prisoner.

It was Isidoro Botto. The loss of his fine cart had been the first step towards a poverty he could not bear; two years of war had stripped him of the possessions of which he had once been so proud. One of Bonnet's infantry columns, marching through the mountains, had stripped his fields of their crops; Frenchmen and Spaniards between them had commandeered his cattle, his barn had been burned, and Botto was now on the point of starvation, just as were most of his compatriots in the debatable land which could be reached but not occupied by French armies. And his brief experience of soldiering when Soult invaded Galicia had quite cured him of any tastes in that direction.

His brown cloth clothes were in rags, but that might have been the result of the mishandling he had just received from the *guerrilleros;* his hands and his feet were tied, and one eye was closed and blackened by a blow. On El Bilbanito's arrival he scrambled awkwardly to his feet and tried to stumble towards him, but his feet were tied too closely, and he only succeeded in falling on his face amid a roar of laughter from the others. His elbows flapped and his legs kicked absurdly. Some one grabbed his collar and hauled him to his feet.

"You won't hang me, Your Excellency?" he said; there were tears on his cheeks. "You won't have me hanged?"

"I will," said El Bilbanito.

"But you can't, you can't," expostulated Botto. The enormity of such a proceeding seemed to make it an impossibility to his mind; but all the same there were horrid doubts within him.

"I can," said El Bilbanito.

"Oh, Your Excellency — "

"What is the proof against this man?" asked El Bilbanito of Jorge.

"He was out late a week ago. He must have gone down to

the French outposts. He knows the path by which the French came — he used to use it for his sheep. And two days back his mother tried to buy food with this."

Jorge handed over a silver coin to his captain, who scanned it closely. It was a Saragossa dollar — money struck by the French for use in the occupied districts.

"And anyway," concluded Jorge, "he has confessed. He admitted his guilt when we were going to hang him over there."

Jorge jerked his head to indicate the area where this story begins.

"Yes, it is quite true," said the tearful Botto. He was hysterical with terror. "But don't hang me. You will lose if you hang me. I can do it again. I can tell them another path by which they can come by night. And then you can be waiting for them. Your Excellency — Señores — "

Botto's hands were tied, and this handicap to his gesticulatory powers combined with his fright to reduce him to silence.

For a moment El Bilbanito was tempted. With his inward eye he could picture the ambush at dawn, the slaughter of the wretched French conscripts, the triumph of the day. But no man could survive two years of guerrilla warfare without being able to see the disadvantages of the proposed plan. The employment of double traitors, tempting though it might be at first sight, was fraught with too much danger; no one could be certain on which side the balance of treachery would eventually rest. Moreover, in this special case, there were practical difficulties. Half the district knew that the man had been arrested and brought into the guerrilla camp; if the French were to hear of it, it would either be impossible or dangerous to use him. Moreover, if Botto were given the opportunity of another visit to the French outposts, the chances were that he would stay there, and the opportunity would be lost of either using him or hanging him. The man's proposal was absurd.

"No," said El Bilbanito, turning away.

Botto shrieked with despair.

"Hang him," said El Bilbanito to Jorge.

Willing hands laid hold of the wretched man. They dragged

him screaming to a tree. A boy climbed it eagerly and slung a rope over a bough. They fastened the rope about his neck. Botto, gazing at the sky through the noose, saw, like a drowning man, his past life rising before him, from the peccadilloes of childhood to the horrors of the recent past, to his only experience of fighting at Vigo, to the dragging of the gun through the mountains. That memory gave him a fresh wild hope.

"The cannon!" he shrieked. "I know where the cannon is."

El Bilbanito heard the words and turned sharply on his heel. They chimed in so exactly with his thoughts of half an hour ago, when he had been asking himself where he could find artillery. He hurried back just as they swung Botto off his feet, just as the last shriek of "The cannon!" was cut in half by the tightening noose. At his signal, they lowered Botto to the ground again; fortunately the jerk had not broken his neck.

"What was that you said?" demanded El Bilbanito.

Botto tore at the noose with his bound hands; his eyes bulged; even when they loosened the rope, he had to gasp and swallow for some minutes before he could speak.

"We buried a cannon," he said at length. "A big, big cannon, when I was with Father Prieto. Before you came here, Your Excellency. I am sure no one has found it since. I am the last of those who were there."

"Where was it you buried it?"

"Over the mountains, a hundred miles from here. I can take you there, Your Excellency."

"Where was it?"

"On the side road to Lugo, two villages beyond Monforte. A great big cannon, Your Excellency."

"In what place did you bury it?"

"In a quarry just outside the village, Your Excellency."

"H'm," said El Bilbanito. "Are there many quarries there?"

"I don't think so, Your Excellency. There will be no difficulty — "

Botto choked anew as he saw the trap into which he had fallen, and he began to beg again for his life.

"Oh, you won't hang me now, Your Excellency?" he

screamed. "You must take me with you to find the cannon. You can hang me if my story is not true. It is true, by all —"

"What else have you to tell me?"

A little spontaneous inventive power might at this moment have saved Botto's life. If he could only, with some verisimilitude, have laid claim to further knowledge, and offered to barter it against a promise of pardon, he might have prolonged his wretched existence, for a space at least. But he was not endowed with creative ability. He had to stop and think, to try to devise something, and El Bilbanito, watching him closely through his narrowed eyes, saw the truth, saw that no further useful revelations were to be expected.

"Bah!" he said, and he called to the men who still held the rope: "Up with him."

It was only five minutes more of life that Botto had gained for himself, and the five minutes were now ended.

El Bilbanito was grimly satisfied with himself as he walked away. He had a reputation for ferocity to maintain; he hoped the incident had made a suitable impression on his band. It had been rather amusing to have the poor fool blab out all he knew and then hang him after all; it would not be difficult to find the gun, in a quarry two villages beyond Monforte on the road to Lugo, without him. And it was just as well the man was dead. That saved a good deal of the possibility that the news that the *guerrilleros* would soon be armed with artillery might leak out to the French — trust a guerrilla chief to know the value of surprise. There might be traitors among his own followers, all the same — El Bilbanito's pensive expression hardened, and he put his hand to his pistols at the thought — well, the recent hanging would make them cautious, at any rate.

El Bilbanito's mind went on making plans, devising how he could make best use of this possible gun. It would have to be a hard, sudden stroke. El Bilbanito's motives in making his plans with such care were only very slightly selfish. True, he certainly wished to regain his prestige among his followers. And there was a good deal of the spirit of the true craftsman in wishing to make the best job possible of the work he found to his hand.

But also there was Spanish patriotism within him, a hatred of the French invader, a desire to bring back the king whom the French had kidnapped, a passionate resentment against the nation which had meddled so gratuitously with Spanish affairs, a longing for revenge upon the enemy who had brought such calamities upon the country. Spanish pride and Spanish patriotism were in this case working hand in hand with the instinct of self-preservation.

El Bilbanito's decision was reached quickly enough. He signalled to Jorge.

"Call the men together," he said, curtly. "We march in ten minutes."

That was all the order necessary in a guerrilla band. They marched with all they had, and they were unused to having explanations offered them by their high-handed leaders.

Chapter IV

THE route which El Bilbanito's Cantabrian band had to follow was complicated by the fact that most of the main passes in the Asturias and in part of Galicia were commanded by French garrisons, but El Bilbanito was perfectly capable of devising a route which would steer clear of them, and that without a map and without a moment's reflection. Two years of guerrilla warfare had taught him every mountain path in the province; at any moment he could say instantly which passes were likely to be blocked with snow, and which fords impassable with floods, according to the season. That kind of knowledge was part of his stock in trade; it was in consequence of it that he was able (on most occasions, at least) to elude the pursuit of the French columns which were sent after him on the rare occasions when the garrisons of the plains were able to scrape together a surplus of men for the purpose.

There were moments during the march when his heart misgave him slightly. If the expedition were to prove a wild-goose chase, his men were likely to get out of hand. The possibility had to be faced, but he had encountered mutiny before and the likelihood did not worry him unduly; he only saw to it that his pistols were invariably primed and loaded. If he wanted the gun, there was no other course open to him than the one he was following. Had he merely sent a small party to find if the gun were there, he knew perfectly well that before he could bring it up to join him, it would be commandeered by some other band or by the hunted group of refugees who called themselves the Galician Junta; and if he went for it himself, he would not only meet the same difficulty but his band would elect another leader in his absence. Besides, a hundred miles of rapid marching would do his men good; they were growing fat and lazy and it was important to conserve the incredible marching capacity which they were capable of displaying.

The villagers of Molinos Reales resigned themselves to the inevitable when a new band of *guerrilleros* descended upon them from the mountains. They were used to it by now, and *guerrilleros* were at any rate one degree better than French. El Bilbanito billeted himself on the house of the alcalde, and distributed his men among the stone-built cottages which clustered about the church. Every householder found himself with one or two men to feed and house, and if these men's boots and clothes were worn out, as they mostly were, he had to resign himself to handing over the small contents of his wardrobe to them and donning instead their cast-off rags. The worst of *guerrilleros* was their habit of descending without warning from the hills; if regular troops or French came along, there was nearly always sufficient time to hide what few valuables were left, drive the sheep and cattle into the mountains, and assume an aspect of poverty even more abject than was really the case.

El Bilbanito allowed his men the luxury of twenty-four hours under roofs, with as much food as they could coerce from their unwilling hosts. He himself, with Jorge and two chosen aides-de-camp, went off immediately to the quarry which the alcalde indicated to them. The fact that there was such a quarry certainly boded well for the confirmation of the story of the man they had left dangling from a pine tree on the borders of León. And the basin of the quarry was level with the road, surrounded only on three sides by the steep-cut sides — a further indication of probability. And there, in the centre of the basin, was a huge pile of broken stone, which must have been there some time, because two or three blades of grass were growing on it.

With a little feeling of excitement El Bilbanito pulled a stone or two from the heap, and then, remembering his dignity, desisted.

"Pull that heap down," he said to his followers, and, turning his back, he strolled away with a magnificent assumption of indifference.

He heard the clatter and rattle of the stones as Jorge and the others set to work, and when he heard their cry of delight he turned hastily back and rejoined them. The gun was there, surely enough. Already its huge long barrel was visible above the dwindling pile, and they were digging away the stones from about its carriage.

El Bilbanito examined it carefully. Its metal had assumed a dull green colour with all the moisture to which it had been exposed, but that was a reassuring sign. It proved that the gun was of bronze, and bronze will endure centuries of exposure; an iron gun would be honeycombed with rust by now. Indeed, the ironwork of the mounting, the screw controlling the wedge below the breech, the staples of the carriage, the rims of the wheels, were red and rotten and crumbling. Even the stout oak and chestnut of the carriage had suffered. Lichens had grown up on them. But the gun itself, the irreplaceable, was intact. El Bilbanito ran his fingers with joy over the relief work along the barrel, and slapped its fat trunnions, and with the needle that his dandyism caused him always to carry he dug the dirt out of the touchhole. Then he hastened back to the village.

The alcalde was confronted with a demand for carpenters and smiths. He spread his hands deprecatingly. He explained in his barbarous Gallego dialect that skilled workmen of that sort were scarce nowadays. But El Bilbanito would listen to no excuses. The village carpenter was sent for, and within an hour the alcalde, escorted by Jorge and half a dozen men, was on his way over the hills to the next village in search of a smith of repute who was known to live there. El Bilbanito with a working party and the armourer of the band — a gunsmith who had strayed into the band from Aragon — hurried back to the gun.

The armourer knew nothing about artillery, nor did El Bilbanito, but they were men of experience and common sense, of inventive capacity and ingenuity, as befitted survivors of two years of mountain warfare. Men who had bridged crevasses with an enemy in hot pursuit, who could swing loaded mules over precipices and set them unhurt on their feet at the bottom, were not likely to be deterred by the difficulties of handling a three-ton gun. El Bilbanito set his party — partly his own men, partly impressed villagers — to work on the construction of tall shears over the gun. The armourer sketched the elevating apparatus for future reference. The carpenter examined the carriage, noting measurements and dimensions; as he could neither read nor write he had to notch them cabalistically on pieces of wood, but he was used to doing his work like that.

Plans were complete by the time Jorge returned with both a smith and a carpenter, whom he had torn from their homes with the comforting assurance that it would not be more than a week or two before they would be allowed to return. The armourer was already improvising a forge, and a detachment detailed by El Bilbanito was conducting a house-to-house search for all the iron which could be discovered, *braseros* and suchlike. By the next morning the smiths and carpenters between them had constructed the necessary pulley blocks, the shears were reared over the gun, and El Bilbanito was anxiously supervising the swinging of the vast mass of metal cut out of its carriage.

Jorge selected, with the aid of the carpenter, the best pieces of weathered oak from the latter's stock. Jorge knew nothing about timber, but, as he explained with his eternal grin, he made sure of getting the best and most valuable pieces by simply insisting on taking those which the carpenter was most voluble in explaining would not do.

The gun swung in its slings over its carriage. Thanks to the quadruple pulleys in the blocks, a dozen men had sufficed to lift it far enough for the trunnions to clear the deep notches in which they rested. The wreck of the carriage was run from beneath it, and then, ever so carefully — El Bilbanito would have shot the man who was clumsy — the huge thing was lowered to the ground, and El Bilbanito turned his attention to urging on the smiths and the carpenters to complete their work of fashioning a new carriage.

The man was in a fever of excitement. He knew, even better than unfortunate Father Prieto had suspected two years before, what prestige the possession of artillery would bring him among the *guerrilleros* of the province. But more than that, he carried in his mind's eye that mental picture of the fat plains, and the helpless garrisons dotted over them — helpless, that is to say, in face of an eighteen-pounder — and the ruin he could wreak upon the long vulnerable lines of communication stretching far to the rear of the French armies in the field.

All day long and for days afterwards the little village rang with the beat of the hammers on the extemporized anvils. There were iron rims to be made, fitting so exactly the broad wooden wheels which the carpenters were making that only when they were strongly heated would they slip over the felloes, so that when they were cool they would hold the wheels together, despite the strain to which they were to be subjected. The screw handle which forced in and out the elevating wedge beneath the breech had to be painfully forged by hand out of bar iron, and, more difficult still, the threaded sockets in which it had to revolve. Axle pins and so forth were easy enough — the Galician smith had passed his days on that sort of work.

Even El Bilbanito had to grant an occasional rest to the weary ironworkers. He chafed at their taking six hours for sleep, but he allowed them to do so each night. He confiscated for them the best of wine and provender, and he sent his detachments far and wide to secure for them a sufficiency of charcoal. In four days the work was completed — a perfect new carriage was made for the gun. Perhaps it was not quite so prepossessing in appearance as the old one had been at its best, but it was a wonderful piece of work. The cheeks, on which the trunnions were to rest, were of four-inch oak, and the notches themselves were faced with beech. The axle was of oak too, six inches in diameter. The spokes of the wheels were of the finest ash that could be found; those wheels were the wonder of a district which had never seen other than plain solid discs cut from trees. El Bilbanito grudgingly gave his approval when he came to inspect it finally, but he reserved his final decision until a trial should be made.

The carriage was run out to the quarry, the gun slung up again by the shears, and the carriage pushed beneath it. Then the gun was slowly lowered into position, with the armourer rushing back and forth to see that it was properly done. Slowly the trunnions entered into the sockets and bedded themselves down. The vast breech settled itself upon its block, and the sling ropes slacked off as the carriage took the strain. The woodwork creaked at the first imposition of its three-ton burden, but everything held firm. The armourer clamped down the iron hold-fasts over the notches and passed on to examine the rest. Everything was perfect. Zero on the newly forged scale exactly corresponded with the groove on the gun's breech — or within a quarter of an inch, which was good enough for siege artillery work. The trunnions fitted the sockets exactly; there was no trace of rocking or rolling. When the elevating screw was wound out, the wedge below the breech slid sweetly backwards, and the muzzle of the gun rose steadily, and the notch on the breech moved regularly down the ranging scale. The gun, so the armourer declared, was ready to work, and El Bilbanito issued his order to prepare it for firing.

The armourer was delighted; it would be a further opportunity of demonstrating his attention to detail and anticipation of instructions. One of the two reserve powder kegs was brought up and opened. A liberal measure of powder was scooped up and poured into the muzzle of the gun, a rammer which the armourer had prepared of a bundle of rags on the end of a pole was pushed up the barrel so that all the powder was packed into the breech, and then a piece of blanket was stuffed up after it to hold it firm. Next the armourer produced his masterpiece — a big round boulder selected from the bed of a stream and bound round with leather so as to fit the bore of the gun. This was pushed in on top of the wadding, and the gun was loaded.

At the armourer's order, half a dozen men laid hold of the trail, two others worked with levers at the wheels, and the gun was swung round until it pointed out of the quarry, across the road. The armourer mounted on the trail and fussed with the laying screw — which gave the necessary amount of fine adjustment in the lateral aiming of the gun which mere pulling round of the gun and carriage could not give with certainty. Looking through the notch on the bar of the backsight he had made yesterday, the armourer aligned the groove on the muzzle swell with a patch of white rock showing through the under-growth of the mountain side across the valley. Then he turned the elevating screw until the mark on the breech corresponded with the figure "250" on the elevation scale. The armourer had never in his life fired at such a range as two hundred and fifty *varas,* not even with the long Tyrolese rifle his lordship, the Marquis of Lazan, had brought him to repair before the war, but he estimated the distance as well as he could by the light of Nature. Next he scooped a little more powder from the keg, and with it filled the touchhole. Last of all he produced flint and steel and tinder, caught, after many attempts, a spark upon this last, and transferred it to a length of slow match which he blew into a glow. All excitement, he was about to lay the match on the touchhole, when the harsh voice of El Bilbanito called him back. He was not to be the man to fire the first shot from the gun.

El Bilbanito took the match, hardly hearing the armourer's pattered instructions. He had sense enough without them to stand clear of the wheel in the recoil, and he knew well enough that the way to fire a gun was to apply a match to the touchhole. Leaning far over, he pressed the spark against the loose grains of powder visible round the edge. There was a sharp fizzling noise, instantly drowned in an immense, a gigantic bellowing explosion. The enormous volume of the noise quite dazed El Bilbanito; it was so much bigger than he had expected. The gun rushed from beside him in its recoil, crushing the fragments of rock beneath its wheels, and a huge cloud of smoke enveloped him. Through the smoke he could hear a wild cheer from his men.

Then the smoke cleared away. He was still standing holding the smouldering match, and the gun was four yards away. His men were gesticulating and pointing, and, looking in the direction they indicated, he saw that a little cloud of dust still hung over the patch of rock at which the gun had been aimed. The armourer had indeed achieved a miracle.

And the gun stood there with a faint wisp of smoke still trickling from its muzzle, immense, imposing, huge. It almost looked as if it were filled with contempt for the little marionettes of men who capered round it, little things whose lives could be measured, at the best, in scores of years, and who were quite incapable, unaided, of hurling death across five hundred yards of valley.

Chapter V

It was not until the gun had been tried and proved that El Bilbanito allowed himself to send out the letters he had looked forward so eagerly to dispatching. Haughty letters they were, as befitting the only chieftain in Galicia who possessed an eighteen-pounder. All save one were addressed to the other *guerrillero* leaders in this debatable land. They announced the brief fact that El Bilbanito now disposed of siege artillery and was intending an attack upon León; any one who cared to come and serve under him would be welcomed. That the offer would be eagerly accepted El Bilbanito had not the least doubt; no one could lead the life of a *guerrillero* and not yearn to push down into the plains; so great would be the desire that the chiefs would swallow their pride and consent to act as his subordinates — or, if they did not, their men would desert and flock to join the leader who could offer them with so much certainty plunder and victory beyond anything achieved up to now.

The other letter was just as peremptory and was addressed to the Junta — the hunted local Government — of Galicia. It, too, announced that El Bilbanito now owned a gun, and it demanded instant supplies of powder and eighteen-pound shot, with plenty of pack animals to carry them, and ample forage, and muleteers. As an afterthought El Bilbanito included in his comprehensive demands a request for money, food, and clothing — not that he particularly hoped to get them, but because there was a faint chance that the Junta might have some stores, for once in a way, and he felt he was just as entitled to a share as any one else.

While he was awaiting answers to all his letters, El Bilbanito took in hand the business of getting the gun back over to the edge of the plains. All the energy which Father Prieto and his party had expended in carrying the gun so far was not merely wasted, but was the source of a great deal of trouble, for El

Bilbanito wished to bring the gun into action not many miles from the point where its regular gunners had abandoned it. And there was the question now of those French posts on the high road through the mountains; they would have to be circumvented. The gun would have to return by the route which El Bilbanito and his men had followed — over the rests, by the footpaths. The alternative was to use the gun to help storm the French posts, and from that El Bilbanito turned resolutely away. When he struck, he wished to strike at the heart; the reduction of the mountain garrisons would take time, and the plain lands would receive warning before he could be in among them.

Far and wide El Bilbanito sent his men in search of draught animals. They were hard to get nowadays. In one village, where he came in person and demanded oxen, the priest took him and, pointing down the valley, showed him a plough being dragged over a field by a strange team indeed — a little white ass, a man, and four women, the human beings bent double with the strain and only preserving their balance by supporting themselves on their hands, while an old white-haired man exerted his feeble strength at the handles. El Bilbanito laughed and took the ass, and the women were white to the lips as they saw him and his men go off with it. Spring was near at hand, the ploughing was not a quarter finished, and they would starve before the year was out.

The asses and the one mule and the six oxen they collected at last served their purpose in getting the gun under way. Two wheels on an axle served as a limber to which to attach the trail, and for some miles the gun moved nobly along the high road. But soon they reached the point where a footpath came down the mountain side and joined the road. It was up this path that the gun had to go. El Bilbanito had ordered it, and he was here with his pistols to see that it was done. A mass of rocks was carried down to bridge the ditch. The motley string of animals struggled over it, the gun crashed after them, and the struggle began.

These lower crests of the Cantabrian Mountains, on the borders of Galicia and Asturias, are covered with that dense growth of spiny bushes which is best known to English people by its

Corsican name of *maquis,* but which the Galician peasant calls the *monte bajo* — an impenetrable tangle of small evergreen trees of different species, growing precariously on the rocky slopes. The mountain side, too, is not a continuous uphill, but is broken up into a precipitous switchback with a general upward tendency, but alternated with down slopes as steep as the roof of a house.

Ten men went on ahead with axes, cutting the undergrowth at each side of the path to allow the animals following them to push along it two abreast. Beside the team walked the drivers, one man to each animal, with whips and goads, ready at a shout from El Bilbanito in the rear to stimulate their charges into fresh frantic efforts. Forty men walked beside the gun and limber, distributed along the drag ropes; they had to be ready to pull forward or back, or to turn the gun round corners, as the difficulties of the path dictated. Then came a dozen men carrying two thick trunks of trees, and ready to drop these behind or in front of the wheels to act as "scotches" where necessary.

It was El Bilbanito's personality which carried the gun over those mountains. His men would soon have abandoned the task as hopeless, despite the assistance which their leader got for them by conscripting the aid of all the peasants, men and women, whom he could catch. There were times when an hour's labour meant only ten yards of progress. That was up the steeper inclines, when they had first to disperse and gather small rocks to make some sort of road surface, and long ramps up and down at points where the path charged over some steep minor ridge of rock at gradients which would compel a man to go on hands and knees. On these steep slopes men and animals would rest to get their breath, while the gun was held up by the scotches, until a warning shout from El Bilbanito caused the men at the drag ropes to take the strain again, and the drivers to hitch their goads ready in their hands. Then El Bilbanito would shout "Pull!" and the men would tug, and the whips would crack, and the animals would tug and flounder about on the uncertain foothold, and the gun would move ever so little — a yard or two at most — up the slope before the effort died away and the scotches were dropped hastily behind the wheels again and the gasping beasts of burden — on two legs or on four — could rest again.

The animals would fall and break their legs between rocks, but others could be got as the party moved on; a peasant threatened with instant death would generally reveal where an ass or an ox could be found. There was rarely any need to apply torture. Even cows had to be used — to this day the Galicians and Asturians use cows for draught purposes — but cows, with all the contrariness of their sex, persisted in dying under the strain without even the excuse of broken bones. The men did not die. They cursed El Bilbanito, they cursed the gun, and the cattle, but they lived. During this period El Bilbanito slept more securely than before; he knew that mutiny breeds in idleness, not in hardship or hard work. The men might curse, complain, grumble, but they were secretly proud of their efforts. There was a thrill in looking back down a seemingly endless mountain side and in knowing that they had dragged a gun all the way up it. Unremitting toil of the most exacting nature had always been the destiny of those peasants, even in peace time, and now in war their labour was made more attractive for them because each man wore a plume of cock's feathers in his hat and belonged to the noted *guerrillero* band of El Bilbanito, which was soon to sweep the plains of León by the aid of the gun.

In the mountains above Bembibre they found the first results of the letter writing El Bilbanito had done before setting out. As they came lumbering down into a village, a band of ragged *guerrilleros* came forth to welcome them from the houses in which they had been billeted. Foremost among them were two men not at all of the Galician type. They were tall and slender, with mobile humorous faces, and both of them had blue eyes and black hair — a most unusual combination. El Bilbanito knew them by reputation. They were the brothers O'Neill, Hugh and Carlos, who at the head of their Asturian band had distinguished themselves the year before, when the Spaniards had tried to raise the siege of Astorga. Their surname explained their colouring — they were the descendants of some Irishman, possibly one who had "left his country for his country's good," or who had joined the Spanish Army to avoid the tyranny of Cromwell or of William III a hundred and fifty years ago. Men with Irish names teemed in the Spanish ranks; most of them were more Spanish than the Spaniards by now, and few could speak English.

The two O'Neills bowed to El Bilbanito with much ceremony. They could appreciate what he had achieved in bringing the gun thus far, and they could appreciate still more the advantages the possession of the gun conferred. El Bilbanito, on the other hand, was equally glad to see them. He needed a large force for his projected raid into León, and so was glad of the reinforcement; still more was he glad of the promise it held out of further additions to his force.

Carlos O'Neill was clearly all a-bubble with excitement as he stepped up to the gun and examined it.

"My brother was in the artillery once," explained Hugh to El Bilbanito.

"Indeed?" said the latter, with increasing interest. A trained artillery officer was a most desirable acquisition.

They watched him as he looked over everything, examining the elevating and training gear, the detail of the carriage work, the soundness of the metal of the gun itself. Then he came back to them.

"Well?" asked El Bilbanito; for the life of him, he could not keep a trace of anxiety out of his voice.

"May I congratulate you, Señor?" said Carlos. "It is a magnificent weapon. Your Excellency must have good workmen to put together so good a mounting. They were artillerymen, I take it?"

"No," said El Bilbanito. "I have none with me."

"Indeed?" said Carlos in his turn, and the two brothers looked at each other.

"So you expected *us* to supply artillerymen when you wrote and invited us to join you, Señor?" said Hugh haughtily.

El Bilbanito shrugged his shoulders.

"You or the others. It was of no importance to me. I should contrive something, anyway. Call your men out and set them at the drag ropes. Mine are in need of a rest."

The inevitable quarrel between the chiefs might have flared out there and then. The Spaniard does not assume authority gracefully; he suffers from the defects of his qualities and becomes overbearing when he finds himself in the position of leader. But at the moment the situation was eased by the rapid fraternization of the two bands. The O'Neills' men had in fact forestalled El Bilbanito's order, and, swarming out of the cottages, had already relieved the new arrivals of their duties at the gun. At the moment they were going slightly downhill, and they were on a path which might almost be called a road, from its width and regularity, so that the change was effected without difficulty. The two O'Neills had to break off the conversation in order to get their belongings from the house, hurriedly, for fear of being left behind. It was undignified, they felt.

They felt better when they came clattering up on their horses to catch up the column, for El Bilbanito was on foot like the rest of his men, like a true mountaineer. Carlos O'Neill, especially, could look down on El Bilbanito trudging along behind the gun, because his horse was an immense animal, a seventeen-hand grey, a most surprising sight in this band of fine mules and diminutive horses.

"Horses!" said El Bilbanito. "They will be useful when we leave the road again. Our team is weak, as you see."

"No, Señor," replied Carlos O'Neill indignantly. "You will not have Gil to pull in traces. I value him far too much."

"I shall have him if I think it necessary," retorted El Bilbanito.

"No, no, no, never," said Carlos. "Take your hand away from your pistol, sir!"

El Bilbanito was determined to display his authority and to nip any incipient rebellion in the bud. But as he drew and cocked his pistol Hugh O'Neill's riding whip came down on his wrist, and the weapon exploded harmlessly. El Bilbanito flung the empty pistol into Carlos' face.

At the sound of the shot, the two bands of men on ahead with the gun stopped and came running back, and the animals, grateful for the rest, began to munch the grass at the roadside. Carlos O'Neill had dismounted, and the big grey horse stood behind him, looking over his shoulder like some wise councillor whispering in his ear.

"You shall die for that blow," said Carlos, wiping the blood from his cheek. Hugh O'Neill came round beside him; the *guerrilleros* began to draw up on each side of the road, the two bands facing each other. Muskets were being cocked; there seemed every likelihood of a bloody little battle on the spot.

"As you will," said El Bilbanito. "Here and now."

Jorge was at his elbow. Carlos drew his sword.

"Holy Mary, Mother of God!" said Carlos. "The fellow has no sword!"

"Not I," said El Bilbanito. "We settle our quarrels with the knife, we men of the mountains."

"Do you expect *me*, with the blood of kings in my veins, to fight like a brigand with knives?" demanded Carlos.

"Of course, if you are afraid, Señor — " said El Bilbanito.

Carlos looked round him. His ragged Asturians for once had no sympathy with him. They knew nothing of the etiquette of the duel, and they took it for granted that knives should be used; as far as their knowledge went, the knife was the national weapon of Spain. El Bilbanito was very sure of his ground.

"It is nothing to me," said Carlos, his fighting blood aflame. "Lend me your knife, you."

Even his brother could not remonstrate. An O'Neill could not be expected to refuse a challenge to fight with any weapon, at any time, against any opponent. All Hugh O'Neill could do was to watch to see that no unfair advantage was taken, and to hold himself ready to challenge El Bilbanito himself if — inconceivably — his brother should be defeated.

The sky was wintry and grey, and a cold wind blew down from the snow-covered peaks which closed in the horizon. At the edge of the road stood the gun, huge and immovable, with the weary animals harnessed to it in a long double line. The *guerrilleros* were ranged in an irregular oblong, enclosing the piece of road where the quarrel was to be fought out, and in an angle of the oblong stood Hugh O'Neill, with the reins of the two horses over his arm; ever and anon he patted Gil's neck to reassure him in this matter of his master. In the middle of the oblong the two men seemed to dance a strange, formal dance. Each held his cloak over his left arm with the end fluttering loose; in his right hand each held a knife, the long, slightly curved weapon of Spain, blade upwards, thumb towards the blade as a knife ought to be held. Each was bent a little at the knees and hips, and taut like a spring. They sidled round each other right-handed, their eyes narrowed with the strain of watching every movement of the enemy. Feint and countermove followed each other like the steps of the dance which a casual observer might think they were dancing. Here and there in the ranks of the spectators men coughed nervously. In a fight with knives, one man must die as soon as the opponents come within arm's length.

El Bilbanito had no fear of the result; he had fought too many of these duels, and, as he would simply say, he had not been killed yet. This man O'Neill handled his knife and cloak like a tyro, and caution was only forced on El Bilbanito on account of O'Neill's long reach and vigilant eyes. Yet they would not save O'Neill, not with El Bilbanito in front of him. If a feint did not throw him off his guard, he could goad this beginner into making an attack which would lay him open to a deadly counterstroke. El Bilbanito moved farther to his right, and O'Neill turned to face him. But even while he turned, quick as a flash El Bilbanito leaned to his left and dashed within O'Neill's guard. By a miracle, O'Neill caught the knife on his cloak; it went through the cloak and through his arm; with satisfaction El Bilbanito felt the blade jar on the bone. He caught his enemy's right wrist in his left hand, and bent his knees and braced his thick body for the throw which would follow. The fight was won.

Perhaps his grip slipped; perhaps O'Neill's arms were stronger than he expected. O'Neill's wrist slipped from his hand. El Bilbanito was conscious of a violent blow on his side, which deprived him of his breath. There was a sharp pain in his chest, but it soon passed. El Bilbanito never knew that he had lost that fight; he never knew he was dying. With a strange dull curiosity he noticed his knees grow weak under him, and he felt himself, without knowing why, sink slowly onto the stones of the road. The light hurt his eyes, and he turned gently onto his face and lay limp. And over him stood Carlos O'Neill, with the knife in his right hand, red to the hilt. El Bilbanito's knife still transfixed his left arm, from which the blood came in spouts, and ran down his wrist and fingers.

Chapter VI

THERE was Spanish regular infantry in the village which looked out over the plain. They were the Princesa Regiment, but they were not in the least like the old regular army, the men who had worn the white Bourbon uniforms, with the cocked hats and the tight breeches and the black gaiters. These men wore the rough brown homespun cloth of the country; the coats were cut away in tails at the back, and the trousers fastened with straps under the foot. And they wore shakos, too, so that altogether they looked like gross caricatures of English soldiers.

The appearance of caricature went further than the clothing, for the men were at drill, and drilling grotesquely. The lines were ragged, and there was no attempt at keeping step, and when finally the Colonel gave the word to form square, there was hesitation, muddle, until in the end the regiment fell together in one vast, pudding-like mass, bayonets pointing in all directions, while the Colonel and the Adjutant raved from their saddles. In despair of ever sorting out the confusion by drill-book methods the Colonel called out company markers, and gave the word for the regiment to fall in on them, and while the men slouched to their places, the Colonel made ready in his mind the speech he determined to deliver, in which he would paint in vivid terms the fate of the Princesa Regiment if ever it tried to form square in that fashion with Kellermann's dragoons charging down upon it.

It was unfortunate that at the moment when the Colonel began his lecture there should come distraction from the mountain tops. Over the crest high up on the left a little procession came into view. The men and animals and vehicles composing it were dwarfed to specks by the distance, but in the clear mountain air they could be seen clearly enough, while even the sound of their progress, the shouts of the men leading the team, could be heard as a faint shrill piping. The spectacle was far more interesting than the Colonel's hysterical lecture on tactics; every eye was turned up the mountain side, and soon every face was, and then in the end, while the Colonel almost wept, the whole regiment broke up and lounged over to watch the fun.

The process of bringing the big gun down the mountain side was really exciting. There were four long drag ropes stretched out behind it, with thirty men to each, and every man lying back, taking the strain and only allowing the gun to descend foot by foot to the accompaniment of the directing shouts of the leaders. In front a quaintly assorted team of draught animals was being led down, while round about the gun a dozen wildly energetic men were running back and forth, rolling the bigger rocks out of the way, working like fiends with levers when irregularities of surface tended to tip the gun on its side, and dropping scotches in front of the wheels when the drag rope teams became disorganized and there was a chance that the gun might tear loose and come charging down the mountain on its own. Then, when the angle of slope altered and the gun was faced by a short uphill, the excitement redoubled. The team had to be harnessed up to the limber, a good momentum imparted — to the accompaniment of deafening yells — to the gun on the last bit of downhill, and then the drag rope crews had to rush round so as to pull forward instead of back, to carry the gun as far as possible up the slope until the momentum died away and spasmodic efforts were substituted for it, each painfully dragging the gun another yard or two up until the next crest was reached. Altogether it was a most entertaining spectacle.

When at last the gun reached the road, the regiment eyed it and its escort with curiosity. The gun was huge, enormous, in their eyes, accustomed only to the little field six-pounders which were all the Spanish Army could boast nowadays. It came crashing and clattering down the road on its vast five-foot wheels with a most intoxicating noise. The odd team which drew it — three mules, six asses and a couple of cows — did not appear so strange; they were used to seeing the military train drawn by assorted teams. And the men who came with it were not so unusual a spectacle either; they had often seen *guerrillero* bands before, and more than half of them had been *guerrilleros* themselves before they had been caught and clapped into the ranks of the Army.

At the head of the band rode a tall young man in a captain's uniform on a small brown horse; beside the gun rode another man in the blue coat of the artillery, much patched and very ragged; and the fact that his left arm was in a sling accounted for his having mounted his horse on the wrong side on reaching the road. His horse seemed to have been proportioned to the gun, so colossal an animal it was, a huge, bony grey, like some horse out of a picaresque romance.

The Princesa Regiment witnessed the meeting between the Colonel and these two officers, and saw them escorted with much politeness to regimental headquarters beside the village church while the Colonel's grooms attended to their horses. And then the regiment found itself, as frequently happened, with nothing to do. The men fraternized with the *guerrilleros,* and examined the big gun with curiosity, and idled about as only Spaniards can, until their idling was interrupted by the sudden appearance of the *guerrillero* captain in the little square outside the church. He clambered onto the breech of the gun, and all through the village they heard him shout, "Princesa! Princesa!" and they came running to hear what he had to say.

Chapter VII

"I AM Colonel de Casariego y Castagnola, of the Princesa Regiment of infantry," said the Colonel, introducing himself, "and my adjutant, Captain Elizalde."

"I am Captain Hugh O'Neill, late of the Ultonia Regiment," said O'Neill. "May I present my brother, Don Carlos O'Neill, of the Artillery?"

The introductions were most ceremonious; it was not until they were comfortably seated in headquarters that any topic of business was mentioned.

"I understood from my orders," said the Colonel, "that a certain El Bilbanito was bringing the gun here."

"We have El Bilbanito's men with us," replied Hugh O'Neill, "but El Bilbanito himself, most unfortunately, did not survive the difficulties of the journey."

"But how sad," said the Colonel. "How did he die?"

"It was a sudden indigestion," interjected Carlos O'Neill.

"Very sudden," elaborated Hugh.

"I have heard of the disease before," said the Colonel. "Was it steel or lead he was unable to digest? Or perhaps — perhaps he suddenly found himself unable to breathe?"

"It was something like that," said Hugh airily.

"Quite so, of course," said the Colonel, with his glance drifting over Carlos O'Neill's bandaged arm. "And now to business."

The Colonel did not seem in too great a hurry to start, all the same. He took a long pull at his cigar, and he made a searching examination of its ash, before he could bring himself to say what he had to say.

"In consequence of El Bilbanito's lamented decease," he began slowly, "I must address my orders to you, Señores. Those orders are . . ."

"Yes?" prompted Hugh O'Neill, when the pause grew too long for his patience.

"My orders are that I take the gun out of your charge. The Junta has decided that it is too valuable to risk on the plains. They have decided to employ it in the fortifications of Ferrol, whither I am to escort it at once."

There was a shocked silence for a moment before O'Neill's anger blazed out.

"What?" he said. "Take it all the way back again? Take it away from us? Never!"

"Those are my orders from the Junta, Señores," said the Colonel firmly. "It is my duty to obey them. And may I remind you that it is the duty even of *guerrilleros* to obey the established Government?"

"It is simple plain foolery," said Hugh.

"I could think of a worse name for it," said Carlos.

"Perhaps I could too," said the Colonel, "but I would not say it to my superior officer."

"So they have sent no ammunition, nothing?" demanded Hugh.

"Naturally not. Why send ammunition from Ferrol when it is at Ferrol that the gun is to be used?"

"But El Bilbanito made all sorts of plans to use the gun on the plains," said Hugh.

"I am aware of that," said the Colonel. "El Platero with two hundred men is waiting to meet him between here and La Merced. Cesar Urquiola has brought up his cavalry. Even Mina has sent a battalion of his Navarrese to the rendezvous."

"With a thousand men and the gun we could raid as far as the great road," said Carlos O'Neill.

"I think it extremely likely," said the Colonel. "You could set all León in an uproar. La Merced has only two hundred men in garrison, with two six-pounders."

"Indeed?" said Hugh, professional interest quickening. "I thought it was stronger than that. We can take it easily, then."

"You might, if you had a gun to do it with. But unfortunately, Señores, as I am the first to admit — you will have no gun."

"But you cannot take our gun from us, Colonel. It would be criminal folly to waste this chance."

The Colonel had to brace himself before he could reiterate his determination. It was sad to disappoint these two young men; it was sadder still to throw away an opportunity which even the Colonel's limited military instinct told him was ideal. But he had his orders, and he must abide by them.

"I must repeat, gentlemen," he said, slowly, "that I start for Ferrol to-morrow with the gun."

Carlos O'Neill's chair fell over with a clatter as he got to his feet.

"We won't permit it," he said. "You shall *not* have our gun."

"This sounds like insubordination," said the Colonel.

"So it is! The gun's ours and we shall keep it!"

"Don Carlos, that is not the way to speak to your superior officer. I might punish you severely if I did not make allowance for your youthful enthusiasm."

"You will *not* have the gun. Not if I die for it."

"Don't say words of ill omen like that, Don Carlos. Remember — gentlemen, you force me to say this — that outside I have three battalions of my regiment. Fifteen hundred men altogether. And you have — two hundred? Three hundred? If you force me to take strong measures, you see that I can carry them out. And if your insubordination is maintained outside the privacy of this office, I shall have to take official notice of it. I shall have to call a court-martial to try you for mutiny. There is only one penalty for mutiny, gentlemen, and you know what it is."

For the moment the Colonel thought he had won his point. Neither of the young men spoke. Carlos O'Neill even replaced his arm in the sling whence he had withdrawn it in his excitement. Then Hugh O'Neill rose from his chair, where he had been seated all through the interview. He said nothing, but walked slowly to the door; the Colonel and his adjutant followed him with their eyes. So lackadaisical were his movements that no one could have suspected him of any plan. He opened the door, walked through, and shut it behind him. The Colonel was genuinely sorry for him; he thought that, overwhelmed by sorrow at being deprived of his beloved gun, he had gone out to work off his despair in drink or, possibly — for mixed Spanish and Irish blood plays queer tricks — even in exercise. The Colonel was disillusioned only when he heard O'Neill's voice ringing out like a trumpet, "Princesa! Princesa! Oh, Princesa, come and hear about this new treachery in high places!"

The men came running to hear him. They massed themselves round the gun onto which he had climbed. Irish eloquence winged his Spanish words. He told of the mountain sides over which they had dragged the gun, and of the mustering of *guerrilleros* at the rendezvous, of the coming of El Platero and of Mina. He told them of the helpless garrisons in the plain, the prisoners who would fall into their hands, the plunder which was there for the taking, the welcome they would receive when they freed the towns from the hated French dominion. He got a roar of laughter from the plainsmen among them when he said that he was tired of the bellyaching mountain cider and wanted to drink honest wine again — it was a deft argument, which appealed both to those who looked on wine as a necessity of life and those who considered it a rare luxury.

Colonel Casariego made his appearance in the mob just as O'Neill was working up to his climax, telling the men that folly or worse at headquarters had decided to waste all these glorious opportunities. The Princesa Regiment was ordered back to rot again in garrison at Ferrol, and they were to drag the gun back with them over the mountains. Carlos O'Neill sidled up to Colonel Casariego as he made his way towards an excited group of his officers. Before the Colonel realized what was happening, something was dug uncomfortably into his ribs, and, looking down, he saw it was the muzzle of a pistol. At O'Neill's back were half a dozen of his gang.

"I think we will go back to Headquarters, Colonel," said O'Neill politely.

The only satisfaction Colonel Casariego found as he sat miserably in his Headquarters with a sentry at his door, listening to the hullabaloo outside, was in the periodical arrival of his senior officers, who came to the house under O'Neill's escort, in ones and twos, and were incontinently locked up with him. The three majors commanding battalions, the older ones among the captains, the adjutant and the quartermaster, all came to share his captivity. What was significant was the absence of the junior officers. It was no surprise at all to the Colonel when Hugh O'Neill made his appearance again and announced to the waiting officers, "Gentlemen, the Princesa Regiment has decided to follow me to the plains. Any of you officers who care to join me and serve under me, retaining your present rank, will be welcome. I only ask your word as gentlemen to give faithful service to me and the cause of Spain."

There was only a moment's silence before Captain Albano rose.

"I am with you sir," he said.

And one after the other the majors, and the captains, and the quartermaster came over to O'Neill. Only Colonel Casariego was left, sitting solitary at the table. There was nothing left for him to do but to make his way back to the Junta and confess his failure, to tell of the desertion of his whole regiment. He bowed under his misery. His face went down into his hands, and he wept. O'Neill shut the door quietly and left the old man weeping.

Chapter VIII

CAPTAIN LUKE BRETT, of His Britannic Majesty's forty-gun frigate *Parnassus*, was in his cabin reading the Bible, for he was a religious man, when a midshipman knocked on the door.

"Come in," said Captain Brett.

"Please, sir," said the midshipman, "Mr. Hampton says there is a fishing boat coming off from the land, apparently signalling to us."

Captain Brett looked instinctively up at the telltale compass over his head.

"Tell Mr. Hampton I'll be on deck directly," he said.

He put the marker carefully between the pages of his Bible, and followed the midshipman to the quarter-deck. Last night's gale had died down by now. The *Parnassus*, close-hauled under easy sail, heaved and swooped over a quartering sea, with every now and again a spatter of spray tumbling in over the starboard bow. Captain Brett's all-embracing eye swept over the ship; in that one encircling glance, as his officers well knew, he could inspect every detail of the routine of the deck. He looked at the trim of the sails, at the gleaming white decks, the shot in the racks and the hammocks in the nettings, the course of the ship, the working party overhauling cable on the forecastle. Away on the port side could be seen the brown cliffs of Spain, with Cape de las Peñas in the distance.

The First Lieutenant was looking forward through his telescope, and Captain Brett, following his gaze, saw a little speck appear on the crest of a wave, disappear in a trough, and appear again, bobbing violently. It was an open fishing boat running down wind under a brown lugsail to intercept them. As the Captain looked through the telescope which the Lieutenant handed him, he saw a speck of white run up to the top of the little mast and down again, up and down.

"Yes, they're signalling to us. Bear down two points, Mr.

Hampton. Heave to and let them come alongside when we reach them."

"Shall I have a bo'sun's chair ready, sir? You know what these dagoes are."

"As you wish, Mr. Hampton."

Lieutenant Hampton's suggestion was proved to be a very sensible one, for the man who was swung eventually on to the *Parnassus'* deck from the yardarm clearly could not have climbed a rope. He had one arm in a sling, but that was not the most important of his disabilities. He was green with seasickness as a result of the violent motion of the fishing boat; moreover, to Mr. Hampton's huge disgust, his feet were no sooner on the deck than he vomited again, helplessly, holding on with his one hand to the rope of the bo'sun's chair over his head.

"God damn all dagoes," said Mr. Hampton.

When the paroxysm passed, the man looked about him. He was a tall, slender man, dressed in something resembling a uniform — a much patched blue coat with some gold lace still adherent, and white breeches and boots and spurs; perhaps it was the first time that spurs had ever jingled on the deck of the *Parnassus*.

"*El capitán?*" he asked, inquiringly.

"I am Captain Brett, of this ship."

Clearly the man spoke no English; the words meant nothing to him, but at sight of Captain Brett's uniform, shabby though it was, and air of authority, he decided that Captain Brett was the man he sought. He produced from his pocket a small leather wallet, and with infinite care he drew a letter from it and offered it to the Captain. It was an innocent-looking enough letter, although it would have been his death warrant if he had fallen into the hands of the French with it on his person. The Captain glanced through it, examined the signature with care, and passed it on to his lieutenant, who read:

OFFICE OF H.M.'s MISSION TO THE ASTURIAS
GIJON
10th June 1810
This is to make known to officers of His Britannic Majesty's forces by

land or sea that the bearer of this recommendation, Captain Carlos
O'Neill of the Spanish Artillery, is an officer in the Partisan forces of
Spain, and to charge all such officers to render all assistance to Captain
O'Neill as their duty permits and as they may judge will further the
common cause.

HENRY BERKELY, Major
H.M.'s representative in the Asturias
Second Foot Guards

"That's Berkely's signature, all right," said Captain Brett.
"I've seen one of these things before. And what's this he's trying
to show us now?"

Captain O'Neill was trying to draw another paper from his
wallet, which fitted it so tightly that in his one-handed condition he found difficulty in drawing it out.

"Allow me, Captain," said Captain Brett; the fellow's bow-
ings and scrapings had actually infected him too.

Captain Brett drew out the paper; it had been long folded
and was in danger of tearing along the creases.

"Oh, it's his commission," said Captain Brett.

It was indeed a noble document, embossed at the head with
the arms of Spain and bearing three seals at the foot; it was
printed in type resembling a flowing italic hand, but quite in-
comprehensible to Captain Brett because it was in the Spanish
language. But he could see that written in by hand here and
there through the document, in gaps purposely left, were the
words "Don Carlos O'Neill." It was obviously a genuine document and established the identity of the bearer.

"If his name's O'Neill, why the devil doesn't he speak English?" asked Lieutenant Hampton.

"He's a Spanish—Irishman. I've seen his sort before," said Captain Brett. "He had better have a drink while we find out what
he wants."

The gesture of offering a drink is an easy one, actually within
the capacity of a stiff-necked naval captain; while he made it,
Captain Brett heard a chuckle from the midshipman of the
watch at his side, but Lieutenant Hampton, that resolute dis-
ciplinarian, saved his captain's dignity.

"Fore to'ga'n masthead, Mr. Norman," he said. "And stay there until sunset."

And the midshipman went, crestfallen, while Captain Brett escorted Captain O'Neill with ceremony to the companion ladder. But once down below, where everything heaved and creaked and swayed, O'Neill's misgivings overpowered him. Unceremoniously he turned and rushed up the ladder again and fell limply across the leeside bulwarks.

"Poor fellow!" said Captain Brett. "A glass of my old port ought to do him good."

The Captain's steward brought chairs and bottles and glasses, and, once seated, with a glass of brandied port inside him (where, for a miracle, it stayed), O'Neill seemed to get better.

"Now, Captain, tell me what I can do for you," said Captain Brett.

The words meant nothing to the Spaniard, but the tone in which they were spoken did. He got out of his chair and looked round the ship. The twelve-pounders down on the main deck clearly, from his attitude, were not what he sought. But he went across to the big eighteen-pounder quarter-deck carronade, looked at it with delight, took out the tampion, examined the bore, and then slapped the gun with pleasure, pointed to himself, and then at the distant shore.

"He wants to take our eighteen-pounder away with him!" said Lieutenant Hampton.

"I don't often swear," said Captain Brett, "but I'll see him damned before he does."

Both officers shook their heads violently, and O'Neill's face fell, until he realized that they misunderstood him.

"What's he looking for now?" asked the Lieutenant.

"He's found it," said the Captain.

O'Neill, after staring anxiously round, had seen hanging by the wheel the slate and pencil of the log of the watch. He rushed and seized these, and began hurriedly drawing with the slate on his knee. After three minutes he showed them the results of his work — a neat drawing of a big gun on a military carriage. He pointed to the picture, and then he moved his hand in a circle round the muzzle of the carronade, and then out to the mountains again, and then to his chest.

"He's got an eighteen-pounder on shore," said Captain Brett, and nodded and smiled, trying not to look quite as foolish as he felt.

Thus encouraged, O'Neill started drawing again.

"What in God's name is this?" asked Hampton, who was looking at the drawing upside down as it progressed. "Grapes?"

"No, shot, of course," said Captain Brett. It was a picture of a pyramid of cannon balls.

Brett opened the shot rack beside the carronade, and lifted out one of the eighteen-pounder shot and offered it inquiringly to O'Neill.

"Sí, sí, sí," said the latter, nodding ecstatically.

"At last!" said Brett.

But O'Neill was drawing again, excitedly.

Now that they were on the track, only a cursory glance was necessary to recognize the new drawing as a picture of a powder barrel.

"He wants powder and shot for an eighteen-pounder siege gun on shore," decided Captain Brett. "He can have them."

One paragraph of his orders laid stress on the need to help the Spanish forces, and to co-operate with them wherever possible. It was only English sea power, reaching out across hundreds of miles of ocean, which sustained the Spaniards in their interminable struggle with the French Empire. But for that, the Spanish insurrection would long before have been quenched in blood, as had been the Tyrolese revolt, and the Lombard revolt in preceding years.

"I don't know how he thinks he'll get them, sir," said Hampton inquiringly. "The French have got every port garrisoned between here and Ferrol."

"He knows some quiet inlet or other, never fear," replied Brett. "Look, he's drawing again."

The new picture was unmistakably a mule — not a donkey or a horse, because O'Neill's pencil point laid great stress on the ears and tail. Then O'Neill spread the fingers of his one sound hand ten times, and pointed down the coast.

"He's got fifty mules waiting somewhere," said Hampton.

It was Captain Brett who solved the difficulty of finding out the exact place; O'Neill could think of no method of conveying his meaning, for all his pointing and gesticulating.

"The chart, Mr. Hampton," said Captain Brett.

With the chart of the coast spread out before him O'Neill had no difficulty in pointing out the exact little bay he had in mind. Everybody this time was nodding and smiling, pleased with the progress made despite all difficulties.

"He's drawing again," said Hampton.

O'Neill was making an addition to his picture of the mule; when he passed it over, it had along its side five cannon balls held in a sack over its back.

"That means ten altogether to each mule," commented Brett. "They always overload the poor brutes."

Next the cannon balls were rubbed out by O'Neill's wetted finger and replaced by a powder barrel. O'Neill pointed at the mule so adorned and then spread his fingers.

"He means he wants five loads of powder and forty-five of shot — four hundred and fifty rounds. Let me see." Captain Brett was not of a really agile mental quality, but he succeeded in solving the problem of mental arithmetic presented to him.

"Yes, he's about right. That is not quite enough powder, but I suppose it is easier for them to get powder than eighteen-pounder shot."

"That's four tons of shot, besides the powder, sir," said Hampton, who also had been doing mental arithmetic. "It'll mean sending the cutter — that boat of his isn't nearly big enough."

"That is so," said Brett.

The two officers looked at each other and then found themselves glancing uneasily at O'Neill, as if he could read their thoughts, although not understanding their speech.

"It might be a trap, sir."

"Very true, Mr. Hampton. You will have to use all precautions. Have the four-pounder mounted in the cutter and loaded with grape. Get that boat of his in tow, and I will stand in after dark. You can cast off *here*" — Brett's stubby finger indicated the mouth of the inlet — "and I will wait for you."

"Yes, sir."

"And call the gunner and see to breaking out the shot and powder he wants. Offer him a few rounds of canister and grape as well as round shot. He may need 'em, sometime."

"Aye, aye, sir."

"If it *is* a trap, Mr. Hampton, that boat will be just ahead of the cutter as you go in. Fire the gun into it, and then come back, bringing this gentleman with you. We will see how he looks at the yardarm."

"Aye, aye, sir."

There is no need to follow Captain Brett and Mr. Hampton through the complicated task of explaining to Carlos O'Neill in dumb show the fact that he was their prisoner until the cutter should leave the inlet after nightfall unharmed. The rising moon found the *Parnassus*, a shimmering white ghost of a ship, hove to off the mouth of the bay. Captain Brett, leaning on the quarter-deck rail, had felt so much confidence in O'Neill's obvious honesty that he was not in the least surprised or relieved when he heard the splash of oars returning down the bay and knew that the munitions had been safely landed. Mr. Hampton came on board to make his report.

"Yes, Mr. Hampton?"

"Everything was as he said, sir. The mules were waiting on the beach. I saw them loaded and start up a little path up the cliff."

"Very good, Mr. Hampton; hoist the cutter in."

But it was a different story five days afterwards, when Captain Brett came on board again after going on shore for orders at Ferrol.

"Oh, Mr. Hampton," he said, "do you remember that man O'Neill who came on board when we were off Cape de las

Peñas? If ever we see him again, we are to put him in irons and bring him here for trial."

"For trial, sir?"

"Yes, they want him for treason, and mutiny, and — bless my soul, there's no end to his crimes. Berkely gobbled like a turkey at the mention of his name."

"Was that recommendation of his a forgery, then, sir?"

"No, but it was a year old. We noticed that. And since Berkely gave it to him — just before he came off to us, in fact — he has got half the Spanish Army to mutiny and taken them off on the opposite course to what Berkely ordered. The Junta is sick with rage about it."

"But what did he want the ammunition for, sir?"

"For his eighteen-pounder. It's the only siege gun in all Galicia, it appears. The Junta wanted it for themselves, it appears, and O'Neill thought otherwise."

"He seemed to me to be a man of sound judgment, sir."

But Captain Brett did not try to countenance any criticism, however veiled, of the government of His Majesty's Peninsula allies.

Chapter IX

WHILE Hugh O'Neill was waiting for his brother's return, he came to know all the sensations of a man in a powder magazine with the building on fire. The idiocy of the Junta in not sending the ammunition which El Bilbanito had demanded was imposing delays on the invasion of León, and delays were dangerous. There was no fear of the French; with Wellington loose again in the South and every French resource at strain to hold him in check, the French were content to sit quiet in their garrisons in the North and hope not to be attacked. Every movable body of troops in León was on the march for the Tagus, as O'Neill well knew, and he had little fear that any news of the concentration in the mountains would leak out to them. Nor was there much to fear at the moment from the Junta. That was two hundred miles away, at Ferrol, and it would be long before the news of the defection of the Princesa Regiment reached it; it would be longer still before they could move up troops — if they had any to spare — to interfere with him.

The danger lay round about him, close upon him. Troops which had mutinied once might mutiny again. He had seduced them from their allegiance by a promise of an invasion of León; with every day that the invasion was postponed, their turbulence increased. The fact that there was no ammunition for the gun would be attributed to his negligence, and no mob ever stops to listen to excuses. O'Neill, a year or two ago while he was still with the Army, had seen San Juan, a real general, hung up in a tree by his mutinous troops and then used as a target. Something like that would be his fate if he had to hold these undisciplined villains in check much longer.

It was a blessing that Carlos had been able to move off at once in search of ammunition. The Princesa Regiment's mule train had been at his disposition, and fortunately Carlos still had the recommendation to the English which Colonel Berkely had given him nearly a year before. The sea was only thirty miles away, across three ranges of mountains. Hugh O'Neill tried to be pessimistic in his estimate of the time Carlos would be gone. He decided that Carlos might be back in a week, and he set himself to keep things quiet for that time. He called out the Princesa Regiment for manœuvres and worked them until they were ready to drop. He sent the *guerrilleros,* both those of his own band and those of the deceased El Bilbanito, on expeditions hither and thither, to harry the wretched villages for food — he had nearly two thousand men to feed, and the whole district had been plundered and replundered for years. He sent urgent messages to El Platero — the silversmith — and to Joaquin Alvarez, Mina's lieutenant, and to Don Cesar Urquiola, begging them to have patience and await his arrival at the rendezvous. But all the same it was a mighty relief to the young man when a boy rode up on a pony with a note from Carlos. He was on his way back with the ammunition, and would reach them shortly. O'Neill called down a blessing on the British Navy and issued the order to his motley forces to make ready to get on the move. The animals were harnessed up to the gun and they set out on the last stage of the journey through the mountains.

The gun, the big lumbering thing, was responsible for much already. Here, on the edge of the mountains, was assembled the biggest concentration of irregular troops the war had seen as yet. Besides the Princesa Regiment there was O'Neill's band and El Bilbanito's. There was Alvarez with his Navarrese, whom Mina had sent from their Pyrenean hunting grounds. There was El Platero with his Biscayans, and Urquiola with his Castilian horsemen — the only guerrilla troops who had dared to carry on the war in the plains. They were of a different type from the mountaineers, lean, dignified men, who wore their clothes and their beards with an air. Pennons fluttered at their lance points when they trotted up to meet the descending column, and their spurs and accoutrements jingled bravely. Yet Urquiola and El Platero and Joaquin Alvarez all greeted O'Neill with deference when they came up to him as he rode beside the gun. It was not the two thousand men whom he commanded who made them so respectful; it was the gun. Its thirteen feet of length, its five-foot wheels, its immense breech, all indicated its colossal power. One and all, those men had chafed at the restraint imposed upon them by the little fortresses in the plains. This gun would knock those places to pieces.

On the evening when the forces were all met, O'Neill and his brother walked out to where the mountains definitely ceased, along a path which ran along the top of a huge green spur jutting from the mountains into the plain. Here, where the hill fell away in a steep escarpment, they could look out over the plain, and note the winding rivers and the scattered villages, and the rich fields and the numerous roads. It was from this very point that El Bilbanito had stood gazing out over the plain, a long time ago, and wishing that he had artillery with which to descend into it, but neither of the young men was aware of that, and perhaps if they had been, they would not have considered it a matter of ill omen. Their hearts were high, and they laughed as they laid their plans. Carlos O'Neill even considered it now worth that loss of his dignity which he had suffered on his visit to H.M.S. *Parnassus,* worth the seasickness and the childish drawing on the slate and the gesticulations which had (in his opinion) consorted ill with the gravity of a Spanish gentleman with the blood of kings in his veins.

Chapter X

MAJOR JONQUIER was a Dutchman. He was a fat, pale, fair man with pale blue eyes, slightly protruding. He was not much given to thought; he never meditated upon the strangeness of the fate which made Holland a part of France, and which had carried him off from his land of dykes and windmills, and had set him down in command of a mass of French conscripts in the sun-soaked plains of Spain, and had bestowed upon him the high-sounding title of Governor of La Merced, and had set him to hold Spaniards in subjection to a Corsican who was known as "Emperor of the French."

He was a man of phlegmatic temperament, but he was a little annoyed when a message came to him, just when he was comfortably dining, to the effect that there were enemies in sight. With a sigh he got up from the table, and rebuttoned his tunic, and refastened his stock, and buckled his swordbelt round his bulging waist, and drained his glass of wine, and took his telescope from its hooks on the wall, and then, sighing again, he addressed himself to the climb up the steep stone stairs to the first floor, and he positively grunted with the exertion of climbing the vertical ladder which led to the roof. If the sentry had allowed his imagination to run away with him, he would get a week's *salle de police* for disturbing him at this, the most sacred hour of the day.

Determined to get the business over and done with without delay, he did not linger on the roof, but walked straightway over to the bell tower, bowed his head to enter by the low door, and climbed ponderously up the little ladder to the little square platform at the summit, where the French flag flapped languidly in the slight wind. The sentry was there, and the Sergeant of the Guard, and the addition of Major Jonquier's portly form made the platform uncomfortably crowded when he squeezed through the trapdoor.

He extended his telescope and looked about him, and the Sergeant of the Guard pointed excitedly towards where the mountains towered up from the plain.

"Hum!" said the Major to himself, and again "Hum!"

There was something which looked like a snake a mile long advancing up the road from the mountains, where the sun was about to set in scarlet glory. From the length it must be a small army, but it was so wreathed in dust that nothing could be definitely ascertained, except that through the dust occasionally could be seen the flash of weapons. But ahead of the column the Governor could plainly see more of the enemy. There was a small column of horsemen on the road, and out to right and to left of it were smaller groups of cavalry winding their way along the field paths parallel to the road. Clearly there was a strong force of the enemy advancing to the attack of the fort, screened, as the best military opinion dictated, by an advance guard of cavalry. As the Major's glass swept the plain again, his eye caught sight of something fluttering where the cavalry rode. They were lance pennons — it must be Urquiola and his mounted brigands come up from Castile. Once before they had penetrated this far. There must be a concentration of *guerrilleros* — an event often expected but never witnessed before.

Major Jonquier began issuing his orders even before he left the platform. The messenger was to ride at once to León with news of the attack. Major Jonquier was quite certain that the messenger would not do any good; he knew that in all the province there was no relieving force which could be sent to him at present. The monthly convoy of supplies with its heavy escort was only due to arrive in three weeks' time. But the garrison — an unreliable lot — would be more cheerful if they knew the messenger had ridden off.

Meanwhile the Major was equally certain that he could hold off for three weeks the attack of any mob of irregulars, who of course would be without artillery. He came down into the fort and began a rapid inspection of the defences.

La Merced had been a convent, a large square building of grey stone built round a central courtyard. Its position for the defence of the bridge was ideal. It stood on a rounded hillock just away from the river and a complete hundred yards from the roadway where it joined the bridge. At one time the land on which it stood had been enclosed by a high stone wall, but this had been torn down because of the protection it might offer an attacking force, and had been replaced by a high strong palisade of wood, of which the posts stood just far enough apart to prevent a man squeezing through. This palisade would delay any storming party, and as it stood within comfortable musket range of the convent, it formed an important part of the defences. The building itself, like many Spanish convents, offered windows only towards the courtyard; the four exterior walls were quite blank, save for the loopholes which the garrison had knocked in them all round. The stone which had once formed the park wall had all been carted up to the convent and built into two little bastions at opposite corners, in each of which was mounted a six-pounder, one commanding the bridge and the road. Each gun could fire along two faces of the building, so that if the attackers were even able to climb the palisade, they would find themselves merely at the foot of the blank walls, pelted with musketry from the loopholes and scourged with an enfilading fire of grape from the guns. No wonder Major Jonquier felt easy in his mind as he went along the corridors, seeing that everything was in order.

One of his two companies of infantry was on duty, the men standing at the loopholes looking out; the other company, instead of making the most of its period off duty, like sensible men, were gathered about in groups in the barrack rooms, or peeping out of the loopholes, discussing the new development. But then, they were only recruits, not veteran troops.

Major Jonquier went out on to each bastion in turn. At each gun were five artillerymen. The linstocks were burning and the guns were loaded ready with grape. With a grunt of satisfaction he waddled back again into the convent. He peeped into the courtyard. His six cows were there, in improvised wooden stalls — Major Jonquier was a man who insisted on milk in his coffee and butter on his bread. He saw that the sentries keeping guard

over the doors of the cellars in which were the stores were at
their posts. He gave orders for carcasses — bundles of rags
soaked in oil — to be made ready on the parapets. If these were
to be lighted and tossed over, they would give all the light necessary to shoot down the attackers in the event of a night attack. Night was already falling rapidly, and it would be dark
before the raiding army reached the convent.

He went back into his own room and shouted to his servant
for his dinner. That servant was a perfect fool. He had the incredible imbecility to bring in to the Major the omelet which
had been ready to serve before the alarm — it was a nightmare
of an omelet now; as the Major said, with oaths, it was the colour, shape, consistency, and toughness of the sole of a shoe. He
drove the man out to the kitchen again to prepare another.

It was no excuse for the man that he was a Spaniard and would
be hanged for certain if the place were taken. The place was
not going to be taken, and an omelet was a more important matter than a Spaniard's neck, anyway. The second omelet was only
a slight improvement. Major Jonquier groaned as he ate it; the
man's nerve must have been completely ruined by his fright.
But the braised beef with red pepper would be better — Major
Jonquier had prepared that dish with his own painstaking hands
before this bother about *guerrilleros* had begun. He ate it hungrily, heard with annoyance that there was no soft cheese to
complete the meal, and contented himself with hard. He finished
his wine and shouted for his coffee and brandy. He stretched his
legs beneath the oak table and tried to feel like a man who has
dined satisfactorily. It was a useless effort. A dinner interrupted halfway through can never be a good dinner. The bleak
grey stone room was too Spartan by far for his tastes, and it was
so infernally cold, despite its miserable *brasero* of charcoal, that
he had to wrap his cloak round his legs. The tallow dips gave
only a suspicion of light. The coffee was not coffee at all, but
only a horrible chicory substitute which the continental block-
ade forced him to drink. His cigar was perfectly foul. Major
Jonquier thought of his native Holland, of white-tiled stoves
and oil lamps and good coffee and a black cigar with a straw

up the middle. The only thing which was satisfactory was the brandy, and even of that he did not think it advisable to drink more than three glasses after his couple of litres of wine. The horrors of war were decidedly unpleasant.

He could not even drink his brandy in peace because that young fool Captain Dupont insisted on coming in to tell him that the *guerrilleros* were in earshot. The Major growled like a bear, climbed up to the roof again, and peered through the night over the parapet. Decidedly there was activity out there in the darkness. The Major and the Captain could hear voices, shouting, and laughter. The neighing of a horse came distinctly up to them. Then a new sound reached their ears — the chink of spades and pickaxes. Some working party out there was digging vigorously. Major Jonquier decided it must be on the summit of the mount lower down the road, a quarter of a mile away. What they could be digging was more than he could guess — barricades, probably, across the road, as a defence against cavalry. He knew by experience that those *guerrilleros* from the mountains, who had half of them been miners in the days of honest work, would dig like badgers on the slightest provocation, huge, useless fortifications, always in the wrong place.

He was tempted to go down to the bastion and order a shot or two in that direction, but he decided against it; ranging and aiming were too difficult in the dark. He impressed upon Dupont the need to keep the sentries well awake, so that they would hear if any one tried to chop down a section of the palisade under cover of the darkness. He himself repeated his tour of inspection and testily ordered the young men of the company off duty to get to bed and go to sleep. The whole garrison would have to be on duty an hour before dawn. Major Jonquier confidently expected that the *guerrilleros* would try their usual tactics — a wild rush in the grey of the early morning.

They could do so if they liked. He could predict the result, having fought *guerrilleros* often enough before. Many men would die at the palisades. A few ardent spirits would perhaps hew a little gap. A few others would haul heavy scaling ladders up the slope, but they would not even reach the foot of the wall.

They would be shot as they climbed under their burdens, and then finally the whole mob would break and run and probably not stop until they reached the mountains again. It would be a salutary lesson for them, and for another few weeks he would be able to dine undisturbed and sleep in peace. As it was, he went and lay down on his bed with all his clothes on, even his sword as well, leaving strict orders that he should be called before daylight.

In the dark morning, when his servant came to wake him, he started out of bed as soon as he was called. Pulling his cloak close round him in the biting cold, he walked out into the dark corridors. The passages rang with the sound of the heavy boots of the men coming up to take their posts at the loopholes. All of them were shuddering with cold. Jonquier turned to the Sergeant at his side.

"Have the soup heated and brought to the men at their posts," he ordered.

He went up on to the flat roof where Dupont was nervously pacing about. The young fool had evidently not been to bed, and the Major was about to reprimand him severely when his words were cut short by a new series of sounds down by the road. There was a cracking of whips and a clanking of chains. Lights showed, flickering, over by the mound.

"What in hell — ?" said Jonquier, peering vainly through the darkness. The lights moved vaguely about. Some one shouted hoarsely. There was a terrific bustle over there.

"Oh, well, we shall know soon enough," said Jonquier philosophically.

The eastern horizon was just beginning to grow a little paler, and it became evident that it was going to be a misty morning.

"Keep your men awake up here, Dupont," said Major Jonquier. "And remember never to leave any side of the fort unguarded, however hard they may be attacking the other ones."

He lowered himself down the ladder and reached the first floor. The men were all at their posts here, and as he descended a private came clattering along with a pail of soup, and another followed behind with a basket of bread.

"If they attack," he said to the nearest group, "don't get mud-dled. Don't drink your muskets and fire your soup out of the loopholes."

The men laughed. Every one liked old pot-bellied Jonquier and his funny guttural French.

"And aim low," said Jonquier more seriously. "Aim for their legs and put an end to their fandangoes."

He waddled down the staircase to the ground floor. Every one down here had finished breakfast.

"Feeling better for your breakfasts, men?" he asked. "That's good. Now you won't . . ." He made the same joke as he had made on the first floor and got the same laugh.

"And aim low," he went on just as before. "Aim . . ."

Jonquier was doing his duty. He was cheering up his soldiers and embedding the pill of good advice in the jam of banter.

He went to a loophole and peered out. By now it was nearly full light, and the mist was beginning to shred away. If the *guerrilleros* were going to attack, they were losing their best op-portunity. The big bulk of the fort must be fully visible to them by now. It was strange that they should delay. He walked through into the big grey stone room which had been the re-fectory and which ran along the whole of one side of the build-ing, facing towards the mound down by the road.

"Feeling better for your breakfasts, men?" he asked. "That's — "

A terrific crash interrupted him. The building shook, and the whole hall was filled with stone dust and flying chips of stone. Some one screamed. Something fell on the stone floor with a clang and rolled towards Jonquier. It was a big cannon ball — a most certain indication that La Merced was doomed. Jonquier looked at it as though death itself were rolling towards him over the floor — as indeed it was. A big section of the two-foot thick wall had been knocked in, leaving a nearly circular hole two feet in diameter between two loopholes. The unhewn stones of which the wall was composed had been sent flying to all parts of the room. A man with a shattered wrist was still screaming, as much with fright as with pain.

"Stop that noise!" said Jonquier, pulling himself together. "Go down into the storeroom and get one of the servants to bandage that arm for you. Get to your posts, men."

With all the appearance of nonchalance that he could assume, he walked to the hole the cannon ball had made and looked through it. There was still a slight mist outside, but it would hardly last five minutes longer, with the thirsty sun drinking it up. Down there by the mound the mist seemed thicker. No, it was a cloud of powder smoke which was gradually dissipating. Jonquier could make out the raw brown of the newly turned earth; five seconds later the smoke had drifted sufficiently away for him to see, vaguely, a rude breastwork which had been dug. And pointing out through the embrasure of the earthwork he could see the muzzle of a big gun. Even as he looked, the gun disappeared in a burst of white smoke, and in the same instant the building shook again to a splintering crash, as the shot hit the wall twenty feet from where he was standing. The concussion threw him to the floor.

There was panic in the long hall, but Jonquier dragged himself to his feet in time to check it.

"Back to your posts, you cowards!" he roared. "You, Sergeant, shoot the next man to flinch."

The men hesitated, but Jonquier stood firm.

"Each man must lie down by his loophole," he said. "And stand up and aim straight when the rush comes. I am going to turn the guns on their battery. We'll not be hit without hitting back."

On the first floor he saw young Lieutenant Lecamus fidgeting with his sword hilt and biting his lips with nervousness. Even as they met, the building shook again as another shot hit the wall below.

"Go down to the refectory and keep the men there up to the mark," Jonquier ordered. "And pull yourself together first, man."

He brushed the grey dust from his salient abdomen, and, wheezing a little, hurried on to the bastion. Here the gunners were standing to their gun.

"Why the devil haven't you opened fire?" he demanded.

"No orders, sir," said the Sergeant in charge.

"Orders? Who waits for orders in a siege? You're not fit for your job, Sergeant. Slew the gun round and open fire with round shot on that breastwork. No, don't stop to draw that charge. Fire the grape out."

The gun roared out its defiance, but it was a much more insignificant sound than the deep-mouthed bellow of the big siege gun which the *guerrilleros* had somehow acquired. In the smoke the artillerymen sponged out the gun, rammed in cartridge and ball, and the Sergeant crouched over the breech to aim. He stepped aside and jerked the lanyard. Jonquier saw the earth fly from the wing of the breastwork.

"High and to the right," he said. "Reload."

Then the big gun on the mound fired back, and this time the shot hit the solid mass of the bastion six feet below their feet.

"Ha!" said Jonquier. "We've taught them to leave the wall alone."

The Sergeant fired the gun again, but this time it was a clean miss. No one saw where the shot fell.

"Reload," said Jonquier. "I will lay the gun next time."

As he spoke, the big gun on the mound thundered forth its reply, and the ball screamed through the air close over their heads.

"Devilish good gunners down there," said Jonquier to himself. "And a devilish good gun."

He crouched over the breech, looking through the notch on the elevator bar and the groove on the muzzle swell. In the bit of the interior of the breastwork which he could see through the embrasure, he saw bare-armed figures labouring over the siege gun. He aimed carefully and signed to the Sergeant to fire while he moved aside to note the effect. This time earth flew from the face of the earthwork close to the embrasure.

"We'll hit him next round," said Jonquier. The gun was wiped out, the cartridge rammed, and a gunner was about to thrust the ball into the muzzle when the reply came. Eighteen pounds of solid iron, flying at three hundred yards a second, hit the little six-pounder square on the mouth. The air was full of flying bits, and the gun was flung back off its carriage. It was split clean open for half its length, one trunnion broken off, the carriage knocked to pieces. The gunner with the cannon ball fell dead with a fragment of iron through his neck.

Jonquier looked down at the wreck and ruin. He was of the type that failure merely makes angry, not despairing. The blood surged into his face. He clenched his hands and stamped his feet. But by an effort of will he prevented himself from shaking his impotent fists at the enemy and compelled himself to speak calmly and carelessly.

"Our gun receives an honourable discharge," he said. "Get your muskets and lie down, you men. Save your fire when the rush comes until they are at the foot of the wall."

He climbed back out of the bastion on to the roof again and walked over to the other bastion. As he went, he felt the fort tremble again as another shot hit the wall down below. The Spaniards had recommenced, pitilessly, pounding at the main building to open a breach.

The reason why the other gun had not opened fire was obvious. The angle of the fort projected between it and the siege battery. There was nothing to fire at. Jonquier played with the idea of hoisting the gun up to the roof, running it across, and lowering it down to take the place of the injured gun, but he abandoned it. Even a six-pounder is a difficult and ponderous thing to hoist about, and the breach might be achieved and the assault made while the gun was still out of action. Besides, this gun had been mounted to sweep the bridge; the whole reason of La Merced's existence was to guard the bridge. Removing the gun from this bastion would leave to the Spaniards practically free passage over the river.

He looked down towards the bridge and the river and caught his breath. The enemy were already over the river. He could see little knots and groups of men on the farther bank. Presumably they had crossed lower down during the night by small boats. Now a little group of men ran on to the bridge. Some of them waved their arms. Jonquier wished he had his telescope

with him so that he could make out details, but he was only three
hundred yards from the bridge and could see well enough. One
member of the group seemed to be walking unwillingly, as if he
were being dragged along. Another leaned over the parapet of
the bridge as if he were fastening something to it. Then, with a
bustle and a scurry, the unwilling man was hoisted up and flung
over the parapet. Jonquier heard the artillerymen standing beside him breathing suddenly hard. The unwilling man's fall from
the parapet was abruptly checked. It ended with a jerk, which
threw his arms and legs into the air in grotesque attitudes like those
of a child's toy. Then he swung idly like a pendulum in a little arc,
turning first his back to the fort and then his face, and his bald
head shone in the newly rising sun. Then Jonquier recognized
him; it was Julio Coppola, the renegade Spanish postboy, whom
he had sent out the night before with the news of the attack.
Jonquier shrugged his shoulders. Even if he had got through, it
was much to be doubted if help could have come for another
fortnight; but all the same, it was annoying that the Spaniards
should have hanged him so publicly, because otherwise he might
have told his men that help might come any moment, and so
stimulated them to beat off the attack.

"Don't hang about gaping like this," he snarled to the artillerymen. "Sweep that rabble off the bridge."

The men seemed to wake from an evil dream, and sprang
guiltily to the gun; the whole hanging had only taken a few
seconds. While they were aiming, the Spaniards were scuttling
back across the river like naughty boys discovered in mischief.
It was almost too late when at last the gun fired. The grapeshot
plunged down to the roadway of the bridge, ploughing it up and
sending chips flying from the parapets. Only one shot found its
target. One of the men, hit in the leg, was thrown to the
ground, and, prostrate, continued to writhe comically towards
safety. The others were all safely hidden in the undergrowth
along the river bank.

"Reload," growled Jonquier, "and keep that bridge clear in
future."

He went back over the roof and down to the refectory. The

room here was thick with dust, but enough light came in through the gaping holes in the wall to show the damage which had been done. There were big ragged rents everywhere along it; the floor was littered with the stones which had been flung in. As Jonquier stood gazing round, another cannon ball arrived, sent flying a big stone which was projecting into one of the holes, passed across the room, knocking a table into splinters, and crashed through the inner wall into the kitchen beyond. The men were crouching as close to the floor as they could, lying still like dead men, all save Lieutenant Lecamus, who was walking up and down, trying to be brave.

"Can't I take the men out of here?" said Lecamus, as plaintively as he could whisper. "They would be safe enough in the cellars, and we could call them out when the attack comes."

"If we once let them down into the cellars," replied Jonquier, "there will be no getting them out again when the attack comes. You know that as well as I do. It will do them good to be shot over a little." He did not add "And you too," although he thought it.

The pitiless pounding went on. Monotonously, every few minutes, a fresh hole appeared in the wall. The Spaniards were breaking it from end to end, and a good gun they must have had, and reliable powder, because there was very little variation in the height up the wall at which the balls hit — three feet or so. Then, with a rumble and a crash, a whole section of the wall, completely cut away at the bottom, came tumbling down, cascading partly into the room. Jonquier sprang forward. He was sure that the sight of that wall falling would draw the Spaniards to make their assault. One good attack, beaten back with heavy loss, would take the heart out of them and stiffen up his men. But the attack did not come. Looking out from the breach, Jonquier saw no enemies. The gentle wind had blown a long smear of smoke across the country from the enemy's battery, and that was all. The dazzling sunshine revealed no column of attack. The enemy were all hidden away out of sight, behind the mound, and under the embankment of the road.

"How much ammunition have the bastards got?" asked Jonquier of himself. "Are they going to pound the whole place into ruins before they attack?"

The only answer to the question was another shot, which hit the wall towards one end and brought down yet another big section of the crumbling structure, and another shot after that, and another, remorselessly.

Then at last came a break. Jonquier heard the high notes of a cavalry trumpet twice repeated. Two men appeared over the earthwork on the mound and began to walk steadily towards the fort, first down the slope, and then up the gentle incline to the palisades. One had a bit of white cloth on a stick; the other blew his call upon his trumpet.

"All the etiquette of war!" sneered Jonquier to himself. "A flag of truce and a trumpet like one gentleman to another."

He was about to step through the breach to meet them, but checked himself. There was no need to make too much disclosure of the practicability of the gap. He turned back through the kitchen and the hall, and went out through the main door, and round the building to where the trumpeter and the flag of truce were standing at the palisades.

The trumpeter was a Basque, to judge by his round blue cap — some Pyrenean smuggler, doubtless. The other wore some fragments of the blue uniform of one of the mercenary regiments of the Bourbon kings of Spain. Jonquier stopped five yards from them and stood waiting for them to speak. The officer turned to the trumpeter and said something to him, and in turn the trumpeter addressed Jonquier, speaking the vilest French.

"You must surrender," said he.

"I shall not surrender," said Jonquier.

The trumpeter and the officer conferred, and then the trumpeter turned to Jonquier again.

"If you surrender," he said, "we shall grant you your lives. If you do not, you will all be killed. That is what the laws of war say."

"I do not discuss the laws of war with brigands," said Jonquier. "I am an officer of the Emperor. And I trust that when

General Kellermann's dragoons arrive this afternoon, I shall have
the pleasure of seeing you on the end of a rope."

That was the best he could think of in the way of stimulating
the besiegers to make a premature assault. He turned his back
and walked away, striving to be as dignified as possible in the
eyes of his men, whom he knew would be watching this interview from the parapets and loopholes. He trailed his sword and
he stuck out his chest and cocked his shako.

"This is your last chance," called the trumpeter harshly
through the palisades after him.

Jonquier made no sign of having heard and left them to turn
away with no appearance of dignity. Even trifles like that may
affect the spirits of troops.

It is hard to say what motive made Jonquier so obstinate in
the face of death. He cannot have had overwhelming confidence
in his troops to beat off an attack. He had no hope of relief. He
was fighting in a cause in which he did not feel any interest.
Possibly it was sheer blind obstinacy, the obstinacy of a man
who finds a piece of work to his hand and will not abandon it
though it kills him. Perhaps it was fighting madness, or its lat-
terday equivalent, professional pride. But it was hard to associate
either of these qualities with the fat little man — whose blue
tunic rode up in horizontal creases over his belly — despite the
military splendour of his red epaulets and glittering buttons.

Lieutenant Lecamus awaited him anxiously in the refectory,
and the men stood about, wishful to hear what he had to say.

"You had better lie down, men," was what he vouchsafed,
"they will be opening fire again soon."

And then, when they had obeyed, disappointed, he continued:

"You'll soon get your revenge for being shot at. Each of you
can kill six of them, while they come up the slope. But one or
two each will be enough to set them running back again."

His words were emphasized by the bellowing roar once more
of the siege gun on the mound. But no shot hit the fort.

Curious that they should have missed, thought Jonquier.
There came another roar from the gun and still no sound of
the impact of the ball. He went up to the roof where Captain

Dupont still stood with his company crouched behind the parapet. From the roof he could see the explanation. The enemy were
firing grape at the palisades. They were making good practice
too. Jonquier saw a blast of grape hit the ground six feet before
the palisades, tear it up, and then, continuing on, cut off short
a full dozen of the stout posts. Five rounds of grape cut enough
gaps in the palisade for fifty men to make their way through at
once.

Still Jonquier did not care. From the parapet of the roof,
from the bastion, and from the breach itself he could turn a
hundred muskets upon the attackers when they came up over
the glacis. If his men held their weapons straight, the enemy
could not break in. Struck with a new thought, he sent Captain
Dupont's drummer flying down to the servants huddled in the
cellars — renegade Spaniards, all of them. They were to bring
up to the roof all the spare muskets and ammunition. All the
men there could have two muskets each, and the servants could
help with the reloading.

Until this reinforcement arrived, Jonquier was in a fever lest
the assault should be launched before the new arrangement was
settled, but there was no need for this anxiety. The gun in the
breastwork had opened fire again with round shot and was re-
suming its remorseless, monotonous pounding of the walls.

Jonquier left to Dupont the marshalling of the trembling
civilians and went down again to the breach. The whole side wall
was now blasted away and was represented by a long heap of
stones piled up from ground level. The sun was pouring into
the long room, illuminating the chaos within — shattered furniture, huddled corpses, scattered stonework.

The firing was now being directed at the corner of the building, where the walls were trebled in thickness in a solid pillar,
to support the weight of the floors above. At every impact of
a ball the building trembled, and they heard the fall of a little avalanche of stone outside. Jonquier wondered grimly what
would happen when the pillar gave way. He looked out through
the breach to where the gun was firing away, remorselessly, one
shot every four minutes. There was only death or captivity in

store for him if it continued. Yet there was no means of silencing it. Jonquier thought of a sally; he might gather the greater part of the garrison together and charge out and try to capture and damage the gun. But he put the project away as hopeless. There was no possible chance of it succeeding. Two hundred men could not charge across four hundred yards of open country against two thousand enemies. To attempt it would only precipitate the end. The only thing to do was to fight it out to the last where he stood — a determination which suited his temperament admirably. He set his teeth with sullen ferocity.

There was not much longer to wait. One last shot knocked away so much of the supporting pillar that it collapsed with a rending crash. The whole building was full of the sound of smashing rafters. Stones and plaster rained down from above, as the whole angle of the building collapsed. The dust hung thick as a fog round the fort. It seemed for a brief space that the whole structure would fall like a house of cards. The men at the loopholes on the first floor and on the roof were flung down, as the floor heaved beneath them. Then, with a horrid sound, the bell tower which surmounted the angle buckled in the middle and came crashing down onto and through the roof, flinging the look-out sentry in a wide arc a hundred feet to the ground.

Jonquier wiped the blood from his forehead, where it had been cut by a flying chip of stone, and peered through the dust.

"Stand to your arms, men!" he roared. "Here they come!"

Masses of the enemy had broken out from their cover behind the mound, at the roadside, in the ditches. They were racing up the hill. Their wild yells reached Jonquier's consciousness as only a shrill piping — rage and excitement having forced up his blood pressure to such a pitch that his hearing played him tricks. His own stentorian shouts, the reports of the muskets, seemed to him no louder than the sound of children at play.

"Don't fire until you can see the buttons on their clothes!" he yelled. "Aim low!"

But half his men were too numb and dazed to fire. Others loosed off their muskets at hopelessly long ranges. A solid wave of stormers reached the palisades and burst through the gaps.

Only one or two fell to the firing. The others poured forward up to the breach and began to pick their way through the littered stones.

"Back with them!" yelled Jonquier.

With his blood aflame he leaped onto the breach. Somehow he had lost his shako, so that his sparse fair hair gleamed in the sunshine. He plunged down the ruins, sword in hand, but none followed him. He struck some one down and found himself in the midst of enemies. For yards on either side of him Spaniards were pouring up the breach. Some gathered round him and he slashed at them impotently with his sword — an odd, ungainly figure he made with his big belly, plunging about on the heaped stones, cutting at his wary enemies. He felt the blade rasp down a musket barrel. Then he became conscious that some one was shouting at him, the same word, over and over again. They were calling on him to surrender.

"Never!" he said and slashed once more.

Ten yards away a Spaniard dropped on one knee and took aim. The musket cracked and Jonquier fell on his face among the piled-up stones. His little short legs moved pathetically for a moment.

And the breach was won and La Merced was taken. The Spaniards raged through the corridors and the halls and the chapel. They were as merciless as only men can be who have taken a place by storm, as merciless as may be expected of men with uncounted defeats to avenge, with uncounted oppressions to make payment for. Some of the groups they met here and there tried to fight, and some tried to surrender, and each attempt was equally unavailing. The wretched French boys died on the bayonets, or were shot at close range, so that the flash of the muskets scorched their clothes. They were hunted down in the cellars like rats. They were killed as they huddled round the chapel altar. They were flung over the parapets of the roof and were finished off as they writhed with broken bones at the foot of the wall.

Chapter XI

So La Merced was taken, and the passage was won across the Orbigo. Great was the plunder. The cellars were heaped with food — there was enough there to supply the starving Spaniards for a week at least. There were chests of silver coin, the accumulated tribute wrung from unhappy León. There were clothes for the naked and weapons for the unarmed. There was a six-pounder field gun to add to the artillery train of the besiegers, and there were welcome supplies of powder. And lying among the ruins, easily to be found, were the cannon balls that the siege gun had fired at the place. Some were in fragments and useless, but quite half were still round enough to be used again. Ninety rounds had sufficed to batter in the walls of La Merced, and there were still four hundred to load onto the ammunition mules.

And the wine, the vast barrels of last year's vintage, was a delight to these men, who for months had lived lives of severe hardship. It was not long before every nook and cranny of La Merced was filled with shouting, quarrelling groups, who drank and fought and fell asleep and woke to drink again. The natural abstemiousness of the Spaniard and the peasant was forgotten in the flush of victory. By midnight three quarters of the victorious army were dead drunk. The tiniest fraction of the French Army would have won a resounding victory over them, if such had been near, but there was none. There were some among the Spaniards who kept their wits — especially those who had first reached the treasure chests. They must have borne in mind the cry of the irregulars at the beginning of the war — *"Viva Fernando y vamos robando"* — "Long live King Ferdinand and let's go robbing" — for during the night several little parties of men made unobtrusive departure from the fort, with heavy haversacks, which might have emitted the musical jingle of coined silver if they had not been so carefully packed. The disintegrating effect of victory upon undisciplined forces was thus early marked.

But the morning and the rising sun found at least the most important unit of the attacking force still at its posts. The gun still stood in its redoubt, glaring motionless over the earthen parapet. The heavy timbers which had been laid beneath its wheels were splintered and cracked under the shock of the recoil of its ninety discharges. Heaped up beside it were cannon balls in depleted pyramids, opened barrels of powder, all the litter which the gun's crew had hastily left behind, when they ran forward to join in the plunder of the fort. The commanding officers of the army, even, were not there. They were in a peasant's cottage a mile away.

It had been a deadly shot that Jonquier had fired, the one that had flicked those masses of earth from the parapet. Hugh O'Neill had received the full blast of pebbles and sand right in his face, driven with enormous force, as he had stood in the redoubt directing the fire. They had borne him away stunned; the quick blood had masked his face so that Carlos O'Neill did not know the extent of his brother's injuries, while he stayed to continue the battering, and to conduct the parley with the French commander, and to let his yelling hordes loose in the assault when the corner of the fortress collapsed. He did not know how badly Hugh was hurt until the afternoon, when he mounted his big horse and rode back to the cottage, intent on cheering his wounded brother with the news of the success.

Hugh was in no mood to be cheered by any news whatever. Consciousness had returned to him, and all he could think of was the agony in his face and eyes — his eyes were sightless pits of pain from the sand which had been flung into them. There were no medicines, no dressings. The men who were with him could only lave his ragged face with cold water and hold his arms, when his hands sought in his madness to increase the damage done, while he screamed and choked with the pain, uttering horrid unintelligible sounds from the tongue and through the cheeks that the stones had riddled, revealing the shattered stumps of the teeth the stones had broken.

He would have asked them to kill him and end his agonies, Carlos guessed, if he had been able to articulate, and more than once he thought of using the pistol in his belt on this brotherly mercy, but he could not bring himself to do it. He could only sit there beside him, listening to the horrid sounds, until at last pain brought its own relief and Hugh fell unconscious again. Mortification and blood poisoning might in the end save Hugh from his fate, of dragging on his existence blind and with a face no one could see without shuddering, a blinded officer, dependent until the end of his days upon charity.

The gun called insistently for all the attention Carlos could give. The blow must be struck hard and quick, now that the way had been opened for it. There must be no dallying now. The French dominion over the plains must be shattered before they could draw together sufficient forces to parry the blow. Carlos had never been anything other than a soldier. His childhood had been passed in barracks, and his adolescence in the ranks. His father and his grandfather and his great grandfather before him had been soldiers. Family tradition and the professional pride of the soldier by birth forbade him to think of abandoning his task. The possibility never occurred to him. His brother might die of disease or starvation, but he himself must go on. The Government he served was notorious for its inefficiency and its ingratitude, but the soldier does not bear that in mind. He knew nothing, or next to nothing, of the peasants he wished to set free — the monasticism of barracks gave few opportunities to a soldier of meeting the people who found the money to clothe and feed him — but that was beside the point; it was as inconsiderable as the fact that he knew nothing of the men he was to kill. His sole task was to go on fighting. He was undoubtedly glad that the fortune of war had brought him his present important command instead of the obscurity of an artillery captaincy, just as in the old days he had been glad that Fate had given him the dignified occupation of man-killer instead of relegating him to the lowly ranks of farmers or doctors or shopkeepers, but this again had no influence on his decision to continue with his duty. Heredity and environment left him incapable of considering any other course. He must go on fighting as a river must run down-hill.

So that in the morning the soldiers and the brigands who were sleeping off their debauch in and around La Merced were roused by their commander with bitter words. The lash of his tongue drove them back into the ranks, and set the teamsters hurriedly harnessing up the draught animals to the gun, and the muleteers loading their mules again with cannon balls and barrels of powder. The column was formed quickly enough, the Castilian lancers riding ahead, the infantry trailing along the road with no more trace of formation than a flock of sheep. They were over the river at last, pouring forward onto the rich plains, chattering and laughing and singing, while in their midst rode O'Neill on his huge grey horse. He was silent and dry-eyed, although he looked back to the cottage where his brother lay awaiting death in charge of the half-dozen lightly wounded. Behind came the gun, rumbling and clattering along the stony road, with its long team extending fifty yards ahead of it, and the attendant gunners walking at its side, while after it ambled the fifty pack mules of the ammunition train, with their balanced nets of cannon balls or barrels of powder rubbing their raw backs rawer still.

It was a typical day of the Spanish spring, with winter left behind. The sky was a hard blue, with scarcely a cloud, and the sun that glared down upon the plains bore more than a promise of its midsummer tyranny. As far as the eye could reach, the plain rolled away on all sides in gentle undulations, green and pleasant now with the young corn, and only broken here and there by the scattered villages of greyish-brown brick.

Over the plain and into the villages the invasion swept like a flood. Urquiola and his lancers came clattering in. Haughtily they made their demands. Who was there who had shown signs of acquiescing too readily in the French dominion? The villagers pointed to one and another whose fate was sealed. What carts, what draught animals were there? Each village must find food in proportion to its size, twenty loaves to every house, one sheep to every three, delivered immediately in the carts. Money? Communion plate? Powder and shot? All was swept in. Young men of military age? They must join the ranks. The liberation of the plains proceeded satisfactorily.

At the next river there was a force of the enemy, only half a company, a hundred men. They had no fort here to guard the bridge, there was only an entrenched redoubt covering the approaches, in which the garrison could retire on the approach of an enemy; normally the men lived in billets in the village. The garrison had taken refuge here the day before, as soon as they heard the noise of the bombardment of La Merced, like a minute gun proclaiming the end of the French dominion over the province of León.

They had no artillery and little food, and they knew that the message they had sent to the town of León asking for help would bring small response, and they had had a chilly night huddled in the trenches, and when they saw three thousand enemies pouring down the road towards them, their hearts misgave them. Jonquier had died rather than yield; the elderly Lieutenant in command here preferred to yield rather than die. He guessed what must have happened at La Merced, and when he saw the big gun run up and preparation made to batter a gap in his flimsy earthworks, he had one of his white shirts hoisted on a pole in sign of surrender. He had a strong card to play. The bridge behind him was of wood. He would burn it unless their lives were to be spared.

O'Neill rode up to the redoubt on his grey horse, with his interpreter running by his stirrup, and granted the terms demanded without argument; time was valuable now. The garrison marched out, feeling a little sheepish, and laid their arms on the ground while the Spaniards clustered round them. The French had been promised their lives, but they had been promised nothing else. They were stripped of most of their clothes, of their invaluable shoes, of their haversacks and pouches. Finally, half naked and barefooted, they were handed over to a sergeant to escort to the rear.

What their fate was to be was rather worse than the elderly

Lieutenant had ever contemplated. Ferrol was the nearest place where the Spaniards could lodge prisoners in security, and Ferrol was two hundred miles away, beyond the Cantabrian Mountains. French prisoners, barefooted and half naked, guarded by men without the least interest in keeping them alive, would fare badly in a mountain march of two hundred miles through a hostile population. But they were fools, of course, to have expected anything better.

Then the column pressed on, over the wooden bridge. The Asturians and the Galicians, and the Navarrese whom Mina had sent, were prodigious marchers. The regulars — for what the name is worth — of the Princesa Regiment kept up as best they could. The sun began to sink towards the west, behind them. Still they toiled on, down one long incline and up the next. Every little crest they reached displayed the same interminable landscape before them, in which the villages came as welcome but only transient breaks. Still they tramped along the narrow road, sandy here and rocky there, while the sun beat upon their backs and the dust caked upon their mouths, and O'Neill sat silent on his horse in the midst of them.

In the late afternoon there came a sudden flurry of excitement. One of Urquiola's lancers came riding up to the column, and the news he bore caused O'Neill to drive in his spurs and gallop forward hastily to the head of the line. There was cavalry out ahead of them; it might be Kellermann's dreaded dragoons come up from Estremadura. The rumours that León was bare of troops save garrisons might be false. A thousand dragoons, led by the man whose charge had won the Battle of Marengo, would sweep this flimsy infantry away, capture the gun, and bring this expedition to a ridiculous end.

However, O'Neill found his alarm unjustified. There was only a single squadron of French cavalry out on the plain; presumably they were the recruits with remounts whom report had described as detained in León on their way south. Urquiola's two hundred lancers hung round them, neither side daring to subject their shaky troops to the trial of a charge. O'Neill could see the

French commander riding in front of his men, shading his eyes with his hand as he peered forward into the setting sun to ascertain what was this unexpected army pouring into León.

At sight of the French, a yell of defiance went up from the marching infantry. The Spaniards shook their fists and waved their weapons, and called to their enemies to come on. At the sound O'Neill's lips wrinkled in a sneer, although he did not let his men see it. Three times already he had marched with Spanish armies which had yelled defiance at the sight of the enemy and which had called just as eagerly for battle. And every one of those three Spanish armies had been shivered into fragments at the first charge of the French cavalry — brave words forgotten, heroic determinations thrown away, weapons cast aside, running terrified in all directions. O'Neill had no illusions about the quality of this fourth army. Mina's disciplined Navarrese might stand firm. The others would run. He could only hope to achieve anything with this mob by the inglorious method of avoiding all collisions in the open country, attacking garrisons while he might, and hurrying to the shelter of the mountains at the first approach of a field army.

The commander of the French cavalry, having noted the length of the column on the road, and the gun and the wagons at the rear, and the bearing of the troops, and all else concerning which he would have to make report to his master, wheeled his men about and trotted off, Urquiola and his lancers trailing after him at a safe distance. And at the same moment the milk-white spires of León Cathedral, tinged to pale rose in the reflected light of the sunset, showed at last upon the horizon. Not for two long years of war had any Spanish army — save those marching back to captivity in France — set eyes upon them. It was with some consciousness of achievement that O'Neill gave orders for the march to end, for pickets to be sent on up the roads while the men found shelter in billets or bivouacs where they could, and for the gun to be halted under his own supervision in the roadside inn which he decided should be his headquarters for the night.

Chapter XII

O'Neill dined that night in the company of his senior officers; El Platero sat at the foot of the table, uncouth in his stubby black beard — he never seemed to have more or less than four days' growth — and with him were the majors commanding the three battalions of the Princesa Regiment, and Don Cesar Urquiola, and Alvarez, who commanded the Navarrese, all of them light-hearted and gay. They ate the tough chickens with relish and they drank the best wine the worried innkeeper could provide.

This latter individual fluttered round them anxiously. It was nervous work satisfying the wants of the new conquerors; the fact that there was not the least chance of his being paid for this dinner, or for the accommodation of the two hundred men who were billeted in the outbuildings, was the least of his anxieties. His inn had been a favourite rendezvous for young French officers riding out from León, who had even been known to pay for their meals, and he feared lest this should be held to indicate that he was a "Josefino" — one who had become reconciled to Joseph Bonaparte's rule over Spain — and if that were the case, his existence would end abruptly in a noose of a rope.

No wonder he did his poor best to see that his visitors were comfortable, and he eyed with increasing trepidation the stony melancholy of O'Neill, who sat heedless of the gaiety of his companions, drinking glass after glass of wine with no visible effect. The dim candlelight shining on his face showed his expression to be desperately unhappy. He looked out over the heads of his officers and seemingly through the blotched whitewashed walls into the darkness beyond. It was only that morning that he had left his brother blinded and with his face in tatters. And the Irish blood in his veins, small in proportion though it might be, made him specially liable to these fits of brooding melancholy.

Yet there were moments of satisfaction even during this

nightmare depression. They came when his glance wandered out through the window, out to the courtyard lit by the lanterns of the headquarters guard. For there, solid and immovable in the centre of the court, stood the ponderous mass of the gun. O'Neill found something supremely comforting in its presence. He had come to love that colossal eighteen-pounder.

Outside, at the door of the inn, an argument arose. The sound of it drifted into the main room where the officers sat. They could hear men expostulating, and a deep booming voice, unknown to them, overriding the expostulations. Finally the door opened and a Franciscan friar entered. He was a huge, burly man; his hood fell back over his shoulders, revealing a close-cropped head of black hair and a wild tangle of black beard. His greyish-brown robe was in rags so that his bare legs could be seen. His sandalled feet were filthy with road travel. Behind him were visible the frightened innkeeper and an equally frightened Jorge, who were responsible for admitting him.

The huge Franciscan — his head seemed to brush the low ceiling — gazed down at the men around the table and addressed himself without hesitation to O'Neill.

"You are the General of the army?" he demanded.

"Yes," said O'Neill.

"I have a message for you."

O'Neill signed to Jorge to withdraw and close the door, but the friar checked him.

"It does not matter who hears my message," he said. "It is one of good cheer. Go up boldly against León. The walls will fall before you and the atheists will die — will die — will die. The hand of God is at work in León, and those whom God may spare for *you* to kill must be killed without mercy. They were all killed at La Merced?"

"Yes," said O'Neill.

"All? Every one? That is well. But you spared those others to-day at the bridge of Santa Maria. That is evil. The atheists must be slain, and you have spared a hundred of them to fatten in idleness."

El Platero laughed; he knew — none better — how inappropriate a description this was of the prospective fate of the wretched prisoners sent back to Galicia. But his laugh ended on a wrong note, as the Franciscan turned his terrible eyes upon him.

"The hand of God may reach those who laugh in the hour of the Church's agony," said the Franciscan solemnly.

Then he looked deliberately at each person at the table, and each one dropped his eyes before his glance.

"Kill — and spare no one," he said. "Remember that the hand of God is at work in León. I am going on to be the instrument of God elsewhere."

With that, he turned about. They heard him stride down the little passage, and they heard him bless the sentry at the main door as he passed him.

"Who the devil is that?" asked El Platero.

"God knows," replied Urquiola. "Here, innkeeper, innkeeper!"

The worried host came in, wiping his hands nervously on his grey apron.

"Who was that friar?" snapped Urquiola.

"Really, sirs, I do not know for certain. They say — "

"Well?"

"They say that he was one of those that fought at Saragossa. Brother Bernard, the world calls him. They say he is more than human. A year ago Marshal Bessières at Valladolid offered a thousand dollars for his head, and as you see, gentlemen, he has not paid it yet. He was in the city of León for three weeks past. He walked in the streets, but the French did not arrest him. They say he can make himself invisible to French eyes, but I do not know whether that is true."

"Neither do I," said El Platero, with grotesque solemnity.

"That will do, innkeeper," put in O'Neill, unexpectedly, and the innkeeper withdrew, relieved.

O'Neill sat brooding at the head of the table. Suddenly he looked up.

"Gentlemen, I hope you have enjoyed your dinner," he said.

That was one way of dismissing them. El Platero remembered he had to go round the outposts to see that his men were awake.

Urquiola had problems of forage and farriery to solve. The officers bade O'Neill good night; he hardly condescended a monosyllable in reply, still sitting there, with his hands resting on the table, looking into vacancy. They were all a little piqued at this aloofness and grumbled at it as they emerged into the keen night air. The thought was in the minds of all of them that this boy of four and twenty had no business usurping the command over grown men of experience. They had not minded obeying Hugh O'Neill, but this young Carlos . . . It was a pity he was the only artillery officer of them all. Still, that did not make him entirely indispensable. The men would follow him while he gave them victory and plunder, but at the first check . . .

O'Neill, who had not slept for two nights, allowed his forehead to droop down to the table. Among the three thousand men whom chance had brought under his command, there was not one to whom it occurred to see that O'Neill had a bed to sleep in. The groom who had brought in his saddlebags was now comfortably drunk in the cow stall where Gil was tethered. It did not occur to his Spanish mind to seek out any additional duty. It was left to the innkeeper to suggest bed to O'Neill and to bring in a sack of straw and lay it on the floor for him — the innkeeper slept in the pleasant warmth of the kitchen, with his wife and serving maid and ostler and five small children. Now that Hugh O'Neill was disabled, there would be no one to dress the wound which El Bilbanito's knife had made in Carlos O'Neill's arm three weeks before. Fortunately a clean stab heals best when bound up in the blood, so that Carlos had no need now for the sling, and the wound itself was nearly healed and hardly troubled him.

Yet O'Neill's night was disturbed. There were numerous people who urgently wanted to see him, people who had somehow, despite guards and curfew orders, contrived to escape from León and had walked or ridden out to where, as rumour had soon spread the news, the headquarters of the raiding army were to be found. Most of them were pitifully anxious to interview O'Neill. They pressed actual gold — and gold was a very rare commodity in Northern Spain at that time — into Jorge's hand to bribe him into ushering them into O'Neill's room, and once there, they were ready to talk at incredible length. They all had something to explain, they all sought to compensate for past misdeeds. The Spanish interpreter to General Paris, Governor of León, wanted to explain why he had accepted this employment, and why he had translated Paris' brutal proclamations into Spanish. It was done with the most patriotic motives, he assured O'Neill, and in proof of it he was ready to tell O'Neill all he knew about the organization of the French garrisons in the province. The Mayor of León came out; he wanted to explain that he accepted office under the French occupation solely to be able to soften down the French demands upon his long-suffering people. Now he was delighted to be able to tell O'Neill all about the arrangements made for guarding the town in the event of a siege. There were other men most unjustly suspected of having favoured the French cause who were anxious to clear themselves of this charge by denouncing others — some of whom had already made their appearance at headquarters with reciprocal denunciations. Even the principal brothel keeper of León came with a plausible explanation of the hospitality offered to the Army of Occupation.

All night long there was a constant trickle of people out from the town, and O'Neill had to deal with them all. Delegation of authority is a difficult matter with an improvised army, and especially so when internal jealousies are present. O'Neill could leave the cavalry scouting to Urquiola, and the outpost work to El Platero — they could be relied on to do such work well. But it was a very different matter when it came to the business of a staff. The men who might be expected to do staff work well were not to be trusted at all in an army where any one might hope to succeed to the command if he guided chance the right way. O'Neill was acutely conscious that he did not possess the gift, almost essential to a leader of irregulars, of making men love him. Unlike Hugh, who could crack jokes in Gallego and Asturian, and who won the hearts of every one he met, Carlos could only speak his own Castilian and left every one in his army indifferent as to whether he lived or died. He had to watch every move of his subordinates, and he had to lock within his bosom any information which came his way — and he had to reserve for himself, in consequence, the labour of gathering such information.

He was a good soldier, nevertheless. He knew what information he needed, and he did his best to acquire it. In two years of desperate warfare, he had amplified the theoretical knowledge acquired from his father, and in barracks, and in the military college at Zamora. He knew just how much he could ask of his men and how far they could be relied on. Most important of all, he knew what he wanted to do and was utterly determined to do it. There would be neither divided counsels nor dilatory execution in the handling of O'Neill's army.

This was confirmed again the next morning, when an hour before dawn saw the invaders roused from their billets and assembled on the road; by two hours after sunrise Urquiola's lancers were prowling round the walls of León and the infantry were forming up in a mass outside the Benavente Gate. General Paris within the walls was a wily old soldier. He had a thousand men under his command, and he knew well enough that it was an insufficient force to defend a long medieval wall against a serious attack and at the same time hold down a rebellious population of fifteen thousand or more. He intended to make his real defence within the citadel he had built up inside the town, but at the same time he had not the least intention of abandoning walls and city before he was sure that the attackers were capable of capturing them. He was not to be bluffed into yielding an inch prematurely.

It did not take long to convince him that the attacking force was in earnest and had the means to enforce their will. A column of troops, in the brown clothing which now indicated the Spanish Regular Army, marched off round to the east side of the town. Paris' telescope saw that they had scaling ladders with them. Meanwhile, up the road to the Benavente Gate, he saw a big gun come lumbering up. His cavalry reconnaissance had made no mistake when it credited the invaders with siege artillery. The gun was brought up to within a quarter of a mile of the gate and was swung round into position with the utmost deliberation. A train of mules followed behind with ammunition. Through his glass Paris could see an officer on a grey horse directing operations. Presumably that must be the O'Neill he had heard about.

Paris could do nothing to discommode the Spaniards while this was going on. He had no artillery at this point which could have the slightest effect. The flimsy medieval wall was not wide enough to bear big guns, even if he had any to spare, and even if the Emperor who had sent him into the country had condescended to supply him with them. He had two or three two-pounders — "wallpieces" — but they were not accurate enough to have any effect at a quarter of a mile. The besiegers had chosen the weakest spot in the whole circumference.

O'Neill dismounted from his horse and straddled the trail of the gun. His target practice against La Merced two days before had given him an exact knowledge of the capabilities of the gun. It was a beautiful weapon, shooting with an accuracy which had surprised him, accustomed as he was to the rough-and-ready equipment of the Spanish regular artillery. As he looked along the sights, he knew exactly where the shot would hit, and his expectation was fulfilled. The cannon ball crashed into the huge wooden gate exactly over the lock. The timber shattered in all directions. Methodically, O'Neill changed his target. Half a dozen rounds left the whole gate hanging in splinters. The gate had been built up with sandbags behind the timber, but sandbags could not be expected to stand long against eighteen-pound cannon balls hurled against them. At every shot, the shape of the heap changed, as the contents of torn bags at the bottom poured out and full ones from the top came rolling down. Before long the steep-sided mass of sandbags had degenerated into a mere mound, easy to climb and difficult to defend. O'Neill sent one of Urquiola's lancers flying to the Princesa Regiment with the order to attack. Alvarez drew his sword and ran to set himself at the head of his Navarrese. With a yell they all poured forward. To the right of the gate went El Platero; to the left Jorge led the other *guerrilleros*. Their duty was to open musketry fire on the defenders of the wall while Alvarez burst through the gate with his solid column. Yet as they charged forward, they saw spots of colour appearing on the top of the wall. Men up there were waving their arms, waving flags, waving scarves, dancing with delight. General Paris had withdrawn his garrison into the citadel in the nick of time. He was not going to try to defend that wall against an assault and an escalade, with a furious civilian population at his back and only a thousand men all told.

Chapter XIII

THE successful army poured through the steep and narrow streets. The population was mad with joy. Bright shawls waved from the windows. The streets were full of cheering mobs. The men clapped their deliverers on the back, and the women tore their arms and equipment from them and carried them themselves. Patriotic persons and those with guilty consciences rolled barrels of wine out to the street corners and stood with cups in their hands, beseeching passers-by to drink. A bevy of women surrounded O'Neill, stroking the big grey horse, spreading scarves under his feet, kissing O'Neill's hands and even his boots and breeches, if his hands were not attainable.

O'Neill was too preoccupied with urgent business to enter into the spirit of the thing. He had to shout his orders over the heads of the people to where Urquiola rode beside him. The half-dozen troopers who accompanied him went clattering off, each despatched on a separate errand. He was too much of a soldier to allow civilians to delay him when he had a course of action mapped out. The municipal deputation which came to meet him was heard with scant attention, and they pulled long faces when a few brief words in reply told them the number of shoes, and of suits of clothes, and the amount of solid hard cash the city was expected to contribute to the cause, and that within three days. Every householder must be ready to lodge and maintain two soldiers from now on, indefinitely. But O'Neill's final order excited a different kind of interest. There must be a scaffold and the municipal garotte erected within two hours in the Plaza Mayor, and the town executioner must be in attendance.

The news of the request sent a buzz of excitement round the town, for no Spanish fiesta could be really complete without a public execution; when the chapter of the Cathedral heard of it, the arrangements for the celebration of the thanksgiving mass were abruptly cancelled; the clergy would not risk their dignity in hopeless competition with the spectacle.

O'Neill rode off to where, against the north wall, the garrison had concentrated to stand a siege. León could not boast a military citadel, like Burgos, but General Paris had done his best to compensate for the omission. The thick-walled prison and the town hospital stood side by side beyond the Plaza Menor, in complete isolation; he had torn down, long before, one or two houses which offered points of vantage to any who might attack. He had built solid works connecting the two buildings and strengthening weak points. Here with a clear space all round him, with six weeks' provisions in his cellars, and four field guns to keep the mob at a distance, he felt confident that he could beat off any attack until the concentration of outlying garrisons or the despatch of some other army of relief should set him free again.

Paris would have felt happier in his mind if the *guerrilleros* had not possessed a powerful siege gun — as was the case everywhere else, his arrangements had only envisaged a spasmodic attack by an enemy without artillery — but even as things were, he felt few qualms. He had more troops and more guns than Jonquier had at La Merced, and an infinitely stronger fortress whose peculiar construction afforded several concentric rings of defence.

O'Neill, reconnoitring cautiously from an upper window of a house on the corner of the Plaza Menor, recognized the difficulties before him. He could breach those walls with the gun, doubtless, but one breach would not suffice. When that breach was won, the gun would have to be brought up to it to breach the wall behind, and when the prison was finally taken, there would still be the hospital. If the French fought with spirit, there would be bloody fighting and tedious battering — weeks of it, presumably — before the whole place was taken. One gun would do its work so slowly, and in the progress of the siege there was always the chance — particularly at close quarters — of a lucky shot from the besieged, or a well-timed sally, dis-

abling the gun completely. It would be a hard task to keep his
wayward followers up to the effort and the self-sacrifice involved. If once they tired, or if he could not continually gratify
them with success, his army would fall to pieces. There was
some excuse for the gloom which still clouded O'Neill's brow
when he rode back; he bore too heavy a responsibility for a
young man of twenty-four.

At the corner of the Plaza Mayor and the Rambla more
women were awaiting him. But these had not come to kiss his
hands, or to spread shawls under his horse's feet. There were
two or three small children, and a young and lovely woman,
and one or two older women with white hair. They fell on their
knees as he approached and held out clasped hands to him. Un-
consciously he began to rein Gil in as he neared them, but his ear
caught a few words of their petition, and at once he loosened his
reins and drove in his spurs, so that Gil plunged forward again.
They were asking for the life of a man; apparently they had
discovered for whom the garotte was being prepared. O'Neill's
black eyebrows came together, scowling. A young man with the
fate of a kingdom in his hands, called upon to dispense the
power of life and death, does not welcome arguments about his
decisions. He had judged the men guilty and they must die.

The young woman scrambled to her feet and ran and seized
his arm, but he shook her off so that she fell on her face in the
road, and the orderlies clattering behind him had to swerve to
avoid her. He saw the white lips of the old women moving in
prayer, but his ears refused to hear their words.

Alvarez and Captain Elizalde had done good work in the
scant time allowed them, here in the Plaza Mayor. The scaffold
and the garotte stood ready in the centre, with the executioner
and his assistant gracefully at ease — the executioner was seated
in the chair to which he would shortly bind his victims. On one
side of the scaffold were the half-dozen drums of the Princesa
Regiment; on the other, in a vivid mass, were the clergy in their
vestments, with the Bishop at their head, ready to give their
blessings and countenance to this display of justice. Round the

sides of the square, and thronging the windows of the houses, were the population of the town — a thin line of soldiers prevented them from encroaching too near the scaffold.

Alvarez came up and saluted.

"Everything is ready," he said. "Shall I give the word?"

"Yes," said O'Neill.

"There are one or two others," said Alvarez, "besides the ones you had arrested last night. The mob brought them to me, and the town council said they were traitors. I put them in with the rest."

"Quite right," said O'Neill hoarsely.

Alvarez turned and waved his arm to a group of his men who stood, apparently awaiting this signal, round the portal of the Cathedral. They disappeared inside. In the beautiful Cathedral tower a bell began to toll, its deep note vibrating oppressively through the silence of the square. A procession emerged from the Cathedral door. Pablo Vigil, Alvarez' lieutenant, came first, strutting along, much elated by the dignity and solemnity of the occasion. Then, three by three, came the victims and their guards, each man who was to die between two *guerrilleros*. Some were old men and some were young; mostly they were of the type of portly citizen.

O'Neill recognized in most of them the men who had come to plead with him for their lives the night before. He remembered the arguments they had used, one after the other, and the bribes they had offered. Most of them had knelt to plead with him; some of them had wept when, after hearing all they had to say, he had called to the guard and had them locked up.

They had no dignity now, for Alvarez had stripped them to their shirts for greater shame. The wind flapped the garments round their thighs; one or two of them, unable to walk for weakness, were being dragged along by their guards. One of them was shrieking in a high treble. Round the square they went, right round to the Cathedral door again, and then out to the middle, where stood the scaffold. The guards flung the first of them onto the wooden flooring, and the executioners fell upon him and hoisted him, nerveless but resisting feebly, into the chair. They made fast the straps and clasped the iron collar round his neck. The executioner applied himself to the lever, while Alvarez, his showman's instinct working double tides, signed to the drummers. To the roll of the drums, the wretched man's limbs contorted themselves horribly within their bonds. It seemed as if all the thousands watching caught their breath simultaneously. The executioner put all his weight upon the lever and the screw broke the man's neck.

At that moment, something crashed into the square, ploughing up the cobbles, and, ricochetting, crashed into the face of a house. The French were firing field guns from the citadel. There was panic in the square. The crowds of spectators began to push and struggle to get away; the soldiers broke their formation; the executioners hesitated in the midst of the business of taking the corpse out of the garotte. A flash of hope illuminated the features of the unhappy men waiting their turn to die. One of them actually, on his knees and with clasped hands, began to render thanks to God in a cracked voice.

A second cannon ball, pitching near where the first had fallen, intensified the panic. It seemed as if all Alvarez' carefully planned ceremonial was to be stultified. But O'Neill's voice, blaring like the bellowing of a bull, steadied the mob. He sat his horse rigidly in the centre of the square, keeping the big brute still while another shot fell only twenty yards from him. As he pointed out in his terrible voice, only a small part of the Plaza Mayor was exposed to the fire of the guns of the citadel. They were firing straight up the Rambla, and their shot could only reach the small portion of the square which lay in a direct continuation of this road. If the weak-kneed fools in that corner would only move — *quietly* — over to the other side of the square, they would come to no harm and business could proceed.

So it was done. While one side of the square was deserted, the crowds thronged the other three sides, and the executions went on with decency, the drums rolling, the bell tolling, and O'Neill on his horse like an equestrian statue watching the work being done.

This was as severe a blow to French rule of Spain as even the taking of La Merced. When the news of the executions at León went round, no Josefino would feel himself safe. Every Spaniard would think twice before he made himself a tool of the usurper. French rule in Northern Spain could never be so secure in future. The knowledge was a source of satisfaction to O'Neill, but unhappily it is to be doubted if he had been entirely influenced by the need to achieve this result when he ordered the executions. Two years of savage warfare, the overwhelming responsibility of his position, the horrible wounding of his brother, and the present strain upon his nerves had brought out a vein of cruelty which had lain unsuspected within him. The mixture of blood which so often makes for cruelty may have been partly responsible as well, and at La Merced he had ample temptation to acquire the taste for slaughter. O'Neill on his horse was conscious of an inward delicious satisfaction at the sight of the contortions of the men in the garotte, even though he kept his face unmoved. It boded ill for the enemy he had to fight and for the people he had to govern.

With the conclusion of the killings and the approach of evening, the city of León gave itself up to riot and revelry. During eighteen months of French occupation, the people had been subjected to a severe curfew ordinance. The evening life of the streets, in which the Spaniard takes so much delight, had been denied to them, but now, with the French shut up in the citadel, they could swarm here and there as they wished. They did not care that all the Rambla, from the Plaza Menor to the Plaza Mayor, was dangerous ground — the French sent a blast of grape up it whenever there were sufficient saunterers to justify the expenditure of a round of ammunition. They did not care that the peace of the evening was occasionally broken by musket shots, for the Navarrese were distributed in a semicircle in the houses round the citadel and were taking long shots at any sentries who might be visible within. They did not care that the gun, wreathed incongruously in greenery by patriotic ladies, was being dragged by devious alleys to a corner where a working party under O'Neill's own supervision was toiling to build up

solid the lower rooms of two houses to act as a battery for the
bombardment of the morrow.

All the troops were not on duty. There still remained a thousand or two to join in the music and the dancing and light-
hearted merriment, and to console those ladies whose husbands
were at the wars, and to give pleasure to those others who were
fortunate enough to have husbands who were careless or stupid.
Any one might have thought, who saw the gay throngs, that
the war was over, that Spain was set free, instead of that a handful of irregular troops had gained a precarious hold over one
little patch of the vast expanse of Spain. No one minded. No
one could mind who, for the first time for eighteen months, was
not compelled to go to bed at sunset. The night was all too
short for them to wring all the pleasure they wanted out of its
passing hours.

Even morning found them still gay. They demonstrated the
ability of the Spaniard to make merry all night and still be able
to face the day without depression. There was talk of a bull-
fight. The aged, patriotic and wealthy Conde de la Meria was
rumoured to have sent out of the town in search of bulls which
Don Cesar Urquiola's Castilian gentlemen could ride down with
their lances in accordance with the high tradition of Spanish
chivalry — the day of the professional bullfighter on foot was
not yet come, by half a century.

A few of the more military minded and inquisitive among
the inhabitants wandered down to the alleys round the Plaza
Menor to see what was being done in the matter of the siege of
the citadel. They found the soldiers busy barricading the alleys,
knocking loopholes in walls, making ready to beat back the
sorties which O'Neill judged would be launched upon them as
soon as the big gun should open fire. To capture or disable that
gun the French would pour out their blood like water.

He himself had hardly slept again that night. He had lain
down and dozed in snatches now and then in the midst of the
working parties. The lower rooms of the two houses he had
selected were now filled with earth; the gun had been dragged

into the narrow passage between them and earth had been heaped round it so that only its muzzle protruded, concealed as far as might be. At a hundred yards — the range which circumstances dictated — even the light guns of the garrison might disable this, the only siege gun at his disposal.

His heart almost misgave him when he looked out at the massive defences he had to penetrate, the palisades and earthworks and walls, the ditches and escarpments. He remembered with bitter amusement the words of Brother Bernard — "Go up boldly against León — the hand of God is at work in León." Brother Bernard could not be very well versed in siege warfare. There was no chance even of starving out the French, for O'Neill knew that General Paris had filled the cellars of the citadel with food long before. Many people had pressed upon him information regarding the stores there. They had counted the barrels of flour, and the tubs of salted meat, and the sacks of grain, and the barrels of wine which had been accumulated there during the occupation. It was the Spaniards who had had to make up that store; there were people in the town who had had to labour in the milling of the flour. And while the hundred and fifty thousand rations were being accumulated in the citadel, the French had lived on further rations drawn from the luckless countryside. There was not the least chance that the stores might turn out to have been depleted by rash indents upon them to save trouble. Why, before O'Neill's very eyes arose the smoke of the French fires, cooking their morning soup. The two tricolour flags flaunted themselves from the flagstaffs at each end of the long fortress. O'Neill set his teeth and turned away to supervise the completion of the arrangements for the siege. He saw no sign of the hand of God being at work.

By noon he had everything ready. The gun was ready to open fire; its ammunition was hidden away behind masses of earth where no stray shot could find it out. Close at hand a hundred men stood with trusses of straw. These were to be thrown into the prison ditch when an assault was made, after the palisades had been shot down and a breach battered in the west wall of the prison. How many casualties would be incurred, even if

the attack succeeded, O'Neill did not like to consider — and
the greatest success which could be anticipated could only result
in the capture of one twentieth of the citadel. All the open
space of the Plaza Menor would have to be crossed under a fire
of point-blank musketry and of grape and canister from the
artillery. But still, these losses would have to be faced. Perfectly
conscious of what would be the result to him of a severe check,
O'Neill went down to the gun to open fire.

The noise of the gun in that confined space was appalling.
O'Neill and the gun team felt as if their heads were being
beaten open with sledge hammers every time the gun went off.
But the practice was good. A few rounds of grape tore a huge
gap in the palisades, and then O'Neill began with round shot
on the angle on the hospital. He would not direct his fire upon
the main gateway, as the approach there was exposed too much
to cross fire, and he shrewdly expected that within the courtyard, unseen, lay a field gun crammed with canister trained upon
the entrance. He preferred to attack a spot not so easily defended. Round after round crashed against the wall. The bricks
flew at every blow, but owing to the angle of impact, it took
some time before any hole was apparent in the wall.

It was strange that so little return fire was directed upon the
gun by the defenders. There was a light gun in an embrasure
some way down the wall from the point of attack, but it only
fired twice, and each time the aim was dreadfully bad. The
shots only brought down a shower of bricks from the face of
a house twenty yards from the gun. O'Neill could not understand the reason for this silence. A further shot from the big
gun brought down a little cascade of bricks from the angle of
the wall. O'Neill left the gun for a moment, and went up to
the first floor of the house beside it, in order to inspect the
progress of the bombardment without having his view impeded
by smoke.

There seemed to be no sign of life in the citadel. Then suddenly he noticed that one of the two tricolour flags was invisible
now. Some one must have hauled it down. As he looked, wondering, he saw the ponderous hospital gate swing open. He

rushed back down the stairs, shouting to his men — the anticipated sortie must be about to be delivered. Yet so quickly did he move, and so slowly did the door swing open, that by the time he was on ground level again, it was only half open.

But no stream of soldiers yelling "*Vive l'Empéreur*" appeared. There was a distinct pause while O'Neill stood and wondered. Then some one came staggering out round the gate. He walked unsteadily a few yards towards the gap in the palisades and fell down. After him came a few more men, reeling and tottering. One of them, walking like a blind man, fell with a crash over the recumbent figure and made no attempt to rise. Another suddenly doubled up with pain, sat down, and then fell over on his side. Not one of the group succeeded in reaching the palisades. The wondering O'Neill, completely puzzled, suspected a trap and yet, unable to see wherein it lay, stepped out into the open. He strode forward across the open space, and his men began to follow him. Not a shot was fired from the citadel. O'Neill pressed forward through the broken palisades and reached the men writhing on the ground. He could gain no enlightenment from them. He went on, sword in one hand and pistol in the other, through the gate, and under the *porte cochère,* into the courtyard.

Here the sight presented to his gaze was horrible. The courtyard was heaped with men in the last stages of agony. They lay here and there, raving in delirium, torn with pain, vomiting and retching. Some were dead, and they seemed the most fortunate. A field gun, just as he had expected, stood defiantly in the centre of the court facing him, but its crew lay dead around it. The *guerrilleros* would take no farther step forward; they clustered about the gate peering into the yard; most of them were praying and crossing themselves.

O'Neill shook off his superstitious fears. Alone, he opened the door beside him and entered the building. The long room in which he found himself seemed full of groans and cries, and as his eyes grew accustomed to the lessened light, he saw more men in agony writhing under the loopholes, and throughout the citadel he found more tortured humanity — dying men on the staircases, dying men on the parapets, dying men everywhere.

As Brother Bernard had promised, the hand of God had been at work in León — or rather, the white arsenic which he had caused to be mixed with the flour of the garrison's stores had had its effect.

Chapter XIV

THE Leonese knew pity. When they heard the news, they came, men and women alike, to try to care for the unhappy men whose bowels were being seared and torn by the poison within them. But arsenic knows no pity. It slew and slew and went on slaying. Many of the men who did not die at once survived only a few days, lingering until the secondary effects of the poison extinguished the flickering life in their wasted bodies. Only a few score of the garrison survived, bent and crippled. It had been a most notable slaughter, redounding to the credit of Brother Bernard. If a few more patriotic Spaniards would arise who could kill a thousand Frenchmen apiece, the invasion of Spain would end abruptly.

But the fall of León, the capture of the citadel, was an event which was of first-class importance in the course of the war. At the news of it, the whole province shook off its sullen fear of the French and took up arms. Every village contributed its band of half-armed irregulars; it was a rising more violent even than the one which had opened the war — the one which Bessières had extinguished in blood two years before. The other small garrisons scattered through the province were forced to take shelter within their little fortresses, round which prowled the rebels in their thousands, unable to do any harm to the stone walls, but watching and waiting, with the patience of wild animals and the same thirst for blood.

Nevertheless, these peasants had a proper respect for the outward signs of authority, and when a glittering cortège, all hung with orders and dazzling with gold lace, rode down from the mountains of Galicia and across the plains of León, it was received everywhere with deference. The horsemen who composed it seemed to be in a hurry to reach the city of León, and they rode fifty miles along the sandy roads with hardly a halt, clattering up to the town and through the gates with all the pomp and dignity they could display. They drew up outside the palace of the Conde de la Meria, where soldiers lounged before the doors.

"Go and tell Captain O'Neill," said the leader to one of them, "that the Duke of Menjibar, Captain General of León, has arrived."

The soldier made his leisurely way into the palace, and the horsemen sat waiting in their saddles. They had to wait a long time; there seemed to be no great hurry to welcome the Captain General of León or to offer him the subservience which his rank demanded. It was only after a considerable pause that the doors opened and O'Neill emerged. He was still wearing his shabby artillery uniform, but he bore himself very erect. His black eyebrows nearly met above his blue eyes — a danger signal to any who knew him. He took time to walk down the steps and out to where the Duke of Menjibar fumed in his saddle.

"There is some mistake," said O'Neill slowly. "Perhaps the message was delivered to me incorrectly. I know of no Captain General of León."

The Duke of Menjibar was a stout little man with fierce black moustaches. He beat impatiently on the pommel of his saddle.

"I am Captain General of León," he said. "Do you doubt my word?"

"I doubt either your word or your sense," said O'Neill.

"I hold the commission of the Junta," said the Duke. "Must I show it to you to be believed? It will go hard with you if you compel me to."

"From the Junta of Galicia?" asked O'Neill. "There is no Junta of León, nor has been for two years back."

"The Junta of Galicia represents León as well," said the Duke.

"Oh," said O'Neill. "So that discredited gang, loitering at Ferrol a hundred miles from the enemy, presumes to nominate a Captain General for a province it has never set eyes on. I suppose it wants some of the gold we have captured. Or it wants to filch the credit for the conquest of León."

"That is not the way to speak to me, Captain O'Neill. Remember, there are grave charges against you already. Do not add to them."

"Charges?" repeated O'Neill innocently. "Against me?"

"Don't try to fool me any longer," said the Duke testily. "Leave — "

O'Neill's gesture interrupted him. He glanced up at the windows of the palace, whither a wave of O'Neill's hand had directed his gaze, and his words died on his lips. At every window there were soldiers, and every soldier had a musket, and every musket was pointed at the Duke and his followers.

"I have a further message for you from the Junta," said the Duke hastily, playing the last card of his instructions. "In recognition of your services, the Junta is pleased to ignore the charges of mutiny preferred against you by Colonel Casariego. They will be glad to promote you to the rank of Major General, and they will solicit for you from the Central Junta at Cádiz the Order of Carlos III and the title of Conde de la Merced. That is, if I am able to report to them your willingness to act under my orders."

O'Neill's smouldering anger burst into a blaze.

"You try to threaten and you try to bribe," he blared out. "I won't hear another word! Come down from your horse, you poor thing. Come down, or by God . . . ! And you others, come off your horses! Here, Jorge, take them away. Put them in the dungeons under the prison. Set Vadilla and fifty men on guard over them. By God, you fools, I have it in mind to cut off your noses and ears and send you back to your Junta, to tell them what I think of them. Perhaps to-morrow I shall do so — you can wait till then. With your stars and your epaulets — and you've never set eyes on an enemy in your lives. Jorge, take the horses away too. We need remounts."

This was treason of the wildest sort. The news that their Captain General had been clapped into a dungeon would rouse the Galician Junta to transports of rage beyond even those caused by the defection of the Princesa Regiment. Yet O'Neill did not stop there. Even before the keys were turned upon the raging Duke of Menjibar and his suite, he sent messengers to

summon the great men of the city. Coldly, he invited them to
elect a Captain General for León, and coldly he accepted the
office which they hastened to proffer him. With rolling of drums
and blaring of trumpets, the city bailiff proclaimed him Captain General of León, and the printing presses were set to work
reproducing his decrees.

That was not the only function which the Plaza Mayor witnessed during the hectic five days following the fall of the citadel
of León. There were more Josefinos routed out from their hiding
places, to be garotted with great ceremony on the scaffold in
the centre of the square — scaffold and garotte stood there per-
manently now. From the surrounding country others were sent
in too. The peasants of the plains turned fiercely upon all who
had shown any sign of approval of the French occupation. Day
after day little groups of prisoners were brought into the city,
and a word from O'Neill sent them to death in the square.

He never thought of trying them, of hearing what defence
they might advance. The mere fact that they were brought to
his notice, that they crossed his path, made them worthy of
death. His pride, his sense of power and of his own importance,
were swelled to monstrous proportions. He held the unquestioned
power of life and death over a wide province, and the knowledge maddened the young man like a drug. His cruelty grew
with its indulgence. That threat of his to the Duke of Menjibar
about cutting off noses and ears was the smoke which indicated
the fire beneath. His imagination was dark with mental pictures
of horrible public tortures. It was only for five days that the
carnival of death went on in León, but those five days are still
spoken of with lowered breath in the city, and are remembered
even though the cruelties of the Carlist wars and of the revolu-
tions are forgotten.

Perhaps this knowledge of the impermanence of his position
helped to madden him. It could only be a question of days before the French could collect together an army which would
sweep him back into the mountains, where his army would break
up again perforce into fragments, where he would be relegated
to the humble position of *guerrillero* chief with perhaps a hun-

dred followers — and they none too loyal — and where the
Junta of Galicia could call him to account for his actions. The
thought of it brought the blood to his skin and set him vibrating
with rage, so that he wished, like Caligula (of whom he had
never heard) that all the world had but one neck, which he
could sever at a stroke.

The other garrisons of the province had to be reduced, and
that was clearly the work of the Captain General. Especially so,
seeing that to do this called for the use of the big gun, and the
possession of that gun was the outward sign of the lordship of
León, like a king's sceptre. After five days in León, five days of
executions and confiscations and requisitions, O'Neill marched
out again. He took his army with him and his big gun. He left
behind him his puppet council; for he could not trust his army
save under his own eye, while he knew there was not the slightest chance of those terrified civilians doing anything to thwart
him.

There were only six small places which held out against the
Spaniards in León, small fortresses guarding strategical points,
after the fashion of La Merced and Santa Maria. The garrisons
knew the details of the revolt; they had been brought by terrified Josefinos flying to them to take refuge. They knew how
every soul in La Merced had been killed, and how the citadel
of León had fallen, and how every man for miles round was in
arms against their dominion again, and how O'Neill was a devil
in human form, with an insatiable thirst for blood, and with a
siege gun of unbelievable power and accuracy. They were cowed
by the news before even O'Neill came up against them. Santa
Eulalia surrendered the moment that O'Neill appeared before
it, and Mansilla and Saldaña and Carrion as soon as the big gun
began to pound their flimsy defences to pieces. Each place was
sacked in turn, and the French prisoners were sent back towards
Galicia — Heaven knew what chance they had of ever reaching
it, and of being sent across the sea to the sybaritic comfort of
the English hulks and of Dartmoor Prison.

Old General Dufour held out in Benavente for two whole
days; he had a garrison of five hundred men and two concentric

rings of defence. But he had no luck. If he had succeeded in beating back an assault, he might have taken the heart out of the besiegers, but the wild attack of the peasantry and of the *guerrilleros* lapped over his walls and up through the narrow breach. Dufour died sword in hand at the last breach, as Jonquier did, and his men died in holes and corners as the attackers raged through the place.

O'Neill left the place behind, silent, peopled only by the dead, and passed on with the big gun lumbering behind and the peasants flocking to join him. His circular tour had consumed less than a fortnight. In thirteen days he was back in León, marching his army in triumph through the cheering streets and dragging behind him the wretched Spaniards who had been found in the captured places; men and women, peasants and landowners, tailors and cobblers, prostitutes, mistresses, and wives. León gave itself up to a fresh orgy of blood and pleasure.

When they forgot to rejoice, the Leonese found plenty at which to grumble. O'Neill had ten thousand men at his command, now that he had swept the countryside. These ten thousand men had all to be fed and clothed and paid. O'Neill considered that the well-being of his soldiers weighed far heavier in the scale than the suffering of the civilians. Only the best — if there was enough of it — would do for his men; the best boots, the best clothing, meat every day, although before they became soldiers they had rarely eaten meat oftener than once a fortnight. Any one with a little hoard of money or silver plate was compelled to make a free gift of it to the State, which meant to General O'Neill. There was still some to be found, despite the exactions of the French, and O'Neill had little difficulty in discovering it, for his reign of terror produced the inevitable crop of informers. Even the French had not thought of garotting the man who buried his spoons, but then the French could not call such an act "treason," as O'Neill did.

In the forcing heat of present conditions, all the characteristics of a military autocracy developed instantly; the inevitable bloodthirsty leader, trusting no one, with an eye on every department of state and a toadying mob of informers to help him; the usual inner ring of personal guards — lately the bands of Hugh O'Neill and El Bilbanito; the usual soldiery, rapidly learning their power and steadily increasing their demands; the usual ruined civilians, too terrified to murmur openly. In three weeks the government of Carlos O'Neill had reached the pitch which it took Imperial Rome a century to attain.

Possibly O'Neill was the only one of his army with an acute sense of the impermanence of it all. He was aware every minute that by now the French armies would be making a convulsive effort to gather together enough troops to strike him down. Wellington might be loose in the South, hot in pursuit of Masséna's army, reeling back from the lines of Torres Vedras, Soult might be staggering under the fearful blow dealt him at Albuera, King Joseph at Madrid might be trembling on his throne, but all the same they would spare no effort to dispose first of this menace to their communications. Every man that could be collected would be hurled upon him soon, and O'Neill, unlike his men, had not the slightest doubt as to the result.

Characteristically, he went forward to meet his fate, instead of waiting for it to come to him. Moreover, his best policy was to advance. A rebellion on the defensive is doomed for certain, as his military instinct assured him. Perhaps if he were enormously lucky and enormously active, if he rushed upon the great Royal Road which ran through Burgos and Valladolid, he might burst in among his enemies and prolong the struggle long enough for something unexpected to turn up and save him. Any other policy, whether he chose to wait round about León or to try to lead his forces back over the Cantabrian Mountains to reduce the French garrisons along the Biscay coast, meant ultimate certain ruin.

There is room to doubt whether it was these considerations which influenced him in his decision to advance. O'Neill was a fighting man. His whole instinct called upon him to rush upon his enemies, to meet his fate halfway, to go down, if go down he must, with his face to the foe rather than his back.

Chapter XV

TEN thousand men were on the march towards the Royal Road. O'Neill's messengers had summoned them from their billets in the town, and from their cantonments in the villages round about. Not even O'Neill, fount of dynamic energy though he was, had been able to make an army out of them. There was some faint trace of organization; there were the battalions of Mansilla and Saldaña; there were the first and second and third of León, officered somehow by untrained local magnates. Alvarez' band and El Platero's band and O'Neill's band had absorbed all the recruits they could, and more. Don Cesar Urquiola had five hundred cavalry now under his command, mounted on horses captured or requisitioned. But it was much more of a mob than an army.

The very act of concentrating on a single road had led to an incredible muddle. Units approaching by byroads had found their paths blocked by others marching across them, and, sooner than wait, had casually intermingled with the other stream. Some had been late and some had been early. The mass that poured down the road displayed no trace of military organization, despite the cavalry out ahead and the train of artillery in the rear, the six field guns, and the one big siege gun, and the long files of baggage mules. Handling ten thousand men is a very different matter from handling two thousand, and when the greater part of the ten thousand is a mere undisciplined rabble, the task calls for a genius, which was exactly what O'Neill was not.

The fates turned against him. The pleasant spring weather which had prevailed for some time now changed on the very day that the march began. It seemed as if winter had come back again. A cold wind blew from out of the mountains, and it brought with it torrents of icy rain — the kind of rain which can be experienced only in Spain. The road was churned into mud, the ditches overflowed, the wretched soldiers were soaked to the skin. The end of the day's march found them only ten miles from the city, and many of the men went off in the night to seek the comfort of their homes. Of the remainder, few were fortunate enough to have a roof over their heads, and spent a comfortless night lying out in the drenching rain.

And the next day it rained, and all night too, and all the day after; and by this time the eternal commissariat difficulty had arisen again. O'Neill had depended — for lack of any better system — upon supplies gleaned from the district over which they were marching, but it had been plundered and replundered, and when the news of the approach of the vast column was passed round, every one fled from its path as if it bore the plague with it. Three days of rain and two of half rations made even that contingency not unlikely. The effect upon O'Neill was bad indeed. He raged against the delays and the desertions. The evil temper which the blinding of his brother and the responsibilities of his position brought him vented itself in unpleasant ways. He rode his big grey horse up and down the column and struck at the men with his whip, and they did not love him for it. The townsmen among them, and even the long-suffering peasants, did not take kindly to blows. But with the rain soaking his clothes and the icy wind whistling round him, he could not control his temper, even if it had been possible after his weeks of enjoyment of unfettered power.

A mile behind the rear of the column he found the big gun stuck in the mud, buried up to the axles of its five-foot wheels, and Jorge and the rest of El Bilbanito's band toiling to free it. They were all free to work on this one gun, because the others had already been abandoned. It might have been more sensible to leave the heaviest behind and press on with the lightest, but it would not have been in accordance with the tradition of this army. Moreover, with further sieges in prospect, it really would not have been wise to abandon the big gun; they could manage without field guns, but not without the big eighteen-pounder. That was only an academic argument, all the same. No one would have dreamed of abandoning the gun which was the emblem of their new power and future hopes.

Yet they were having a difficult time; the draught mules floundered in the mud, unable to gain a foothold, with the steam of their exertions rising from them in clouds, while Jorge and his men slaved with levers and dragropes to get the gun on the move again. They countered O'Neill's imprecations with dumb insolence and with angry mutterings, according to their several constitutions. Jorge wiped the blood from his neck where O'Neill struck him, but said no word. His mouth still smiled — his mouth was made for smiling — but his brow was black with anger. Some one shouted a curse after O'Neill when he wheeled the grey horse round again and galloped off amid a spatter of mud, but the wind and the rain deafened O'Neill's ears and dulled his senses, so that the curse passed unheard and the man's life was not imperilled.

At midnight that night O'Neill in his headquarters in an inn shouted for the guard, and Jorge came in — circumstances and recent history had imposed upon the combined bands of El Bilbanito and O'Neill the two rôles of siege artillerymen and headquarters guard, with Jorge as general factotum. Jorge, looking round the room, was able to amplify from observation what he had guessed from the loud quarrellings he had heard through the door. O'Neill, white with rage, was seated at a small table at one end of the room; the candlelight lit up his face and revealed the ungovernable rage which distorted it. The other officers were standing here and there about the room, some of them sullen, some of them uneasy, but all of them obviously as angry as O'Neill himself, even if through fear or caution they could not show it. Clearly O'Neill had been dealing out reprimands regarding the marching, and clearly they had been resented.

"Arrest that man!" said O'Neill in a high-pitched voice.

The wild gesture of his arm indicated El Platero, standing mute and solitary in the middle of the room, with his usual four days' beard disfiguring his cheeks. There was a cornered look in his eyes, and he looked here and there sidelong, his hand on his knife. The other officers moved restlessly.

"Arrest him!" repeated O'Neill, his voice rising even higher in the scale. "Lock him up. I shall have him shot."

Jorge stood fast. With one hand he felt the weal on his neck where O'Neill's whip had drawn blood that afternoon. He was slow of thought, was this big-limbed boy, and when he thought, his lips pouted in a rather inane grin.

"Don't stand grinning there," snapped O'Neill. "Take him and put him under guard until morning."

Jorge still stroked his neck. He had arrested many people already at O'Neill's bidding, and sometimes he had made history thereby — the Duke of Menjibar, and the pitiful men who had come out from León the day after La Merced fell, and men in León whom O'Neill had deemed to be traitors; men who had struggled and men who had wept, and women too. He had obeyed because it had never occurred to him to do anything else. But now something else had occurred to him, and the pleasure of reaching a decision broadened his grin.

The others saw his face and their attitudes changed suddenly. They all seemed to draw in a little, ringing O'Neill round like dogs round a wolf. Still no word was spoken until O'Neill broke the silence.

"Why, what is this, gentlemen?" he asked. Bewilderment was taking the place of rage. His voice rang flat now instead of sharp.

El Platero laughed with the relief of tension, but it was left to Urquiola to express the changed views of the assembly. He stepped forward towards O'Neill, resting his fingertips on the table. His spurs rang in the silence. They even heard the creaking of his long gaiters of soft leather reaching up to mid-thigh.

"El Platero will *not* be shot," he said. "He will not be arrested."

Now, too late, O'Neill tried to reassert his authority.

"Is this mutiny?" he roared, glaring round the room.

But in those few seconds the baseless fabric of his omnipotence had fallen to the ground, and nothing could build it up again. Every one had realized that there was no need for any one to obey him — at least, as long as Jorge commanded the guard, and Jorge was unfaithful to him. His choice of words, even, was unfortunate, for it put into the mouths of the others words which they might have flinched from using.

"Yes, it *is* mutiny," said El Platero, and that clinched the matter.

Captain Elizalde sidled up alongside O'Neill and took his sword from his sheath, and the two pistols where they had lain handily on a shelf behind him, O'Neill offering no resistance in his surprise. Only when they were out of his reach did he think of falling sword in hand upon these mutineers and slaying them where they stood; now it was too late.

"Well, gentlemen, what shall we do with him now?" asked Urquiola.

"Keep him to work the gun," said Alvarez — a surprisingly rash suggestion from one so experienced and cautious.

"Never!" said El Platero. "You'll not risk my neck like that. Hang him and save trouble."

"Hang him," said one of the infantry majors, whom O'Neill had insulted before his men yesterday.

The candles flickered in a draught, casting strange shadows on O'Neill's face as he stood there, stock-still, listening to this debate over his life or death.

Don Cesar pulled at his thin, old-fashioned beard, looking from one to the other.

"Can he hurt us if we set him free?" he asked mildly.

"Certainly he might," said El Platero. "I'll not trust him. Remember how his brother brought Princesa over to him. He might get us in his power again. Think what he would do to us then — look at his face."

At El Platero's gesture, they looked at O'Neill's face as none of them had dared up to that moment, and all of them caught the tail end of the expression which had flickered over it. At the thought of the treatment he would like to deal out to them, O'Neill had been unable to keep his face immobile; the mental picture had swept away his stunned apathy.

"Hang him, I say," said El Platero, rubbing in his lesson.

"Send him back to León," suggested Major Volpe. "They know how to use the garotte there."

Several people brightened at that suggestion, because the majority were not at all anxious to risk the obloquy which might reasonably follow the execution of the man who set León free.

"You cannot be sure they would use it on *him*," persisted El Platero. "Though there would be a few who would be glad to."

"To Ferrol, then," said Volpe. "The Junta wouldn't hesitate."

El Platero shook his head.

"Too far," he said. "Too risky."

Don Cesar interposed again, mildly:

"What about the gun, gentlemen? Artillerymen are scarce."

"I can work the gun," said Jorge. Those were actually the first words he had spoken since O'Neill had called him in; up to that time his silence had made history, and now this brief speech of his obviously threw much weight into the scale.

The others looked at Jorge; they were trying to decide if here was another O'Neill, if by entrusting the gun to him they would be setting a new yoke on their necks, all impatient of authority. They could not believe it of this thick-limbed, stupid boy who had forgotten his own surname.

"Of one thing I am sure," said El Platero. "I have never yet wanted to bring back to life any man I have hanged, but twice at least I have regretted allowing a man to live. I don't want this to be the third time."

El Platero was clearly of a more thoughtful and philosophic turn of mind than his appearance would lead one to expect, but then he was older than most of them, and had worked at a highly skilled trade before ever he had become a *guerrillero*.

"What would the men say?" asked Alvarez.

"Mine would not ask questions. You know best about your own. As for the others — if O'Neill is dead before we leave this room, what would they care? What could they do? But if we let him go out from here alive, by this time to-morrow we may all be rotting on trees — if there are enough trees in this God-forgotten plain."

"He would have to answer for my life to Mina," said Alvarez.

"Mina? Do you think he cares about Mina? Mina is in Navarre, and we are on the borders of Castile."

"Why not ask O'Neill what he has to say?" put in Delgado, the junior major of the Princesa Regiment.

"Yes," said Elizalde eagerly.

All eyes turned towards O'Neill again, where he still stood at the table. He had listened almost unbelievingly while they bandied back and forth the pros and cons which would decide whether he should live or die. It was hard for a man to realize that one minute after being undisputed Captain General of León he was in the most pressing imminent danger of dying a criminal's death. But Jorge had never taken his eyes off him, nor his hand from his knife.

O'Neill could only stammer at first. He may have wanted to plead for his life, but he could not do so. It was difficult to find his tongue in the face of this startling change in his position. It was Hugh O'Neill who ought to have met this situation, not Carlos — but Hugh would never have allowed matters to reach this pitch.

"He has little enough to say, you see," sneered El Platero, "this Captain General."

Jorge took a step forward.

With a huge effort, O'Neill pulled himself together. He glanced like a hunted animal from one face to the next, and he found small comfort there. It was their lives or his, and O'Neill knew it too well. He could not gloss over that obvious fact in a ready speech, for he was a man of no words. He could not promise amnesty and forgiveness so as to get himself out of that room to where he could change his mind safely, although possibly a man of glib tongue and no scruples might have persuaded the assembly to agree. He was a man of action, not of words. Finding himself in a trap, his whole instinct was to struggle madly, hopelessly even, like an animal. His fingers closed upon the top of the table in front of him; it was a small, massive piece of furniture, clumsily made out of thick slabs of wood. With it he could dash out brains, smash bones, hack his way to the door. At the prospect of action, the fighting madness inflamed in his veins. He tightened his grip on the table, tautened his muscles, made ready to spring.

Jorge uttered an inarticulate shout of warning just as O'Neill charged. Like the fighting animal he was, O'Neill was guided by his instincts to launch himself upon the decisive point. Whirling the table horizontally to save time, he struck Jorge to the floor before the knife was well out of Jorge's belt. Then, with incredible agility and strength, he shifted his grip upon the clumsy weapon so that he held it by the legs and could make use of its heavy top. Don Cesar Urquiola caught him by the belt from behind as he went by; he tore himself loose and plunged for the door. Some one fired a pistol and missed; in the low narrow room the report sounded like a cannon. Elizalde barred his way; the table top crashed down on his shoulder and felled him. Delgado was before the door with his sword in his hand. O'Neill struck at him, but the table caught on one of the low beams of the ceiling. He struck again and dashed him out of his path. He was reaching for the door handle, when Jorge flung himself along the floor like a snake and gripped his ankle. O'Neill and the table fell together to the floor, on top of Delgado and Jorge and Elizalde. Their bodies tossed and heaved in a wild wrestling match. El Platero rushed in with knife drawn, but before he could strike effectively, a fresh upheaval engulfed him and he, too, fell to the ground, entangled in the struggling bodies. First here and then there the mass of undignified humanity thrashed across the floor. Some prodded at it ineffectively with their swords. Don Cesar held himself aloof from a rough-and-tumble which consorted ill with his Castilian dignity. Some one else saw O'Neill's head emerge from the muddle and kicked it shrewdly with a heavy boot. Others saw their opportunity and, falling on their knees, struck with their knives, over and over again.

And there, on the earthen floor of an inn, the Captain General of León — self-appointed — died. The military despotism he had set up was thus marked, in the best traditions of such a form of rule, by a palace revolution initiated by the defection of the Captain of the Bodyguards.

It had taken much to kill an unarmed man. O'Neill's body bore as many wounds as any Cæsar's, as he lay there in a wide pool of blood in the semi-darkness. Only one candle had survived the struggle, and this stood in its candlestick, with a long sooted wick protruding from its flame, stinking abominably. El Platero snuffed it carefully, and then relit the other candles from it. The other men were recovering from the struggle, breathing hard. Volpe was trying to adjust his tunic, which had been torn right across the breast. Elizalde, gasping with pain, was sitting in the blood on the floor, nursing his shattered shoulder. Don Cesar bent over the body sprawled upon the ground.

"He solved the problem for us," said Don Cesar.

It was perhaps a more kindly epitaph than a dead despot deserved.

Chapter XVI

As though the very elements wished to mark their approval of recent events, the next morning dawned bright and promising. The icy wind had dropped, the rain had ceased, and the sun broke early through the mist to warm the aching limbs of the marching soldiers, and to harden the miry roads, and to comfort the hearts of all. The Army of León was on the march, just as if its General had not died during the night. It continued to sprawl forward across the plains like some shapeless monster — an acephalous monster, now — like some vast amœboid organism trickling over the plains towards the great road from France to Madrid, along which ran the life blood of the French Army.

The many leaders had been wise to keep their several sections on the move. No one was likely to ask questions about a dead general in the course of a long and sultry march, or while recovering from it afterwards — and while the prospect still dangled before them of new conquests to be achieved. Not the stupidest man in the whole army could be unaware of the existence of that road and of its supreme importance in the war; nor could he fail to thrill at the prospect of closing it to French supplies and messages.

Besides, there was little motive for asking questions. El Platero's men obeyed El Platero's orders, and Urquiola's men Urquiola's. No one was specially interested in O'Neill's continued existence. The men who had once formed O'Neill's band, and those who had once formed El Bilbanito's, had grown accustomed to their combined duties as headquarters guard and men of the artillery train, and in consequence, to obedience to Jorge. Their experiences as *guerrilleros* had taught them that too great an interest in the doings of their superiors was unhealthy. Some men had opened their eyes wide at sight of Jorge astride the big grey horse which O'Neill had ridden, but they knew better than to open their mouths as well. There had been no love for O'Neill.

As for Jorge, he was as happy as a king. The sun shone, and he had a good horse under him, and he was undisputed master of the gun. He had come to love that big eighteen-pounder. There seemed to be some fraternal bond between him and it. There was an odd physical resemblance, certainly. Although Jorge, at eighteen, had hardly come yet to his full strength, his figure was immense and square, with vast thews, and on foot there was a roll in his gait queerly like the gun's motion on a rocky road. He loved the gun for its deadly precision, for its crushing power. Its pig-headed obstinacy when being pulled over broken country was to Jorge's mind (which was also somewhat inclined to obstinacy) much more of a virtue than a vice.

As Jorge rode along beside the gun team he felt — even if he was not yet conscious of them — unwonted prickings of ambition within him. He hoped — he even nearly believed — that he was on the high road to eminence as a soldier. Certainly the council of war which had been held the night before over O'Neill's dead body included him in it as a matter of course. It was assumed without question that he was to be responsible for the artillery; as chief of a detachment he could rate himself on an equality with Don Cesar Urquiola, a gentleman of the bluest blood of Castile, or with Alvarez, the most famous of Mina's lieutenants. He could even look down upon the inexperienced country gentlemen who found themselves in command of the battalions of local levies. At a conservative estimate he was not lower than fifth or sixth in the unstated hierarchy of the army. With a little good fortune he might find himself soon in command of all the ten thousand men of the Army of León, able to proclaim himself Captain General if he wished, and with a long future of military glory before him. The prospect more than compensated him for the saddle soreness and stiffness which almost prevented him from walking at the end of the day.

These physical disabilities did not deter him at all from limping round among the men that evening. The mercurial temperament of the mountaineers had risen with the improvement in the weather; perhaps also with the unexplained disappearance of O'Neill; and the mountaineers' light spirits infected the graver men of the plains. The guitars of the South and the bagpipes of the North blended in a raucous discord as the men danced in their bivouacs and billets. There was laughter and merriment, and, perhaps because there was food in plenty in this halting place, perhaps because — as seems barely possible — Jorge's new-born pride communicated itself to the others, every one was newly filled with confidence. On the next day's march the men roared out songs as they tramped along, and the drums rattled and roared with a gaiety they might almost have learned from the French, and Jorge rode along among them, shrinking from contact with the saddle, but rapt in blissful dreams of future triumphs and glory, as unwarrantable as they were ill-defined.

Now they came to the road at last. El Bilbanito had hardly dared to think of reaching the road. O'Neill, before his megalomania overmastered him, had thought of it as a very desirable but hardly attainable ideal. It was Jorge who had finally brought the gun there. It ran as straight as a bullet flies, as far as the eye could reach in either direction across the plain. Fifty miles to the north it had quitted the mountains of the Basque provinces, where Mina and Longa and El Marquesito threatened it; fifty miles to the south it charged the slopes of the Guadarrama, where El Empecinado lurked. For two years no Spanish force had ventured to approach it here, in the heart of Old Castile.

The great roadmakers of the world would not consider it to be a very remarkable road. It was narrow, it was not too durably paved; its gradients were not engineered with particular skill. But for all that, it was a very remarkable road for Spain; if only for the fact that it was the one beneficial public work undertaken during two centuries by the dynasty for which Spain was at that moment so lavishly pouring out her blood. It was the link which joined Spain to Europe; the stages along it, Vittoria, Burgos, Madrid and the rest, marked the flow and the ebb of the Moorish conquest just as they were to mark later on the ebb and the flow of the French conquest. It was at once the main artery and the main nerve of the French Army of Occupation. Along it came the recruits, the stores, the money, and the information which enabled King Joseph to rule in Madrid, and Masséna to confront Wellington in Portugal, and Soult to hold down the opulent South.

In the mountains to the north and south experience and necessity had taught the French to fortify almost every yard of its course; here in the plains there had been no need so far, and small indication of any eventual necessity. But at this vital strategic point, where the road was joined by the byroad from León, and where it crossed the Salas River by a long stone bridge, Bessières had taken the precaution of building a fortress. Here convoys could rest in security, and here was a convenient depot wherein could be concentrated the tribute and the supplies wrung from the surrounding country.

It proved its value now; when the news had come that León had risen in revolt, that the garrisons had been massacred, and that a new Spanish army was pouring down towards the road, the little garrisons of Old Castile had gathered here for protection; the convoys bound south and the convoys bound north had halted here, and measures had been taken to offer a desperate defence while messengers had sped north and south with the alarm, to summon the inevitable armies of relief.

Jorge, filled with a most delicious sense of his own importance, trotted forward on the big grey horse, Urquiola and Alvarez at his side, to reconnoitre this new object of attack. The army stopped to rest, higgledy-piggledy, along five miles of road, save for Urquiola's lancers, who were riding in groups over the plain. The fort did not look as formidable as La Merced, because it did not stand on such a dominating height, nor as the citadel of León, because it could be inspected from a much greater distance. Jorge could see long walls of grey stone, and storehouses within and a central citadel. At the foot of the walls might be a dry ditch, and in the bottom of the ditch might be palisades. Jorge rode forward to confirm these suspicions, Urquiola and Alvarez jingling beside him. There came a puff of smoke from the wall; a cannon ball pitched close to them in a cloud of dust and bounced onward over the plain.

"That was heavy metal," said Alvarez, eyeing the length of the range.

Jorge said nothing. He was so interested in this business of reconnaissance that the fact that he was under fire made no impression on him. He rode on through the sparse corn. Another jet of smoke showed on the wall. This time the ball pitched almost in front of them and ricochetted past them.

"Garcia told us that they have eighteen-pounders mounted on the wall," said Alvarez.

Jorge pressed on through the dust cloud which obscured his view. It was from this side he must make his attack; the other was guarded by the river. As far as he could see, apart from that, one starting point was as good as another on this naked plain. But there might be something, some fold in the ground, some dry watercourse, which might facilitate the attack.

A third shot from the fort screamed close over their heads; they felt the wind of its passage.

"Haven't you seen enough yet?" growled Alvarez anxiously. "There's no sense in being shot at without an object."

He quieted down his plunging horse and addressed himself to Jorge more directly than ever.

"Come back now," he said. "They'll hit us next round."

Jorge shook the hand from his arm and rode diagonally forward still, his attention all concentrated in the unwonted stream of thoughts passing through his mind.

"Then go on, if you want to," said Alvarez. "I shall not come; my men have still need of me. Shall we go back, Don Cesar?"

Urquiola turned his horse without a word, and the two trotted back. Jorge rode on. He approached the river bank on one side of the fort, wheeled the grey horse about and rode round the fort until he neared the river on the other side. They gave up firing eighteen-pounders at him as he came nearer, and opened instead with handier field guns. Several enthusiasts on the wall took their muskets and tried long shots with them; even at three hundred yards it was just possible to hit a man on a horse with a musket, if one fired enough times. Bullets kicked up the dust round his horse's feet. They roused him from his abstraction in the end by wheeling an eighteen-pounder round again and

firing at him with grape. It was long range for grapeshot, but
the aim was good. The bullets tore up the ground all round
him; it seemed for a second as if the grey horse were wading knee-
deep in a river of grape.

Jorge woke like a man from a dream. Miraculously he had
not been hit, nor his horse. He shook his reins and cantered
away, to where half the army had gathered to watch the per-
formance.

"Well?" asked Alvarez, anxiety in his narrow eyes. "Can you
take the place?"

Alvarez and Urquiola had decided that they neither of them
liked the look of the fortress of Salas at all, and they were anxious to thrust the responsibility of a decision upon Jorge's shoulders.

"Of course I can," said Jorge. It never occurred to him that
his marvellous eighteen-pounder could fail.

"Then get to work," said Alvarez. "I will take my men northward up the road to cover you."

Alvarez had by no means sufficient trust in the eighteen-
pounder — or at least in Jorge's management of it — to risk his
men's lives and his own reputation in the attempt.

Jorge found himself there on the road, just out of range of
the big guns, with the siege of a powerful second-class fortress
on his hands. He had never even seen a real fortress before. But
the other commanding officers gathered round him for orders
with pathetic confidence. They looked upon him — as Alvarez
and Urquiola did not — as O'Neill's successor. They were quick
to toady to him, quick to defer to authority, or quick to evade
the responsibility which Jorge assumed without a thought.

Jorge peered down the road under his hand. He was under
the necessity of working out for himself the highly technical art
of siegecraft from first principles. "Parallels" and "approaches"
meant nothing to him at all, but he knew that no troops could
advance against that fortress over that naked plain under the fire
which would be turned on them. But he had heard of trenches
— he had even seen one or two minor trenches dug during the
sieges O'Neill had conducted. By a trench the men could ap-

proach the fort; but naturally the trench must not point directly at it, or the artillery would play straight down it. The trench must point towards some point just outside the fortress, and then at a convenient distance must change direction and point towards the opposite side, and so on, approaching the fort in zigzags. Then, when the trench was close to the fort, the big gun must break the walls, and the infantry rise up out of the trench and storm the breach. A very technical art seems simple when stated in simple terms.

Jorge, positively inspired, rose to greater heights still. If the trenches were to be begun out of cannon range — a mile and a half from the fort, say — and carried forward in zigzags by work at one end only, it would be months before the approaches neared the walls. But Jorge had not been a *guerrillero* all these years for nothing. He had acquired an eye for ground. There were two successive, almost imperceptible undulations in the plain; the crest of either would shelter men from fire. The nearer one was no more than half a mile from the walls. If the trench were to begin there, on a long front, much time and trouble would be saved. True, men coming to and going from it would be under fire, but what was night for if not to conceal besiegers? And when circumstances permitted, they might dig a communication trench for use in daylight.

The first trench would have to be dug at night, too, and Jorge had had a fair experience of military operations at night — trust a *guerrillero* for that. He knew how incredibly easy it was for them to go wrong in the darkness, and he was keenly appreciative of the necessity of making every possible preparation beforehand. If the trench was to be dug at night it must be planned and marked in the daytime. Jorge abruptly issued orders for the cutting of a number of pointed stakes and for strips of white cloth to be tied to them. As night fell, in the last feeble glimmering of daylight, he went out himself to the second fold in the ground and drove those stakes in a long line beneath the tiny crest of the insignificant ridge.

Chapter XVII

A TALENTED engineer officer, set to besiege the fortress of Salas, would have acted just like Jorge. The only difference would have been that the engineer would have had a vocabulary with which to describe his actions. On the first night of the siege, his report would have stated, he would have "broken ground" and "thrown up his first parallel" in "dead ground" half a mile from the fortress. But, just like Jorge, he would have sent forward a "covering party" in skirmishing order to guard against a sortie, and, having lined up his "working party" along the stakes previously driven in, he would have bade them dig like devils, throwing the earth forward in a "parapet," along the very line which Jorge's untutored eye had selected as most suitable.

Perhaps because Jorge's methods were so strictly orthodox the besieged discovered his nocturnal activities at once. They fired a few cannon balls at his workmen, but, not being sure of their aim in the dark, they took to a much more effective weapon. There were four big howitzers within the place, and with these they began dropping shells just over the line of the ridge, whose range was naturally known to them to a yard. They did a good deal of damage. They blew down parapets, they killed workmen half a dozen at a time.

But Jorge's men stuck to it. Some of them were miners, and most of the rest of them had been tillers of the soil until recently. They were accustomed and hardened to digging; more important still, they had never so far besieged a place without taking it. They, in their ignorance, were far from sharing the doubts of Alvarez or Urquiola. They dug with enthusiasm. They dragged their dead comrades out of the way and went on digging. It was not long before the howitzers lost the range, so that the shells only rarely interfered with the work. By dawn there was a long narrow seam of trench all along the fold of the ground, and six hundred men were comfortably settled into it. They were in a state of siege as long as daylight lasted, as much as the garrison of the fortress was, because the artillery fire cut them off from supplies from the rear, but they did not mind that to-day. They rested content and began to reduce the trench to that happy state of filth which made things homelike, while two small working parties began the one to push a communication trench slowly to the rear and the other to sap forward towards the fortress from one flank of the trench.

On this advancing trench, the garrison turned all their guns, big guns, field guns, and howitzers. They knocked down big sections of the parapet and killed a good many of the working party. Even Jorge saw that what the besiegers ought to do was to build a battery somewhere along the line of their "first parallel," arm it with big guns, and so keep down the fire of the fortress. But Jorge had only one eighteen-pounder, and he was not going to risk it in a duel so unequal; he had to reserve it for breaching the wall when the approaches were completed. Perhaps, when the field guns struggled up from the rear, he might use those, although they would be too small to do much damage. Meanwhile men's lives must be sacrificed in the absence of artillery. The murderous work at the sap head proceeded steadily. The sturdy miners dug furiously despite their losses.

Partly their enthusiasm was kindled by Jorge's example. He worked as hard as any; he seemed to be quite indifferent to danger. As a matter of fact, he actually was indifferent. He was so intensely interested in this new enterprise that he quite forgot about the danger he was running. It was something new to him to hold this high command, to bear this great responsibility. It was peculiarly gratifying to see his siege works growing under his eyes. It satisfied his creative impulses.

But while he was so engrossed in the bustle and toil at the sap head, he was suddenly interrupted by a messenger who came pushing his way down the trench to him. The other officers urgently requested his attendance at headquarters. Jorge cursed aloud, but comically, somehow, so that the men digging beside him laughed. With a parting incitement to work harder still he left them, and they cheered him as he went — so much had his popularity grown overnight.

Jorge made his way along the trench, scrambled out over the back, and ran the gauntlet of the enemy's fire as he hastened across the open country. But nobody bothered to fire guns at a single man on foot. At the roadside were Urquiola and Alvarez and Delgado, with half a dozen of Urquiola's lancers; and a man in peasant's clothes was sitting on the ground, his face grey with fatigue. Behind him his small horse, grey with dust, hung his head in exhaustion. Urquiola handed Jorge the note the man had brought, and Jorge looked at it upside down and handed it back.

"What does it say?" asked Jorge, who naturally could not read.

"It is from Brother Bernard," said Urquiola, "the man who put the arsenic in the flour at León."

"I am glad to hear from him again," said Jorge. It was wonderful how his new activity was bringing him out of his previous dumbness.

"There is a regiment of the French Guard marching down from Biscay, he says," said Urquiola. "He is out with all the peasants he can raise — which are not very many."

"Nor likely to be," said Jorge. O'Neill had swept every man he could catch into the ranks of this army now gathered before Salas. "And how many Frenchmen did you say?"

"A regiment," said Urquiola testily.

Jorge, groping in his mind, was just able to recapture his recollection of what a regiment was — two or three battalions; altogether from one to two thousand men.

"Of the Guard," added Alvarez sombrely.

"Yes," said Jorge, "I expect Brother Bernard finds his hands full."

Jorge in his *guerrillero* days had come up against the Guard once or twice, and he knew what kind of soldiers they were.

"Brother Bernard says that there is no stopping them. They march where they will. He asks us for help. He asks us for cannon."

"Cannon?" said Jorge. In his mind's eye he saw the army's field guns embogged and deserted, left without teams fifty miles away. It would be a week before they came up.

"It must be guns," said Alvarez. "What can we do against a regiment of the Guard here on this cursed plain?"

Alvarez could never mention the plains without bitterness. He had learned his soldier's trade under Mina in the mountains of Navarre. But Jorge, just as well as Alvarez, could picture the attempt to engage the Guard on the plains. No Spanish troops, however numerous, could face them. They would shatter any infantry force opposing them; they would beat off any cavalry. They might march unchecked even into Salas, and the addition of their strength to that of the garrison would render a siege impossible; it would, in fact, imperil the whole army.

"How far off are they now?" asked Jorge.

"They were thirty miles away at dawn this morning, when this man left Brother Bernard," said Urquiola.

"Thirty miles? Then they may be here at nightfall. And we must meet them as far from here as we can."

"We know that," snapped Alvarez. "Can you move your gun at once?"

"Yes."

"Then, for God's sake, come now. Don Cesar, are your men ready?"

"Bring my horse!" shouted Jorge to his orderly. Within three days it had grown to be perfectly natural to Jorge to call to a man to bring his horse. The thrill of pleasure which the giving of the order had originally caused him, already growing stale, was quite unnoticed now in the excitement of the moment.

The evils of a divided command were not at all apparent at this crisis. The situation was too simple, the need was too urgent, every one was too enthusiastic in the cause for opinion to be divided or for irresolution to display itself. Soon, drawn by thirty mules, yoked two by two, the big gun was off up the great paved road. On this admirable surface, and under the goadings of the excited muleteers, the mules made prodigious speed. At quite three miles an hour the big gun was dragged along; it crashed and rattled over the inequalities of the *pavé*, rolling about like a ship at sea. After it came thirty mules of the pack train, plodding stolidly along under their vast burdens of cannon balls and powder — some of them (those with careful drivers) bearing a net of forage as well.

Don Cesar's lancers were already clattering up the road far ahead, and hot on their tracks marched Alvarez' Navarrese. The garrison of the fort saw them go, but it was only a detachment, after all. There were still several thousand men in loose formation round the place. A sally at present would be objectless and dangerous.

Chapter XVIII

THE Fourth Regiment of the Fusiliers of the Imperial Guard — the premier regiment of what was colloquially termed the Young Guard — had had a disturbing march. They had been sent over the mountains from Biscay in consequence of the wild rumours which had drifted into that province regarding the situation in León. Even the men in the ranks had heard the fantastic stories; they had heard whispers of universal revolt, of huge Spanish armies, miraculously sprung from the ground, of fortresses taken, and even unbelievable tales of the poisoning of the whole garrison of the citadel of León.

The fact that no messengers came in from León did not do much towards confirming these rumours. The French garrison of every Spanish province was accustomed to being quite isolated from every other province for weeks at a time, thanks to the activities of the *guerrilleros* who lurked in the mountains. It was a usual assumption that no message was safe unless four hundred men at least escorted it. But the rumours had grown insistent, and at last the Military Governor of Biscay had felt compelled to act upon them. Only by pinching and scraping, and by careful redistribution of his garrisons, had he been able to set free a single regiment and launch it over the passes with orders to get into touch at all costs with the troops guarding the main line of communications. Wellington was loose in the South, he knew, and the knowledge was enough to make any French general nervous; moreover, when every available man had already been drawn off to oppose him, there was always this difficulty about finding a sufficient force to reopen communications.

The march of the Fusiliers had all the nightmare quality which characterized the march of small bodies of French troops in Spain. There had been the usual sniping from hillsides, and the usual number of sentries found in the morning with their throats cut. They marched along roads without a soul to be seen; they entered villages without a single inhabitant — everything was left deserted at their approach. The hard-bitten veterans of the Guard took care in every village to see that nothing of value was left behind when they quitted the place, although the loot was poor because every village had been plundered half a dozen times already. It usually happened from carelessness or malice that the villages were set on fire as they marched out.

Down in the plains the conditions seemed more ominous than ever. The number of irregulars hanging round their flanks as they marched apparently increased. They could see gangs of fifty or so marching parallel to them, ready to run at the first attack, but equally ready to cut a straggler's throat or to cut off a small body of marauders, and much too fleet of foot for the heavily laden infantrymen to catch. The march seemed to the men in the ranks like the passage of a swimmer in the sea. No individual droplet of water could offer him any measurable resistance; but the water would close behind him as readily as he cleft it in front, and if he tried to swim too far the water would overpower him in the end.

Then they reached Saldaña, and they knew matters were serious, for where the tricolour had once waved they now saw the red and gold of Spain, and where they had anticipated welcome, they now received musket shots and yells of defiance from the fanatics who had shut themselves up in the place. There was no retaking the place; as the Spaniards had discovered long before, these little fortresses were impregnable to infantry without artillery. The Fusiliers swerved aside and marched to Santa Eulalia, and Santa Eulalia was in the hands of Spaniards, too. Surely León, the capital, with its garrison of a thousand men and its formidable commandant, would still be holding out. But when they marched up the road to León, they found the gates shut against them, and the walls manned by excited mobs who fired off muskets at them at impossible ranges but who could still be relied upon to beat off any attack unsupported by big guns. That impression as if a sea was closing about them was intensified. Already the sea had engulfed many of the rocks where they had hoped to rest awhile.

On their march back to Carrion they met the first real opposition in the field. A few score misguided peasants tried to hold the crossing where the road passed one of the ravines which seam the plain. But it had been folly to suppose that a mere ravine and a few brave men could stop two battalions of the Guard. The Fusiliers rejoiced at the prospect of action. In front one battalion threatened the crossing. Half a mile away the other battalion swarmed down the side of the ravine, fought their way waist deep across the raging water, up the other side, and came down on the flank of the opposition almost before the poor fools realized that their flank might be turned. Some they caught and bayoneted, and the rest ran like hares across the plain — half a squadron of dragoons would have cut them all to pieces, but with Wellington loose in the south, there was not even half a squadron of dragoons to spare in the north.

It was only by the greatest exertions that the officers could prevail on the maddened soldiers to spare two or three of the men they caught. It was of the utmost importance that information should be gathered, and it was only from prisoners that information could be got. The prisoners did not tell willingly, but they talked after a time, after "the question" had been applied to them — a most significant expression. Kept rigidly apart, and questioned by men who had learned how to extract information from recalcitrant Spaniards, and then requestioned on points in which their tales differed, they told all they knew.

Pieced together as far as might be — for the wretched men had only fragmentary knowledge themselves — the story they told was like some fantastic romance of the old chivalry in which the supernatural was inextricably blended with the truth. They told of a marvellous man called O'Neill, who had marched down from the mountains with a great army, and with a new sort of gun which had blown in the gates of the city of León from five miles away. He had ranged the length and breadth of

León, killing all who had offered him opposition, Spaniards and Frenchmen alike. The peasants' hearsay account of the executions in the Plaza Mayor took on the aspect of the multiple human sacrifices of a King of Dahomey. They knew something of the killing of the garrison of La Merced, and a little of the more prolonged, processional massacres of the garrisons which had capitulated and had been marched to the rear. Along with all this, and recurring like a refrain in their account of slaughter and destruction, they kept referring to some one else, vaguely identified as Brother Bernard, who apparently achieved by magic and prayer what was necessary to complete the work which O'Neill's strength had begun. It was from what they told that the Fusiliers were able to guess, with sickening hearts, at the poisoning of the garrison of León. And the peasants agreed that it was on account of orders issued by Brother Bernard that the peasantry were out in opposition to the Fusiliers. He had passed over the country with magic speed, and where he passed the men took arms and stood to fight the French. Finally, as to O'Neill, he had gone on with a great army, a very great army indeed, an enormous army — so said the peasants, whose eyes had not been trained to appreciate the difference between a force of ten thousand men and one of a hundred thousand. He was gone to Madrid to hang King Joseph, and he would take King Ferdinand out of his dungeon and set him on the throne again.

Colonel Baron Laferrière, listening to all this muddle of fact and fiction, had to decide what to make of it. He had to discount some proportion of the obvious exaggeration about the size of O'Neill's army; he had to guess where its next blow might be struck; he had to make up his mind as to what was his duty to do next. Not without reason he was convinced that his men could march through any mass of hastily raised Spanish levies. He made up his mind that the best thing he could do would be to march by crossroads over the plain to the great road. There he would at least be at the place where his troops would do most good; he could complete the circle and march back to

Biscay, if he were wanted there, and, most important of all, he would carry the news of the rising and some facts about it to Burgos on his way.

After a few months of warfare in Spain, every French officer learnt how necessary it was to take every opportunity to carry news — news in those isolated provinces where *guerrilleros* haunted every road was the most precious military requirement that existed; the march of every column had to be modified so that it could escort despatches as well as carry out whatever other function allotted it.

So the Fusiliers of the Guard turned eastward, and marched along the country tracks over the plains. They were a very fine spectacle, in their smart blue tunics and their white breeches and black gaiters. The stream of tall black bearskins, ornamented each with a long, gaudy red feather, poured along the rough tracks; in the centre of the column between the two battalions the band blared away nobly, and the drums thundered and rolled, and overhead on its long staff the silver regimental eagle flashed as it caught the sun. These were the men who had marched into every capital in Europe, the men who had decided the fate of Europe at Wagram. Colonel Baron Laferrière was the man who had headed the charge at Jena which brought down in ruins the greatest military monarchy of the world.

It was ironical that they should now be ringed in by armed peasants. The men of whom the kings of the world went in terror were glad to halt for the night in mud-built villages, where they made their meagre supper of corn looted from the barns, pounded between stones and toasted into tasteless griddle-cakes. And a knife between the ribs killed a sentry of the Guards just as surely as it would the youngest conscript in the Imperial Army.

They were thirteen hundred strong, and the men who scrambled through the fields beside them, who took long shots at intervals into the column, who pestered and worried them so remorselessly, were perhaps less than two hundred. If there had been ten times as many, they would have effected no more, and perhaps their numbers would have tempted them to attempt more and fail; but that was cold comfort to Colonel Baron Laferrière when he saw his big sunburnt men, veterans of Marengo and Austerlitz, tumble over when the muskets squibbed off in a distant ditch.

It was near evening, at the end of one of these nightmare days, when they reached the great road at last. Southward it went like a bullet across the dreary plain towards Madrid; northward it plunged into the mountains, blue in the distant horizon, where lay Burgos, and their friends, and a meat ration, and a rest from this continual sniping. While the men were cooking their evening meal — tearing out doors and window frames for fuel — Colonel Baron Laferrière thought he heard a significant sound to the southward. It was gunfire, he thought, and a man who had heard artillery firing on fifty battle-fields over Europe could not be mistaken. But when he called the other officers' attention to it, they could hear nothing, nor could the Sergeant Major, when he was consulted. Even the Colonel could hear nothing again now. He felt he must have been mistaken, although he could not really believe it. Truly he could hear nothing now; Jorge had by now turned his horse away from the fortress of Salas and the garrison had ceased trying to hit with grape the fool on the grey horse who had ridden so close up to their walls.

Yet in the night the Adjutant came and woke the Colonel where he lay wrapped in his cloak in the flea-ridden inn. Out in the courtyard several officers and men were listening intently. As the Colonel joined them, he was quite certain that he heard the distant thud-thud of guns. A chorus of exclamations from the listeners confirmed him in his belief. The Sergeant Major lifted his head from the drum on which he had laid it and announced positively that there was firing somewhere to the south. Every one listened again. In the still night the sound came to them clearly enough — the garrison of Salas was firing at the first parallel which was being thrown up under Jorge's direction.

Colonel Baron Laferrière had no difficulty next morning in deciding what he ought to do. Thirty miles down the road was the fortress of Salas, one of the most important posts on all the Royal Road. The gunfire — men still affirmed that they heard it, despite the bustle of the regiment's getting under arms — showed that Salas was beleaguered, presumably by the Leonese rabble which this unknown O'Neill had organized. Salas, Laferrière knew, was well provisioned — many were the convoys he had helped to escort thither — and with an adequate garrison ought to hold out indefinitely. Yet he could not be sure that the garrison was adequate. It was of the first importance that he should march on there to reinforce it, breaking through the mob of besiegers. Then Salas would be safe until a real relieving force came up from the south.

The orders that Colonel Baron Laferrière gave on parade that morning turned the head of the column down the road towards Salas, instead of up it towards Burgos. It was then that Brother Bernard sent off his only horseman with the news to the Leonese army, while he himself mounted on his little white mule — his feet almost touched the ground on either side — to stimulate his peasantry into delaying the march of the French. Brother Bernard was quite as well aware of the importance of Salas as was Colonel Baron Laferrière.

The Fusiliers of the Guard marched southward down the great road. Still the pestilent irregulars pursued them. They acted more recklessly than usual, all the same. Several of them stayed firing until too late from the ditches and dry watercourses in which they had hidden themselves, and were caught by the advance guard and killed. All through the morning the Fusiliers saw in full view the leader of these pests — a monk in a greyish-brown robe astride a white mule. Once he approached so close that the Colonel departed from his rigid rule of paying no attention to irregulars, and, halting the column, had the leading platoon fire a volley at him. But he trotted off quite unharmed through the gust of bullets; it was a waste of five minutes and fifty rounds.

Then, as the weary morning wore on, and the heat of the sun grew more crushing, a new enemy appeared. A long column of horsemen came trotting up the road towards them, and, as they drew near, they spread out over the plain in little squad-rons, ringing in the marching column from a safe distance. The Colonel cared nothing for them; they were no danger, but merely an additional nuisance. There were no Spanish cavalry in existence which could charge five hundred men together, and these poor levies, on their Lilliputian horses, could do his regi-ment no harm as long as it kept closed and ready to form square in the event of a rush. But they were undoubtedly a nuisance. The Fusiliers had to abandon their comfortable marching order in column of sixes and form quarter column of companies astride the road, slowing their rate of march and worrying the men with the need for careful dressing and distancing. And the endangered flank-guards and advance-guard had to be called in, so that the irregulars on foot could creep in close to the column and fire into the vulnerable masses.

Chapter XIX

JORGE left the gun and the ammunition train making its slow way up the road, and, digging his heels into the grey horse's sides, galloped on ahead whither Urquiola and Alvarez had vanished over the grey-green plain. Thoughts and ideas were pouring through his mind like a millstream. He knew nothing of textbook principles of war; he had never heard of "the intelligent combination of the three arms" or any of the other ideals held up before aspiring generals. But he knew that ahead of him was an enemy whom the cavalry could not break, whom the infantry could not face, but who would be quite helpless before a skilful employment of the big gun which he so dearly loved. So engrossed was he with the plan of action which he was evolving in his slow brain that he never noticed the agony which riding caused his skinned and blistered body.

He was looking for a safe ambush for the gun — a place from which he could open fire unexpectedly and at close range, and yet have time to fire a dozen rounds without having to fight for his life. As he urged the big grey horse up the road, his eyes swept the plain to left and to right, in search of the sort of place he had in mind. He found it a couple of miles higher up.

Here a steep-banked ravine seamed the plain, crossing the road at an acute angle. It was not in the least impassable to infantry, but it would be an awkward obstacle, causing delay and disorder. The massive stone bridge by which the road crossed it was far too solid a structure for him to think of destroying in the hour which was all he had to spare; but the destruction of the bridge was not essential to his plan. For on the near side of the ravine, where it flanked the road beyond the bridge, stood a solitary cottage, of the usual sun-dried brick, with beside it some sort of cow house of the same material.

Jorge urged the big horse through the crops towards the cottage, clattering up to the door. There were two young women

working in the field near at hand who looked up, and an old
bent woman came out through the door at the sound of his
approach, with two small children clinging to her skirts. Jorge
gave them neither word nor look — possibly he did not even
see them — and the children looked at him wondering as he
wheeled the big grey horse here and there, riding round the
cowshed and the dungheap, taking in the details of the position
before he turned his horse's head back to the road and rode like
the wind to set his plan in motion.

Alvarez, wondering how he could use his Navarrese infantry
with their untrustworthy leaven of Leonese levies in this featureless plain against this solid mass of disciplined troops, heard
the hoof-beats of the grey horse as it came up to him at frantic
speed. Jorge reined the sweating animal up beside him; his eyes
blazed strangely out of his face caked with dust and sweat. He
poured out his plan. Excitement lent him unwonted eloquence.
Even Alvarez, the sceptical and cautious, took fire. It was at
least a plan, while Alvarez had none to offer. Within five minutes four hundred of Alvarez' men were marching back down
the road again as fast as they could set foot to the ground,
under the burning sun, to the bridge they had crossed an hour
before.

Jorge gave no thought to the scene before him. He did not
spare the Fusiliers of the Guard the grace of a glance. The visual
imagination which excitement and action had roused in him had
pictured the whole scene before he set eyes on it — the long
beautiful lines of bearskins and plumes moving regularly across
the plain, the eagle flashing overhead, the bayonets gleaming
through the dust; and the knots of horsemen prowling round
out of range, helpless and disconsolate.

He found Urquiola riding with a hundred of his Castilians,
grimy pennons fluttering from the lance points. Two years before Urquiola would have charged them, to red ruin and certain
death, but in two years of war Urquiola had learned that it
was folly to charge on these weakly horses against unshaken infantry. But it was a bitter pill to swallow, to follow these
French like jackals, picking up the stragglers who fell out with

sunstroke, and apart from that acting more like an escort of honour than like an enemy, as they made their triumphant way to Salas.

To Urquiola Jorge poured out his plan again. With a sweep of his arm he pointed out the features of the land — it was strange how quickly Jorge had acquired the General's eye for country — and next minute another detachment of lancers were trotting off along the route Jorge had pointed out, turning the end of the ravine so as to be on the farther side before the French could reach it. Then Jorge galloped back down the road again to where the gun was lumbering up towards him; he was wild with panic lest he had not time to get all things ordered before the French should reach the ravine.

The children at the cottage had not yet ceased from asking questions about the man on the big grey horse who had galloped up and galloped away again — questions which their grandmother could not answer — when things began to happen which ended their questions. A long double line of mules came tugging and straining over the field to the cottage, drawing after them an immense cannon. The sweating men who goaded the mules said something to their grandmother which sent the poor old lady into a terrible panic. Their mother and their aunt came running in from the field and began despairingly to bundle together pots and pans and the treasures of the household, but when the man on the grey horse came up they had to leave off doing this and hurry out of the cottage with the children, aimlessly out across the fields. The children whimpered and struggled vainly as they were dragged away. They wanted to stay and see what was going to happen and to hear the big cannon fired; already, with shouts and gaspings for breath, it had been hauled through the yard and wheeled round beside the cottage wall, so that its long grim muzzle pointed out round the corner. There were other men, too, who came clattering into the cottage, and broke holes in the walls, and who loaded their guns with long ramrods, and who turned the precious goats loose, and who yet had time and thought to spare to wring the chickens' necks and hang the bodies to their belts.

Jorge had found time for everything. The gun was well concealed between the cottage and the dungheap. The cottage was garrisoned; the banks of the ravine were lined with skirmishers. Urquiola and his lancers were waiting ready in line two hundred yards away. Jorge loaded the gun with care. He was meticulous about the ladle of gunpowder which was scooped into the gun muzzle and rammed carefully down. He saw that the touchhole was filled with loose powder. He rammed down with his own hands one of the long cylindrical tin boxes filled with musket balls, which constituted the projectile known as "canister" — Jorge had never seen canister used in action before. Close beside the gun stood an additional dozen rounds of canister, a dozen of grape, a dozen of roundshot. A ladleful of powder was ready for instant reloading. There were two slowmatches ready burning — Spanish slowmatch was unreliable material, with a distressing habit of going out at a crucial moment. The mules had all been sent half a mile away, so that in the event of disaster they would not be captured, and the French would have no means of dragging away the big gun. For the last time Jorge looked along the sights of the gun and saw that it bore exactly on the point of the road nearest the cottage.

The Fourth Regiment of the Fusiliers of the Guard came marching steadily over the plain. The afternoon was well advanced now, and they had been marching since dawn under a burning sun. They had eaten nothing since morning, and all they had drunk had been the contents of their water bottles. One or two men had collapsed under the strain. One or two men had been killed by long shots. One or two wounded were being carried on the officers' horses — no wounded could possibly be abandoned to the mercy of Spanish irregulars.

But the honour of the Imperial Guard was involved. At the thought of that, the big, sunburnt, moustached soldiers pulled themselves erect again under their heavy burdens, as a child will wipe his eyes when told that no really big boy ever cries. Their officers told them that their troubles were nearly over, that Salas lay only six miles ahead, and that in Salas they would find rest, and security, and food, and a bottle of wine for every man. They marched on hopefully.

At the sight of the ravine, and the bridge, and the cottage,

with the enemy drawing in closely at this point, Colonel Laferrière realized that it was here that the enemy had decided
to make his decisive stand; and the Colonel's heart grew propor-
tionately lighter. The ravine was not the sort of obstacle which
would stop his hard-bitten men. They would shatter the enemy's
line at the bridge, and with any sort of good fortune they would
deal the enemy such a blow that they would not be molested
again that day. He would have to guard his rear while attacking
in front, and it might be better to give his men ten minutes'
rest before sending them forward, but his troubles were over,
he thought. At his word the long lines of plumes stood fast, and
the men wiped their sweating faces, and saw to the priming of
their muskets, and looked forward expectantly to taking their
revenge on the Spaniards.

Then the drums rolled, wilder and wilder in the *pas de charge*.
The officers moved out to the front, with their swords flashing
in the sun. The long lines came forward like walls. The company
of *voltigeurs* ran out ahead, the green plumes waving gallantly, to
the edge of the ravine, and the solid lines followed them. Jorge
squinted along the sights of the gun. He blew the smouldering
slowmatch into a brisker glow, and pressed it into the touchhole.

An eighteen-pounder round of canister contained four hundred musket balls. The thin tin box which held them served to
lessen their spread just a little, like the choke bore of a shotgun.
Four hundred bullets were flung at once with precision into the
flank of the advancing lines. No infantry battalion — not even
an English one — could have fired a volley of such deadliness. The
Guard staggered with the shock.

The gunners tried to peer through the billowing smoke to see
the effect of the shot, and those who could see raised a cheer at
the destruction it had caused, but Jorge, cursing at the top of his
voice, recalled them to their duty. Already he had wiped out the
gun. He ladled the powder into the muzzle and forced it down
with the rammer and the wad. He swung a new canister into the
gun and rammed that. He flung his weight upon the breech, as if
by his own unaided exertions he would run the gun up into position again. They helped him wildly. The muzzle of the gun peered

forward round the corner of the cottage again. Jorge looked along the sights, turned the lateral adjusting screw half a turn, looked again, and then, grabbing a handful of powder, scattered it over the touchhole. He caught up the slowmatch and fired the gun. It roared out deafeningly, with the smoke pouring over them all. One born fool had forgotten to get out of the way of the recoil and lay shrieking with his leg under the wheel, but no one minded about that. Their business was to load and fire the gun as fast as it could be done.

The massed Fusiliers reeled as though every single man had been hit. Jorge had made "intelligent use" not merely of the "three arms" but of the general's fourth great weapon, surprise. No one had anticipated that blast of gunfire from the edge of that cottage. Not for the last year had the French in Northern Spain encountered artillery in Spanish hands in the field. An eighteen-pounder canister can tear fearful gaps in massed infantry; and canister fired in from behind a flank, when an attack is about to be made to the front, is the most staggering of all.

There were a few young soldiers among the Guard; they tried to edge away from the merciless fire. The stoutest hearts — and the thickest heads — were bent on pursuing the attack, and pressing forward to the ravine across which the *voltigeurs* were already exchanging shots with the Spaniards. The more intelligent and less disciplined tried to alter the direction of the attack so as to rush the gun which was doing the damage. Into this wavering confusion came the fourth discharge to complete it. The Colonel fell dead from his horse. The eagle fell in a wide arc, as the standard bearer collapsed, riddled with bullets. Some one else — one of the men who can be found to display Quixotic gallantry in any regiment — raised it up again.

But the mischief was done. After lurching in indecision, the Guard began to move slowly away, along the ravine, away from the gun. No one directed the movement, no one ordered it, but all followed it. The old formation had disappeared. There were no more rigid lines. Even the two battalions were hopelessly intermingled. It was only a vast mob which stumbled over the plain.

The Spaniards yelled with triumph. They closed round the

shattered regiment like jackals round a wounded lion, firing at close range into the clumsy mass.

Jorge eyed the lengthening distance between his gun and the target and called for grapeshot. An eighteen-pound round of grape contains only thirty balls, each a little more than half a pound each, but thirty balls, each claiming its two or three victims, can smash a hole in a mass of human bodies. Jorge felt the inspiration of warfare boiling up inside him more furiously even than before. He called to his gun's crew to go on firing, rushed round the cottage to where the grey horse was tethered, and hauled himself into the saddle. Next moment he was galloping to the ravine. The good horse steadied himself at the obstacle and then leaped it like a stag. Jorge lost stirrups and reins and all, but he grabbed the saddle, regained his seat by a miracle and came flying up to where fifty of Urquiola's lancers were trotting cautiously after the French. Jorge shrieked "Come on!" to them, as he tore by, and they followed him. The lances came down to the horizontal, the sound of the hoof-beats rose to a roar through which the sound of the wind in the lance pennons could be distinctly heard.

A fresh blast of grape crashed into the mass of men and Jorge rode for the gap. Some of the Frenchmen — men who had beaten off the charge of the Russian Imperial cavalry at Austerlitz — faced about and raised their muskets, but it was only a few spattering shots which met the charge. The grey horse, badly wounded, rose on its hind legs and then came down among the Fusiliers, kicking and struggling. Jorge, dazed, stupefied, without even a weapon, rolled in among them. But the lancers with that example before them charged home for the first time in their lives. The very pennons were soaked in the blood of Frenchmen. The impact of fifty galloping horses clove the mob into two parts, and each part disintegrated into smaller parts, into little groups that surrendered, into little groups that closed back to back and fought to the last, into isolated men stricken with panic, who tried to run away over the plain through the victory-maddened Spaniards.

It was a pitiful sight to see the fine tall guardsmen in all the glory of bearskins and scarlet plumes and manly moustaches asking for their lives from the tatterdemalion semi-savages who seized them, but it was just as pitiful to see the others who scorned to ask for mercy being shot down one by one by the prowling *guerrilleros* who would not close.

Chapter XX

THE gun had won another victory. Previously it had only beaten down walls; but now it had beaten down discipline, organization, *esprit de corps*. It was a most resounding achievement. A whole regiment of the Imperial Guard had been destroyed. There would be a gap in the next army list to be issued in Paris. In the Almanac Imperial the name of Colonel Laferrière would have to be erased from the list of bearers of the Grand Cross of the Legion of Honour — his star was now borne upon the breast of a woman of the fields, who had received it from her lover who told a great tale of how he had won it in single combat hand to hand with the Colonel himself. The eagle was in the hands of the victors, and was borne in triumph at the head of Alvarez' men, when they marched back to Salas.

Despite all this, Jorge did not seem to be spoilt by success. He was the same grinning giant, cracking the same jokes with the men who cheered him as the author of their triumph. For Jorge, although he might yearn for military distinction, could not visualize himself as a great man and had no touchy sense of his own dignity. When some enthusiast offered him a captured horse — most valuable personal plunder — to replace the dead grey, he was actually embarrassed by the magnitude of the gift, but fortunately he remembered he had in his pocket the purse which he had taken from O'Neill's body, and he filled the man's hands with gold; he had never seen gold, save in the Cathedral of Santiago, until the war began, and he was conscious of a feeling of strangeness as he made the gesture. He shook off the awkwardness by a couple of jokes about those parts of his body which had no skin left on them, as he climbed up into the saddle.

It was only ten hours since he had set the gun in motion up the road from Salas, but it seemed like a week. The fields were littered with dead men, and there were heaps of wounded to mark the place where the blasts of canister had reached their mark.

Some of them were still able to call for help; they had been thirsty before they had been wounded, and only God knew how they felt now. But they would not be thirsty long. The irregulars were going over the plain, systematically, stripping the bodies, emptying pockets, and bringing rest to the wounded. Brother Bernard was among them. He took his spiritual duties seriously. As far as Latin and the wounded men's Spanish would permit, he confessed the wounded, and performed all the necessary offices before he cut their throats.

No one saw anything odd about that; irreligion had never been fashionable in Spain, and it was important to save souls, while as Brother Bernard's followers had never heard that there were such things as customs and usages of war, they assumed that it was purely a matter of taste whether a helpless enemy's life should be spared or not. That Brother Bernard should cut a man's throat — in warfare, of course, not in civil life — meant no more and no less to their opinion of him than that he should wring a chicken's neck.

And Jorge was only eighteen, and he had been fighting since he was sixteen. Death was a commonplace to him, and he did not set the value on life which old age does. It did not move him in the least to pity to think of all those splendid men dead by his own act, and the huddled mass of prisoners doomed to a lingering death on the long march back to León and the mountains. He was merely elated at his own success, and he was still more pleased when he found that the whole force — Alvarez and Urquiola included — were awaiting his decision as to what should be done next. He had no hesitation in deciding to move back at once to continue the siege.

Alvarez and Urquiola had enough consideration for their own dignity not to come and ask for orders; but when Jorge gave the word for the gun to be got back onto the road for Salas, they went off hastily to their own contingents and issued similar orders. They knew that their men knew who had won the victory, and, at least until the glamour wore off, they knew that it would be as well to conform to his movements.

The victors rejoined the besiegers of Salas before the one survivor of the vanquished joined the besieged. Lieutenant Aubard, assistant adjutant of the Fourth Fusiliers of the Guard, had not meant to desert his regiment. He had wanted to die with them, although it was dreadful to die in such a fashion in an obscure skirmish in Spain, with the Emperor eight hundred miles away. There had indeed been occasions when young Aubard had imagined himself being killed in action, but it had always involved a charge under the Emperor's own eye, on a field which would decide the fate of the world, with half a column devoted to his exploit in the *Moniteur* afterwards.

Aubard was the only man of the Fusiliers left mounted when the square broke. A rush of the Spanish lancers carried him away. He fought his way clear and rode to join the nearest rallying-group, but it surrendered before he reached it. He rode to join another and was chased by a dozen yelling lancers. His splendid thoroughbred soon outdistanced their Lilliputian mounts, but he found himself a long way from the nearest French infantry by the time he had shaken off his pursuers. Then some irregular infantry began firing long shots at him, and he had to make a wide detour round them. Then more of the lancers crossed his path and headed him off. He saw the silver eagle which towered above one group of the Guard fall a second time, and it did not rise again.

He sat his horse disconsolate, the sword he was so proud of dangling idly in his hand, as he saw the last flurry of the battle under the scorching sun across the grey-green plain. Presumably he still could, had he chosen, have ridden into the Spanish ranks and hacked away with his sword until some one killed him, but it was not easy to decide to do it. No one could blame Aubard — he did not even blame himself — for wheeling his horse round and riding away from the scene of the defeat.

He was only twenty, and he wept as he rode away. The tears rolled down his cheeks. All that he had once been so proud of now seemed to be a mockery. His nodding bearskin and its scarlet plume, his blue uniform with its silver lace, his little scrubby moustache, so carefully tended — for no one might disfigure the ranks of the Guard with a bare upper lip — were all hateful to him now. It was not until an hour later, when his life was in danger again, that he forgot his unhappiness.

Aubard found a place where he could get his horse across the ravine. He rode hard for Salas; he nearly rode straight into a party of foragers from the besieging force, and was chased away along the Salas River. Forcing himself to be calm, he reined in his horse when he was once more safe and looked back at the distant fortress. The dust along the high road indicated the spot where the covering force — the force which had destroyed the Fusiliers — was marching back to join in the siege again. Besides them, there seemed to be several thousand men still round the fortress.

But to reach Salas was his only hope. Alone, and wearing his conspicuous uniform, he could not dream of riding back across León, or of riding forward over forty miles of unknown country to Valladolid. His one chance was that there was no strong force of the enemy on the other side of the Salas River opposite the fort.

Aubard reached Salas in safety in the end. He had to ride a long way up one bank of the river before he found a place to cross, and then he had to ride a long way back down the other side. Then at nightfall he had to turn his horse loose and scramble down the ravine to the rushing water in its rocky bed, and in the darkness he had to make his way, stumbling and slipping in his heavy boots along the stream to where the fortress towered above the bank. Then he climbed the bank with fearful difficulty — expecting every second to be observed and shot from the other side — and then, cowering at the foot of the wall, he had to call quietly until he attracted a sentry's attention, taking his chance lest the sentry should be one of the kind that fires first and challenges afterwards. He was nearly weeping again, with hunger and fatigue and cold, before they opened a postern to him and led him in to where General Meyronnet was waiting for news.

For Aubard had achieved something at least that day. He had brought the first authentic news out of León, the first real information which for three weeks or more had been able to trickle through the cordon of irregulars which the rebellion had called into being.

Chapter XXI

GENERAL COUNT DARPHIN woke with difficulty and realized that some one was pounding on his bedroom door.

"Who the devil's that?" he shouted, inhospitably.

"It's me, Guillermin," said some one on the other side of the door.

"Oh, to hell with you," said Count Darphin to himself, closing his eyes and promptly forgetting that Colonel Guillermin was anywhere near.

"Can't I come in? It's important," persisted the pestilent Guillermin.

"Er — what?" asked Darphin, waking up again with a jerk.

"I want to come in," said Guillermin.

"Confound these enthusiasts," said Darphin to himself. He heaved himself out of bed, scuttled in his shirt across the floor and unlocked the door, and scuttled promptly back again and dived back into the warm comfort of the bed. It was still some time before dawn; only the faintest light was creeping in through the windows, and it was most savagely cold.

Colonel Guillermin came in slowly; although it was at such a ridiculous hour of the day, he was dressed in the full uniform of the Imperial staff — the blue breeches with the gold stripe, the blue tunic covered with gold lace, the cloak trimmed with grey astrakhan; under his arm was the smart grey busby with its panache, and trailing at his side was the heavy Oriental sabre which fashion had just decreed should be worn by staff officers.

"Take a chair," said Darphin, shutting his eyes again. "Make yourself quite comfortable and then tell me what it is all about. More wails from the Army of Portugal again?"

"There are some complaints from the Prince of Essling," agreed Colonel Guillermin, "and something must be done about them. But I have something much more important to tell you."

"Well, what is it?" said General Darphin, quite resigned.

But no words came to his listening ears for quite a time, and in the end Darphin opened his eyes again and craned his neck to peer over the sheets at him. Colonel Guillermin was gazing fixedly at the tumbled mass of black hair that lay on the pillow beside Count Darphin.

"Oh, never mind about Chuchita here," said Darphin testily. "She knows nothing of affairs, do you, my *poupée?*"

From under the bedclothes came the sound of the slap with which the General gave emphasis to his question and at the same time demonstrated his affection.

"No," said María de Jesús — Chuchita for short — very sleepily, and the bedclothes heaved as she snuggled herself into a comfortable position with her head on the General's shoulder.

"So hurry up with this news of yours," said the General.

"The news is from León," said Guillermin; something in the quality of his voice would have told the General that the matter was of burning importance, pregnant with disaster, except that the General was still too sleepy to be receptive of minor details.

"News from León at last?" he said. "What is it?"

"León is taken. Paris is dead — poisoned — and all the garrison with him. La Merced is taken. So are Mansilla and Saldaña. And the Fourth Fusiliers of the Guard were cut off in the plain and every man except one killed or taken. And there are ten thousand Spaniards besieging Salas at this moment."

By the time the recital was finished Guillermin could have no cause for complaint regarding Darphin's lack of interest in what he was saying. Darphin was sitting bolt upright, having gradually pulled himself up to that position while Guillermin was adding horror to horror. And simultaneously with the rising of his body, his jaw had fallen until his mouth was wide open. The natural disorder of his hair, of his heavy moustaches and whiskers, added to the ludicrous consternation of his expression.

"How do you know this is true?" demanded Darphin; but he showed his appreciation of the importance of the matter by flinging off the bedclothes — without a thought for the revelation of Chuchita's naked charms that ensued — and stepping out of bed.

"Meyronnet has sent the news from Salas. One of the Fusiliers got there after the regiment was destroyed — Salas is still open on the side of the river."

Darphin pulled on his breeches.

"Have you told the Marshal yet?" he asked.

"No," said Guillermin with a trace of bitterness in his tone. One of the cast-iron rules that General Darphin, as Chief of Staff to Marshal Bessières, had instituted, was that no one should dream of reporting direct to His Highness; it was significant that Darphin should have forgotten his own orders.

"I shall tell him at once," said Darphin. "Send to Dumoustier to tell him not to march this morning as last night's orders told him to. Send to Kellermann at Palencia to say that he must be here with all his dragoons before nightfall to-night. Call Serras back too. The Marshal will confirm in writing, but those messages must go in five minutes. Hurry!"

General Count Darphin had been a staff officer during nineteen years of continuous warfare. In the old revolutionary days, the guillotine, and after that the Emperor's own drastic methods, had winnowed out the incompetents. Darphin knew his trade from beginning to end. The news that five thousand Frenchmen had been lost, that the communications were broken on which a quarter of a million French soldiers depended, left him unshaken. He might be growing old, careless, lazy, but there was nothing wrong with his nerve. Now that news had come through at last which cleared up the mystery as to what had been happening in León, he took no longer than the time necessary to button his tunic to issue the orders which would set matters right. Yet he had to brace himself before going into the Marshal's room with the news. His Highness Marshal Bessières, Duke of Istria, Commander in Chief of the Army of the North of Spain, Colonel General of Cuirassiers, Grand Eagle of the Legion of Honour, was not at all a sympathetic person in the matter of receiving bad news before breakfast. And Darphin positively shuddered at the thought of the letters, wild with wrath, which would come pouring in from Paris when communications should be reopened and the news should reach there of the destruction of one of the beloved regiments of the Guard.

While buckling his stock Darphin reached a new decision. He turned to where Chuchita lay motionless on the bed; he strongly suspected that she was motionless, enduring the cold of the morning on her naked body, because any attempt to pull the clothes up over herself would have reminded Darphin of her existence. Darphin was not nearly as much of a fool regarding Chuchita as Guillermin thought he was.

"I am sorry, Chuchita," said Darphin slowly, "but I don't want the news of this concentration to reach the Spaniards. It pains me to have to tell a lady that I do not trust her, but that is what my duty compels me to do. You will oblige me, my dear, by not going out of this room before this evening. In fact, I am going to post a sentry at the door, in order to make certain of it. I regret very much causing you this inconvenience, but I am quite sure you appreciate the importance of the matter. Now calm yourself, my dear, and I will send some breakfast up to you."

Perhaps it was Darphin's military training which had taught him when to make a judicious retreat; however it was, he decided, in the face of the expostulations with which Chuchita proceeded to overwhelm him, to finish dressing himself outside the room. He caught up his sword and his boots and scuttled through the door, and turned the key upon the bad temper which Chuchita was beginning to display. Rather than face it, he would prefer to endure the smiles of passers-by in the corridor while he pulled on his boots and buckled on his sword to the accompaniment of the drumming of fists upon the locked door.

And he held to his previous determination too, of posting a sentry at the door with orders to allow no one in or out. It was quite a shame that his motive should be misconstrued, that the Sergeant of the Guard should grin noticeably when he received the order. Fortunately General Darphin had forgotten any Latin he ever knew, and quite missed the point of the *sotto voce* remark of one of the aides-de-camp: "*Quis custodiet ipsos custodes?*"

To make quite certain that no hint of the blow that was intended should reach the Spaniards in the field, he next sent orders to the guards at the gates. Until further orders, no Spaniard was to be allowed outside the walls. Any citizen of Valladolid who wished to take the air must breathe the insanitary odours of his own alleys; any countryman who wished to enter to sell his produce could only do so by resigning himself to an indefinite stay in the town.

With that settled, he went off to the barracks where Dumoustier's division, on receipt of the orders conveyed by Colonel Guillermin, had been dismissed from parade. Dumoustier's division was the finest of all the French Army of Spain, eleven battalions of the Young Guard, Voltigeurs, Tirailleurs, and Fusiliers. Dumoustier himself was sitting down to a second breakfast when Darphin entered — until ten minutes ago he and his men had been under orders to march south to join Masséna's army opposing Wellington.

"You will march north, not south, General," said Darphin to Dumoustier. "And you will not be starting until to-morrow night, after Serras and Kellermann come in."

"And why this change of plan?" asked Dumoustier.

"León has broken out and wants taming all over again. You are just the man for the job, aren't you, General?"

"I have a reputation for taming provinces," said Dumoustier.

He nodded his head slightly as if he were remembering past achievements; his eyes narrowed, and his lips revealed cruel white teeth under his black moustache. If Darphin had had any doubts as to the suitability of Dumoustier and his Guard division for teaching. León a lesson it would never forget, they would have been instantly dispelled by the sight of the expression on Dumoustier's face. And when the Guard should hear of the annihilation of the Fourth Fusiliers . . . ! If there is any truth in the assertion that the contemplation of the sufferings of others helps us to bear more easily our own suffering, General Darphin must have found much relief in thinking about what was going to happen to León while he bent his steps back to that dreaded interview with his commander in chief.

The latter was already worried enough by the news that Wel-

lington was loose in the South; to hear that the devil was un-
chained in the North would rouse him to paroxysms of rage. For
the splendid army which Masséna had led into Portugal the year
before had now come reeling back again, starving, naked, with
a third of its men and two thirds of its horses dead of exposure
and starvation before the Lines of Torres Vedras. Wellington,
whom every one had thought to be out of the game for good,
was back again on the frontier of Spain. He was starving Almeida
into surrender; he was threatening Ciudad Rodrigo with the
same fate, and without prompt help from Bessières, Masséna
could do nothing to stop him.

So that letters had come pouring in to the Duke of Istria from
the Prince of Essling, demanding clothing, food, guns, horses,
and, above all, men, so that the insolent islanders could be thrust
back into the mountains again. Phrases from the letters ran
through Darphin's mind — "You feed me only with promises";
"You have used all sorts of pretexts to evade my requests"; "Your
letters are inconceivable"; "All the troops in Spain are of the
same family"; "You are responsible for the defence of Almeida";
and so on interminably. And now at this very moment, when
Dumoustier and Serras and Kellermann were all ready to march
to Masséna's aid, and Masséna had been told to expect them,
there came this news from the North.

There could be no hesitation about what to do. Every available
man must be turned back to clear the communications. Not a
man could be spared to help Masséna. What he would write when
the news was broken to him Darphin could visualize with extreme clarity. Not so definite but even more dreaded was the
thought of what he should write to Paris regarding the shortcomings of Bessières and — for the greater includes the less — his
chief of staff. The thought of it made Darphin's blood run cold;
and he knew, even as he walked jauntily across the palace courtyard, that his chief would be equally apprehensive and consequently irritable.

To Darphin's credit it should be added that his fears were not
entirely selfish. There were vague apprehensions regarding the
future of France which worried him just as much, however un-

acknowledged they might be. He could not conceive of an end to the glorious Empire; that the French dominion of Spain, even, should ever be seriously threatened was beyond the limits of his imagination. He would have laughed to scorn any one who should suggest that no more than two years from now Wellington would sweep the French from the entire Peninsula in one brief campaign and come pouring triumphantly over the Pyrenees to deal the death wound to the Empire on the soil of France itself. All that would have seemed the merest rubbish to Darphin. But at the same time the thought of Wellington steadily extending his conquests, laying hold first of Almeida and then of Rodrigo, with the French powerless to keep him back, seemed strangely ominous and depressing to Darphin.

In that, of course, Darphin's military instinct was correct. The fall of Almeida was the beginning of that ebb tide which was to continue until the Allies should reach Paris. And Almeida fell because of the success of the revolt of the North. And it was the gun which was the cause of that success.

Chapter XXII

JORGE was pressing forward the siege of Salas with all the vigour that was in him and which his example could rouse in his men. He was having to learn the craft from first principles, but his was just the sort of temperament to which first principles make most appeal, and his immutable courage and endless cheerfulness set an example which his men were not slow to follow. Under the steady, deadly fire from the fortress, the "approaches" crept out from the "first parallel"; two nights after the defeat of the Fusiliers of the Guard the "second parallel" was begun and nearly completed, despite the fire of the besieged, and after daylight had come, it was finished at the cost of much blood — a long, well-planned trench with a solid parapet, which established the besiegers no more than two hundred yards from the walls. The howitzers within the fortress dropped shells into it with monotonous regularity, and the eighteen-pounders battered the parapets into ruin, but the Spaniards were not discouraged. They had been victorious too often lately for that. They pitched the corpses out over the back of the trench, and they rebuilt the parapet as fast as it was pounded down.

During the course of the day, Jorge laboured over mathematical problems — as mathematics were a complete mystery to him, he had to solve them by rule-of-thumb methods. Yet he was successful in his endeavours, for he was a man of hard common sense, and his experiences of the last few days had inspired him. When darkness fell, fifty men crept over the parapet of the advanced trench and began to dig furiously, throwing up a thick parapet to enclose a small square battery on the base lines, which Jorge, at the risk of his life, had marked out with stakes and tapes during the daylight. Ten men were levelling a section of the trench behind it. Ten more were levelling a section of the first parallel, so as to provide a passage for the big gun — a hundred men were dragging that up with dragropes.

Jorge managed somehow to be at all these places at the same time. If, when daylight came, the gun had not reached the second parallel and the shelter of the battery, it would be pounded to pieces by the guns of the besieged as it stood exposed to the open ground. Similarly, if it reached the second parallel and the battery was not ready for it, the same thing would happen. Everything must be completed to schedule. Jorge hurried back and forth, from the road to the second parallel, from the second parallel to the road, to keep every one at work.

The besieged heard all the bustle and did their best to interfere. They rained shot and shell on the place where the sounds indicated that the battery was being dug. They changed their target and fired at the place where they could hear the noise of the dragging up of the big gun — one lucky round shot killed ten men in a line at one of the dragropes. They pushed out a sortie across No Man's Land, but of course Jorge had foreseen that possibility and had had a "covering party" lying out there since nightfall; the brisk musketry fire that promptly spattered up caused the attackers to be withdrawn, lest a trap had been laid for them.

Jorge had simply excelled himself. The big gun reached the first parallel just as the gap which was being made for it was completed; it was dragged across and the trench instantly redug. He brought up a burdened carrying party with the huge balks of timber — the rafter beams of a house — which were to act as a flooring beneath the gun's wheels just as the redoubt was nearing completion, and no sooner had he got these laid when the gun itself was dragged in and put into position.

It was time enough, for it was nearly morning. Sweating with exertion and excitement, Jorge made sure all was well. The men digging outside continued to cast up final spadefuls of earth on to the immense walls, even when the growing light and the furious fire opened on the battery by the fortress made the work terribly dangerous. The work was finished as far as was necessary. The battery could boast of earthen walls immensely thick. It was not a thing of neat geometrical symmetry — unskilled en-

thusiasts working in pitch darkness could not produce that —
but it would suffice. The gun rested on its timbered platform
two feet below the level of the ground. For five feet above ground
level rose the walls, progressively thinner from below upwards.
The embrasure through which pointed the muzzle of the gun was
very narrow — the merest slit. That was all that was necessary,
for the gun was only destined to fire at one single small portion
of the wall, while the narrower the slit, the less chance there was
of lucky shots coming in through it.

Jorge had done well. An ordinary officer of engineers would
most probably have consumed two nights in the construction of
the battery, and a third in bringing up the gun. Jorge had tele-
scoped three nights into one and had gained forty-eight hours.
Already he was back on the road starting a fresh carrying party
up the trenches — men carrying four round shot apiece, slung
over their shoulders, and barrels of powder. Hurrying back to
the battery, Jorge issued instructions as to where this ammunition was to be stored; it must be in little parcels here and there
along the trench near the battery, but not too near; already a tor-
nado of fire was opening upon the battery, and men, crouching in
the bottom of the trench, were hurriedly filling sacks with earth
with which to rebuild the walls as they crumbled beneath the
cannon fire.

Then Jorge hurried off again and started men at work upon
the new approaches. Two more trenches were to be run out from
the second parallel, and then connected by a "third parallel"
close to the ditch. Here the storming party would assemble to
attack the breach which the gun was to make; breach and parallel
would have to be completed simultaneously. Jorge knew nothing
of the refinements of siegecraft; he was not aware of the fact
that in a properly conducted siege not only were the approaches
carried up to the ditch, but the sides of the ditch and the obstacles
in it should be levelled by mining, and the artillery fire of the
besieged quite subdued before the breach should be stormed.
These refinements were beyond Jorge's power, if not beyond his
imagination. All he aimed at was to get a body of men near

enough to a hole in the wall to have a chance of penetrating. The storming would be a bloody business — so would the approaching — but Jorge could not help that.

So all day long the approaches crept forward over the bare earth. Men were killed in them who had hardly had time to throw up ten spadefuls of earth. Men were buried under avalanches of earth and sandbags — the others only stopped to dig them out if to do so carried forward the work in hand. Dead bodies helped to give thickness to the parapets. The approaches at least served the purpose of multiplying the objectives of the besieged, so that the battery was not under such concentrated fire. Here the French were trying to drop shells into the work; but it was not so easy to drop a shell with indirect aiming into an area only ten feet square. French powder was not consistent enough, French shells were not cast truly enough, to make such accurate shooting likely — it was far otherwise with the magnificent English powder and shot which Jorge had at his disposal. Shells burst all round the battery; they burst on the very parapet, but the only one which fell inside failed to explode at once, and an imperturbable Galician vaquero, who found the thing at his feet, cut off the sizzling end of the fuse with a blow from his spade.

Meanwhile the gun had begun to fire back. Its bellowing roar, so well known to and so beloved by all the Spanish Army, punctuated the fighting at regular intervals. Jorge was back with the gun again. It was he who squinted along the sights before each shot. And his inventiveness was developing hourly. Out of his own brain he had devised a system to limit the force of the recoil and to minimize the labour of running up the gun each time. Behind the gun he had built up the timber platform in an inclined plane. At each shot the gun rolled backwards up it, hesitated, and then rolled forward again, as gravity overcame the force of the recoil until it was almost in its correct firing position again. It almost doubled the speed of fire and halved the labour of handling the big brute.

Jorge was half mad with exultation and excitement. His face and hands were black with powder so that his eyes were unnaturally noticeable. He roared out bits of songs as he worked the gun. He slapped the big hot breech caressingly after each discharge. He did not seem to be fatigued, although he had fought a battle the day before and spent two consecutive nights in the most exhausting labour. He blazed away with the gun exultantly.

The effect of the battering upon the wall was small but all that could be hoped for. The solid stone splintered but little at each successive blow, but Jorge had thought out a scheme of battering which, significantly, exactly corresponded with the methods employed by the best schools of artillerymen. He was aiming at the foot of the wall, and he hoped, traversing the gun a little to right and to left, to undercut a section of it until the mass above it should come tumbling down, presenting a slope that should be easy of ascent; with luck the ruin should even fall into the ditch and lessen the difficulties of passing it. He had no idea how long this would take; all he knew was that he had the gun in position to contrive it sooner or later, and he was prepared to go on firing it until it happened.

He only left the gun at intervals to hurry along the trenches to where the murderous work of continuing the approaches was being carried on; he did this when he feared that the breach would be achieved before the third parallel could be completed. But sooner or later, while he was at the approaches, he became convinced that the third parallel would be completed before the wall should be breached, and so he hastened back to speed up the firing of the gun.

There were other interruptions. El Platero and Delgado and the others kept making their way up to the battery with complaints and requests. In the heat of all this fighting Jorge found himself beset with unending distractions. There were nearly ten thousand Spaniards grouped round Salas, and Jorge found himself in the semi-official position of commander in chief. He had to decide which sections of the army should man the trenches, and which portions of the trenches. He had to make arrangements for feeding them, sending out foraging parties on both sides of the road to bring in whatever provisions could be found. He had to see that provisions and water were carried up to the men in the trenches. He had to see that there was a sufficient force in support of the men in the trenches, lest the garrison should sally out and ruin everything. Jorge found himself not merely commander in chief, but his own chief of staff, his own artillery commander, his own chief engineer, his own chief commissary.

It was a matter of interest as to how long he would stand the strain. And it was a significant fact that in the sweltering heat of the battery, with the gun bellowing its loudest and with shells dropping all round, Jorge was able to devise far more complicated arrangements and issue far more practicable orders than ever he would have been able to do if he had been peacefully herding sheep in the way he had spent most of his short life.

When night came, and he could no longer see the impact of the shot against the wall, so that he reluctantly decided to cease firing, he suddenly realized how exhausted and hungry he was. He braced himself to make his way again to the approaches, to warn the men there to make the most of the hours of darkness to push the works forward and to send patrols out to cover them, and then he picked his way back to the road, where makeshift tents had been put up for Alvarez and the others, and where the men not in the trenches were preparing for another night's uncomfortable bivouac.

He asked for food, and they brought him some, bread and meat and wine, but he fell asleep as he ate. The wine in his cup cascaded over his breeches, as his head fell forward on his knees, but he did not notice it. He rolled over on his side, snoring with a noise like a badly blown trumpet, and Alvarez, who had come to love him, took off his own cloak to cover him. He lay there and neither his own snores nor the constant passage to and fro of men and animals close by his head could wake him.

Yet at midnight something else woke him, so that he sat up with a jerk, with all his attention at stretch, like a wild animal. There was musketry fire from the trenches. It was no mere idle firing either, as might have been expected if two patrols had met or a sentry had allowed his imagination to be too much for him. It was a well-maintained blaze of musketry, and Jorge guessed what was its import. He leaped to his feet and ran for the trenches, stumbling in the darkness over obstacles innumerable. He fell headlong into the first parallel, where men were peering over the parapet at the flashes of the firing, but he was on his feet again and shouting loudly before any one could put a bayonet through him.

"Come with me, Princesa," he yelled.

The men knew his voice. All along the trench in the darkness they followed the example of their neighbours and scrambled over the parapet and ran wildly forward, falling at length into the second parallel.

General Meyronnet in Salas had become really alarmed at the rapid advance of the siege works. At midnight he had sent out a strong sortie, which had overrun the patrols, had taken the approach trenches, where men were now busy shovelling down the parapets as fast as they could, and which had pushed a determined attack home upon the breaching battery, intent upon capturing and disabling the one big gun which the besiegers possessed. Jorge and the Princesa Regiment arrived just as the attackers reached the second parallel. In the battery itself a grim fight was fought out in pitch darkness, where no one could tell friend from foe, but struck and spared not. Jorge had been weaponless when he reached the battery, but somehow a spade had come to his hand and with this he fought murderously, sobbing with excitement, until he suddenly realized that the clamour had abruptly ceased with the flight or death of every Frenchman who had broken in.

In the darkness he felt his way to the gun and ran his fingers anxiously over it. It was uninjured; he found the touchhole and made sure no one had driven a spike into it; he ran his fingers along the chase to the muzzle; there was no crack or sign of injury. The trunnions were intact.

Satisfied in this, he only wanted to sleep again. He cared nothing for the fact that in the approach trenches there could still be heard shouts and shots, as the last of the raiders were driven out by the Spaniards swarming up from the rear. He seated himself on the ground with his back to the trail of the gun and his shoulder against the wheel. He raised his head long enough to send an order to Elizalde regarding the manning of the trenches, and then he let it fall forward on his breast again, and the sound of his snores filled the battery. Daylight revealed the extent of the damage. Great sections of the approach trenches had been tumbled down, so that it was impossible for men to reach the head of the sap under the fire of the besieged. There were a good many corpses littered between the trenches and the fort, and El Platero and several of his band were missing — the patrol he had been leading had been overwhelmed in the first rush, and El Platero was now somewhere in a dungeon of the fortress. If the place should be forced to surrender, his life would be a valuable counter in the negotiations; if the besiegers should be driven off, every one knew what would happen to El Platero.

Jorge did not allow himself to be cast down; the sortie could have done far more damage than it did. He started the gun again at its work of battering, and went off to the approach trenches, where he set the example of beginning the dangerous work of rebuilding the broken sections. The besieged had gained half a day for themselves by their sortie — it took that long before the sap heads could be reached again and the trenches pushed forward on their long-drawn zigzag course towards the fort.

At midday something definite at last followed the discharge of the gun. There came a little avalanche of stone down from the face of the wall, the first indication that the gun was making any impression on the wall, twelve feet high and ten feet thick. Jorge rushed along to the sap head and stared at the wall. There was a little seam running up it now, like the trace of a watercourse on the face of a cliff. At this distance of a hundred and fifty yards, it was hard to be sure of details, but at any rate it was not now a smooth vertical ascent. There were at least projections and irregularities. A single man, active and unencumbered, might possibly climb it. That did not mean that an assault was possible in the face of a garrison a thousand strong, but it was at least a promise that a breach could be made sooner or later. And under the steady battering which went on during the rest of the day there were two or three further little avalanches. The wall was positively crumbling.

Jorge went back to the sap head to gaze at the wall again.
It was dangerous work to show one's face there, for the garrison
had lined the wall with musketeers, and at a hundred and fifty
yards there was always a faint chance of a lucky shot — to say
nothing of the fact that the besieged were always ready to pour
in a torrent of grape if a fair enough target were offered.

Jorge came to the conclusion that another day's battering
would pound ten feet of the wall into a practicable breach. He decided that that very night he must connect the advanced trenches
with another parallel, a hundred yards or less from the ditch.
And on the next night they would assault from there, with some
chance of success. He left the men digging away at the sap head
and proceeded back to the point on the road which a regular
officer might have called "headquarters," but which was actually
only a convenient sort of rendezvous for every one who had nothing special to do. His mind was busy with details; mentally he
was allotting the various parts to be played that night by the
different sections of the besiegers. Alvarez would have to take
his men forward towards the wall as a covering party — irregulars were the best for that sort of night work. Princesa would,
as usual, have to provide the four hundred men necessary for
the digging; Elizalde would have to allot the task to whichever
battalion he thought fit. In the second parallel and the first parallel there would be — Jorge was interrupted in his thoughts by
a hand laid upon his arm. He turned and found one of the boys
who composed the gun crew; he was out of breath with running
after him and his lips trembled.

"The gun, Señor!" he said. "The gun!"

"What about the gun?" demanded Jorge, with sudden fear at
his heart.

The boy stammered and gesticulated, but he could not utter
a word more of sense. With a curse Jorge turned away from him
and began running heavily back to the battery, and what he
found there was worse than he had anticipated. There were dead
men there, but Jorge cared nothing for dead men. The gun, his
beautiful big gun, was out of action. The carriage still stood,

somehow, although half of one tall wheel was shattered. But the gun itself was tilted up at a grotesque elevation, and at the same time was twisted over on its side. One trunnion had been smashed clean off — the raw irregular surface of the broken metal was visible. The elevating gear and the training gear were now only represented by splinters of wood and distorted bars of metal. On the chase a wide area of the ornamental relief work had been ploughed off.

Jorge stood glaring at the ruin. He could not see how it happened. The explanation was brought home to him a second later. There was a howl like that of a thousand lost souls, and a wind that flung him back against the battery wall. A big cannon ball had entered by the embrasure, as its predecessor must have done, but this one had gone clean across the battery from front to back without hitting anything. Jorge peered through the embrasure. On the top of the fortress wall, silhouetted against the evening sky, he saw a black hump close above the point where the breach was being made; it had not been there when he had looked half an hour before, from the sap head. It was a big gun, foreshortened, pointing straight at him.

For all the anguish which afflicted him Jorge could picture what the French had been doing — he knew much about the handling of heavy artillery nowadays. Finding that no gun of theirs would bear so as to fire into the embrasure, they must have set to work instantly building a ramp up the inside of the wall, with a platform at the upper end just below the top of the wall, and they had dragged one of their eighteen-pounders up the ramp to the platform. As soon as it reached there, they had swung it round and begun firing into the battery. Now that Jorge looked closer, he could see men's heads bobbing about, round the gun, as they reloaded it. Instinct caused him to pull down his head and crouch below the embrasure as the next shot was fired. There was a crash behind him, a ringing noise as though a great bell had been struck with a sledge hammer; a sizzling fragment of metal sang over his shoulder and buried itself in the battery wall close by his face. Jorge turned to see that the wreck of the gun was completed. The ball had hit the under side of the chase, making a great dent, and flinging down the gun from the wrecked carriage. Its breech had fallen on the ground and its muzzle perched up on the axle; the lettering round it, in its old-fashioned Latin characters, still said, "And our mouths shall show forth Thy praise."

Chapter XXIII

AT nightfall there was a good deal of activity among the besiegers of Salas. The gun would never fire again and the rumour of that had gone round the ranks, but they were in too high spirits still to be discouraged at the thought of that. Every one could appreciate the desirability of capturing a fortress which completely commanded the whole line of communications of the enemy, and flesh and blood were to finish off the work the gun had begun. Salas was to be stormed that night. The men were to attack in the darkness, over a deep ditch, up a wall like a cliff. The wall was seamed by one tiny crack; besides that, they had a dozen ladders taken from the farms near by. Nevertheless the men had not the least doubt that they were going to succeed; their commanders naturally did not communicate their doubts on the subject to them.

In gloomy conference they had settled the details — Alvarez was to assail the breach, and Elizalde was to attack at one side and the rest of the Princesa Regiment at the other, while Jorge led the irregulars round in an attack upon the river face of the fortress. In the darkness they moved the columns of men up to the second parallel — that was difficult enough in itself — and some time after midnight they streamed out to the attack.

There is no need to dwell upon the details of that repulse. The French in Salas had given proof enough already of their activity and vigilance and courage. Only against a craven enemy, demoralized and unready, could the assault have succeeded. The summit of the wall blazed with the fire of the besieged as the Spaniards approached. Grape and canister from the guns mounted to sweep the foot of the walls tore the Spaniards to pieces. Tar barrels and bundles of oily rags, all aflame, were flung down from the walls and served to give sufficient illumination to the musketeers upon the wall. Live shells with short fuses, dropped down by hand, blew apart the little groups of Spaniards who reached the foot of the wall. Fanatical courage brought them up to the attack over and over again; until towards morning the courage suddenly evaporated, as it will do with undisciplined troops, and they broke and fled away from the walls in blind terror, leaving even the trenches deserted, and only the dead and wounded piled upon the glacis as proof of what they had dared before this panic overtook them.

In the grey morning Jorge came back from the wall where he had raged berserk but uselessly, and found Alvarez and the others at the roadside. He halted his men and bade them rest — the survivors of El Bilbanito's band, and O'Neill's band, and El Platero's band were very, very few now — while he went up to the conference. Alvarez' right arm was in a sling and his clothes were in rags. Elizalde was in as bad a condition. Only Urquiola was as spruce and smart as ever, because his cavalry had taken no part in the assault.

"Delgado is dead," said Elizalde.

"Yes," said Jorge.

"So is Volpe."

"So are half my men," said Alvarez, "but I write no poems about it."

Jorge looked back at the fortress, at the low grey wall just visible over the rolling plain. Even at that distance he could see the speck which floated above it — the tricolour on its invisible staff.

Alvarez broke in upon the reverie into which Jorge was imperceptibly drifting.

"Holy Mary," said Alvarez. "Here comes a bird of ill omen."

They looked southward down the road as he pointed; a big man on a little white mule, his skirted legs trailing on each side so far down that his feet almost brushed the road, was riding up towards them. They saw the brownish-grey habit, and the massive black beard. It was Brother Bernard.

No one wanted to listen to Brother Bernard at that moment. They moved restlessly under his reproaches when he heard the news, like lions beneath the lion-tamer's whip. They sulked and they snarled. They had done all that men — men without a gun

— could do, and they resented bitterly his recriminations. They thought of the dead men along the foot of the wall, and Jorge thought of the gun, broken and grotesque, deserted in its battery.

"And the French will be here to-morrow from Valladolid," said Brother Bernard.

Alvarez looked up with a start.

"*Who* will be here?" he demanded.

Brother Bernard had not been idle, it appeared, while they had been pouring out their blood round the walls of Salas. He had seen the army of relief start out from Valladolid. He had watched them all one day; he knew just how the army was composed, and he had ridden hard all night to bring the news. Every unit, every general in the French Army, was known to Brother Bernard. The names he let fall were as well known to his listeners. They had all heard of Kellermann and his dragoons — Urquiola had been hunted by them times without number across the plains of Castile which Kellermann ruled. And Dumoustier and the Guard division; Dumoustier was a name Spanish women used to frighten their children. Serras too; small imagination was required to picture Dumoustier and Serras turned loose to subjugate León. Twelve thousand infantry, three thousand cavalry and a dozen guns; there would be fire and rape and slaughter from here to the Cantabrian mountains.

And the connecting link which might have held the army together in face of this danger was broken. The gun was a gun no longer, and the courage and good spirits which the gun had brought into existence had vanished last night under the walls of Salas. Alvarez was thinking about the charges Kellermann's dragoons could deliver here on these naked plains.

"I shall take my men back to Navarre while the road is still clear," he said. "I know the byways past Burgos. Mina only gave me leave to help El Bilbanito for three months, and the three months are ended."

The others looked at him, but he was quite brazen about his motives.

"I risked my men in a forlorn hope last night," he said, "but it would be worse than a forlorn hope to try and defend León against Kellermann and Dumoustier. And only the hope of seeing Navarre again speedily will keep my men together. I shall march in an hour's time."

Urquiola looked automatically at his big silver watch.

"If Kellermann has left Castile," he said, "my place is there. Our business is to be where the French are not. In a week's time, I shall be raiding up to the gates of Madrid."

"And what about León?" asked Brother Bernard.

Urquiola hesitated before he enunciated the heartless truth. "León must look after itself," he said.

The madness which underlay Brother Bernard's enthusiasm for the cause broke its bonds. He raised his clenched hands high above his head.

"Woe unto you," he said. "May God . . . "

Urquiola and Alvarez bore his curses as philosophically as a resigned husband bears the scoldings of his wife, and listened as heedlessly. The bonds of union had snapped with the disabling of the gun; and moreover, there were sound military arguments in favour of a prompt dispersal in face of the overwhelming force of the enemy.

And while Brother Bernard was calling down upon Urquiola and Alvarez the enmity of God, Jorge slipped unobtrusively away. It was not his duty, nor that of any irregular, to stand a siege by a French army. Jorge was determined not to be shut up in León or Saldaña or La Merced to await inevitable death or captivity. He thought of his native Cantabrian mountains. He had a horse still, which was far more than he had had when he descended from them. The relics of the *guerrillero* bands would follow him, if he promised to lead them back home. The Princesa Regiment — what was left of it — and the Leonese levies could obey Brother Bernard if they wished. As for him, he was off home. He had had his fill of commanding an army.

Over by the deserted trenches, foul with dead bodies, a patrol from Salas climbed cautiously over into the battery. They examined curiously the huge bronze gun which lay wrecked upon the splintered flooring. A scholar among them looked at the half-defaced heraldic traceries upon it, but he did not know which ducal house it was which bore those arms. He was able to puzzle out the Latin of the legend round the muzzle, and he translated it for his comrades, who were much amused. But still, the gun had played its part in history.